THE INFINITE NIGHT

THE INFINITE NIGHT

THE HAPPY MARAUDER

BOOK 1

JORDAN GRAY

ISBN: 979-8-9917209-0-8

1st edition, 2024

To my Dad,
Without you, none of my dreams
would have come true.

The universe I am creating is meant to encompass the full spectrum of experience in doing so it may not be appropriate for everyone. Here's the top of my head list of topics that some may find as reasons not to read my book.

- Ableism
- Abortion
- Abusive relationship
- Ageism
- Alcohol
- Amputation
- Animal abuse
- Animal death
- Anxiety
- Assault
- Attempted murder
- Attempted rape
- Blood
- Bones
- Branding
- Bullying
- Cheating
- Child abuse
- Child death
- Cults
- Death
- Decapitation
- Depression
- Drugs
- Eating disorder
- Emesis
- Emotional abuse
- Eugenics
- Famine
- Fire
- Genocide
- Gore
- Gun violence
- Hallucinations
- Hospitalization
- Misgendering
- Misogyny
- Murder
- Needles
- Occult
- Pedophilia
- Physical abuse
- Plague
- Poisoning
- Police brutality
- Profanity
- Prostitution
- PTSD
- Racism
- Rape
- Religion
- Self-harm
- Sexism
- Sexual abuse
- Sexual assault
- Sexual harassment
- Sexually explicit scenes
- Slavery
- Snakes
- Spiders
- Stalking
- Starvation
- Suicide
- Terminal illness
- Terrorism
- Torture
- Violence
- War

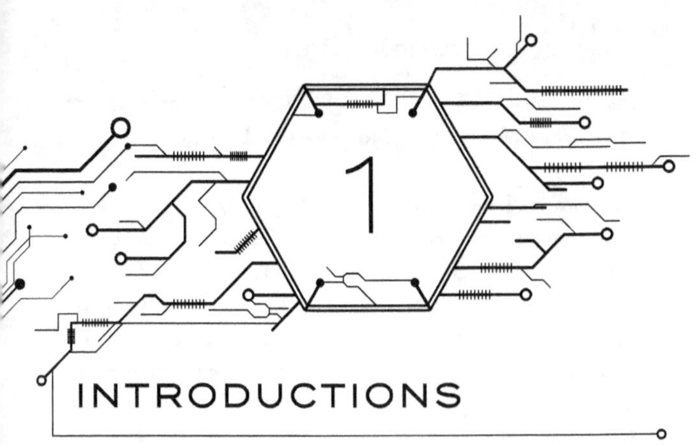

INTRODUCTIONS

520.100.2153 Elevator District, Vanguard
City, Vanguard Prime. Vanguard

OH, HEY. IT'S working… Oh, it's recording already. Well, you my little, uh… Oh, it's here on the inside of the case! Door Corp Secure Personal Log and Data Vault. I don't know how you wound up in a dumpster, but it's my lucky fucking day. You were in the package and everything.

The instructions say you're compliant with orthodox file transfer protocol, blah blah blah, bio-resonant charging, and organic camouflage. Gross! It says that you're going to harvest my dead skin cells. I guess so no one sees me wearing you around my neck. Whatever. Right now, you look like an ordinary necklace with a pendant. Almost like a military tag but with no emblem or serial number or whatever. In a few weeks, you'll just be a part of my chest and neck.

Enough of that. I already registered you, and I'm going to tell you my story.

I'm effectively unplugged from the world. I can't afford a handset or a much less the bills that come with them. No social media. No bank accounts. No news feeds. No subscriptions. Any of that. All I have as a record to prove that I exist at all in this fucked-up world is you.

My name is James August Childs. I got my name because the clerk at the Vanguard Institute for Developing Children had no fucking imagination. I was found on James Street in August, and I was a child. Fucking clever, that one. My birthday is 500.227.2150, assigned seven years from when those CE pricks dumped me at the institute. I don't know my biological birthday.

CE is civil enforcement, the name for the police here on Vanguard.

You should know that Vanguard is a military autocracy. The civilian economy isn't under direct military control, which is really complicated, and I don't know how it works exactly. I can't tell how it ranks against other civilized worlds because I don't know what's propaganda and what's truth. I know conscripts from all over come to settle in droves and shit on me because they're citizens, and I'm not.

All the government is an extension of the military, and it doesn't matter how rich you are, you start as a conscript and must do a minimum of two years of service to earn your citizenship and vote. Does that make it a virtual democracy? I don't know...

People not raised in an orphanage usually pay for training, so they can survive conscription.

If you're not a citizen—like me—you can't vote or own anything that requires a deed or title. If you can't prove ownership, don't bother going to CE if you're robbed. Non-citizens also have the lowest priority for emergency services. The public feeds say that eighty-something percent of non-citizen emergency calls expire without being answered.

The talking heads and politicos are more concerned with us

"stealing jobs" than if we starve to death. But we're "stealing jobs" because we make forty percent less.

I'll stop there, so I don't go on a rant.

Um… Other things you should know about Vanguard… It was settled when the Vanguard fleet refused to participate in some invasion on the orders of the government at the time. There was a civil war, and in less than a century, Vanguard settled and became a trade hub. Now, it's one of the largest shipyards in the area.

That sums up my knowledge of the local sociopolitical situation. Oh, and Vanguard Prime has close to one hundred and twenty billion people concentrated in cities to limit our environmental impact or some shit.

ANOTHER DAY

SO, I SHOULDN'T have skipped yesterday's sleep to fuck with you and get you registered and all that. I dragged my ass all night.

The night started off like shit.

I just realized you don't know what I'm talking about.

Uh, let's see.

I left my closet of an apartment to go to work and saw the line outside The Corner Bar. It's like two blocks away, and the proximity is ninety percent of the reason I work there.

Vanguard City is situated at the highest peak on the equator of Vanguard Prime. It's a stupid place for a city really. It's constantly covered in a foot of slush. The black stone buildings and roads make the bottom layer of snow melt during the day. Those of us reliant on public transportation have to walk through knee-deep drifts every time the winds kicked up, which is most of the time. The short walk is not a pleasant one.

A line outside a bar should be a good thing, right? Not at The

Corner Bar. That bar is not a nice bar with cute little baristas running around in their underwear.

No one runs around in their underwear in Vanguard City. It's too fucking cold.

At The Corner Bar, a line means a star liner made port, and all the porters who spent the last month getting bitched at by entitled rich fucks want to take a shit on someone. That bathroom where they take the aforementioned shit is The Corner Bar, and I am one of the requisite toilets.

In reality, the prices on the ground are a fraction of what they are in space, and that makes all the space peasants royalty when they come down.

The Corner Bar is built into the back corner of a factory that makes computer parts or some shit. The bullshit name of the place is overshadowed by the amount of traffic it draws from the factories and the elevator.

Speaking which, it's only an elevator is if it goes to space. Because it changes your *elevation*! Those boxes that take you to your apartments and offices are lifts. Get that straight, I will die on this hill.

The interior really drives home how much of a dive that place is. Starting with the big mesh drain and sloping floor is disturbingly reminiscent of a slaughterhouse. The floor once had a traction-clean coating and is now a composite foundation with a long history of violence and desperation.

When I got there, The Corner Bar blasted sensory overload in the form of deafening electronic seizure music and pulsing laser light show. People with histories of epilepsy should not enter. The furniture was all assembly-line garbage, tables, stools, and chairs. Seriously. I had to pick them up from down the block because someone above me bribed the recycling guy to let me take it.

"You're a half hour late! You're bouncing tonight!" Cody, the night manager, barked at me over the drone of a machine-gun dance beat.

I had just slipped in through the delivery freezer and was hoping to get logged in and behind the bar before he noticed. Bouncing would mean I wouldn't make shit for money tonight unless one of the other bartenders fell behind or got hurt. It was a harsh punishment, but it was better than getting fired.

I turned to give the expected argument because I really need the money, and Cody's usually later than me. But then I saw that his left eye was red and swollen, his knuckles were bloody, and his left pinky stuck out at an odd angle. The wild look in his eye told me he was still on an adrenaline high. His two-hundred-plus-centimeters of lean pale wrath did not leave room for back talk.

—*ABORT! ABORT! ABORT!*— my brain screamed at me.

I had to do something diplomatic and now. The best idea I had was to pull a random beer from the nearest case and open it for him.

Cody took the beer in his good hand and offered me his bad hand to accept my apology. We had done enough first aid on each other that we knew what to look for.

I squeezed the finger and hand, and he flinched. I didn't detect any jagged edges that indicated a broken bone. I gripped his pinky finger firmly and met his eyes. He chugged his beer as I jerked the finger back into place. He coughed but recovered quickly. The soft pop made me shiver with the spinal brush fire of bones knocking together, triggering the memories of when it had been my hand.

I left the freezer, and the harsh, sterile light of the kitchen made me wince. The kitchen was a shiny canyon of industrial grade cookware and economic servitude.

I clocked in, took a long, centering breath, and got to work. Outside the kitchen was a cesspool of addiction and violence, and it was my job to manage it. I checked the surveillance while I was still at the terminal. There wasn't any fighting actively going on, so I grabbed the bussing cart and got to it.

It was less than an hour on shift before some porter punks got into a fight over who got which hooker or some shit. I let them tire themselves out and kicked them in the back if they got too close to the other patrons. I also put every drink they spilled on their tabs, mostly because I was irritated.

One would think a bouncer would break up the fights. One would, of course, be wrong. My job is making sure the fights stay at an entertaining level. Not a murderous level. More importantly, spilled drinks go on the fighters' tab.

A few hours went by until the highlight of my night arrived. It came in the form of two-hundred-kilos of augmentation addiction.

Now, I'm not a bigot who has anything against anyone with prosthetics. But there's a huge difference between someone who got in an accident and lost a limb and this shiny douche-canoe. He's the kind of guy that uses this seasons enhancements to show that he's better than me.

Fuck him.

Anyway, I got a little off track. This guy had display projectors built into his shoulder, and he hijacked the sound system. His playlist was a complete rip-off of stuff circulating social media. He claimed he started the trend. His chest was stylized to make his pecs look like neo-classical subwoofers from the early information age. It would have been more of an impressive display if he didn't split the tracks with a monologue about how "this part is custom" and how "this part is only available on planet No One Gives a Shit About." The guy was a total douche right up until he literally exploded.

I couldn't imagine the amount of fluid coming out of a person who was made mostly of metal. He covered the bar, the ceiling, and the patrons—staff included. That cleared the bar because it smelled terrible. Think cat piss and old rotting pecans. A mess was one thing, but losing two-thirds of my already reduced tips were the sprinkles on the shit-flavored cake.

I just sighed, kicked on the sprinklers, and got the water hose.

Pro tip: urinal cakes will get the smell off anything.

Now, I'm on the tram, picking at the graffiti and talking to you. I feel a little insane trying to monologue my day. I'm trying to figure out the sub-vocalizing feature so i stop getting strange looks..

Oh, I forgot to mention that when the cyborg splattered, his head hit the ground, and I'm pretty sure he was blinking SOS at me. His emergency retrieval team was there in impressive time. I'm pretty sure he survived.

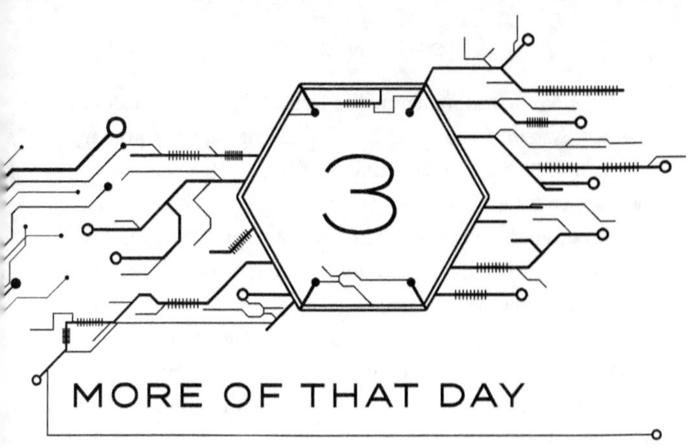

MORE OF THAT DAY

520.101.1548 Industrial District, Vanguard
City, Vanguard Prime, Vanguard

SO, I FELL asleep on the tram and didn't make it to my primary job, Telex's, until after 0900. A ten-minute tram ride turned into an hour and half nap. I regret nothing.

Telex's Articulated Vehicle and Supplies is a distribution warehouse for industrial equipment. The warehouse's exterior is a giant display of advertisements for products and services which we are associated with in one way or another. The annoying speakers try to whisper sweet promises of a better life if I choose their dick to get fucked with.

Once inside the warehouse, I found flat illumination and the steady hum of industrial climate control soothing. The matte tones of composites and metal made me feel safe because there was none of that torturous sensory overload. The matte coating was broken with the standardized markings of black and yellow for caution areas, red for danger zones, and other standard industrial markings. The bright lights from thirty or forty meters away were saturating but not blinding.

The equipment dominating the interior spaces was a Bullet Casings System. Logos aside, Bullet Casings are the primary standardized shipping containers of the sector. Each cube has its own little story of cosmetic damage that documents its journey around the cosmos. The containers are rather intuitive with smart foam, adjacent interlocking, and a dozen other little features that help with inventory management. The omni-rack system can shuffle the whole warehouse around in minutes.

My job is to prep items going into the casing and more importantly into the specialty transport for big shit that doesn't fit in a casing.

I made my way to my second home: the garage. It's a big open main bay with heavy equipment in various states of repair. Three overhead cranes unofficially divide the garage into sections for trucks, heavy equipment, and specialty welding. The smell of welding and grease might as well be mother's cooking. Tucked behind the milling and machining equipment, are the cradles where we keep our AVs.

What is an AV? Excellent question. I'm glad you asked. An articulated vehicle or AV is a car with joints? While technically true, that doesn't really describe them. Ours are four-meter-tall walking forklifts with stilts that give a maximum actuating height of about ten meters.

The stilts are oversized and overpowered and can get us to jump almost thirty meters. They do make the lower leg and ankle look comically disproportionate. If you ask how we don't kill ourselves hurling twenty tons of metal around, the answer is motherfucking skill!

Our AVs are an older robust design, and the controls are completely analog. They may be from a power plant or factory where the EM would fry anything more delicate than a toggle switch. Nothing but a safety cage and a harness lets us walk the tightrope of an industrial accident.

Pure beauty.

The only imperfection is that as they are industrial-use equipment; we have to keep them in the standard safety yellow.

If you think of the Vitruvian Man and combine it with a traditional vehicle lift, you have a cradle. Five meters of metal and bracing let one person work on an AV. The ones for servicing customer AVs in the garage are fully automated, whereas ours use cranks, counterweights, and safety pins. I can't complain against free.

Sure, there are a lot more versatile models out there, but we know these machines inside and out. We even have tails with tools and cutting torches that make the term –*permanent*– more of a suggestion.

I neared our workstation, which was just a screen on an arm where I would find the day's workload. Instead, I found Telex— the proper, the short, squat fucker who decided to remind me that his name is still on the side of the building.

"You o'er an hour late, an' you still tank you gets a full days pah? You out ya damn mind," Telex squished out between his fat dark cheeks while still slurping on slurping his coffee.

I don't know how he can see with his bloated cheeks ballooning right up to his forehead.

"Well, if you're going to dock me a half a day's pay," I said, "I'll take another two hours off, and we'll meet in the middle."

"Bah! You leave, an' you don' come back!" he practically shouted. "You have big delivery today. Dey clear out da shed. Nowa more overstock. Youha go to the elevator today. BEHAVE!"

I was too tired for his bullshit. I had been doing this same song and dance with him for two years and had reached the point where I was going to shoot the conductor if he didn't play something different.

As frustrated as I was, I couldn't leave because I didn't have anywhere to take my AV. The shitty part was Telex knew it.

"Looky here, you squat piece of shit," I said. "What's the delivery time on this? Noon?" I hadn't seen the docket yet, but Telex always swung his dick around when he made promises that I had to keep. "What's the late discount? Twenty percent? Thirty?"

He looked chastened, and I knew I had struck home.

"If I walk, you're going to start missing payments, aren't you?"

His face was stone, but his pupils dilated and contracted with real fear.

"Overextended yourself this time, didn't you?"

A strong hand gripped my shoulder, calming me. It was Shantu, perhaps my only real friend. The simple gesture told me that I was going overboard and that I should back off.

Shantu took the docket from Telex and scrolled through it.

"Get us the company chit encoder." Shantu's voice was ice.

Chit encoders change digital currency into hard coin currency. They are also capable of encoding deeds, registrations, and any other document of ownership. They are the linchpins of the fast-moving interstellar economy, consolidating several bureaucracies into one device.

"You are funny if you tink I stoopid enough to gib you dat," Telex retorted.

The encoders are justifiably difficult to replace and will involve an investigation by the Vanguard Commerce Authority. It is the bureaucratic pain in the ass that Telex is afraid of.

Shantu scrolled over the docket, and his expression darkened. He stiffened. "Take the big truck to the yard." He stared into my eyes and then repeated his order firmer.

That was our game. I am the overtly indispensable pain in the ass. He's the rational one who can manage me. He doesn't have my gifts with an AV, but this world is short on people I can trust to watch my back.

I left him to deal with Telex.

The big truck is a semiautonomous mechanical centipede

designed by a three-year-old on drugs. It was "stacked" where it had the same spatial footprint as your everyday shipping truck. Its load being modular drive drove, uh, modules. From the outside, it just seemed like neatly arranged wheels in metal. The cab portion only looked slightly more robust than a standard truck with larger tires that had dispersion polymers. That just meant they squished more underload.

Each drive module is individually powerful enough to tow a fully laden standard truck. The square segments are half as wide as a standard trailer—just motors and battery crammed between four tires.

The big truck is advertised that "the load isn't a problem, the ground is" with pictures of mountains being crushed flat.

The cab segment is kept meticulously clean by the detailing guys. The polymer coated chains that hang from the headache rack are usually only used a few times before they become too scuffed for the show truck. The overhead rack has neatly arranged polymer dunnage blocks that we don't use to maintain the aesthetic. Instead, we swap them out for battered but usable ones in a shipping container.

I ran the startup checks and pulled it from the center truck maintenance bay where it lived as a showpiece.

Shantu better be getting something good out of Telex while I dealt with the big truck. New parts! Company feed! A fucking raise!

I would settle for permission to build walls around our AVs, so I could sleep here again. We used to sleep here to the sounds of industrial work, but some asshole mechanics started fucking with us when we slept. So, that didn't end well. Let's just say we weren't allowed to sleep here anymore.

I parked the big truck in the yard's loading zone. Since I had been with Telex, the yard was just an open lot that changed uses with the wind. He hosted equipment expos, auctions, parking, and more. Anything that needed a lot of space.

I ran back to my AV. I was going through the slightly more extensive startup checks for my AV when Shantu came running. "Dude, how fucking bad is it?" I asked as he passed my AV cradle.

"He sold the neodymium forge."

The forge was almost two hundred tons of rare magnets that fell out of orbit a long time ago. It had a few years of scrap metal covering it now.

I couldn't help but process my emotional connection to this place. while trying to think my way through the work.

Telex, for all I hate him, had a mind for business. Anyone who came to the main gate had to turn right and look at all the shiny new equipment, cranes, drills, excavators, trucks, and every kind of drone that he could have out in the weather. They had to pass the garage, where shipping trucks could go ahead and get serviced while they were here, before they picked up or delivered their order.

Genius.

I have to give it to that shithead. More than once I got a call to park a truck because it came in for service, and the owner opted to buy a new one instead of repairs.

Directly behind the new stuff was used equipment in a fuck ton of shipping containers. The containers were currently stacked so high they swayed in the wind.

Behind all that was a pile of shit that Telex didn't want to send to recycling because it was "too valuable." Under that pile of shit was the neodymium forge.

"Fuck me. Really? I'll clear a path for the straddle crane if you want to start putting together the mag bottle."

"He sold it like five seconds before you walked in," Shantu said over the local comm. "There's a huge bonus if we get it up on this lift. We have until 1500 to get to the elevator for the hazardous cargo carriage."

I didn't ask what the bonus would be. I trusted Shantu, and I didn't need the distraction.

Gather around kids, so I can explain this shit.

Straddle crane. I think you can figure that one out.

Mag bottle. Take an electric motor. Cut it in half in line with the rotating axis until it'll lie flat. Then attach a bunch of sensors that can measure magnetic fields. Put it in a hexagon housing so it'll be modular, and you have equipment that can contain big ass magnets without pulling people's implants out. These modules are about a meter tall, and I hoped they had the juice to do the work.

"Well, fuck," Shantu said over the local comm. "They're getting a solid meter of bonus shit because I can't get close enough to do fuck else right now, if I'm reading this right."

We call it the local comm, but they're analog radios. The kind you print for children, so they can pretend to be soldiers.

I dove onto the heap, flinging materials to cut a path for the big crane.

A half hour later, I was cursing Telex's very existence because we weren't making the progress we needed, and this was his fault.

"If we make it, I'm going to beat Telex's head in and fuck the hole!" I yelled like the universe was going to throw me a bone.

"This is the company channel, asshole," Shantu said. "Everyone can hear you, and it's monitored."

"Do you think I give a fuck?" I shot back. "Whose testicles are turning inside out to keep him from sinking the company?"

"EM fields aren't ionizing, you dipshit. The only reason your balls don't work is because you have a pussy. Now, quit being a cock bite and get the fuck on with it. I'll be there in a second to help you with the reach around."

"Fuckstick!" I yelled at him.

"Fucknuts!" he yelled back.

It's when he says shit like that that I know why we've been inseparable for as long as I can remember. I'm not sure how we met though. Might have bunked together at the institute.

Without Shantu, I don't think I would have made it out of the institute. Don't get me wrong, we took our share of poundings, but we didn't end up with a debt we couldn't pay or worse.

Never mind that.

We were working on getting this ten-meter, magnetic, anal fistula out of the ground. According to my feed, the neodymium forge was a part of some capital ship cannon. The originating ship broke up in orbit a long time ago. Also, I'm not sure what makes a ship capital.

Telex's predecessor bought the land here because that chunk of space garbage made the land affordable. The problem with this particular piece of garbage was that it had a magnetic field that could pull the fillings out of your teeth from about ten meters. We, of course, had been throwing metal scrap at it for years. Just to watch it get crushed under an invisible fist.

Now we needed to move the mountain of scrap half welded to the damn thing.

"So, who the fuck decided they wanted this thing? Why the fuck do they want it in six hours?" I asked over the general warehouse channel, mostly to vocalize my foul mood.

Fuck it. I ran to the key locker in the garage and grabbed the control console for two planetary exploration drones we had on display. I had been playing on the simulator in the lobby for months and wanted to see if their big lasers were as good as advertised. Never thought I would get a chance to use one.

"You're going to be in so much shit for spinning those things up," Shantu said.

They were colonization equipment used to search for minerals and shit.

Full disclosure, I was planning to draw a dick in the scrap heap. But because I'm a professional, I put in the cuts I needed for the crane first.

Safety tip that movies lie to you about: lasers do not go *pew*. Lasers go *–fuck your eardrums.* Go get struck by lightning. You'll understand.

Shantu and I tried to run back into the garage for hearing protection, looking like drug addicts on a bad trip. I'm sure it was hilarious watching us struggle to cover our ears with our hands while sliding over the ice as the drones kicked up a snowstorm.

I was doing safety squints from my AV and questioning so many of my life choices.

Choice number one: why didn't I grab the safety glasses that were on the shelf next to the hearing protection?

Choice number two: how many times do I need to get blasted in the face with snow and ice before I put up a windshield?

I directed my anger appropriately at Telex because all this was his fault. "Telex can drink liquid shit out of my ass if he thinks there's another way to get this fucking thing delivered to the elevator in six hours."

"Well, time to be awesome!" Shantu exclaimed, putting an end to my bitching.

It was our private agreement. No matter the situation, we would always choose the best end to the story. From there, we dove into it.

An hour drifted by as we furiously worked to turn a giant pile of scrap into three slightly smaller piles of scrap.

The second hour drifted by, and our furrows were looking good enough for Shantu to peel off. He set the big truck to unstack while he pulled the mag bottle modules from their shipping containers. He then ran to climb to the crane. That ladder was like thirty meters straight up to the controls. Fuck that.

I finished getting the scrap out of the way to let Shantu get the crane into position. He dropped the crane's big magnet and expertly extracted it from the soil with a muddy SHLURP!

The modules for the big truck were getting themselves into

position. He must have the control panel up in the crane. He then released the ten-meter diameter hemorrhoid, and the truck sunk a half meter into the freshly churned ground.

The big truck slowly moved to the paved driveway. There, it shimmied and CLUNKED! The sound echoed across the driveway as the modules fought to lock together. The whole assembly became a stable vehicle.

Shantu and I manually loaded our AVs, securing them in fore and aft with significantly more care than the neodymium forge received. I hopped in the driver's seat, and he pulled a tablet from the console while checking the invoice.

"Tell me Telex didn't submit the transport permit," I said.

"No. Jeffery did," he replied, not looking up.

I thanked my lucky stars and checked the queue for the hazardous cargo and the live feeds from our route through the pilot systems. My stress levels rose as I calculated a small margin for error and an overreliance on luck to get us there in time.

"The rest of the order was a literal truckload of part codes. No special handling instructions." Shantu swiped furiously. "Fuck it. Go. Nothing else needs to be on the hazardous cargo carriage. Bullets will take everything else to the elevator, but it looks like we have to unload it ourselves."

The ride to the elevator was the most nerve-racking trip I had ever made. We took up two lanes and a shoulder, and there was enough manually piloted traffic to send me into a rage.

I used the control board for the big truck to check the traffic at the gates, looking for people who we knew could get us an express lane. They would charge, but that was Telex's money and Shantu's problem.

The power drain by the mag bottle was costing us speed. Irate traffic let us know their shitty lives were our fault. Watching our ETA march closer and closer our time slot frayed my nerves.

We made it. But just barely.

Shantu took the chit encoder and met the elevator rep, and that was that. They would get their equipment and deal with it from here.

An elevator that goes to space sounds impressive, right? Not so much. Imagine an airport with only one plane. I know there are lower levels for passengers, but I've only ever seen the top where heavy freight is taken. Aside from the massive cable strands shooting straight up into the sky, it looks like any other big parking lot with cranes and ground control towers.

I know there's a massive feat of engineering going on here, but it was cold out, I was hungry, and the only heat was in the truck.

Shantu banged on the door and yelled over the elevator's ambient noise. "The other trucks are already here. If we can get the locker unloaded before the elevator crew gets there, we can bill it out ourselves and get motherfucking paid!"

Specialty delivery at the space port was a niche that allowed us to charge additional fees that the local labor took as a threat to their job security. We mostly tried to stay in our lane. However, right now, I had to decide between rent and food.

"Which bay?" I asked.

"At 117 top."

I didn't even notice we were at the first bay.

The bays are zones on the ground for cargo. Each one represents a degree from the elevator's center and is a little over hundred meters on the outside, which put us over a kilometer away from the bay we needed to be in.

"Fuck! Race you there!" Shantu said without acknowledging the pain in the ass it was going to be to get there.

"Calm your tits! I'm pinging ground control, so they don't have a conniption." I used the big truck's control panel, but he was already sprinting away. "Fuckstick!"

"Fucknuts!" he yelled back with a giggle.

I jumped in my AV, set the stilts for full extension, and took off after him. With our AV's long leaping strides to clear the bay, we were treating millions of credits worth of spacecraft equipment as hurdles. We traversed the complex's kilometers in minutes. I know at some point, we used the lifting drones as stepping-stones, infuriating the crew of that bay, but we were gone before they could do anything.

Despite Shantu's lead, I beat him.

At the carousel we did the dock-hands jobs sorting bullets onto skids that had different destination around elevator. A skid is just a flat drone used to move inventory around. Think of a flatbed tow truck but lower and with no cab.

We didn't hesitate to open the carousel lockers and start toss inventory. We did the job of ten people just to hurry the flow of enough to make sure our cargo made it to customer.

"Hot fucking dicks!" Shantu shouted. "We're fucking good."

Fatigue hit me like a freight train. "Dude, I worked all night. Didn't get much sleep before. It's nice to be awesome, but I need sleep."

We walked back to the big truck. I loaded my AV and promptly passed out in the passenger seat, leaving Shantu to restack it.

Well, maybe not so promptly. I'm trying to make it a habit to keep up with my log. If I don't, what's the point of having this thing?

WILL THIS DAY FUCKING END

520.101.1608 Elevator District, Vanguard,
Vanguard Prime, Vanguard City

"DUDE, WAKE UP," Shantu said, slapping my chest frantically. "We're being followed."

After my incoherent babbling sorted itself into something coherent, I managed to say, "Think one of the other elevator crews is holding a grudge?"

"I don't care to find out."

"Yeah. Me either," I said, still trying to get my bearings.

We were on the lower freeway for freight, still headed west. Sunlight bounced off the buildings and pillars where it could. It wasn't a tunnel, but it felt like it, being lit more by headlights than any natural source.

Passenger vehicles down here stand out. Doubly so if they don't look like ragged survivors who would stab someone over a sandwich. To be clear, I would stab you over a sandwich right now. I am so fucking hungry.

This one is one of those common passenger people boxes. The only defining thing about it is that it is clean.

I used the control panel to check the traffic feeds on our route back to the warehouse. I found a place where a building was less than a meter from the interchange, so I set a waypoint for Shantu to follow.

I got to work on stashing the chit encoder in the dash as best I could. If someone got a hold of it, they could drain the company. I sent a message to Telex, telling him where it was. He could lock the thing out remotely. Shit, he could take control of this truck if he wanted to.

"We're going down through the markets," I told Shantu. "If they follow us down there, we're going to be knee-deep in bodies soon."

We can hide in the markets because we know how to disappear down there. Any off-worlder or anyone who doesn't know how to get around is going to stir up the crazy and either get killed or must cut a path of murder through there.

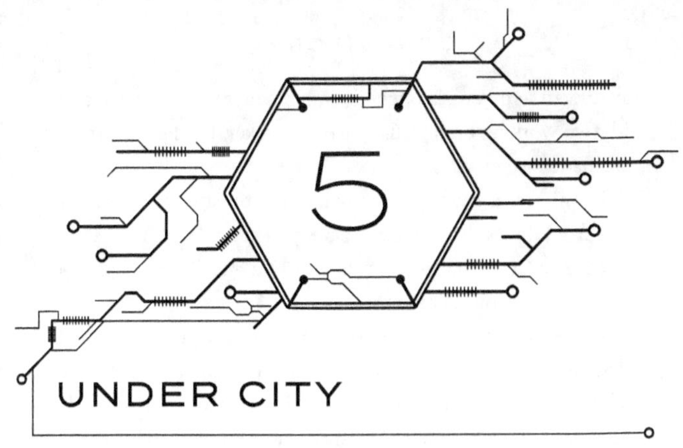

UNDER CITY

520.101.1721 Utility District, Vanguard
City, Vanguard Prime, Vanguard

SHANTU SLAMMED ON the manual brake to stop at the waypoint I had set. The display flashed numerous rear collision warnings before it slowed enough for us to jump out.

The adrenaline rush cleared my mind.

Without thinking, I jumped from the road to the building. The makeshift balconies and improvised environmental systems that grew on the outside like vines became our handholds for more of a controlled fall and less of a climb down. We landed in the refuse-encrusted gutter that millions of people in Vanguard City called home.

The transition from the lower freeway to the under city was like falling into another universe. In a way, it was. Here, every corner and shadow hid monsters that wanted to kill us. It wasn't white with snow like the surface; everything here was wet and covered with black mold.

I drew my rhino and cycled the safety to let anyone listening hear the capacitor prime. My plasma pistol sucked in air and pressurized with a high-pitched whine that would make anyone with two working brain cells butthole pucker. But listening to it purr made me smile.

The rhino was rugged and reliable, and the aperture actuator at the front doubled as the sight gave it its apt name. It wasn't the most elegant weapon, but it was effective and didn't require a license, so CE wouldn't say shit.

Despite its name and reputation, it came to me because it had failed and electrocuted its previous owner. I took it to a topside dealer because I didn't trust anyone down here in the gut. He was kind and professional. I wish I could remember his name because I wanted to be like him.

Competent. That's the word. He was competent.

He didn't look down on me when I asked how much I could get for the gun. He told me he didn't deal in plasma but took the time to show me why it had failed and how to maintain it so it wouldn't do it again.

My rhino's purr, ignoring that it sounded like a little jet engine, felt like I had nursed an animal back to life.

The sun wasn't dumb enough to take all the wrong turns to get down here. We landed in a dark, dingy dead-end alley, knee-deep in garbage that had fallen from the freeway and collected here.

What did that say about us?

Nearby was a corpse. More than a few days old. I could tell by the smell. Those smells twisted everyone's face into a scowl as they failed to pretend, they didn't notice. If they didn't acknowledge the body, it wouldn't count toward the lifetime total of bodies they've seen.

It wasn't even rain that fell on us. It was melting snow from the buildings and roads above.

I didn't like being cornered in this alley. Shantu and I were going to be attacked for setting foot down here by whatever little gang called this their turf. They had to show force or risk losing face to their rivals. These little warring kingdoms gave fantasy dramas a run for their money.

As if on cue, two guys with frost mouth stepped out of a building. Their twitchy movements and the wildness in those eyes told me they were way past recreational users and up to their eyeballs in addiction.

I'm not judging. Maybe it's my luck that frost made me sick. The frost inhaler irritates your mouth with a minty burn that's supposed to function as a self-limiter, but when you do it too much for too long, your teeth and mouth go necrotic. The really bad ones will sniff the inhaler, and it'll destroy their noses.

"You!" the man on the right shouted, startling his partner. "You 'all off de bridge. We ear to rescue you before offin' bad happens. I ought you take our help."

I would have rolled my eyes if I could risk taking them off the pair.

"Thanks, boys. We got it," Shantu said, flicking a five-credit chit at them.

Those five credits bought us a lot of information. Our newfound friends snatched it out of the air, showing no overcompensating or flinching. Their reflexes were in overdrive.

The first one looked dissatisfied at the chit. "No, you don't get it. See, it's dangerous down here. Know what I mean? You need the protection of someone who knows where you can and can't go."

"All right," Shantu said. "Can you get us out of here?"

I knew he was bullshitting. He must've seen something I didn't and judged the fight was over.

He kicked the ground and feigned a trip. I didn't watch him hit the ground. Instead, I leveled my weapon, gripped it with my supporting hand, and relaxed my elbow just enough to handle the recoil. Sight picture where I lock my whole body behind the weapon. Then align with the target. I gently squeezed the trigger until my rhino fired, using the flinch to lock my finger and my wrist into a pseudo automatic fire. I strafed both with plasma bolts and then did another sweep back.

I quietly thanked the nice man at the topside gun range for teaching me how to shoot properly.

The spring-loaded nature of my pistol drills made me kept me from processing the consequences of my actions until it was over.

The junky on the left was just registering that my weapon was firing with pure violent rage before white hot plasma consumed it. His neck exploded in vaporizing gore and blood. Three or four bolts flew between them as I overcorrected, fighting the recoil. My first bolt to the junkie on the right hit his knee, and the joint failed with the follow-up bolt. I let him fall into my fire with a half dozen shots into his abdomen, burning and boiling the organs.

I looked down at Shantu. He was on his back, covering our rear. He nodded and popped up to his feet.

We holstered our weapons and walked away just shy of a run. The rhino's heat soaked through the holster, but it was nice to have some warmth against the cold.

I wanted to see what they had on them—money, drugs, weapons, or maybe a feed. Shantu grabbed my collar and roughly dragged me along.

Out of the alley, we joined the flow of humanity who lived in this borough.

The smell of piss was pervasive. Too many people wore too many layers of scavenged clothing.

Everyone walked differently down here, like they were carrying a big invisible backpack. You had to bend like your back hurts and pull your collar up and hold it closed like your guts were going to fall out if you didn't. It's a stiff hobbling hunch.

Our jumpsuits had already picked up enough grime to match everyone else's.

Only psychopaths live down here by choice, according to people who don't understand the lack of options. It is the lawless underbelly that no one talks about on the news feeds. Leave the criminals to themselves.

We don't talk about the seven-year-old girl who's never left her apartment because she is too pretty to not get caught up in a flesh trade.

We don't talk about the pair of unsupervised teenagers who have started a family well before they are ready.

We don't talk about the kids who become grandparents before they are ready to take care of themselves.

We don't talk about good people who are not willing to abandon each other for the unknown fate of wars they know nothing about.

We don't talk about all the people who live down here because citizens think they have a monopoly on struggle. The two years in the military makes them better than a mother who won't abandon her children.

It doesn't matter how much you have to offer the universe. Unless you do those two years, you don't fucking matter, and you have to live in the gutter.

Shantu and I pressed toward the noise, cover, concealment, and safety. We took turns checking over our shoulders to see if anyone was following us.

Nothing yet.

The noise led us to an abandoned school. A concert must be somewhere in these lost halls. Learning still happens here, just not with principals or teachers. It taught different lessons now, and experience doled out the harsh curriculum. Classes in economy, abuse, control, and addiction were now offered.

We melted into the crowd easier than I like to admit. We had clawed our way out of this but came scrambling back like rats at the first sign of trouble.

Fuck my life!

The ambient conversation about the performance and some fights that were scheduled in the gymnasium fluctuated back and forth. No one gave a shit about us.

Shantu shouldered his way toward the gymnasium, and I grabbed his collar, so I could keep an eye behind us. He tapped my hand twice, and I shook his collar to say, "Sally forth!"

I don't really know how that goes.

Once through the doors, we found two fighting rings cobbled together from spare parts. The matches were underway. Venders lined the walls, selling everything from fight paraphernalia to food and to various sex objects. Not to mention a vice for every impulse-driven idiot.

I jerked Shantu's collar, and we switched places.

I had the idea that a locker room would be a good idea: blind corners and hard surfaces.

Here's something the movies lie about: punching someone in the mouth hard enough to knock them out sucks. If I break my hand, I can't pilot my AV. If I can't pilot my AV, Telex doesn't have a use for me. Telex *will* make good on the treats he makes about firing me.

We used the area between the fight crowd and the vendors, where the crowd seemed to be the thinnest, to get to the locker room as quickly as possible.

I hadn't noticed anyone yet. Maybe they followed the truck. Or maybe they said fuck it once we jumped off the freeway.

In the locker room, we found a rat shit version of a brothel. The smell went from bad to worse—sickly sweet like musty coolant. Soiled sheets mixed with piss and rot. Scented candles struggled to give light and to cover the awful smell.

A man with sores around his mouth stood behind a podium and tried to quote rates for services. I ignored him and tried to find another exit, but I couldn't see past the privacy curtain that was just a dingy sheet and a shipping tarp strung up with an electrical cord.

A bouncer type stepped up, overtly blocking my view with his body. His shiny chain advertised how tough he was.

Looking back, I must have looked like a creep trying to get a peek between the makeshift curtains.

The bouncer produced a large knife as if to say, "No free shows."

I didn't bother with him and snapped my pistol into the chest of the podium guy before he could move.

I locked eyes with him. Bones cracked, but I watched for a reaction. His face went from shock to terror, letting me know that Shantu had made short work of the bouncer. Podium guy put his hands up.

"Exit?" I asked as calmly as I could.

He fervently nodded.

I waved with my gun. "Go."

He grabbed a sturdy-looking bag from behind the podium and ran. The bouncer was up, cradling an arm and limping. They disappeared through the curtain wall.

Shantu shoved me to the other side of the door we had just entered through, and we got into ambush positions. We stood there for long moments, listening to people fuck elsewhere in the locker room.

A confused man entered and stopped short. We waved him to fuck off.

We didn't relax. Either our pursuer had lost us, or they would come through that door any moment now. Maybe the smell would keep them away.

It didn't.

What walked through the door was a crew-cut man with a shitty raincoat over light power armor. Panic hit my brain as I realized the shit, we were in.

His eyes met mine. There was a hard focus there. A military focus. The kind of focus that was casual with violence. I had only seen one person like that before. A CE trading plasma with a gang. Everyone around him had been torn to shreds by a bomb.

I had a narrow window.

I squeezed the trigger.

The shot went wide, and a hard grip tightened against my wrist. Flashes of light let me know Shantu was firing too.

The crew-cut man kept eye contact as he tilted his head, almost like he was popping his neck. A helmet deployed from his collar. He wrenched the pistol from my hand and kicked my chest, launching himself back into Shantu.

I gasped for breath and shook my head to clear my vision. The crew-cut man stood, but Shantu didn't. His matte black helmet now completely covered his head.

We were fucked.

I tried to crawl back into the fight, but my arms and legs were giving me —*ERROR 404 LIMBS NOT FOUND!*— messages. The fog in my head didn't know what to do with the whores and the johns who were being herded out of the room by a woman with two pistols that displayed distorted CE markings.

"You think these kids really have that much potential?" a level masculine voice asked.

"They have a nose for tactics," a deep seismic bass said.

"They're not cruel," a soft female voice added.

"D's got a point," the first voice said. "Look at this move after they jumped off the bridge."

My eyes wouldn't focus.

"Call it a job interview. Let's say you aced your skills assessment."

"Didn't mean to spook you, kid," another male voice that I still couldn't find said.

"Your friend there took a big knock to the head," a happier voice said. "It's best if we don't interrupt our medic. Once he's done, I can call you a ride, and we can have this conversation at the elevator. Sound good?"

I nodded, and he dropped my gun on my chest.

WORKING INTERVIEW

I GOT SOME drugs that cleared my head but made my limbs feel spongy. I couldn't tell anything about the medic who patched Shantu and me up. All I saw was a white space suit with an opaque faceplate. It could have been a top-of-the-line medical drone for all I know.

The strike team—or whatever you want to call them—scattered before I could get a headcount.

A big minotaur escorted us out of the under city. He was more than three meters tall and looked like something from the machine judgment day that never came. The armor walking in front of us was like gleaming laser reflective metal bristling with weapons. The minotaur death robot machine didn't say anything the whole time.

In a wave of common sense I had never seen before, the sea of people in the under city parted for him. The same people who set a CE armored personnel carrier on fire for interrupting a gang war.

Soon, we got to the CE checkpoint to get out of the under city.

"Were you two the idiots who jumped off the overpass?" the CE sitting at the gate asked while checking us over for contraband.

I didn't know what contraband was when there was a tank casually walking through the vehicle port.

"That thing was following us, and we didn't know it was friendly," Shantu jibed back.

"No shit." The other CE in the vehicle waved a sniffer wand around. "I don't even know why I'm doing this."

"Y'all have a good one," the first CE said. His friendly demeanor set me on edge.

"Elevator Embassy Hotel Restaurant at 2200 local, if you can make it," the minotaur said before sliding into a waiting car.

The moment the car took off, Shantu and I lost it. It was just us shouting at each other in a parking lot, trying to get a handle on what the fuck just happened. Eventually, we came to our senses and decided to go back to Telex's and get cleaned up.

EVERY VOTE COUNTS

SO, THE EMBASSY Hotel was the legit embassy. Non-humans everywhere. Shantu and I were the only humans not in high fashion, political, or religious garb. Save the uniformed staff who half jogged everywhere.

"Sir, I will require your weapons. Your party is waiting." The old man in a black and red staff uniform radiated competence. "I assure you that I will personally return them before you leave."

We handed over our pistols and then offered him our knives.

"Seeing as there is cutlery on the table, I see no reason to deprive you of those." He twirled rigidly like it was a dance he was being judged.

Giddy, Shantu and I struggled to not make fools of ourselves in this new environment.

The old man showed us to our table.

Shantu locked his excitement down and angled for control as the crew-cut man locked eyes with us. "You sure seemed to have rolled out the red carpet for us."

The crew-cut man narrowed his eyes as if he was deciding how he wanted to take that. His face then relaxed into a diplomatic smile. "It's funny the perks you get on certain planets when you buy fuel. Never mind that. Have a seat." He gestured to the hostess behind us who was waiting to push in our chairs.

"Allow me to make introductions." The crew-cut man stood and gestured to the table full of different species. "Scout."

A gecko-looking critter with ears that could make an elephant jealous waved.

"Dire-horn."

The minotaur from before stood. "Ship's advocate. Heavy infantry." His voice was more felt than heard, and the ceiling changed shape, dropping some flat panels down to manage the acoustics. Without his armor, his fur was light brown, sandy, silky, shiny, and smooth. I wanted to pet him. His horns were curved forward and up with some kind of decorative bobble on them. He returned to his seat with military professionalism.

"Javelin. Sniper and ship's purser," the crew-cut man said, pointing at a gene-spliced woman with wings and long golden feathers for hair.

Her left arm and side of her face were hard cybernetics. She didn't acknowledge us; her hand gestures; swiping and tapping at nothing, implied she was doing something in her feed.

I want a feed.

"Piper. Pilot and astrogator."

Piper was in a humanoid space suit with the convenient helmet lights on so we could see their androgynous features. "How's it going?" they asked. Their mouth didn't quite match their words.

I narrowed my eyes and tilted my head. Maybe their words were translated by the suit. But I held back from asking to be polite.

"Cyborg?" Shantu asked as subtle as a hammer.

"Blycow," Piper returned, sounding almost amused.

"Hard or soft?"

"Hard."

I'm pretty sure that meant they are silicon-based life and not a program that can change out hardware.

I elbowed Shantu, so the crew-cut man could continue.

"I am Captain Gara Vatosh of the *Free Trade Ship (FTS) The Happy Marauder*," the crew-cut man said. "This is how we decide if we want to invite someone to become a member of the crew."

My default job interview mode kicked in. "Thank you all for this opportunity. Could you describe what our responsibilities would be?"

Shantu rolled his eyes.

"Please," the minotaur boomed, "do not perform for us. We are not a corporate interview automaton."

Shantu snorted, and my face flushed.

That shit is why I let Shantu do the talking most of the time.

"Why did y'all chase us into the gutter?" Shantu asked. "Our contact information was on the side of the truck…"

The crew-cut man–I mean, Captain Vatosh–didn't answer Shantu's question. "Now, walk us through your line of logic when—"

"This fucker"–Shantu pointed at me–"was passed out, riding shotgun, when I noticed we were being tailed."

I buried my face in my hands because there was no stopping him now.

"If you wanted the truck, good luck. It's insured, so fuck it. If we were going to catch a beating, got to make them work for it. Anyone following us off an overpass has an expiration date for us in their plans."

He was talking about how elevator workers get killed to tie up loose ends by smugglers a few times a year.

"Anyway, I can tell y'all aren't from Vanguard, but once you're in the under city, you're going to have to fight. Today's episode of Violence in Vanguard starring yours truly includes two stim junkies packing overloaded SMGs."

"Is that why you dropped?" I asked.

Shantu didn't even take a breath. "Yeah. They were a multicellular yoke job. I couldn't risk getting in a scrap with them; they were at the peak of their ride. You were in position, and you're aces over kings on the snapshot. The best I could do, given the situation, was get out of the way and let you work. I covered the rear and saw him"–he made finger guns at Captain Vatosh–"make his jump. Our only real chance was if we could get lost in the crowds. Our plan in the locker room was good until, we found out the hard way he's a ninja in power armor."

"Tell us what educational subscription leads to such actions," Scout said, his giant ears wafting.

I wondered if his question was part of his species' psychology. I drew a blank on what species he was. I just wanted to play with the floppy ears, but I didn't think that would be polite.

"Honestly, we are avid attendants to the school of hard knocks," Shantu said so fast that I couldn't answer if I wanted to, "and our headmistress experience taught us very well. She was harder on some students, and we learned from them as well. With graduate courses from Murphy and way too much media and video games."

Dire-horn was laughing or trying to warn traffic it was time to move. The dangly bits on his horns jumped with his honking laugh. Parking plazas made less noise after sporting events.

Clear walls effortlessly glided into place, separating us from the rest of the patrons. An animation of leaves falling blended the walls in with the rest of the decor and prevented anyone from walking into the transparent barriers.

Scout tilted his head and perked one elephant ear toward Captain Vatosh.

Captain Vatosh smiled. "Murphy was a legendary human

warrior who was known for saying anything that can go wrong will go wrong."

A quiet moment passed as everyone contemplated the truth in the words.

I broke the silence. "What are we looking at if we join you?"

"Depending on how quickly you get your certifications, six standard months to a standard year before you're operational," Dire-horn said. His gaze pierced us as his horizontal pupils shifted back and forth between Shantu and me.

The rest of the crew's eyes glazed over, or they checked their feeds.

"Pending a medical examination to include a cardiovascular integrity review, you will board *The Happy Marauder* as deckhands. Upon embarkation, you will become a one-eighth share crew."

The waitstaff delivered an appetizer during his monologue. I hadn't even looked at the little interface built into the chair. Who was ordering for us?

The appetizer was a fancy version of cheesy bread with lines of marinara dividing each slice. The flat, thin bread was crispy compared to the oily sponges I was used to. The cheese was a hearty savory variety, not quite sweet but aromatic that took on a life of its own. The cheese set a well-lit stage for the herbs to dance on. I was fucking lost because I had never tasted anything so exquisite.

Resisting the urge to pick up the plate and lick it was the pinnacle of my self-control, but I did lick my finger to prevent the atrocity of letting any of it go to waste.

I'm sure Shantu's face was mirroring mine as he stared at his plate, licking his fingers and wiping up the marinara, oil, and herbs.

Shantu then looked like something had bit him. "Um… Not to be impolite, but who's paying for this?"

FUCK!

This is how people get indentured. Eat a meal and don't bother asking the questions that matter. Find out that it was a million-credit piece of flatbread and go work for five credits an hour for the rest of their life.

"Consider this meal, compensation for your time." Captain Vatosh explained.

"Upon completion of your Interstellar Transportation Safety and Security course," Dire-horn continued, "you will automatically be promoted to load master. Given your background and current qualifications, your shares will increase to one-quarter share. If you fail to complete the ITSS course, you will be asked to disembark at the next port, and one-time passage will be provided for you back to here, Vanguard Prime Space Elevator, or an equivalent legal port of your choosing."

"Is the course difficult?" I asked.

Captain Vatosh answered. "For a human, it's an afternoon worth of reading; a few skills proficiency tests; donning space suits, fire suppression, air locks, and environmental control… That sort of thing. It's a safety thing our insurance requires." His dismissive tone told me I had to be a real fuckup to fail.

Dire-horn continued almost on autopilot, and I briefly wondered how many times he had done this. "Upon your request, your contract may be evaluated up to a half share for critical specialty. Full shares will be offered only to the tier three rated operators upon completion of their first code 681 rated mission."

"Can we get a quick breakdown of the tier system?" I asked.

Captain Vatosh's eyes didn't focus, and his hands kept making gestures like he was in his feeds. "Tier five is an armed mall cop: a weapon, no training, and no experience. The primary goal is customer service. Tier four is a cop: a weapon and training. The primary goal is conflict mitigation. Tier three is a soldier: a weapon and training. The primary goal is threat engagement.

Tier two is special forces: trainers who have extensive experience with specialized weapons platforms. The primary goal is threat neutralization. Tier one is operators: extensive, specialized training and experts in their area of responsibility. The primary goal is to forward the agenda."

He went back to his feeds, and Dire-horn continued on about governing legal codes and statutes. Shantu and I occasionally exchanged glances, checking in. Neither of us were paying attention anymore; it was like a user agreement but spoken by a bass drum.

"We're going to be mercenaries, not crew?" Shantu asked.

"Both mercenaries and crew," Dire-horn answered, seemingly earnest. "Market availability determines what we do. We came to Vanguard to facilitate delivery, so a third party didn't default on the contract. We took payment up front, and now we're here recruiting new crew. It takes a certain kind of person to do what we do."

"And what is that exactly?" Shantu said with a bit of a challenge in his tone.

"Anything and everything." The minotaur seemed affectionate. "The ship is home, and we keep her moving by trading commodities. We make her better with good contracts. It's up to us to crunch the numbers and decide if it is a good contract."

Captain Vatosh cleared his throat, and I noticed waiters standing around the table, waiting to serve the second course. I leaned back in my chair. One waiter took the appetizer plate away, and another placed an entrée in front of me.

The noodles were wide and flat, covered in a white creamy sauce that had just a tinge of sweetness. Black spicy bits stood in a savory contrast. Grilled seasoned chicken made love to my mouth. It was absolute heaven.

Dire-horn stopped talking, and it felt like a large engine cut out. The sounds of silverware made the room seem empty and lonely.

Captain Vatosh filled the silence. "Thank you, Dire-horn. I'm going to cover a lot of practical concerns. Once I'm done, you may ask questions."

We nodded.

"To be clear, we intend to bring you aboard to become full share members. We've collected an extensive library and training modules. The training includes psychological and physical conditioning to maximize your potential and limit your combat liability. Your success is not guaranteed, and failure to adapt will invoke disembarkation provisions. Our operating provisions will be high risk, high reward. Cargo helps reduce the logistic burden but does not yield much of a profit at this scale."

Shantu and I exchanged looks. A conversation as clear as text passed between us.

He was nervous because we didn't know them and should not trust them. I trusted them as much as I could trust anyone who I tried to shoot. I didn't see the logic in a nice meal and brain-melting amount of legal bullshit if someone was going to slave us out.

In the end, we decided to be awesome.

Captain Vatosh watched our exchange; his expression was one of polite respect. "Being aware that the positions we offer you will put you in direct mortal danger, is it still your intention to seek a position aboard *The Happy Marauder*."

We nodded.

"Dire-horn."

A display descended from the ceiling. A simple for and against counter appeared.

"Open forum voting will begin," Captain Vatosh announced.

Javelin's name jumped to the for column right away.

One for, zero against.

"I would like to discuss your criminal history," Dire-horn said.

"Shit," Shantu and I said in unison.

I had forgotten that we were both on probation for another

two years. I didn't know if our legal standing precluded taking work off-world.

"You both are currently on probation for assault, theft of a vehicle, and piloting while intoxicated." Dire-horn paused as if to wait for us to add something.

We were on psychedelics, and it was a night of bad decisions. I hesitated because everything in my head sounded worse than keeping my mouth shut.

Shantu thankfully had something intelligent to say. "It was certainly a wakeup call for us." He glanced at me before continuing. "Our recreational intoxicant use has dropped to nearly zero. We have taken our probation and sobriety very seriously."

Scout's name appeared on the -against- side, and I looked at him. "No offense, but I would rather keep open slots for some veteran operators. Do a tour in the military, and we can pick you up in a few years."

One for, one against.

His tone seemed sincere; I think. How do you interpret the expression of an elephant-eared gecko?

Captain Vatosh glared at Scout. His expression read "don't make promises you can't keep."

Dire-horn seemed to ponder for a moment longer before voting against.

One for, two against.

Piper's name appeared under for. "I think natural talent is invaluable, and their youth makes them more adaptable to changing circumstances." They almost seemed to scold the other two.

Two for, two against.

Shantu and I looked at each other. The media had lied to us about non-biological sapience. They were supposed to be obsessed with quantifiable data and coldly calculating. Evil robots taking our jobs. Blah blah blah.

The display added two flanking columns. —Polarizing Factors— appeared at the top of each new column.

"Is anyone going to leave the ship over this issue?" Captain Vatosh asked.

Attention was split between Scout and Javelin. She shrank into her chair, vibrating with nervous energy.

Dire-horn spoke as if to rescue her from the attention. "I have stated my objections and have voted accordingly. I do not feel strongly enough to harm crew morale to maintain my position."

"Yeah, same here," a voice said from the overhead screen. *Gabe* was highlighted in the against column. "I'm not even going to refuse to train them. I'm just going to bitch to the other two the entire time until they're not green."

Two for, thee against.

Captain Vatosh's eyes unfocused for a moment, almost as if someone was talking to him. His name and *Wraith* then appeared in the for column.

Four for, and three against.

The screen cut out and retracted.

No congratulations?

"All right then," Captain Vatosh said. "Pending medical and legal evaluation, we will set things in motion. Next question: who owns those AVs you were piloting, and what equipment would be necessary to maximize your skill set?"

I paused for a moment to gather a mental inventory. They were built, by us, from the ground up. I had no idea if they even had a vehicle identification code or what would come up if we started tracing parts.

Shantu left me in the dust. "The two we were in are ours. I would like to have a third to make into a cannibal frame. I don't know what you have onboard, but AV Custom Dynamics makes a really good cradle. I don't know if they're worth a damn on a ship, but I like them…"

I stopped paying attention because of the looming magnitude and utter absurdity of it.

Well, it wasn't that absurd. Freighters need a load crew just like liners need porters.

I might be getting off planet!

Fuck! I hope this isn't a strip tease where you can't touch. The food alone was worth it. I don't want to go back to eating pressed calories.

If I can't go into space, maybe I'll find a place on a farm. I can't keep this up anymore. Working two shitty jobs to pay day rates on an apartment I don't even like… Fuck this. Fuck *ALL* of this!

I'm not going to keep working just to be poor and die.

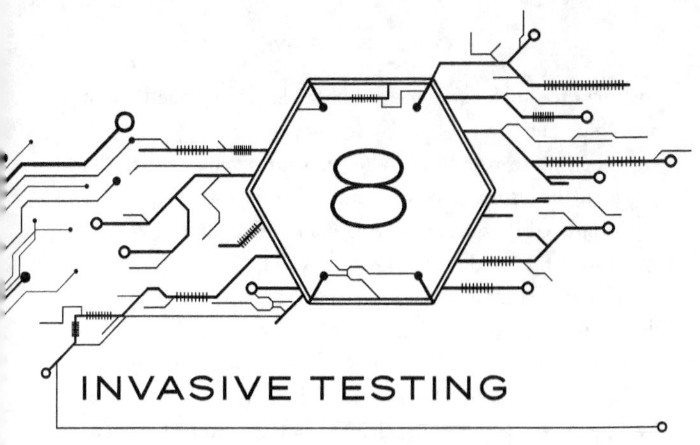

INVASIVE TESTING

520.102.2350 Medical District, Vanguard
City, Vanguard Prime, Vanguard

THIS MORNING BRIGHT-AND-EARLY

my door chimed.

I wasn't ready, but I wasn't getting any readier.

I slept like shit because my brain was like a volleyball, and the players who wouldn't fuck off were my thoughts. I was excited that I had a real job prospect. But I was afraid that the physical is going to tell me I'm dying. Then Shantu would be alone, and that makes me sadder than the thought of dying.

My door chimed again. A suit, flanked by two CE officers, stared at his handset. I rolled back the door feed on the wall panel. The trio stood there for about ten minutes before hitting my chime.

This wasn't a good building, but you didn't need two CE.

"Mr. Childs," the suit said. "I am Expediting Agent Richardson from the Department of Emigration. I am here to process your emigration to *The Happy Marauder*. Please accompany me to the Lui Center for Athletic Medicine."

I quickly dressed and left the door open. I didn't get one foot past the threshold before the suit began launching questions at a machine-gun pace.

"Where were you born? Who are your parents? When did you leave the institute? What's your highest level of education?"

I wondered if he had an augmentation that allowed him to speak so fast. I couldn't even keep up with half of his questions, but ignorance on the topics seemed to be enough to satisfy his documents that I assumed he was completing virtually.

Four people crowded the hallway, and a young lady pressed herself against the wall to let us and the armored CE squeeze by. The lift was approaching claustrophobic with the four of us trying not to touch and failing. It didn't run as smooth as it once did, and the light was a weird green color.

Down the lift and out of the lobby, I saw Shantu entering a sky car identical to the one my suit was sliding into. The cars were the quad rotor flying boxes that all government and cheap people used. The officers hopped on their twin rotor sky cycles to escort us.

Once I was in the car, the suit handed me a tablet with a stylus. "This is recognition that while aboard *The Happy Marauder*, you lose all provisions as a protected citizen."

I signed the legal documents as fast as he could review them.

I'll summarize. The crew are citizens of their respective ships. There will be no one to cry to if my ship is shitty. No recourse if I am screwed out of pay. I am encouraged to research and buy insurance before any embarkation.

Funny. I can't do that because I don't have any money.

But if I get into debt or other trouble with any friends of Vanguard, I won't be allowed back.

Then something in the rapid-fire legalese started making sense. I wasn't a citizen anyway, so it didn't matter. To this planet, I was a piece of trash in the gutter, and it was going to be happy to be rid of me.

My probation would end under the extenuating circumstances provisions if I joined *The Happy Marauder*. The suit provided me with a hard copy of all the provisions for my records.

My stomach lurched with the hard turn we took to land at the hospital. I was robbed! I didn't get to see the city from the air since I was too busy dealing with documents.

It sank in that Shantu and I were really doing something different with our lives. We were not only making it out of Vanguard City, but we were also getting off-world and out of system. I could see Shantu making the same connections. Nervous energy vibrated between us.

The hospital was what you would expect. Clean white walls with displays showing generic medical advice. Like how to spot a heart attack and a stroke. Oh, don't forget the posters with the various body systems. It was empty save one woman entertaining a child with an anatomical human body puzzle.

Shantu and my respective agents tapped us into a kiosk and told us to go to phlebotomy. Then it was an assembly line of testing rooms as each set of medical people did their thing and kicked us out.

During one of the tests, Shantu and I were placed in adjacent machines. We were given masks, placed in harnesses, and forced to climb the ladder version of a treadmill. Ladder-mill?

Anyway, the technician made the mistake of leaving the joule rating visible. We looked at each other and started off as soon as the equipment was ready. I immediately regretted the decision. I lost my breath but managed to pull ahead. I didn't have a chance to beat Shantu with anything physical, but I just wanted the lead for a moment.

It was a small victory but the only one I could get.

Shantu took a steady warm-up pace. It didn't take long for him to almost pass me. But I wasn't going down easily. I surged for as long as I could. My muscles burned, I struggled to breathe, and Shantu steadily passed me.

I then dropped down to a pace I could maintain without having a coronary.

Afterward, we were fed, drained of blood for more tests, and pumped back full of blood. Scanned some more. Talked to someone. Talked to someone else.

I received a message that all our outstanding debt had been transferred to *The Happy Marauder*.

I was spun in a big centrifuge and learned that my resting g tolerance was 6.6, which was good. The people in the booth running the centrifuge taught me how to strain to keep my blood pressure up. My strain rating was 12.1, which was very good from what I was told.

A Vanguard Fleet recruiter offered me snacks and drinks from the lounge's cabinets. I swear they found my porn preferences and stuffed it into a Fleet Formal Uniform. Thick curly blond hair, thick in a good way, with piercing blue eyes. That pissed me off.

"Mr. Childs, if you're longing for adventure," Sergeant Something-Or-Another began in a comfortable tone, "the Vanguard Fleet is somewhere you can make a difference."

I tilted my head, trying to catch her eyes at the right angle. I must have looked like a street kid with sloppy posture and a carefree attitude. There it was: the off glimmer in her eyes. They were prosthetics.

I glared at her. "Idealism, honor, and loyalty are cheap substitutes for market share." I spouted off some bullshit I had seen on the feed about inflation. When that didn't strike a nerve, I made it personal. "You must be from one of the old families, doing your third tour with the fleet here in Vanguard City to check off the boxes so that you can start your political career in ten years."

Her face finally showed anger. "You don't know anything about me."

I held out my hands, letting her see my scars and calluses. "I don't know you because you don't know you. Fake eyes. Fake figure. Fake smile when I walked in through the fucking door. Vanguard of the future? What a fucking joke. You are the epitome of this planet's fucking lie."

She winced but didn't say anything. If all the shows were right, she had been raised with money and wouldn't give her argument until I was done.

So full throttle. "Even your eyes are an illusion to get me to do what they want. If a state-sponsored colony takes four months to get relief from pirate raids, and a mostly automated mining facility can get next-day fucking service, this place is fucked."

I was referring to something I had heard around Telex's and had no idea of the context.

She glared at me. "It's not that simp—"

"No. It *is* that simple. Those colonies are fucking leper colonies."

I don't know what a leper is, but it sounds gross. The service tech who liked to play podcasts in his bay just popped into my brain.

"It's the effortless way to get rid of a political dissonant: pay them to leave rather than to lose their vote because the relay ship was lost to pirates. That mining facility is going to cost some rich fucking family money they can spare but don't want to. So, they would rather call me a hero than pay me what I'm worth. They would rather spend your lives than their own credits on security." I went in for the kill. "Not *your* life. The cannon fodder you're here to recruit. You probably spent your conscription guarding your ambassador uncle."

"What's your problem with me?"

I knew this game. The worst thing I could do was acknowledge that she mattered.

"You personally? Nothing," I said. "I don't know you. Where

the fuck were you yesterday when I was running a forklift and fighting for my life against some junkies? Nowhere! I had to jump off a freeway to take care of myself, and CE didn't even care if I hit the ground. Now some facet of my makeup makes me worth something to them, so they collate my porn preferences and send their closest ass-et to get me. How the fuck is Vanguard going to stand in front of me and ask me to serve when I was banned from conscription for the crime of surviving at the Institute four years ago? How fucked up is that? I claw my way out of the gut and find a ship to take me away, and *now* Vanguard wants me? Sounds pretty selfish to me."

She was dead in her tracks.

I walked out of the room with a smile. I thought taking her pause as my exit moment was an exceptional way to drive my point home.

Outside the lounge, I found an assistant waiting to take me to a psychosocial evaluation. I was taken to a painfully white room. *Saturating* may be the right word. Disembodied voice yelled at me. "Your evaluation is beginning! Repeat the noun at the end of the sentence."

"Sentence?" I looked around the room for the sensors because this was uncomfortable.

Ding.

"You have a dog," it said.

"Dog."

Ding.

"Tallahassee is beautiful this time of year."

"Year."

Ding!

It went like that long enough for me to go on autopilot. Then they hit me with a curve ball.

"I will be raped in the ass by a man."

"What the fuck?"

HONK!

"Please repeat the noun at the end of the sentence."

"Shit, um, man."

HONK!

"Please repeat the noun at the end of the sentence."

"Fuck, uh, sentence."

Ding.

The test varied to different word types and then a fucked-up sentence would disrupt my groove. When the sentence—I rape children—came up, I found out you could skip.

After a frustrating amount of time, the door opened and finally released me from that crap. The door across the hall opened simultaneously, and a geriatric woman called out to me.

"Young man, come here."

Her well-lit comfortable office smelled like getting slapped in the face with a poundcake. She offered me a cookie and milk, and my mouth watered. I was stuffing my face before I realized what I was doing, and she softly chuckled and busied herself with her screen while keeping one eye on me.

"What is this?" I asked.

"A cookie. Chocolate chip. My favorite." Her neck jiggled, and her face folded into a gentle smile.

"I meant…" I barely could speak with the sugary deliciousness filling my mouth.

"I know what you meant. Take a minute to enjoy the cookie." She let me finish a cookie and put a jug of milk in front of me, allowing me to refill the glass. "I'm the case manager for your report. The report and relevant documents about our methods will be uploaded to this." She pushed a tablet toward me. "Some find those tests triggering. I'm here to help."

I shrugged. "It makes sense to get a psych profile before you hire someone. Why a sports medicine facility? Don't they rebuild knees and stuff here?"

The old woman stared at me warmly. I could imagine her doing the same for her grandchildren, letting them work something out.

I got there. "Because sports teams will pay big money to make sure their players will perform?"

She lifted her chin. "You're a bright young man with potential. But the system has you flagged as a sociopath due to your criminal records."

I flinched. I knew I wasn't a psychopath, but I had killed.

Do you become one if you grow hard enough after enough shit?

"I don't want to be a psychopath," I mumbled.

She smiled. "Our testing disagrees with The Institute for Developing Children's assessment to the point that an audit has been triggered."

I could see her face reading mine like an open book. There was a bit of joy in her eyes as she watched me go from introspection to relief. I briefly wondered if she had implants that could read my heart rate, blood pressure, galvanic skin response, and all the shit that can tell if a person is lying.

"I see no reason why any of this would interfere with your potential employment."

She was a warm elderly woman who should be enjoying retirement. Maybe baking for her grandkids or for a shelter. Take in the image of grandma's wrinkles as she serves you soup. So, you know I was taken off guard when she said this:

"So, if anyone tries to fuck with you, call me on that." She gestured toward the tablet. "I will pull my carcass out of my grave before I let anyone stop a young person from pulling themselves up by their bootstraps."

FUCK! She had steel in those old veins.

Grandma had an old soldier's determination where they had decided exactly which hill to die on, and now it was a game of how many they could take down before they died. She was ready for war, and I had chocolate on my face and a milk mustache.

The rest of my day was spent in machines that did things…

They told me. I don't remember.

I know I got a bone marrow biopsy, a limp until it healed, and like fifty different views of my body under different imaging.

Oh, and I put my swimmers on ice because of the high rate of infertility due to space travel. I checked the box that said they could be used in fertility programs if I didn't make it back after a hundred years.

Back in the sky car, the suit asked me, "Do you have an estimate for the volume of space needed for your personal items?"

I shrugged and held out my hands, trying to gauge the space. "Let's see… Call it three meters."

He tapped on his tablet. "Mr. Childs, may I speak frankly outside my purview?"

I was tired and thought a conversation would be nice. "Sure."

The suit looked exhausted—not physically but mentally or emotionally. Something like that.

Anyway, he said, "My job is usually to escort diplomats and the occasional refugee. Some high-risk solar trade executives. We don't usually see a lot of *normal* people. I looked into your background and the ship you are intending to embark upon. The opportunity afforded you is life changing. If I were offered it, I would take it without reservation, even considering the level of comfort my position grants me. I feel the need to tell you to take care. Be mindful of how you invest your time and resources."

He left that hanging in the air as we flew back to my apartment.

I got to look out the window this time. The city was perfect for the noir films that were so commonly set here. White and black. For a city above the clouds, there wasn't anything celestial about it. Black jagged skyscrapers raged against the angry frozen winds. The elevator cable blinked promises of new horizons.

I asked the suit for a lap around the city, and he obliged.

Far below the city, down the mountain, and below the cloud crest stretched the hairs of elevated rail lines that connected us to other cities on Vanguard. If nothing else, the people running this place respected the planet.

I had lived my whole life up here on the peak of this mountain. This was the first time I had seen it from the air, and I wanted to let it linger for just a bit longer. Maybe I saw myself in it: harsh and stubborn but finding a way to reach for the stars.

The suit dropped me off in front of my apartment building.

What hit me was the restraint in his voice to not say certain things. He didn't say "kid, don't get yourself killed" or "don't burn all your money on whores and stupid shit."

He had *hope* in his eyes. That this kid from the gutter of Vanguard City was going to do something with his life other than end up at an organic reprocessing unit.

I felt like he was rooting for me in his own way.

Shantu met me at the front of our apartment building. "We're doing this?" Half a question, half a statement. He looked as if he was coming to terms with our new reality.

"It's a little late to back out now. I don't know if we can back out, legally speaking. I don't know if I would if we could. I don't want us to keep killing ourselves to make a cred. And to do what? Make it another day? Week? Month? It all sounds like a slow death—not a life."

"You get all poetic and shit when shit gets real."

"Fuckstick."

"Fucknuts."

We took the lift to our respective apartments. At my door stood two men with a dolly and collapsible boxes. Clearly nervous, they had their handsets out, failing at acting casual as they tried to look in every direction at once and jumped at every noise.

I rolled my eyes. "I really don't think we'll need all those."

I stepped between the movers and opened the door. One of them unfolded a box, followed me in, and awkwardly stopped at the threshold. I dumped my small pile of work uniforms into the box without warning and hid a smile as he almost dropped it.

I shoved my pistol, my small collection of tools, and the cleaning kit that the guy from the range gave me into a backpack, followed by the few toiletries I had. I disassembled the light fixture and pulled out my small stash of credits and a few illicit items. I offered the moving guy the said illicit items.

When the moving guy declined I tossed my drugs down the garbage chute.

I surveyed my small apartment. The single bed mounted to a wall. The shelf that could be extended to be used as a desk if I was sitting on the bed. That was it.

Fuck this place.

I tapped the panel by the door to end my rental. It wasn't a lease because I couldn't enter into a contract. I placed the key in the slot and acknowledged all the end user agreements.

Before the moving guy could, I lifted my box. It was depressingly light. "I got this," I told the movers and turned to walk toward the stairs.

I saw Shantu greeting his mover and told him, I would meet him at the terminal before walking off.

The thought that I was leaving Vanguard–for possibly forever–circulated in my head. I wondered if this was what kids leaving home for the first time went through.

I looked at my meager box of clothing, most reaching the end of their useful life, and dropped the box next to a beggar. I didn't see the point in carrying it around.

As I wandered away from my former apartment building, feelings of overwhelming insignificance washed over me one last time, and I smiled. The only person who would notice I wasn't there was coming with me.

I turned down the street and headed toward the rail station. I let all the mixed emotions I had about Vanguard and its people fight their own battles inside me. There were so many reasons to love and hate this place. It had been home, and time would tell if it would always be.

Maybe it never was.

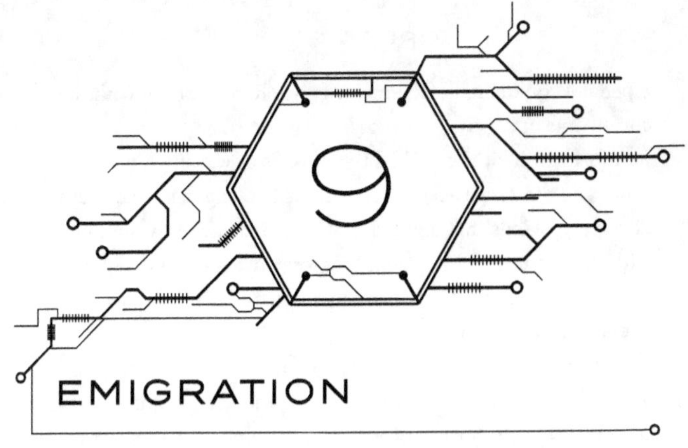

9

EMIGRATION

I STEPPED OFF the familiar tram and into an unfamiliar emigration terminal. It was a beehive of travelers, agents, and personnel.

Everything was clean and in good repair, though not new. What all all the tram stations should look like. No graffiti. No piss smell. No mystery fluid that you knew better than to investigate. People looked comfortable; no one had eyes in the back of their heads.

I moved out of the main flow of traffic to take in the scenes for a moment. Between the ramps, I rested my elbows on the transparent guardrail that gave a good view across three levels. The ramps had moving lights, indicating a magnetic conveyor under the smooth but opaque surface. I watched a traveler steady his luggage cart as it gently but firmly aligned itself to the moving field before being deposited at the next level.

I had lost sight that Vanguard was a huge metropolis. This concourse had a population under three meters and was mostly bipedal. I couldn't tell if the majority was human or not with the cornucopia of coverings, armors, and suits.

Information kiosks flashed their cycles of warnings, notifications, and their own services in a myriad of languages. The vendors were islands that divided the concourse inversely, subdued with simple standardized signs that rotated languages and pictograms. The adjacent single bar line encouraged us to get what we need, consume it, and move on.

A drone swarm circulated a few meters above everyone and gave a false ceiling feel. Together, they formed a giant map with their large mesh displays. Every so often, someone waved at one, and it would politely offer its information, either to be dismissed or to lead the person to their destination.

I was irritated that the tram stations I used normally were never this well maintained. There wasn't enough traffic for the drones, but a kiosk and a cleaning bot would have been nice. Maybe fix the lighting and ventilation. Fuck it. I would just want the tram to run on time without having to fight anyone.

Once I saw the one drone interaction, I noticed how many were interspersed within the crowds, guiding people. Occasionally, someone would do something wrong, and one would honk, dive down, and flash a warning: a not-so-subtle reminder of how heavily monitored this place was.

I watched someone try to swat at a drone's warning sign on the level below me. Two drones darted from above and parted the foot traffic from the hatch built into the ground. A security person in light powered armor popped up from the hole like a plunger to the troublemaker's back.

Security retracted their helmet to reason with the troublemaker. Security then lost interest in de-escalation, picked up the troublemaker, and fell back into the hatch.

Traffic moved on like nothing had happened. Must be nice to not get shot at.

Shantu appeared at my side. "How long have we been coming to the elevator, moving cargo and whatnot? We never knew this was a few dozen meters below our feet."

This is why he's my best friend. He always seems to know what to say at the right time. He only had a backpack too.

God, we're poor. *Were* poor?

"More like a few hundred. I think we might be near a kilometer down." I was guessing because the tram coming to the station was at a decent angle.

I took a deep breath and waved for a drone. I searched for *The Happy Marauder* and found ship information restricted. Shantu nudged me with our itinerary code in his legal packet.

—Please Wait for Escort— and a timer appeared.

"I spent the night at the library," he said. "Everything in space is super expensive because of the cost of getting things out of a gravity well. The cost of a five-star meal on Vanguard will buy you nutrient paste in orbit. No shit. They call it the space tax. Everything costs one thousand times more."

"Does that mean we're climbing out of the sewer and into the gutter?" I said cynically.

"I don't know, dude. Labor in space is in short supply because most people can't survive the space cocktail and have less than five years before they go blind and a bunch of shit. The trend is to sign on with a corporate-owned ship, get experience, and then migrate to a more profitable ship. Even then, there's a lot of movement because of how cutthroat it can be. In certain areas, it boils down to modern slavery because of perpetual debt agreements…"

I let him talk about how fucked up financing aboard ships can be until the escort—a four-passenger cart with a pretty woman in business attire— arrived.

"It's usually not that bad because if you keep your ratings up, better ships will buy your debt for you to take on for a specific role. So, it acts as a big Darwin filter for shitbags."

The woman stepped off far enough to tell us that any seat we wanted was available. Shantu and I sat catty-corner from each other. It was a habit we had developed so that we could literally watch each other's backs and still be engaged in a conversation.

She offered us refreshments and politely talked about the amenities. She then handed us tablets, dropped us off at some executive lounge, and bid us happy travels.

The tablets were coded to our biometrics, and I had Shantu's. We switched tablets and rolled our eyes at the intro animation and disclaimer bullshit.

I checked the all but inaccessible hidden menus, where the spike-encrusted dick was lurking in the form of fine print and billing.

"Our billing is to *The Happy Marauder*," Shantu said, looking over our account information. "There's a list of services they won't cover, but it's all the ultra-premium top tier shit. I think we're good to just do whatever we want if we don't, like, buy wine from Earth or something stupid."

"Dude, I've never had a massage where they didn't offer to put a finger in your butt halfway through," I joked.

"You've never had a massage."

"You're right. Let's fucking get one," I said with a bit too much excitement.

"All right. I put us in queue. I'm not sure what they mean by deep tissue, but it says it's good for your muscles."

The appointment confirmation popped up, and I accepted it. The confirmation was replaced by a timer that took its place at the top left of the screen. We had a few hours to kill.

"Dude, I think we need to get some new clothes." Shantu's eyes gestured around the room.

I looked up from the tablet and took in the room for the first time.

The lounge/lobby was a large open space with discrete

comfortable divisions for dining, drinking, and napping. Staff circulated carts with blankets and snacks. The dark wooden tones, low ambient light, and comfortable indeterminate background music almost lulled me to sleep.

Isolated translucent professional spaces stood as passive lighting. The glass enclosing the space was frosted enough that I could tell there was someone in there but almost nothing else. I assume they were soundproof because the nearest one had someone moving vigorously. I couldn't tell if they just went bankrupt or were playing a game.

What Shantu was getting at was that this place smelled of money. Styles ranged from polite professionals to eccentric performers.

Labor was not in fashion.

I suddenly became aware of our smell: solvents, lubricants, exhausts, and metal.

"Maybe we should get washed up," I suggested.

"Okay. There's a transit package I'm signing us up for," Shantu said without even looking up from the tablet.

"Gentlemen," the concierge woman said. Her tone reminded us that we were holding up two people who were at work.

She never broke her professional distance. "You've decided to take advantage of our uplifting services to help you adapt to your change in circumstance. Wise choice," she said in a bored monotone voice. "Your first stop will be the spa. Would you like to remain together, or would you prefer a more individually tailored experience?"

Shantu and I exchanged looks, shrugged, and decided to stay together.

At the spa, the floral wrapped doors parted as she led us to a room with two baths gently circulating water and petals. Wilderness vistas cycled on the walls, and soft padded benches lined the room. We barely had enough space to walk around the two giant tubs.

Shantu didn't hesitate to strip.

I joined him, less enthused. We were friends, but I didn't like my body. We were caricatures of skeletons who drank too much water; a far cry from the muscled men on the advertisements.

"Relaaax." He stretched out the word. "I'm not going to touch you, and it's not like I haven't seen your dick before."

"Fuckstick."

"Fucknuts."

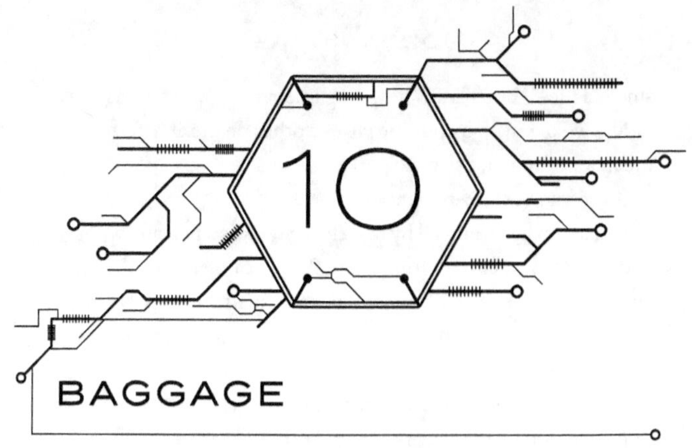

BAGGAGE

Unavailable Context Modified

I'M PUTTING THIS here because you need to know what sometimes happens when I close my eyes.

The last night I slept well, I was a child. Adults were giants to me. I think it's my first memory.

At this point, I thought The Institute for Developing Children was a salvation.

I don't think I had ever had a hot meal before. The big lady in blue was kind but sad. She bathed me with warm fresh water. She let me hold the sprayer as she scrubbed the grime from me. She would say sweet, nice things. I drank so much from the sprayer that my belly jiggled when I moved.

The next lady was in white. She was not nice. She hurt me with sharp things. She asked mean, hard questions. I didn't understand. I didn't know what to say.

I didn't like it.

The big lady in blue let me sit on her lap while I ate two sand-wiches and soup. I was so hungry. She held me and rocked me. She smelled nice. I don't know how long I slept on her, but it was nice.

She woke me up by putting clean clothes on me. Then she put me in a warm bed. I slept so good.

It was the best sleep ever.

I woke up in a room all by myself. There was a bed and a potty and a sink and a cup to drink from. People came in to talk to me and read to me and to give me things that made my tummy hurt. But if I swallowed them, they would give me ice cream.

I like ice cream.

One of the people showed me the black window on the wall that was called a screen, and I could watch whatever I wanted. I could also play games.

I really liked the games.

I liked sleeping in the room alone. The bed was soft and had lots of pillows.

It was quiet.

One morning, bare little feet crossed the hard floor. Feet like mine.

I wasn't in the room anymore. There were other kids all my size, going this way and that. They all had sleep on their faces.

I watched them move, not sure what was going on. I heard them dropping water and running water. Whispers here and there. A grown-up voice told them to shush and to go back to bed since it wasn't time yet. More water and shushes happened until it was time to get up.

We got food, and we were talked at by grown-ups.

We played in two different big rooms. They had one with a hard floor and one with a soft floor and big toys to climb on. The whole time, I was told where to sit and to be quiet and to pay attention.

That's all I can remember about that day. That night, we took turns in the showers, and the grown-ups watched to make sure we brushed our teeth and everything. Then it was time to sleep. I fell asleep easy enough.

Someone put their hand over my mouth and picked me up like a hug. But not a nice hug. A mean hug..

I tried to bite and scream. That's what you do if someone is mean. You bite as hard as you can. But the mean person held my mouth closed so I couldn't.

They hit my head.

And my brain went bye-bye.

They said if I didn't stop squirming, they would hit me again.

If I could've gotten their hand out of my mouth, I would've told them to let me go.

They were hurting me, and my lips were bleeding.

I tried to scratch.

They hit me so hard I couldn't speak. It took all my thinking to figure out how to breathe again. It was so hard to breathe.

I cried, my head hurt so much, and I couldn't move.

Before I could scream, a hand was on my neck. Someone else pulled my hands out. They pulled too hard, it hurt, and I thought they were going to take my whole arm away. My face was in the water near the potties.

They were bigger and stronger and holding someone else down too. Face down in the water just like me, he was fighting too. One of the big boys was sitting on another boy's back, holding him face down. Pulled his pants down. Took his own pee-pee out and put it in where the poops come from.

My pants got pulled down. My pee-pee was against the cold wet floor. I took in a great big deep breath, getting ready to scream the loudest scream ever. Something hit my head, and my head hit the ground.

My head was all dizzy, and something went into my mouth. I couldn't scream or breathe. I tried to push them away, but the big boys wouldn't let me go.

I was hit in the head again, and it made me go to sleep. Not the good kind of sleep. The worst kind of sleep.

When I woke up, my eyes didn't want to see.
The big boys were gone, and I hurt all over.
I crawled over to the other boy. I touched him. He screamed and then cried.
I screamed until I couldn't scream anymore.
We hugged because we both hurt, and I cried too.

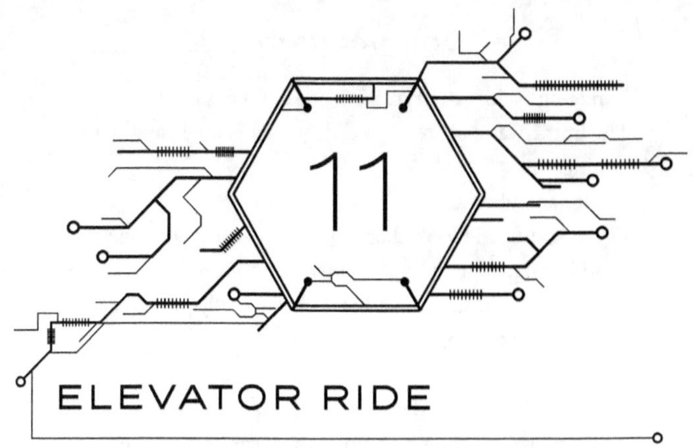

11

ELEVATOR RIDE

520.102.1500 Transit Space, Vanguard
City Space Elevator, Vanguard Prime

I LET THE memory wash over me, done with it for now.

I slipped into the warm water, practically melted into it, and activated the control for the tub. Gentle but forceful vibrations pulsed from the jets.

"Holy fuck. This is nice, man," I said to Shantu.

"Why the fuck is this the first time we've done this?" he asked, his voice trembling with the vibrations.

"Where? There were only four showers per floor at our apartments, and they're disgusting. The ones at work have hot water, but the degreaser leaves me itchy."

"You're not itchy. It's healing. Those bars will scrape paint off a septic tank."

"Whatever…"

A few minutes later, two petite women in medical scrubs stylized to match the decor came in with matching carts. They pulled a bottle from their carts and gave a hearty pump from the nozzle.

"Greetings. This is a degreaser," one of them said.

The bottle was a prop, the real degreaser came from the tub's plumbing.

"Your hand please."

I gave it, and she looked at it and almost jumped. She then cracked her neck, pulled out a bowl that hooked onto the side of the tub, and placed my hand in it. She liberally poured a thick chemical into the bowl, up to my wrists. It smelled like a carbon-ceramic brake cleaner.

The other lady took off on a hurried walk.

"Did she see your dick and morn for its sex life?" I asked.

The woman helping me snickered, spilling the awful-smelling liquid. The ventilation notably increased.

A moment later, Shantu's aesthetician-person came back with two jugs and a few items I couldn't see and got to work on him.

"Shaddap!" The smell must've hit him. "Ugh! We should've done this part before getting into the tub. What is it? Smells like laminate stripper."

She smiled but didn't answer.

"Come on, darling. I'm really vulnerable here. I have a right to know if you're going to electroplate my hands."

The sound that came from her was something between gears grinding against a foreign object and an elderly vacuum survivor. "I'm not supposed to talk."

He met her eyes and did not falter one bit. Didn't even acknowledge the instinct to duck because her voice sounded like rending metal. "Fuck your bosses. I need to know if I get to choose between chrome or gold plating. You look like a classy lady. You're going to hook me up with the gold, aren't you?"

He winked at her, and she smiled bashfully. That was all it took.

"It's an ultrasonic electrolytic emulsion. It'll pull all the, uh…" Her hesitation sounded like a solar flare across interplanetary comms. "All the material from your hands."

My aesthetician glanced at them, who were clearly starting to hit it off, and then back at me. I rolled my eyes and shook my head. I was rewarded with a little smile. She dropped little devices into the bowls, and they hummed. I watched grime and metal particles float off my hands.

I made a show of looking around the room. "Are y'all not supposed to talk because of the, uh"—I gave an uncomfortable shrug—"exclusive…whatever…people who come here?"

She smiled and nodded.

I tossed her a line. "Look, I'm uncomfortable if you don't talk. I mean, I'm naked, and you're digging under my nails with a metal pick."

"Polymer," she said sweetly.

"What?"

"It's not metal. It's a smart polymer." She pressed it against the tub to show how much it could flex.

"Oh. Keeps you from stabbing a client who's being an asshole?" I joked.

She gave a hearty, beautiful laugh. "Yeah. You wouldn't believe how many rich jerks come through here and think they can treat me like subsapient trash just because I work here. At this point, I don't even mind the ones who don't acknowledge I exist…"

She picked up steam from there, complaining about rich, shitty clients. The Vanguard elite were too pretentious and took too many liberties or were just plain rude because they were used to bossing people around.

Interestingly, she had taken classes on how to trim hooves and horns and how to float teeth. She took a rotary tool to grind off burrs to smooth out certain species' teeth, usually minotaur. Weird.

She petted the rough calluses on my hands. "I like off-worlders. They're either polite or quiet because they don't know the local customs. I like their different textures, scales, fur, and pachyderms."

She oiled and massaged my hands, and I stiffened. And not my back, if you know what I mean.

"You don't talk much, do you?" she asked.

I shrugged and waited the right amount of time. "Do you think I really get very many words in while hanging out with that?" I nodded at Shantu, who hadn't shut up yet.

His aesthetician was laughing so hard that her head was resting on his shoulder while she fussed over his nails.

My aesthetician smiled a genuine smile that lit up her face. It wasn't that polite bullshit. "I see your point. How do you deal with that? You have calm energy; it doesn't make sense you two would be so…close." Her pause was pregnant with implications and questions.

"We've worked together for a long time," I said. "Now, we got hired on a ship together, so he's the only person I know going up."

"You're not that old. Unless…?" Her implications were about gene modification and other therapies.

I gave her a super, over-the-top eye roll. It said, "Would you be digging grease from my hands if I had that kind of money?"

She laughed and visibly relaxed.

"What about you and…" I nodded at the other aesthetician.

She mimicked my eye roll.

I made the best innocent face I could.

We talked about our histories and told funny anecdotes. I can't say the distance we kept didn't bother me. Never got too specific. Never made promises that weren't going to be kept.

She tested her limits with me by tickling me while fussing over my toenails. I splashed her, and she giggled. That was my cue to shit or get off the pot.

I grabbed my tablet and checked her employee profile. Prostitution is legal on Vanguard, and I was afraid she was a million credit a night woman who had a profile on me, knew my credit limit, and was going to make sure she got all of it. Once her company profile clarified that, I took a moment to leave a glow-ing review and a decent tip. I then tossed the pad and rejoined the conversation.

She met my eyes and must've sensed my unease.

"What?" I asked.

"What, what?" she countered.

"I was putting in your review and tip before I asked you out because I didn't want one to be dependent on the other. Best pedicure I've ever had in my life by the way!"

She smiled, blushed, and recovered by exaggerating her efforts in digging into my toenails. "The only pedicure you've ever had."

"I mean, you've encouraged me to take better care of myself." I gave her a giant smile.

She turned beet red. "Yeah? Tell me about your life. Where did you grow up?"

My smile left before I could do anything about it. I took a deep breath. "We were raised at the institute, here in Vanguard City."

She took a deep breath. "Oh." Her one word had full acknowl-edgment of all the implications. She recovered with more grace than I could've managed. "How did you manage to get a job in space?"

Shantu answered for me. "We're amazing! That's how!"

I slowly slipped my head under the water as he launched into a dramatic retelling of our "job interview."

When I couldn't hold my breath any longer, I surfaced, made a stabbing motion at my neck, and mouthed, "Kill me now."

My aesthetician giggled while putting away her tools. Shantu's aesthetician seemed to be really into it, hanging onto his every word.

We ignored him and his antics as she asked me what I wanted done with my hair. It was shoulder length, and I had never really managed it.

"I don't know," I said. "I think short is a good idea, given that I'm going to be living in space for the foreseeable future."

She gestured to the wall before me, and the scenic vista was replaced with a few hair styles.

I looked at Shantu, and he looked back, seemingly equally confused. "They're the same," we said together.

The five styles were the same bald fade to short hair on top. I told her that if those were my options, she could surprise me. She got to cutting off large swaths of my hair with gentle massaging motions.

"We're running out of time if you are going to ask me out," she said, prompting me.

"Honestly, I was having second thoughts after you showed me the same haircut on five different people," I joked, and she flicked my ear.

SCORE!

"Would you like to do something with me after your shift?" I asked, trying to play it chill.

"I would like that. I have one more client scheduled. It looks like you are scheduled for a massage, so we might be done at the same time. I'll meet you back here when we're finished. Don't message me through the carriage intranet though. They don't like us using official channels for personal stuff."

She finished her work with my hair, and the tub started its rinse cycle. She patted my head flirtatiously before leaving.

After the women left, two large men with forearms meant to grind rocks into dust entered. Warm water rained down as the molded polymer tub lifted and reformed into a bed. Gel-filled bags inflated, and I repositioned face down. The ventilation kicked up, cycling in cool dry air and sucking the humidity from the room. Sheets flopped over me from somewhere.

"Good afternoon." His fingers worked pure magic into my shoulders.

"Oh fuck." Shantu laughed. "I'm hetero, but I might be falling in love."

The massage therapists kneaded us like a freshly mixed dough. My eyes got really heavy, and I found myself in a new interesting place where I didn't want to fall asleep but it was an almost irresistible temptation.

While I was in a blissful state just adjacent to nirvana, Shantu farted.

Not a little poot. He did not accidentally pass gas or have a sleepy toot. He FUCKING DROPPED ASS! He ripped a chainsaw fart that could cut a starship in half. He is now a war criminal because of that biological attack in a civilian area.

The massage therapists coughed, trying to hold their composure. I was going to ignore it by letting the atrocities take their place and the historians sort it all out—until he giggled.

I leaped onto his back, intent on avenging the wronged and bringing justice to the universe. I slapped the offending orifice as hard and as fast as i could trying to mold my hand print into his cheeks with violence. He was laughing too hard to defend himself. The last of the reserves of his biological attack escaped while I manually modified him into a baboon.

ELEVATOR DATE

SHANTU WAS STILL laughing every time he looked at me—even though he was in noticeable pain as he walked.

We waited just outside the spa for the aestheticians to return.

Even though I had been professionally cleaned, I still felt too dirty to be in a clean, almost sterile environment. The floor was a rubberized material that seemed too soft to handle anything other than people. The long well-lit halls were decorated with dramatic photographs of Vanguardians. I expected them to all be military heroes and CEs in fights against militants. But they were whistleblowers, adoptive parents, ecologists, doctors, and teachers.

A side of Vanguard I had never seen.

"Do you think this is what the rest of Vanguard values?" I asked.

Shantu stared off for a moment. "I don't know who is in charge, but it doesn't feel random. I guess an algorithm could do it. You know what's funny? The war hero stuff comes from the big studios. The state-sponsored films are always about the whistleblowers who threw away their careers to stop corruption… Or the big-budget documentaries. I think this is what the people in charge value." He examined the pictures closely. "I would like to present new evidence, if it pleases the court."

"Proceed."

He pointed at the side where the image was pressed between layers of resin. "This isn't throwaway corporate art. This is creating artifacts. Look at how thick this is. There's a story on the other side that I can't read."

"There's a code, bud." I pointed at the fractal sticker on the bottom right. That code should have everything there was to know about the picture if we bothered to pull it up.

Shantu stopped trying to squish his face against the wall to see through the three- or four-centimeter gap. "Oh, yeah. Anyway, this isn't about advertising. This is about creating artifacts. What someone wants left behind when Vanguard is gone."

"Shit!" I looked up and down the hall, trying to imagine this place falling from orbit and the artifacts people would find…

I used the tablet to scan the code.

Tim Oliveira, a clean-cut, pleasant-looking guy. He was the first to undercut his competitors, breaking the trend of cycling tenants from leases to locally owned co-ops. He started a trend that made the real estate market hostile to big companies, and the housing market shifted to reflect the people's pay.

Citizens' pay.

The women arrived.

"We never got a proper introduction," Shantu said, barely able to get the words out through his own laughter. "I'm Shantu, and this is Jimmy-Dean-Ass-Slapper."

"Fuckstick."

"Fucknuts."

I rolled my eyes. "Just James. Nice to meet you."

Shantu's aesthetician–the one with lighter hair and the mechanical failure of a voice–was named Stephanie. She wore a green dress that was little more than a hint at clothing with an iridescent sheen that only hid her pride and nothing else. The one who worked on me was named Brittany. She wore a modern athletic outfit, more appropriate for running or the gym.

I don't know why I was so relieved.

They first took us shopping. The appalling prices distracted me. I knew that the elevator ride and meals were covered, but I didn't know what else was. I was painfully aware that each credit I spent was possibly going into an account I would have to pay back.

I sent a quick message to *The Happy Marauder*. Javelin replied with a link to an app that had a profile for the ship's environmental systems and inventory of trade goods. The tool tips walked me through how to adjust inventory settings. Like if I bought shampoo, I could make the excess available for sale at the next port.

A follow-up message was from Gabe. A summary of the official policy, sparing me the legalese. It encouraged getting multiple versions of comfort items like bedding and leisure clothing that could be added to the ship's stores. I would get a portion of the profits if they were sold elsewhere. Bulk non-personal items had to be run through the ship's purser. I was expected to get three-years' worth of personal consumables.

I shrugged and showed the message to Shantu.

I played with the app some more. It turned out that their environmental systems did not like certain soaps. I would say who knew, but everyone in space knew about this shit—to the point that they made an app for it.

It was fun using the tablets' augmented reality functions to go up and down the aisle, trying to find a soap and shampoo that we could use.

The women enjoyed using us as human dress-up dolls. Things we had never done before and only had media to use as a reference. I didn't understand the point of a jacket just for dinner but whatever.

We had dinner at the café, not general dining because we're fancy like that. I had a real animal protein hamburger and a milkshake.

"To a new beginning." We clinked our respective drinks.

"I've never had real milk before." I appreciated the sweet rich strawberry milkshake.

"You know that's going to give you the shits," Stephanie said bluntly.

"What?" I said. "No. That's just an advertising myth to get us to buy the synthetic."

"She's right," Brittany said. "I've been working here for two years. It's something to do with the bacteria in our stomachs. Right, um, let me see your tablet."

She tapped on it until she got to an order confirmation screen. It was a dose of a digestive aid. I ordered four.

The polite conversation was enjoyable. The women talked about how competitive it was to get their positions and how some requirements were approaching bigotry but were justified by some analysis. Shantu and I told stories about the minor racket we had going salvaging parts for resale before Telex caught on.

We were then politely encouraged to leave the café we neared departure time.

"We must be getting ready to ascend soon," Brittany said. "Let's get a drink at one of the observation bars."

"I know we get a room," Shantu said. "Let's go drop our shit off and then get a drink."

"Prepare to be disappointed," Stephanie added.

Our room was down one level near the lifts.. The small room

had two single movable bunks folded against the wall with clear pictographs describing how to move them. Straps hung from the ceiling for luggage, and we hooked our brand-new bags to it and activated them, letting them ascend to the ceiling.

The wall opposite the bunks had a screen with waiter access in it. The back wall slightly curved with the hatch. Beyond the hatch was a wet stall that smelled strongly of antiseptic. Three other hatches allowed entry. Water came from the small sprayer hose on the ceiling. In opposite corners were an air and vacuum hoses. The toilet was the vacuum style that sealed to your butt.

"Shit. This is better than my last apartment," Shantu commented. "There isn't a shared bathroom for the floor. And the company is much better." He hugged and kissed Stephanie.

Brittany and I made immature gagging faces. But we took the hint and left them to it.

"I would like to talk about anything other than that," I said to fill the space. "Please bring something up."

I wasn't the best at talking to people. Questions like "Do you hang out with a lot of passengers?" and "What are your sexual preferences?" and "Do you want to tell them to scoot over and get to it?" seemed like terrible ideas.

"I was thinking the same thing. I'm going to have to switch shifts after that little display."

"Why is that?"

"I know too much. She went full rocket jockey on him."

"Wait. *What?*" I said as we made it to the bar. "I thought we were pretty clear about being AV operators." My anger rose. "Pilots technically, sure. But they're fancy forklifts, not spaceships."

She looked at me with sweet understanding. "You don't get it, do you?"

I authorized the pad between us to order drinks, and they came swiftly. She took a long draw from an amber liquid with a sphere of ice in it. "It doesn't matter what you do. You're going to be a spacer. It means your life is going to be different. You're going to see *the stars*." She said it with such hope and longing that I wanted to take her with me. "You're going to do things I can't imagine. Do you know what the percentage is for leaving Vanguard?"

I shook my head.

"Point-oh-oh-one. Ninety-six percent are military. Out of the remaining four percent, ninety-eight percent of those work in shipyards."

"I thought you're an aesthetician. You sound like you have wings." I took a draw from my drink. It was real liquor that grew up in barrels. The harsh burn and sweet tang slapped my throat, but I managed to not cough.

"I'm planet-bound. I'll never break atmosphere unless I'm in a freezer. And I just don't see the point then."

Brittany wistfully looked at the dock moving around out the window. Her eyes were glued on a white smudge that might be a shipping truck full of cryogenically suspended people.

"That's not a window." She pointed at the corner where a camera location was displayed. "We're a couple hundred meters below ground right now. During my tour, I was frozen six times. It's awful. Waking up. Gasping like you just drowned. Shivering like you were running naked in a blizzard."

Technically, they were a few degrees above freezing. Sleeping in a coma, they were in a container filled with gel and chemicals and surrounded by machines that stabilized their bodies. I imagine it wasn't good though.

"I was box meat for my whole first enlistment," she continued. "I signed up for a second and applied for flight school. During the prescreen… Congenital myocardial peripheral insufficiency. Means my heart won't tolerate the changes in gravity. It means I'm normal when I wanted to be extraordinary. I couldn't pull the trigger and get a synthetic. They offered, but I just couldn't do it. Ended up working as a personnel clerk for four years. The itch is still there." She took another pull on her beverage.

I tapped her glass, and we drained our drinks.

"You know I never served, right?" I said.

Confusion followed by disgust washed over her face. "Why?"

"I got in trouble when I was at the institute. I was barred from service as part of the plea deal. Never mind that. If all you need to be extraordinary is a replacement bit, why let that stop you? Is it a religious thing?"

She didn't answer.

"I want to watch as we ascend, if you're not in any hurry."

"Never seen the city from the air?" she asked.

"Just once," I said shortly. Then I felt I was being unfair. "I've been to this elevator a million times, but I've never set foot in it. It's all hitting me. My whole life has been a prelude to this." I didn't wait for her to answer. "I don't know what to expect, but I know I can't turn back. Working sixteen-hour days, stealing naps, and scrounging for food… I don't even know why I have an apartment. I don't sleep there half the time."

That wasn't completely true, I didn't want to get into all the shit that happened when we used to sleep at Telex's.

"I've been in the elevator for a year." She ordered some snacks to munch on. "It took me six weeks before I gave up my apartment. I think I understand too. I stay here because I get to see the stars, and I don't have anything else to do." She shrugged, and it was maybe one of the most honest things I had ever seen in my life.

I kissed her and checked the itinerary timer.

We had over an hour. It was a comfortable silence of all the things people like us didn't need to say. The elevator was crowded now. Drones were busy shuffling people around as standing space became a premium.

I chuckled to myself. "I didn't tell either of my bosses I was leaving. One is going to be surprised when my name shows up as a recipient aboard a ship for a bunch of hardware." I laughed again, and it felt so good. "How's that for a notice?! Send me my shit!"

I maybe was laughing inappropriately loud, but I didn't care. I wasn't going back to work, and I didn't give any notice. Just didn't come back from a delivery one day.

I wondered what Telex was going to do with us just disappearing.

With a slight shudder, the window cut to concrete. It slid down, passing levels where crews were already staging containers for the next trip. The tram station was empty and dark. Level after level, they slid across the screen, and I watched the city sink below me.

I fought vertigo as I looked down at my home. It had never seemed so small. Rails and roads snaked out of the city, disappearing into the clouds down the mountain. I felt like I should have taken one of the trips to see the great forests.

"In school, they taught me that when the first fleet arrived in orbit, they said this wouldn't be a new Earth. That we had to do better," Brittany said. "Humans, that is. That's why we live in cities, underground, and even in one floating city. We wouldn't exploit this planet like our birth world. Shit, we bring water back in comets, so the oceans don't get depleted." There was an odd reverence in her voice. Maybe even pride. "Earth was on an ecological collapse. Even if the swarm wasn't eating it, humans were going to go extinct because we couldn't handle an industrial revolution responsibly. Then the Osheran showed up, didn't ask us for anything, and just saved us."

"The irony is that they taught us all about how military histories, corruption of governments, and cooperation—except a constitutional military autocracy—can be trusted," I said cynically.

"Maybe that's the point. They want us to be prepared."

I shrugged.

When the sky was more black than blue, she took my hand and led me back to my room.

520.111.1200 Transit Space, Vanguard
City Space Elevator, Vanguard Prime

KIND OF LOST track of my logs there for a minute. So, fucking sue me. I was getting laid. Forgive me for not being original, but I'm not going to spoil anything for you hopefuls. We didn't develop any new revolutionary techniques, so use your imagination.

You know what? Some things are going to be mine, not to be shared with the universe. This is mine.

The four of us were fighting for space when the zero g blanket deployed. We were clothed, so don't go getting any dramatic ideas. I'm too shy for that.

Shantu reached over and wacked my chest. "Dude! Get up! I want to see it!" he whispered. He bounced off the ceiling before noticing that we were in zero g.

I was much more careful as I followed him out of the hatch.

Drones pulled people around while the vast majority either walked on magnetic shoes or awkwardly pulled themselves from handhold to handhold.

Vacuum drones chased the poor souls who lost their lunch. The smell of sharp pine or lemon mixed with the vomit. The ventilation system seemed to be at a mild roar, clearly taxed at keeping up with the influx of bodily fluids.

Despite our attempt at courtesy, the women followed us to one of the bars where we could see the rim.

"Well, fuck," Shantu said, floating next to the window.

The station's rotating rim moved somewhere between 100–150 meters a second. Which meant we were looking at a noodle thin blur of a station and ships a few kilometers away.

"Dissatisfied dipshit?" I said. "Let's get breakfast and make our way over there."

Something important to know: food tastes different in zero g. I can't put my finger on it. I don't know if it's the packaging and the way they heat things, but it is *off*.

My coffee came in a squeeze bulb with little injection ports for the liquid sugar and creamer. It was fine. Coffee seemed normal. However, imagine drinking a whole cup—no, a whole pot—of fresh coffee too fast and then eating your breakfast. My bagel sandwich with sausage, egg, and cheese could have been donuts or oatmeal for all I could tell. Super strange.

Anyway, the time for goodbyes came.

"Have fun out there, spacer," Brittany said. "Don't hold a candle for me. It was fun, but this is where we part ways." She gave me a kiss and drifted off.

I would be a composting unit if I said my heart didn't break regardless of how much I stared directly at the reality of it all. I wanted her to say something different. I wanted her to ask me to stay or say she would wait for me to make it rich and come back. But she did it right.

She had more courage than me.

Enough of that.

I gathered my luggage–I'd never had luggage before!–from

the room and waited near the tram that would take us from the hub to the rim. I then learned that porters deal with luggage, so you wouldn't kill someone. We are just going to skip over my embarrassment.

"You good?" I asked Shantu.

He did not look good, but he nodded anyway.

"What a fucking week, right?"

He nodded, all teary eyed.

"Dug out a giant magnet. Got to play with some drones. Jumped off an overpass. Fought some gangsters. Got our asses kicked by a space pirate who sent us to the hospital. Eh!" I elbowed him.

"Not a pirate. A freighter with some mercenary work on the side. We're going to be doing the same shit we were doing but in space."

"Aw. Is Shantu cranky?" I pinched his cheeks.

He smiled while trying to bat me away, and we tumbled in the null gravity. I gave him a great big hug. That, sent us off spinning because I was pinning his arms to his side.

I didn't want to think about a relationship that never was. So, I was going to mess with him until we both felt better.

"All right!" He squirmed against me. "All right! Let me go."

Shantu and I sat,–floated? seatbelted?– there together while shuttle after shuttle passed. I suppose there's something symbolic about us sitting together, each dealing with our own shit in our own way but still there for the other.

I don't know how long we were there or who moved first, but we did what we always do. Stood... well planted our feet, squared our shoulders, and moved forward, leaving others behind.

His eyes were puffy. I pretended not to notice.

We took the tram to transit from the elevator to the space station. The tram had seat belts to deal with the firm acceleration and pivoted to match the spinning ring we were headed toward.

I had issues with orientation because *down* was out from the center of the ring, and we were going *forward,* which was also *up* from the axel-shaped station. The planet spinning *behind* us should be *down.* I just looked at the station tablet and the opaque floor and ignored everything else until we got there.

FTS *The Happy Marauder* was a beautiful design. A light freighter with multicolored containers of freight. The under-laying ship was something much more, like a beautiful woman wearing an ugly work uniform. The drive bell seemed bigger than other ships around the same size.

"Dude, we're getting on a space pinecone!" Shantu said.

I knew his voice. He was forcing the levity.

He found an optical magnifier mounted to the *ceiling,* and I found another one a few meters away. I looked closer at the ship.

From the drive bell *up,* heading toward the nose of the ship, was a hearty organic bulge that I guessed would be the engineering section. A gantry extended from the station, moving cargo into some kind of bay. The scale of the ship then hit me. A full standard shuttle could make it in and out of those bays.

A subtle conical twist to the ship's frame hid under the standardized shipping containers. It really did look like a space pinecone with a greenish tinge from the way light hit it. Bits of equipment, that dotted the hull at regular intervals, made the image of a porcupine come to mind as well. I didn't see a lot of weapons. Though I could feel that this ship was hiding some under tons of shipping containers. Maybe a wolf in sheep's clothing would be more accurate.

The ship's nose had a menacing circle, as if it was a rail gun cover. It would be a monster of a cannon. It could be an air lock for all I knew, but how centered it was around the ship's long axis made me think it was a weapon. Something about how it was balanced in the center of the ship's mass. She reminded me of one of those warrior women with the big sword on their back.

FTS *The Happy Marauder* was a fighter. Her bags may be full but not just any lady gets to walk through this neighborhood like that.

I've seen ladies like that—born to the gut. The kind that will cut you balls to mouth for being in their way. Don't even break stride. Just like that. Done.

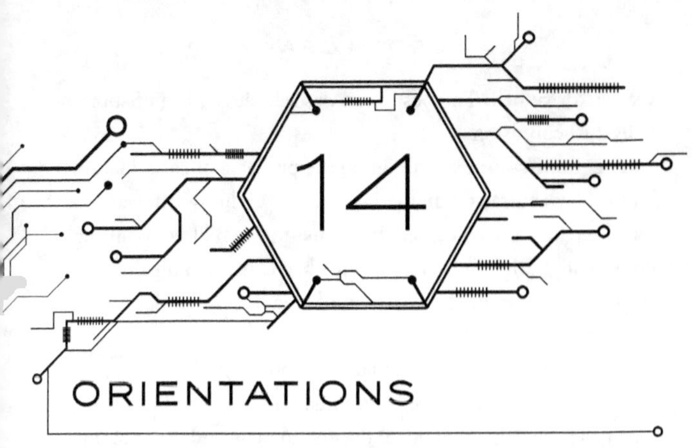

14

ORIENTATIONS

SHANTU AND I took a lift "down" from the station to the docking collar. The gantry meticulously moved around *The Happy Marauder*, placing cargo in cradles while hoses attached at various connection points to actuate the cradles.

The gangway was unnerving. Like walking through a straw. A white floor with only the dimmest glow led from the elevator to *The Happy Marauder.* Then clear plastic in all directions was only occasionally interrupted by metallic rings that were thick with embedded devices.

In the space beyond, ships moved about, illuminated by the green, red, blue, and yellow docking beacons.

In an adjacent docking platform, swarms of docking drones were attaching to a ship. I tapped Shantu so he could watch too. Each individual drone had their own set of navigation lights. Together, they appeared as a shining school of fish trying to eat a whale. I couldn't make heads or tails of the docking ship other than its drive bell. The best I can describe it is a bag of sports balls. Just confusion.

The drone swarm spread out in the pinnacle of coordination and evenly contracted on the bulbous ship. The swarm was too far to see how they attached, but when the ship lit with pulsing coordinated drive flares, I knew they had control of the docking ship. Them spinning the ship around seemed effortless.

Beautiful.

We neared the air lock and finally got a sense of the ship's scale. The hatch alone must have been three meters tall and five wide. The gangway ballooned out at the end to mate with a metal ring from the ship.

"Hey guys! Welcome, I'm Gabe," an overly enthusiastic voice said at the air lock. "I was told you were coming. I'm so excited to meet you."

Shantu and I stopped, staring at a shoni-vonti.

Something from a galactic species class surfaced in my brain. The shoni-vonti were basically sentient plants. That sentiment made biologists wince–as their biochemistry was wildly different from anything from old Earth or Vanguard Prime. They did, however, strip the carbon off CO_2 and were dependent on radiation around the visual range. Good enough for me.

The shoni-vonti had a powerful running leg that stuck out the back of them and smaller walking legs in the front. Their outer arms were powerful enough to rip a human limb from limb while the smaller set curled under and had much finer manipulation.

"Were you that remote vote against us?" Shantu asked bluntly.

I took a step onto the FTS *The Happy Marauder*.

"I lost that vote," Gabe said, "and now we live together. I'm trying to say no hard feelings. I just didn't want the extra work of training anyone."

Shoni-vonti faces didn't have a nose, and their oral cavity consisted of four interlocking mandibles over an overly mobile neck.

Their eyes were solid membranes that doubled as ears.

I wanted to touch them.

Super hard to look at one without staring, which we were totally still doing.

Just fascinating.

"Let me give you the grand tour," Gabe said with so much enthusiasm that I could feel Shantu tense next to me. "First, this is the habitation deck."

The air lock's outer door folded down, and from the marks on the walls, it must be more than a meter thick. The rest of the spartan space was just robust lockers with emergency equipment. I think one was a small arms locker. We transitioned through three more heavy air locks.

"The ship was originally built to transport hundreds of people," he explained as we transitioned into another heavy air lock, "but we've repurposed those decks. There are five free cabins, and they're pretty much all identical. The ship is in transit configuration right now. Most systems don't have a fancy ring like Vanguard, so we'll spin up the habitation decks when we aren't under thrust."

The corridors were a matte off-white and wide enough for a passenger car. Recessed lockers were on either side with the same environmental protection, medical, arms, and emergency repair themes.

I got the feeling there wasn't a room on this ship that didn't have those four lockers.

Also, why was it small arms and heavy weapons? Why not light arms and heavy arms? Or small weapons and big weapons? Someone fucked that up a long time ago.

Maybe this was the drone corridor or deck because most of the rooms, if not all, were marked —Drone Storage— and by their purpose: hull repair, interior repairs, decontamination, target bipedal, and environmental simulations.

The ground had a noticeable air current that made my feet cold. Weird, but what the fuck do I know about starships?

We took a lift up and found our way to the ring hallway. This hallway was wider. Maybe two cars wide. A seam divided it in half lengthwise, and along the noticeable bend were spaced pairs of bars. Above each set of bars was a long screen that said "Unoccupied."

Gabe gestured for us to pick our new rooms.

The door was different from what I was used to. I had to grab the bars and kick, not hard but just a firm press with my foot. The door slid back, and I turned around and climbed down a ladder.

I thought this was a joke. Maybe Gabe was sending me into the sewer or something as new guy hazing.

I was wrong.

Once down, there was a lever to rotate, and it released the mechanism that closed the door. The leaver had positions to open, lock, and close. Next to the ladder was a panel built into the wall that displayed —Place Hand to Occupy Quarters—.

I did that, and my name flashed.

In the room, I was taken aback by its size. It was easily six times the size of my apartment with room to spare. To my left was a painted yellow stripe clearly marked "Keep Clear" around the ladder.

Three people could sleep on the bed without touching each other. I had never seen one so big, save on shows. Was I going to have roommates?

On the opposite wall, the desk at the foot of the bed had a large screen on an articulated arm that was in its locked position. The chair was one of those extravagant ergonomic contraptions that had a lever and knobs for everything. It was currently stuck to the floor with magnetic sliders.

Beyond the bed and the desk was a private shower stall enclosed in glass. The toilet was in the shower. I assumed I could be a lot more optimistic on Taco Tuesday.

The back-left corner was just empty. There was so much room for activities! I didn't know what to do with so much space.

Walking further into the room, I noticed the wall nearest to the door had panels with handles. One was clearly marked with a space suit helmet. I opened it to find a half dozen suits neatly hung in a locker. The drawer below the locker had patches, flashlights, and other vacuum survival equipment, along with a pictogram book on how to use everything. The book had a holographic sheen, making it visible in a wide variety of spectrums. I looked through the other lockers and drawers, only to find some emergency consumables and extra bedding. I put my luggage in one of the empty lockers.

Gabe was practically vibrating with excitement when I left my cabin. "Feel free to make any aesthetic changes to your cabin. For any hardware changes, talk to Flutter. Keep in mind that the ship sprints up to twenty g's, max emergency thrust is eighty-nine, but we can only do that for a few seconds before the drive burns out."

Shantu came out of his cabin, and Gabe repeated the decorating warning.

"Holy shit. Won't that kill us?" he asked a second before I could.

"If we're sprinting at eighty-nine g, something's trying to kill us."

Gabe then took us around the habitation area. It was arranged in a long sloping double helix that I would imagine stretched into two or more rings when docked at a stationary, uh, station.

The upper deck served as a conference room with a large table that was surrounded by chairs. The lower deck was a lounge with a large entertainment system surrounded by couches. It also had a kitchen with a bar that separated it from the dining area. The whole arrangement gave a solid feeling of privacy and conversely openness.

"OH!" Gabe jumped. "Really important! We're moored to the elevator, and it rotates to give us a half g. The ship can stay in drive configuration while we're attached. When we disembark, we're going to be in zero g's until we're clear of traffic and start accelerating. Always, ALWAYS! Keep your stuff locked down, so it doesn't get smashed into your face."

Important safety tip.

I felt like I should be taking notes. "Lock my shit down or get smashed in the face. Got it."

He brought us to the fabrication deck to show off his collection of networked machines that could make just about anything they needed. "This machine was used to make fitted fabric ballistic armor. If we go by a colony, we will crank out whatever they need and make bank. I added settings and templates, so we can also make our own clothes. Go ahead and make some athletic outfits. I'm here to hold your hand."

He flared open his mandibles, and I think that meant he was excited.

"Uh, how much is this going to cost us?" My cynical fear of mounting debt clearly showed in my tone.

He pulsed his membranes, and I took that as him rolling his eyes. The expression was oddly human. My face flushed, but Shantu's slightly open mouth told me he was a half second away from asking the same question.

"Don't worry about it," Gabe said. "Just don't be a dick and deplete the ship's material stores, and you're fine. Anything you don't like, just put it in this hopper, and it'll be recycled."

He gave us a rundown on how to use the equipment while giving gentle suggestions on styles and features. The machine consulted our medical records and gave performance and comfort predictions based on preset parameters.

By the end, we had five sets of athletic clothing. We also made two sets of shoes, one that was so light that it was almost nonexistent, save the support in my low arches. The other set was heartier, almost boots, with more padding and robust ankle support.

I had always resented the fact that I couldn't afford new clothes. My big annual expense had been shoes because I couldn't risk not having decent boots. I looked at Shantu and found the same feelings flashing over his face. We had just manufactured several months' worth of our wages in apparel. The surreal feeling washed over me.

Gabe went on, explaining the limits of their fabrication abilities. Easy explanation: metals and polymers were easy; ceramics and chemicals were not.

But he was quick to dash my dreams about using the equipment to become a space pirate and take over the galaxy. "Any weapons and armor made on the ship could be a dangerous liability versus what's on the open market. The margins for error are too wide in this equipment, and we operate at a lower energy state. Like the rare materials needed for high-end weapons."

In the armory were hundreds of weapons and accessories. Cannons and launchers fit into racks in the ceiling. Small arms fit into lockers around the room, loosely sorted by type.

Gabe let us explore some before announcing, "Something I need to show you two before we disembark. Stand against the wall."

As soon as we complied, an alarm blared for maybe two seconds before a body bag slapped my face and pinned me to the wall. Air rushed around me as I struggled against the oily black plastic. It only gave for a second before becoming rigid. I was cocooned.

Before I could panic, my tomb disappeared.

"They're maneuvering baffles. They deploy when we go into red alert," Gabe said cheerily. "They suck, but it's better than going splat—"

"What the fuck?!" I shouted as soon as the stun wore off.

He stopped and stared off. "Sure thing, Cap. The galley sound good enough? All right. Be there in a minute." He turned his attention back to us. "Your medical review came back. The captain wants to talk to you. Follow me."

Where did he keep his ear bugs?

We hurried back through the workshop and down into the habitation area. The captain and Dire-horn entered from the opposite hall at nearly the same time.

"Congratulations," Captain Vatosh said. "You're officially crew."

"Provisional crew." Dire-horn seemed disturbed about the administrative inaccuracy.

But the captain didn't miss a beat. "You cleared quarantine. Your AVs will be delivered tomorrow. Dire-horn."

Dire-horn presented us with two boxes. Each was a sturdy composite about the size of my fist and was engraved with our names and other identifying information.

Shantu and I were practically bouncing. This was the birthday we never had, and we shredded the seals like the kids we never got to be.

I unfolded the plastic pictogram information pamphlet. These were personal feeds. Not just the handset or tablet. These were custom jobs, probably ordered during my eye and ear exam. The case's lid displayed firmware and diagnostic information.

I don't know how to explain what it meant to me to be given these. I had watched all the citizens just summon information from the ether by waving their hands like magicians. I couldn't get a data plan, and secondhand or unlocked devices were only good for maybe a day before their pirate signal was blocked.

Now, I could get full augmented reality through contact lenses and the self-cleaning, self-positioning sonic devices that fit into my ear canal—affectionately referred to as ear bugs.

I was grateful no one noticed that I almost threw away the control bracelets, thinking it was packaging. The lid's screen prompted me to don the input and haptic feedback devices, referring to the bracelets.

"If you would please activate your devices," Dire-horn ordered.

I complied as tool tips calibrated my devices. Prompts appeared, allowing me to choose my settings for opacity, and constantly displayed information. I choose a minimalist view with subtle gestures. I also set Shantu as a favorite contact and put an icon for messages in the top right, out of my field of view. That way, I had to deliberately look up to see the icons.

Dire-horn cleared his throat. He gestured, and a connection prompt appeared dead center, completely obstructing my vision. It took me a moment to find the setting to make it a small notification icon at the edge of my field of view.

"Please accept the sync with *The Happy Marauder* Local Net," he said.

The initial setup went on with all the formalities that one could expect from a minotaur. Our waiting mail had a pile of legal notifications that outlined our changes in status, medical documents, and insurance. He spent a few minutes giving us access to various ship systems before excusing himself.

A priority message chimed while we continued to go through the myriad of legal bullshit. "Report to the infirmary with all due haste."

I closed the message, looked at Shantu, and shrugged. I accessed the ship's layout and synced it to have a mini map in the top right. It dropped helpful little arrows on the floor to guide me down to the infirmary.

A warning then appeared, informing me about eye strain and damage. It was going to adjust my settings to have the mini map auto-hide if my eyes weren't looking up at it. The prompt had options to override that I wasn't going to take.

"Dude, we're getting mil-spec stems," Shantu said. "They're not playing about making us operators. Artificial HGH.

Vaso-fortifiers. Fuck, man. There are a million credits worth of meds about to go into us."

The data dump of our treatments hit my feed. I skimmed it while struggling to walk.

Shantu laughed.

I ignored it. "Shantu, psychological evaluation is part of our qualifications. Counter interrogation and compromised combat techniques."

"Time to be awesome," he said with a deadly seriousness I hadn't seen before.

"Time to be awesome," I said, bumping his fist.

The infirmary was more cluttered than I expected. Supplies were strapped to the ceiling illuminated by the examination lights near each bed of the dozen beds. Each bed had its own alcove of supplies and equipment marked by the grooves in the floor where an emergency air lock could save patients. Four trauma pods circled a hatch at the far end. —The Skinner— was crudely stenciled over the far hatch.

The Skinner was a device used to extract people out their armor and deliver them into a trauma pod.

We found beds and checked in virtually, and to I looked up at the first batch of injections and found links to videos of tough army guys losing their minds, crying, or getting sick.

I took a deep breath and shared the video to Shantu with a flick of my wrist. "Uh, this is going to suck…"

"No going back." Shantu held out one hand to define where he wanted the video.

"Ain't got anywhere to go back to. If you cry, I'm putting it on the feeds."

A walking starfish that was somewhere between a mahogany and burgundy color came in. It looked like it was trying for human features but wasn't there yet. It only had three fat fingers. The two larger ones had a line down the middle like it had tried to be a human hand but gave up most of the way there.

A video call from Scout appeared. His ears waved. "Doc is in a mood today, so please don't try communicating with him. Take your treatments, and I'll be along when I can. Call Gabe if you need something. And please—*please*—do not leave the beds."

I tried to split the line between formality and friendly. "Yes'er."

I got to do my first virtual dive into my new feed to Doc's species while he prepared our treatments.

Doc is a praportorian. His body instinctively organizes itself to mimic other creatures. Sort-of. A praportorian color is explained by a lot of stuff like atmosphere, biochemistry, and metabolism that I don't understand, so we're going to skip that. It's like watching a starfish make fun of a human for having bones.

My feed showed me points of references that I don't recognize, pointing to a planet that has a continent spanning mass that may or may not be the origin for the species.

He didn't wear the white coat but wore a chest rig woven from metal cable that made the noises like a winch when he moved. The rig looked like someone went recycling–chic with medical equipment.

The praportorian doctor started his series of injections, and I gave no complaints, aware that we were already being evaluated. At first, we tried pretending the injections didn't feel like we were getting pumped full of broken glass.

The faces we made would be funny later. But then, we were sharing pain.

The pain quickly turned into agony as the muscle infusers were applied. Thousands of needles poured fire into my major muscle groups. We grunted and made noises no man should make. I don't know how long we sat in those torture chairs, but when the doctor placed a large needle in our elbows and hooked us up to a machine, I drifted off to sleep before I realized what had happened.

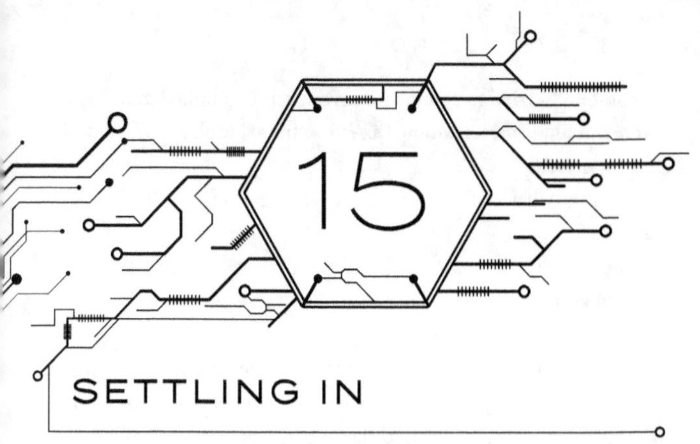

15

SETTLING IN

THAT MORNING, I woke to a man gently shaking my foot. He was backlit, just a talking shadow. I was reclined, so I couldn't tell how tall he was.

"Good morning, boys. You're officially allowed to meet me. Call me Wraith." He stuck out his hand, and I shook it. "I gotta be honest. I was thinkin' you boys would be screaming for ya mommas. I'm damn glad to be wrong. I know that shit right there is tough." He went back and forth between both of our eyes. "I gotta give it to ya. Y'all got some steel in ya nerves. Now, you dun' fucked up because I'm expecting more out of you. Your AVs are being delivered. Get them secured with Flutter, and you'll have tomorrow to yourself."

He then left the infirmary.

How many people hadn't I met?

"Ugh. I feel like hammered shit," Shantu said, sitting, and I agreed with him. "No time to be pussies now."

"Fuck me! This hurts more than all my ass-kicking's

combined." I tried to stand, and my muscles complied, but they were bitching and screaming the entire time. I took a moment to center myself.

"Is this what it feels like to be you? Because… Fuck, it's terrible."

"Fuckstick."

"Fucknuts."

"Who the fuck was that guy?"

"Ship's manifest says Wraith is the morale officer. That's it." Shantu groaned, getting out of his bed. "He's a fucking spy. Probably was running around the city, checking up on us. Shit. Why did we spend all that time with the HR minotaur instead of that guy, so he could vet us?"

"Did he?" My vision was clearing as I tried to walk around. "What a fucking diva!" I turned off the examination lights for the other beds in the infirmary. I then moaned, walking to the door. "This is a professional fucking outfit. I get the impression that if they don't ask, we don't have to answer, and they don't need to know."

Shantu shrugged. We let the conversation die because we were fighting through pain with every step.

He and I followed our feeds up two decks and into the vehicle bay. The large air lock could fit a dozen or so people. I took the time to change my feed settings to display a helper tool that would teach me how to use the ship's equipment, like manual operation of the air locks. I pinged Shantu to do the same, and he gave an agreeable shrug. Each tool tip would remain in a queue until I ran through a practice operation.

A large delivery sled dominated the cavernous cargo hold. Work crews were busy with various tasks, while Javelin oversaw the operation. She used her large, majestic wings to direct workers as her hands worked the chit encoder for the transactions, she was processing.

The tool tip pinged no available data on the device. I cleared it and…

Holy shit!

They were hooking up a magazine of missiles. A work crew looked immersed in their specialty as the machinery integrated into the wall cycled for reasons I didn't know.

I changed my feed to include current equipment status and turned the opaqueness down a notch to avoid data overload. A status window appeared, the integrated magazine was running a lubrication and maintenance check prior to loading. A timer popped up just prior to me looking away.

"How does this look?" Shantu said. Then pinged me with an augmented reality calibration invitation.

I accepted the invitation. He had placed a blue-green wire-frame model for our cradles and AVs near a sturdy-looking cross member. He was drawing how he wanted to weld the bracing for everything in the air.

I walked through the model, and he huffed disapprovingly. I ignored the animated penis over my head, knocked on the cross member, and didn't recognize the noise. "Hey, I don't know what this is. I don't know if we can weld to it."

The penis ejaculated on my face, and I rolled my eyes. "Quit fucking around. I feel like shit, and I want to get this done."

Shantu dismissed the animation. "Where do I go to see what this is?" He browsed the ship's statistics through the local library.

"Keep going there. I'm going to see if our new toys can give us any information." I played with the object's identifying features, cross-referencing starships in the same class as *The Happy Marauder*. "Fuck, do you think this is a test? I got a lot of bad trails on the feeds."

"I don't fucking know, but I did find a project manager tool. Let's see what it does." Shantu turned the half-rendered wireframe into blueprints and added bracing. Error prompts appeared.

I noticed the suggested actions tab and selected it. It scrolled through data about vacuum-state ultrasonic fusion and a short list of suggested materials.

"We are officially out of our depth," I said. "Unless you have a few years of training I don't know about."

"Fuck," Shantu said. "It's composites. I don't know what the fuck to do with them. Who do we talk to about shit like this?"

I pulled up the ship's crew manifest and looked for something like engineering or maintenance.

Success! Ship's engineer: Flutter.

"James, Shantu," Dire-horn rumbled from behind me. He nodded to each of us. "I'll introduce you to Flutter. You will be assisting him in the installation of the stalls."

His choice of words alerted me to my place in the social hierarchy. I didn't know if I was being insulted or not, so I set a reminder to brush up on minotaur social customs.

Flutter, the osheran, was a quad-symmetrical flying football. The thing was a living jiggly ball.

Osheran bodies were oriented around their digestive tract with their mouth centered at the top. The mouth was circular with horrifying gripping teeth that bit into the flora of their native planet. In the modern age, they used their teeth to type and control cursors.

Just below their circular mouth was a large ocular lattice that served in place of an eye. Below that was a pair of rod wings with a connective bone below the surface of their golden-brown skin. That bone defined each of the four slices of the circular being. Each wing reminded me of a bore brush with fine hair. Small static discharges jumped around Flutter.

At the bottom of the being, individual toes ended in powerful claws. And in the center of the foot was its butthole.

Osheran were the reason humans still exist, if I can recall my history class and more recently with Brittany. They were fleeing a planet-consuming species known as the swarm. On their way out of swarm territory, they found us and made a pit stop to pick up the stray kitten.

"The swarm's response to a threat is exponential growth and evolution," I vaguely remember a biology teacher mentioning. "There's a combination of features that make them perfect for killing you, and they'll find it. We don't know why they land on planets or where they go when they leave."

The osheran helped us build our own ships during the long crossings. Because humans are dicks, we went our separate ways quickly. Now, we hardly interact. From what I remember from my species and cultures class, they don't operate on the same emotional bandwidth as humans.

Fascinating.

Command control notifications appeared in our views, and Flutter took control of our project. It dissolved, and we followed along as he generated a new one. He assigned gray items, such as coating removal, to bots, along with cleaning and particulate control. Black items were pending Javelin and/or Dire-horn's approval for external contract work.

Flutter also made us a new garage, complete with emergency lockers and a personnel air lock. He placed an emergency egress priority simulation near the airlock, and unknown data prompts appeared.

"I think he wants us to get in our AVs, so he can decide how he wants the cradles," I said.

"Is that thing a he?" Shantu asked.

"Does it matter?"

"I guess not."

Shantu followed me to our AVs, which were among the myriad of other equipment on the sled. We powered them up and walked them to the indicated location.

A little dual rotor drone buzzed around us, adding information to the project. Flutter adjusted the garage door to be further away from the personnel air lock. The garage door cycled styles—top open, bottom open, split vertically, and so on.

"Do you think that means he's waiting to see what's available?" I asked.

"I do."

It was so cool.

Several heavier bots appeared from wherever they lived, scooting into view on their robust treads. Some were just fans with filters while others had welding equipment and tanks. One bot seemed to be a rolling maintainer for four others. The maintainer bot had spare parts and tool attachments on a rotating rack.

Five or six meters from the air lock, the little army of bots stripped the coating from the floor and the wall. Shantu and I watched the virtual project morph into reality. Items steadily fell off the list, and Flutter's little ballet of bots did their dance.

Shantu pointed out that we were added to the blue list under the other working bots. We shrugged and followed the instructions to gather the noted crates for our cradles. He threw the virtual manual at me with an animation that melted like a bug on a windshield and was replaced by step-by-step assembly tool tips, which made me jump.

"This is awesome! We're installing top-of-the-line cradles for our AVs on a ship!" I giggled.

"I think we're dead, and this is the afterlife for orphans," Shantu said. "We went splat after jumping off the freeway."

"Uh, if that was true, why did it involve a praportorian pumping us full of acid?"

"Good point. I'll think of something later." He jumped out of his AV to work on a bit of preassembly.

Assembly and installation of an AV cradle could have just been another day at work for us. The tool tips kept us from making mistakes, along with the low gravity that put us on easy mode.

"I feel like we're on easy mode," Shantu said.

"Get out of my head." He did a whiny version of my voice over mine.

"Dick!" we said together.

"Fuckstick!" I yelled at him.

"Fucknuts!"

"LIQUID TAINT JUICE!"

He didn't get that one, and we devolved into giggles.

I had assembled these cradles all over Vanguard City. I tried not to think of the hard mode of my life. It was good now, and I was going to enjoy it while I can.

The bots did the base work of preparing the installation site: running power cables, fluid lines, and evacuation lines through hidden conduits.

Something Shantu and I were not used to was dust discipline. The vacuum bots worked overtime, zipping back and forth on their treads that had cloth covers. The supervisor bot changed the tread covers from a bin that was marked with clean and dirty sides.

I looked for what might affect my life on a spaceship, like the maneuvering baffles installed into the ceiling and other shit like that. I was not disappointed when my feed alerted me that I was within a restricted area.

An alert asked us "to leave all equipment as close to its permanent position as possible." Flutter disappeared, zipping across the bay. A team of workers arrived and began installing an emergency shelter.

We locked down our AVs and found a crate to stand on outside our new garage as more sleds and workers started on their tasks.

"Shit, man," Shantu said. "All this for us…" He waved at our AVs.

Workers were installing the modules for the emergency shelter that would encapsulate our AV lifts in a semicircle of flexible material in the event of catastrophic changes in environment.

"Kind of makes you feel special, right?" I said.

"This doesn't feel real, man." He roughly plopped onto the crate. "How long did we have to fight to claim a fucking corner of a garage?" Tears welled in his eyes.

I looked away and pretended not to notice.

"Now they're doing all this just to have us here?"

I plopped down next to Shantu and gave him a hearty pat on the shoulder. I didn't have anything to say, so I just let him know I was there.

"What if we fuck this up? They've already done so much to give us a chance. I just don't want to blow it."

We sat there and talked for an hour. Maybe two.

A message then appeared for both of us. It was an automated order confirmation for environment suits. The store would open tomorrow at 0700.

I poked him. "Would you look at that?"

"What?"

"Nine hours off, and no one is yelling at us." I stood and offered him a hand up. "Let's enjoy our luxury accommodations."

16

NEW SUIT

520.114.0840 Commerce District, Vanguard
City Space Station, Vanguard

THE SHOWER ON *The Happy Marauder* is strange and awesome. It's a wind tunnel thing that pulls the air down through the grate. The simple fact that there isn't a timer begging for credits made me linger. Hot water is so nice.

I'm not proud to say I didn't really get my bed made. More like pulled the sheets out of the packaging, made myself a nest, and passed out. I had the best sleep I can remember though. Still achy from the injections, but in half gravity, it was so much easier to manage.

Fucking EASY MODE!

Other interesting things: sinks are vacuums as I discovered when I brushed my teeth.

Anyway, onto the store to get my first space suit!

Shantu and I left *The Happy Marauder* and went back to the space station for the fitting of the personal hazardous environment protection system (HEPS). The matte brightness of *The Happy Marauder* was a visceral difference to the station's warm shiny lighting.

The distant, professional shopkeeper was customer service level enthusiastic about us. I did the same thing when I served people at the bar. He ran us through the features and maintenance and sent us on our way.

The space suit was a dumb, meaning analog, not unintuitive, and a rugged design that seemed to be popular on the space station. A couple of discrete glow-in-the-dark analog gauges displayed external environmental temperature, pressure, and remaining oxygen and recycler status. Air was cycled through one-way valves and the oxygen medium unit.

The shopkeeper was morbidly disinterested as he showed us the "bananas." They were yellow handles with subdued slots that you pulled to amputate a limb in the event of a breach that you couldn't seal with the patch kit that was built into the thigh. There was a banana at each shoulder and upper thigh.

The HEPS had *connections* for our bodily functions. I'll let you use your imagination. Regardless, sharing HEPS was basically out of the question.

The shopkeeper put us in blue training suits with some cheap shitty gray paint job over the face plate, and we learned how difficult they were to extract from their slots and operate. We had to practice pulling the handle until the light turned green.

It was a total bitch. I couldn't imagine how hard it would be to do this while the air was ripped from my lungs, and I got cryoburns.

Because no one wanted to be responsible for shit, we signed a release of liability.

We waddled back, trying to ignore our new plumbing. Not to get too vulgar, but no one warned us about this. I might have made other decisions.

Here's to new experiences…

Two dozen people wearing nearly identical HEPS were in *The Happy Marauder*'s air lock when the door opened. A tall man with leathery skin stood at the front, barking orders.

"Doff and don your HEPS!" he shouted unnecessarily harshly.

"Huh?" I said stupidly.

Wraith appeared above his head, and his sun-tanned skin looked prematurely aged. He was a few centimeters taller and mean looking. "Take your suit off, and when it is completely off, put it back on as quickly as you can!" His regional accent was gone.

I was tired, sore, nauseated, and generally felt like shit. I opened my mouth to tell him to go fuck himself when Shantu put a hand on my shoulder.

"Do you want to see our dicks?" he asked, "because we're not wearing anything under them."

"Do you think vacuum, fire, or other hazardous environments give a shit about your little planet's sense of modesty?" Wraith's yelling maintained its steady volume and harsh tone. "Do you think your sense of modesty is a salve for pressure necrosis due to improper wear of safety equipment? Now execute my command!"

Something in my head clicked. All the military games and other media slapped my face. He was our drill sergeant, and we were his soldiers. The whole situation took shape, and my anger passed like a warm breeze.

"I got a different idea," someone said.

A body hit the ground before I could make sense of what was happening. Mini-turrets had deployed from the air lock's corners. They were targeting the four closest to Wraith but not Shantu and me, who were crouching. Three pops later, and the body count rose to four.

"Single file. In the cargo bay," Wraith ordered.

"On me!" Gabe jogged off, activating the air lock doors. They actuated dangerously fast.

People scrambled to their feet.

On my way out, I noticed six bodies on the ground.

Someone screamed. I don't know who.

In the cargo bay, I managed to get a clear count of us. Twenty-one. Dire-horn, in his imposing battle armor, watched everything.

Wraith's eyes were wild, and his breathing heavy when he caught up. He then resumed the exercise. Three refused to strip and left. But the nudity seemed such a stupid thing to worry about after watching six people die within two meters from me.

We stepped out of the suits, only to jump right back into them. Fumbling with the quick disconnect for the plumbing while trying to seal them as quickly as possible. He had us repeat it five more times.

"Finally," Wraith said, "you are slightly less likely to die now. Remove your helmets. I want to know that you can hear me clearly. Now, it is my duty to inform you about your life aboard the FTS *The Happy Marauder*. Training and certification have officially commenced." He tapped his handset to make his point. The ITSS course populated my feed, and the tab for my HEPS qualification turned green.

He took a breath. His tone lost its volume but none of its authority. "You are showing minimal aptitude for adaptability. That's all I need. First, your rights: you are free to leave at any time. Account balances will be settled as you disembark. Second, you may seek medical or legal attention at any time. Third, I have been given the task of getting you slugs up to speed, and therefore, your training and qualifications will be added to my record. I will not qualify you for anything I do not have absolute confidence that you can do. Last and most importantly, while in training, all orders are absolutes." His volume rose. "You will not *question* orders! You may request information to better execute orders! DO. I. MAKE. MYSELF. CLEAR?!"

We nodded with a few mumbles.

"Here, upon the *Free Trade Ship The Happy Marauder*, to answer in the affirmative, the proper response is yes sir!"

"Yes sir!" we said.

"Sir, permission to speak?" a voice down the line said. The tone was high and oily.

"Speak," Wraith said with a dangerous tone. It felt like a spring ready to snap and cut someone in half.

The speaker clearly didn't know when to shut his mouth. "Sir, did my records arrive?" His tone was the friendly venomous tone of someone who was stealing your wallet while giving you directions.

"They did. Everyone except you get into a push-up position."

I did, against the protests of my body.

"Cool," "So—"

"Go," Wraith whispered or maybe mouthed.

Several Vanguard Port Authority people stepped out from their hiding places.

"What's this?" the snake salesman said.

I didn't buy it. The guy sputtered, trying to talk his way out of the arrest. The port authority also arrested five others from our group.

"WE! ARE! MARAUDERS!" Wraith said with conviction. "We turn disasters into profit! We control our own fates!"

"WE ARE MARAUDERS!" we chanted.

When the security people finished, Wraith started again. "Sergeant Tok, front and center."

A short squat figure popped out of line and marched with clear military crispness. His heels struck the floor with a metallic snap as he closed the distance. He spoke with Wraith for a few moments before they turned to us.

"Sergeant Tok served with honor in the Walgeylu defense and did two tours in the Pirate Lane," Wraith said. "You will extend him every courtesy as he retains his rank in the Commonwealth Patrol on detached duty under my command. Sergeant Tok, welcome aboard. They are yours to command."

They shook hands, and Wraith left.

"On your feet!" Sergeant Tok boomed. His voice was amplified, clearly synthetic. The feed populated him as Sgt. Tok.

Standing, I saw he was in a more robust environment suit of a different design. His had more curves and was less angular with an opaque faceplate. Not a suit, powered armor with slots for weapons and other equipment. The display color was set to match ours, which was only part of the sting.

He tapped his handset, and his volume modulated to come through our ear bugs. "I am Sergeant Tok. I have worked with *The Happy Marauder* several times during my time with the Commonwealth Fleet Marines, then as a liaison to Vanguard Aggregate Forces. I am not disappointed in the efficiency with which they execute their operations. I have no intention of degrading that efficiency. I will always be a marine, but first and foremost, I am a Marauder. One must improvise, adapt, and overcome new challenges. You are my newest challenge."

Sgt. Tok had us change into athletic clothes and then walked us through stretching and calisthenics. Shantu and I struggled behind when the run started.

The waypoints on our feeds had us going around obstacles while most of the other recruits were tasked over them. A part of me was angry that we were getting special treatment. My mauled muscles, headache, lightheadedness, and nausea were all grateful for the small concession. We still finished last by an embarrassing margin.

After physical training, we were given twenty minutes for hygiene with orders to report to the galley afterward.

I relished the hot water in my private shower. I turned on two of the jets to help massage my aching shoulders, a battered body floating in immense luxury. The mix of sensations was overwhelming.

When I left my cabin, the kitchen's humidity and the scent of food filled the air. The smell of a hearty soup and grilling vegetables hit me like a sledgehammer, and my mouth watered.

Dire-horn, in his imposing nature, wore a floral apron as he danced behind the bar, cooking.

My brain broke.

Shantu shoved me forward. "Quit staring and get a fucking seat." The fatigue was clear in his voice.

"Fuckstick!" I muttered.

"Fucknuts!" he muttered back.

The veteran crew sat near the kitchen while us newcomers took farther seats.

The captain stood and cleared his throat. "I would like to thank Dire-horn for preparing this meal."

A small applause went around the table. He went onto introductions, which I completely missed because the dancing minotaur serving the first course transfixed me. I did catch that Scout also served as ship's counselor, which meant psychotherapist not lawyer. Dire-horn was the ship's counsel, meaning lawyer not therapist.

The captain warned that everyone in training would be placed on a restricted diet in accordance with the training criteria. He rambled on about our immediate itinerary, trade, and political environments. I tried my best to follow, but I didn't really understand what they were talking about. I used a feature of my feed to tag the conversation for review.

"To the new crew." The captain raised his glass. "This is a dangerous job, and we're all here to make money. I, however, will not trade lives for contracts. If you disagree, this is not the ship for you." He toasted. "Liberum volare."

I toasted with the rest of the crew and discreetly researched the toast. It was from a dead human language that translated to "freedom fly" or "fly free." I liked it and shared an approving nod with Shantu.

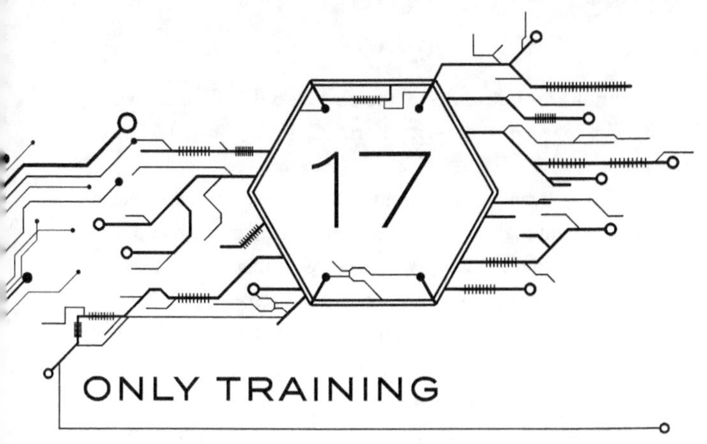

17

ONLY TRAINING

I WOKE UP to a dull red flashing halo in my vision and wailing alarms.

I didn't know what was going on, but I wanted to be in my HEPS before I did anything. I had spent the latter hours of yesterday watching all the horrible ways to die in space.

I flailed uselessly in the absence of gravity. Kicking my blanket toward the far wall sent me drifting toward the locker. I momentarily wondered why cats were so calm in free fall while I flailed headfirst into the locker.

I donned the suit like a drowning toddler and bounced off the shower before I could stop my spinning. My feed was dead. No signal from the ship or anything else. I acknowledged the incessant flashing and found a general ship emergency had activated.

I climbed the wall like a spider before I remembered the boots had magnets. I then stood there awkwardly for a moment before going to the room panel. The menu showed environmental conditions for both sides of the door. It didn't flash any warnings and gave atmospheric information that didn't mean shit to me.

Pro tip: twenty-one percent oxygen, seventy-eight percent nitrogen, and that last percentage can be whatever won't poison you. If oxygen dips below twenty percent or above twenty-three percent: problems. If CO_2 gets above ten percent: problems.

I guess that since the readings outside were the same as in here, I would be okay.

"Now, what was the hold up?"

The shouted question from Sgt. Tok stunned me. He was at Shantu's cabin and appeared to be on Shantu's ass. He pressed further when I hesitated.

"Is my comm not clear?"

I tripped over my words. "It took me a moment to find the display icon for environment…"

"Outstanding," he said, his voice broken up like audio clips. "Now, I understand that you two came aboard together. If you could explain to your moron friend the importance of donning HEPS *before* cracking any vacuum rated seal."

"Conditions may not be safe, Sergeant?" I said simply.

"Good enough." He left us to attack the next person.

His approach would have been more effective if his voice didn't sound like someone was splicing together audio clips from military dramas.

"Ah, fuck." He kicked off the deck, positioned himself on the bulkhead, and launched down the corridor.

A medical emergency flashed on my feed, and a waypoint appeared. Shantu and I tried to follow him but did not have the grace in zero g. We bounced off bulkheads and struggled with handholds.

When we arrived at the designated cabin, Sgt. Tok and Wraith were using adhesive straps to limit a young woman's movements.

A horrifying medic bot clung to her exposed chest, shocking her like in the movies.

Globules of blood floated around the room.

Shantu spoke up first. "What can we do to help?"

Wraith grabbed a device from a compartment on the medical bot and attached it to the young woman's face. "Kick up the ventilation."

Shantu moved as carefully as he could.

Wraith turned to me. "Grab a pillowcase and attach it to that vent with the tape." He pushed the tape toward me. "All right. Firs' lesson in emergency first aid." His accent was thick with strain. "ABC: Airway, breathing, circulation. Airway ain't clear."

He turned on the suction from the medic bot, and the pillowcase quickly inflated. Bubbles of brown mush seeped through the fabric.

"This is a breathing mask." He placed the mask on the woman's face. Tubes from the mask ran to the medic bot. "This is a zero g thorax compressor."

It looked like a fat belt with manual knobs as a buckle. He shoved the belt compressor thing under her back and fed the free end to the buckle.

"This is the activator." Wraith adjusted a knob to activate the device. It formed a divot and compressed her chest. He then adjusted the device over her heart, seeming indifferent to its movements.

A larger, more sophisticated medical bot beeped at us as it entered the room. It looked like a dog mixed with an espresso machine. Four walking limbs and gadgets everywhere. The medic bot deployed a stretcher, and Wraith gently floated her into it.

The woman took a deep hacking breath, flailing violently. The medic bot deployed one of those neck donuts and gently pulled her to the stretcher. It attached a device to her arm, and she calmed.

Wraith deactivated the compressor thing and replaced it in the smaller bot. "Everyone out. We'll take her to the infirmary."

Shantu was green with flecks of brown fluid on his face. I lifted an eyebrow to ask how he was doing.

"It smells so bad." He climbed along the wall to get out.

Thirty minutes later, we received messages to go to the conference room. It seemed every member of the crew was there.

"Crew, as part of *The Happy Marauder* standard operating procedure, we have a meeting after every incident," the captain said. He had his diplomatic face on. "The purposes of these meetings are to identify any shortfalls we may have and how we can improve. Normally, these feeds are restricted, but this is being added to an incident report."

The conference room dimmed, and a virtual request pinged my feed. I accepted it. Johansson, B. appeared in the corner of my feed, along with her vital signs. The video played, showing her bouncing off the overhead, panicking, and sending herself into an uncontrolled spin. She vomited and cracked her head on a wall while she heaved. Her feed detected the impact and sounded the medical emergency alarm before her vitals tanked. She floated spasming and choking on her last meal. Wraith was in the room in less than a minute.

I closed my eyes, but the image became clearer. I had forgotten that it was being displayed on my eyeball via the contact lens they had issued me. The display ended, and the lights came on.

"What went wrong here?" the captain asked no one in particular.

"She panicked," a voice answered from the other side of the room.

"We should have been trained in zero g," another voice said.

The captain's flat expression spoke volumes. "Training."

Dire-horn stood and took his place to head the meeting. "Psychological assessment for novel experiences was necessary.

While far from ideal, it is prudent to perform these types of assessments near major ports prior to the appropriate training. Ms. Johansson, Mr. Barker, and Cutas will be disembarking. They leave with their honor intact as it takes a brave soul to recognize one's limitations."

Blood drained from my face, and my stomach dropped. Three more people were off the ship. It suddenly became clear how easy these tests were to fail.

"Emergency medical response was nothing less than what I would expect," the captain said with such finality that it became a gravitational force.

Fail to meet expectations and get kicked off.

"I don't want to go back," I DMed Shantu.

"Me either. Talk later," he sent back.

"Are there any questions or concerns before everyone is dismissed?" the captain asked.

"Is that how you treat your crew?" a synthetic voice that I didn't have line of sight to asked. "One bad moment, and they're off?"

The captain didn't react. His bland expression spoke of someone who was on autopilot and had given this speech too many times.

"Case study reports." Scout grimaced, probably realizing he was slipping into psycho-babel. "Without going into the research, it's one of the most effective ways to…tell if someone is going to break prior to trauma. Training to desensitize a subject invalidates—"

The captain cleared his throat, and Scout paused.

"Excuse me. I'm accustomed to an academic setting. Many militaries use programs that try to train the fear out of their soldiers. The use of pharmaceuticals…" He paused again and chittered something in his native tongue. "Operant conditioning techniques have, let's say, mixed results. The MO, or how we do business, on *The Happy Marauder* requires a certain psychological profile. We need calm adaptability because we don't have the facilities or the time to take in a larger candidate base. I act as a forward observer but also provide mental health services."

Shantu's voice was flat as he gestured around the room. "We're talking right now, so we don't hold a grudge, and you don't potentially lose good people by pressing too hard?"

"Accurate enough." The captain shrugged. "I make it a point to be clear about the environment we're operating in. The incidents in the air lock and cargo bay were not staged. But the timing was manipulated to make sure everyone was present to provide a visceral example. Beyond that, six violent criminals dead and six others arrested is just how we pay for our parking and maintain a good relationship with the station we are docked at."

The meeting went on for a little while longer, mostly talking in circles. It died out of its own accord.

When we were dismissed, everyone was sent to the cargo bays for zero g familiarity training. "Training" was getting yelled at while installing bracing on cargo containers. I'm sure they were measuring endurance, motor coordination, stress levels, and a hundred other things.

After lunch, we had another doctor's appointment. After a blood draw and another scan, we were kicked out the door with sand-filled goop that almost made me gag. It tasted like the leftover grease from meat mixed with carrots and crushed aspirin. My feed gave me a bland readout of either nutritional or chemical information.

We took the food to the galley. There weren't any official rules about having food outside of the galley but vacuuming crevices was the cost of doing business.

"You all right?" I asked Shantu as he tried to eat the same synthetic crap that I did.

"No. I got puke all over me this morning, and now I have to eat it after it's been sitting in the air vent for six hours."

I almost shot the goop out of my nose by laughing so hard. Fortunately, or unfortunately, it was too thick and got stuck in my nasal cavity. That started a round of laughter from Shantu. The laughter spread around the galley. I enjoyed the belly laugh for as long as it lasted and took a swig of water to get the goop down quicker.

"Huh. My goop makes water taste sweet," I said before downing the rest intermittently with swigs of water. "I'm going to see if Scout can translate this crap for me."

I sent a message and got a reply within a few minutes.

Scout explained, in a language we could understand, the drugs we were on. Long story short: We were from a lower g planet and did a poor job taking care of ourselves. Most of the drugs were to help us adapt to higher gravity and the interstellar immuno-therapy protocol, and a pile of other drugs were to help with side effects to not delay training. He ended his message by asking to have him act as a liaison for the doctor.

Shantu whispered to me in a private channel. "I'm pouring over the training syllabus and their reference documents. I found something."

I met his eyes and lifted my chin.

"There's no end criterion. Our credentials get added to the ship's portfolio, and that's that. If they bring on additional crew, we know we're getting somewhere. We're not going to get any encouragement or anything else until we ask for it to stop and become permanent crew, or we leave the ship and get our training records."

I shrugged. "Time to be awesome."

18

DOUBLE TAP

I AWOKE TO the ship gently accelerating away from Vanguard. There was no physical training scheduled for the morning, so it was breakfast and then weapons briefing for the C-M/L 2851 Double Tap carbine and pistol variant.

I managed to get out of bed without bouncing off the bulkhead with fractional gravity. I wobbled, letting my boots stick to the deck. Growing up on a planet worked against me as I did a weird stomp to adjust my center of balance over the foot that would stay planted. It felt like when you stepped in something sticky and had to pull your foot free.

In the galley, everyone carefully moved, overcorrecting and wobbling in the fractional gravity. Hot food and liquids were restricted to the zero g bulbs. I opened the fridge to find it filled with them. It seemed everyone was on the medical diet that Doc put us on. My feed highlighted the one assigned for me, and I groaned.

I stared at the bulb in its slot, wishing it was something Direhorn cooked.

"I was just as excited to find my ration," Uvwewe, a tall, dark-skinned human, lean and strong. He must be from a high UV word. One of the other new recruits. I had seen him around a bit in briefings, and he lapped me during physical training, but I don't think we had spoken before.

"Enjoy them," Sgt. Tok announced across the galley. "They're worth ten thousand credits each."

I wobbled and found a chair.

"Is that just the space markup?" Alexis asked.

They're one of the drone techs from what I can gather. They're androgynous but with a better build than Shantu and me. I'm almost sure they're human. Dark skinned but not pitch-black like Uvwewe. They have an athletic build, and I get the impression they're coming out of the military by the way they move and talk.

Everyone seems shy about their past, which is fine with me.

Sgt. Tok seemed on the friendly side then. "No. It's bio-tuned. It's not the goop on the inside; it's what you would pay to have a doctor plan your meals and give you medication in them. At least in the marines, we got our medications separate from our food." He shrugged. "Different ship. Same old shit." He raised his bulb and took a long pull on it.

I broke the seal and took a draw on the valved straw.

Uvwewe stared at me.

"What?" I asked around the gob of crap in my mouth.

"What does yours taste like?" he asked. "Mine tastes like orange and roast lamb marinated in a paint stripper. There are small capsules that crunch with a gel that tastes like how burning coolant smells."

I caught on, raising a finger because the stuff was coating my teeth. I gestured for water, and a bulb was passed to me. When I took a pull on the water, the glop didn't mix. Everyone laughed as my face twisted with the sensation of fighting a slug in my mouth. One eye closed, my face contorted as I forced the awful mixture down.

I looked at the bulb like it was pure evil. "Caloric allotment number four and aspirin mixed in fish oil. It's so bad. It has the texture of the red gear lube, and it didn't mix with water."

Shantu wobbled in all bleary eyed, and the room went silent. He took his pull and spit it out. The cleaning bot chased the bolus around and vacuumed it up. "Ugh! What the fuck?!"

The room erupted into laughter.

"It tastes like ass, cherry, and hydraulic fluid," he said once we coaxed the description out of him. "Maybe licorice but like the bad kind."

I guess we are growing together, even if it is over eating hot garbage.

After breakfast, we gathered in the conference room for today's briefing. All the walls were floor to ceiling displays that usually were a plain gray with no backlight. Gabe then brought in a cart of impressive rifles. A weapon appeared on the presentation screen behind him. After the treat-every-weapon-like-it's-loaded spiel, he asked Sgt. Tok to assist him.

"Marauders, for this briefing, I will be familiarizing you with the C-M/L 2851D," Gabe said. He enunciated with authority that warred with his friendly disposition. "When handling weapons in a non-combat situation, a safety person is required in case you shoot yourself. A formal reprimand and a safety violation will be issued on your record. There are three safety check locations on the C-M/L 2851D: the carbine, the combination magnetically accelerated projectile, and laser model 2851 fourth generation, thus the *D* identifier. Colloquially known as the double tap."

His mandibles, the four pieces of basically bones, moved but never tapped or clicked. If they did, they sounded like a human clicking their tongue. It made no sense.

"The first safety check is the primary power cell that fits into the stock here." Gabe handled one of the weapons and gestured to the void in the stock. "Clear."

He presented the weapon to Sgt. Tok, who made a show of looking into the empty space and announced, "Clear."

"The second is the magazine integrated into the forward grip. Currently absent." Gabe gestured into the hole under the weapon's frame and repeated the clear process with Sgt. Tok. "The third is in the chamber." He yanked the top of the weapon back, and a portion of the composite frame slid back. A flag dangled from the hole in the frame. He pulled on the flag, a red plug shaped like a *T* slid out.

"This is the safety interrupt," Gabe continued. "The long portion faces the rear of the weapon system. It prevents a projectile from entering the acceleration chamber. Therefore, it cannot be installed if a projectile is present. It also prevents electricity from reaching the onboard capacitors. Thus, *interrupting* the circuit. Furthermore, it keeps the laser aperture clean during storage. However, the removal and inspection of the loading chamber is mandatory because the onboard capacitors carry enough charge for one magnetically accelerated projectile to reach lethal velocities."

He went on to describe the weapon's characteristics and functionality in different environments. It normally fired a projectile and then a laser so the projectile would both clear the barrel and keep the aperture clean.

The double tap could be used as a cutting laser if you removed the projectile magazine and held the slide back. This forced the weapon into a low power and continuous activation of the laser. It would deplete the standard cell in less than a minute but was a useful feature. Cutting mode should be sustained for no more than twenty seconds, and people should just take turns to avoid weapon damage. Regardless, there was a still thirty percent chance of permanent damage to a battery.

Gabe described it as the workhorse of mercenaries. It was simple, rugged, and reliable. The basic weapon system had been in use for over a century, only changing with advances in materials.

Sgt. Tok and Gabe passed out the weapons. I shook it in the microgravity. It felt sturdy, solid but not so heavy. I'm pretty sure it could make it through someone's skull.

Gabe walked us through the teardown procedure. It was as simple as flicking the compressing lever, lifting the lever, and twisting the lever. The frame and barrel then came apart, giving access to the four ten-centimeter cylinders of voodoo that we didn't open because they were melt-your-face-off toxic. The laser emitter was also a little mystery cylinder that didn't look cool at all. All it had was a circle at one end that would iris when firing. I don't know why in my head I saw circuitry, flashing lights, and glowing crystals.

We then put the whole thing back together. Every piece had intuitive notches or curves so they could only go back together one way.

Which was BORING!

At least my rhino had this cool crystal pressurizing chamber. It twisted apart, and I had to scrub the carbon and other shit out of it. It glowed different colors based on the air when it was fired.

We broke down and reassembled the weapons two more times. Because that was too easy, we pushed everything to the center of the conference table and reassembled all the weapons again. With strobe lights, Sgt. Tok then brought in a little jet engine of a fan and scattered the parts around the room. It was just a tube with handlebars and a rigid filter that he braced against the wall. The walls animated with battle scenes from a movie I couldn't quite place.

"Communicate!" he shouted over the snow blower thing.

"What do you have?! What do you need?! Marauders take care of Marauders. No one else in the deep dark cares."

"Sgt. Tok, may I retrieve parts from the filter?" someone yelled over the rushing air and was rewarded with him handing them the parts.

It was awesome. That was what I call a team building exercise! You got to know someone while assembling a weapon, getting blasted with strong winds, and getting pelted with the parts you were trying to assemble.

After all that, Gabe and Sgt. Tok took the time to show us how to manually actuate the bolt for a function test. They gave us slings, took five seconds to make sure we could handle that, and briefed us on the firing range.

Each station had its own tube of heavy polymer, so we couldn't shoot each other if we wanted to. The backstop was a gel that dissipated the laser, caught the projectile, and displayed a basic target. Sensors in the station, along with our feeds, monitored our proficiency. Sgt. Tok and Gabe didn't accompany us; instead, they went to a monitor and cut us loose.

In the station, I found some earmuffs and goggles and laughed at myself because I wasn't making that mistake again. I still had a persistent EEEEEEEEEEEEE from cutting the neodymium forge free.

I found the bank of power cells and crates of magazines. Not clips. Sgt. Tok was clear to never call them clips.

I'm sure we were being assessed for adaptability or whatever.

When I inserted the power cell, there was a slight electric whine. I was careful to keep the weapon down the range when I inserted the magazine, which locked in with a satisfying snap. I shouldered the weapon and saw how the groove on its top aligned with the clear piece of polymer. Iron sights. Though I don't think there was any iron in the weapon. I closed one eye and aimed.

Nothing happened.

Before I could troubleshoot, a horrendous BANG! reverberated through the chamber, and someone complained that their ears hurt.

I hoped it wasn't Shantu.

"Now you won't forget to wear your hearing protection next time," Gabe said over the intercom.

As others fired, I found the fire mode selector switch and set it to single. I quickly found myself bouncing off the door with a sharp pain in my shoulder. I hit inside the second ring, in case anyone's wondering.

"That's what a kilojoule of energy feels like," Sgt. Tok said into my ear with obvious levity. "There's a harness next to the crate."

Irritated, I donned the harness and found the mounting points. They could have said something. I then laughed because I would have done the same thing.

They let us shoot at the classic grid target. After a few dozen rounds, I used my feed to display a virtual target on the wall, so I could see where I was hitting. Not my shining moment, but I was hitting the target.

By the end of the first magazines, Gabe and Sgt. Tok gave corrections over the intercom for everyone to hear.

"You're anticipating the recoil." Sgt. Tok told me. "Let it be a surprise to you and the weapon when it fires."

The nice man at the topside range had told me the same thing.

Sgt. Tok had me empty the weapon and squeeze the trigger. The feed still showed where the barrel was aiming. Sure enough, there was a jump down and to the left. I reloaded, and he had me empty two full magazines as fast as I could, simulating suppressing fire. When I backed it down to single controlled shots, they were much more accurate.

The ventilation kicked up as the firing range started to smell of ozone. We began practicing going from low ready to firing.

When everyone seemed to have their weapons reasonably dialed in, the lights dimmed, the targets moved, and a scoreboard populated the top.

A red *X* honked when I fired, and my score went negative. I fired again and again, enduring the honks and trying to find the right target. A ka-ching sounded, and Shannon jumped up the scoreboard. The bay exploded with fire as the rules became clear. Honks filled the range as everyone searched for their target. Shannon hit one thousand points, and the game ended. Her name was animated with fireworks.

"Congratulations! Shannon!" Gabe said over the intercom. "You will get a dessert up to two hundred calories."

I didn't know who Shannon was yet. There were just too many new faces.

A bunch of people—not me—threw a fit about how the game wasn't fair because they didn't understand the rules. Okay. I threw a fit. But I wasn't alone. I could hear yelling from other stations.

Sgt. Tok and Gabe didn't even acknowledge us. Instead, they turned on the next game, and an animation of a western carnival game appeared. Someone opened fire. I unloaded, walking the weapon around the backstop and trying to hoard the chain of duck silhouettes. Uvwewe beat me by a few points. I assumed he got the higher value targets in the middle of the screen. I still felt rather proud of myself taking second though.

We kept at it for an hour before returning to the conference room for a repeat lecture on the pistol variant, which was just smaller. The power cell went under the barrel, and the magazine was a traditional grip load. They had a bag of polymer pads to adjust the size grips to our hands.

No tornado this time.

The pistol training took significantly longer because of the trial-and-error period for the pads. We spent the next hour drawing and firing from different holster configurations.

Gabe and Sgt. Tok gave more hands-on adjustments this time. Even Wraith stopped to help. I had particular trouble with my offhand shooting, which would take time. They reassured me that we would have plenty of time to practice. I would just have to "grow into" offhand shooting.

Preventive maintenance was a simple scrub of the contact plates for the capacitor and some oil. We returned the weapons to the cart, Gabe locked it, and Sgt. Tok returned the weapons to the armory.

Gabe then showed us how to operate the equipment that maintained the backstop. We recovered fléchettes from the catch can and poured them into a hopper to be recycled with the ship's ferrous metals stores.

We handloaded one magazine for the pistol and the rifle. Just for the check box.

"You are now qualified to use the weapons. The range and armory are now available to you," Gabe said. "If you take weapons from the small arms lockers, you are expected to restock them. If you fail to do so, you will do inventory and restock all of them. If you fail to do maintenance on the range, you will become my apprentice. I will teach you how to do heavy maintenance. If everyone keeps an eye out, and none of that shit comes to my attention, everyone will have a better time."

Sgt. Tok showed us how to use the automated loaders in the armory. The machine also monitored the wear on the fléchette magazines. Any rejects went into a bin for Gabe to decide whether he wanted to salvage or recycle them.

My feed populated the new qualifications, and I accepted the notifications. A tab appeared on my feed with instructions on how to order specialty ammunition.

"What about my plasma pistol?" I asked Gabe.

"We have a plasma fence; you can pull it out if you want to use it at the range. Your feed will help you out," he said. "They're not widely used because you get what? Fifty shots out a charge with a maximum range of fifty to a hundred meters? Not to mention your weapon needs to be in a compatible atmosphere. That same charge can power a thousand rounds from a double tap with an effective range being line of sight."

Ouch.

I had been carrying my rhino around for years.

Sgt. Tok seemed to notice. "Carry it as a backup weapon. Keep it handy if we're somewhere we don't want to cause a lot of collateral damage."

Gabe shrugged his massive set of shoulders and nodded. "An extra platform qualification is always a good thing."

After lunch, we did the whole thing over again but in our HEPS.

19

PRACTICE MAKES PERMANENT

520.143.0300 FTS *The Happy Marauder*, Interstellar Space

I **KIND OF** lost track of time there. I still want to keep a record, so I'll pick it up here.

Today, I woke to Sgt. Tok shouting over my feed, startling me from my sleep. "Your HEPS is compromised, and this compartment is venting atmosphere. What do you do?"

"Inspect and repair if time permits based on venting speed," I answered. "Vacate the venting compartment if possible, Sergeant."

"You are losing air. Why wouldn't you try to save the atmosphere and survive?"

"Venting implies deliberate ship operation as opposed to breach alarm. No breach was mentioned. Interfering with ship operations could be an act of mutiny and endanger the crew. Active venting of these compartments would imply a spreading fire, boarding party, or the shields have failed."

Sgt. Tok and the senior crew constantly drilled us newcomers on emergency procedures, first aid, manual ship operations, and a bunch of other stuff. We had even gotten used to drinking from a pressure washer.

The Happy Marauder had floated in Vanguard's orbit for a while as it took on cargo, some contracted and some tradable commodities. During this time, we were run to exhaustion for as much zero and low g training as possible. Once loaded, the ship had accelerated at roughly half a g for two weeks—until we were out of the Oort cloud where the Alcubierre drive could be engaged. The ship would add 0.01g of acceleration every day until we became acclimated to 2.5G.

That's all I could get because basic starship theory isn't for another two weeks.

Things had changed. Floors were decks, walls were bulkheads, ceilings were overheads. But it made sense. Port was left because when ships floated on water, they always parked the left side to the port. When ships flew, they added dorsal and ventral like fish.

I love it.

I had put on ten kilos but slimmed down. My gut was shrinking, and my arms were filling out. Not a lot but noticeable. To me at least.

The pacing here is hard, but Gabe and Sgt. Tok explain things plainly. No upsell. No fancy language. Nothing to prove to anyone. Here's what. Here's how. Here's why. Questions? Even if I feel like a fool for asking about vapor pressures, someone sighs in relief because they weren't getting it either. Then someone else tries, or we pull up a video and even cartoons to learn more.

By the way, unless you want to take a deep dive into physics, liquids don't really exist in vacuum. You need pressure for liquid to not sublimate. I thought that was interesting. You're welcome.

Downtime ceased to exist all together. If we weren't in combat training or running emergency drills, we were in correspondence courses that covered everything else. We took confirmation tests in core education and familiarity rating tests in starship cargo handling, starship system operation, maintenance, and repair for non-critical systems. I could now dismantle three different air locks in under a minute—non-standard designs in under five minutes, which is good for a novice.

The wealth of knowledge and skills pouring into me taught me I'm not stupid. I'm not worthless. I'm not just another body in the reclaim. And it doesn't matter what anyone says as long as I accomplish my goals.

The Happy Marauder was quickly becoming my home.

"I've been keeping an eye on the ship's maintenance schedule," Shantu said one day as we ran from point to point around the ship. We were almost up to a full standard g. "Next week, there's some stuff about stress testing and laden maneuvering. I'd put money on that we're getting into high g training."

This is how we were adapting: trying to guess at what we're getting into next.

"Sure," I said. "I'm also getting the feeling that we're going to get into combat training soon. The ship has had several open bids for contracts that are conveniently clustered. There's somewhere they're trying to get to."

"Yeah. Or maybe they're trying to do like three at once and save money on fuel?"

"My money says they're playing the commodities game." That was a new word to my vocabulary. *Commodities.* "Trying to buy and sell whatever. Maybe holding out for a few more people. I would be surprised if they didn't have two or three contracts going at a time with convenient little exit clauses or non-committal legal bullshit. These people don't leave things to chance. Shit, there are three separate fire suppression mechanisms in this corridor."

"Oh right. Shit. Fuck. I didn't get a chance. Looky what I found." He tossed up his map of the cargo bays.

I didn't see it at first. Then it hit me.

"Yeah. You see it now, don't you? We're making ourselves a free running course scaled up for our AVs."

"Fuck! With all the starship shit it felt like we were being made into infantry to repel boarding parties or something." I acknowledged.

"That's the playschool bullshit they're doing to keep us busy," Shantu said. "Checking off the boxes so the forms get complete. They're a couple supersized treadmills and a few rumble packs away from a full training center."

"Very astute. You can stop running," Wraith said in our ear bugs approaching us from down the corridor. "We have a complication. Right now, you cannot move your AVs." His voice was that high society diplomat shit and threw me through a loop. "There is a plethora of regulations that restrict private vehicles being used during training, and the class of vehicle is actively making Dire-horn go bald. Since both of your contracts make it very clear that your AVs will not be added to the ship's inventory, and your planetary advocate was much more thorough than we had expected, I propose you lease them to us. We can have the renewal period every day for all I care. The captain likes the proposal, and Dire-horn will attempt to throw me out an air lock for *such disregard for the integrity of the written word.*"

I didn't listen to a word he said. I had more important questions. "Why does your accent keep changing?"

"It's good practice in perception control. We need an answer sooner rather than later," he said more forcefully.

Shantu shoulder checked me. "Daily lease agreement is set to the cost of something we're already consuming, so they net out to zero or close to it. Just make sure there's provisions for damages, as well as operating hours."

"I can work with that," Wraith said before disappearing down the corridor.

The next morning, we received the lease agreements and signed them. Moments after, we were given the day to perform any maintenance or inspections as needed. I found myself sprinting down to the vehicle bay with Shantu close behind me.

"I don't think they've ever sat up for a day, much less a month," I said.

"I was thinking it was going to be months before we did anything with them."

We made it to our garage.

"Oh, baby. I've missed you!" Shantu pushed my buttons as he put on his seductress act and crawled up his AV like a lover. "We're going to take so good care of you now that we're back."

Barf.

We used the cradles for a balancing and lubrication cycle. Both master drive actuator springs were out of preload spec. It didn't take us long to find, request access to, and use the equipment in the engineering area to retemper the springs.

"Gentlemen," Captain Gara Vatosh said, announcing his presence.

Javelin was with him, her face taking us in.

"We're updating our engagement models to include you. I'm excited to see how you perform with your AVs."

"We need information to decide where to focus your training next." Her synthetic eye seemed warmer than her organic one.

"We tend to focus on small unit tactics, and I wanted some feedback." He had his diplomatic face on. "I want to know how you feel about performing an ingress role."

I didn't know what he was talking about. Too much time passed, and I knew I was making a face as I tried to figure out what an ingress role was.

He pressed forward. "This is what I have in mind." He shared a vehicle modification proposal. "We place attachment points like this." He highlighted four rather subtle pieces of equipment that would be placed on the back of our AVs. "They're the hard points for the smart grapples on our armors. We'll place low signature point defenses on each shoulder and wrap everything up with an active stealth coating." He pushed an equipment change authorization at us. He didn't mention the electromagnets, micro thrusters, and other zero g upgrades, but I didn't mind.

Shantu added an addition that all equipment permanently affixed to our equipment would be ours unless otherwise specified. The return on that was a bunch of fine print that clearly defined "permanently affixed," and at the end of it, we could keep the upgrades. They were just closing off loopholes like how we couldn't weld our AVs to the deck and own the ship. Shit like that.

HOW THINGS WORK
AROUND HERE

A REAL BREAKFAST cooked by Dire-horn and served by Wraith was waiting for us this morning. Not some medical concoction that make me want to lick actuating grease from my AV. Javelin was around helping restock the cabinets from a cart.

"Feel free to make sustenance requests," Dire-horn bellowed because his volume never went below a six out of ten.

"Talk to me on this side of the kitchen if you want any animal products, save a cricket," Wraith added.

"The lüga is no crop pest," he shot back.

Wraith patted his shoulder. Like an old farmer patting his prized bull.

"Sāps," Wraith said, like *sapient* but shorter. Then went full professor. "For those of you who are not familiar with minotaur culture, the lüga is an arthropod and was critical to preventing a particular developmental disorder until synthetics were developed. Therefore, it's the only animal consumed by minotaur.

They don't handle any other animal products."

Dire-horn snuffed approvingly. I guess that's the way to put it. He blew air out his nose in a way that said any offense had been forgiven. I have very low confidence in that though because my sample size in minotaur behavior was one. And that was weak because I didn't see him often.

Us newcomers stared burry eyed at each other in mixtures of confusion and frustration. We worked late last night, and signs of fatigue were on everyone's face. Shantu and I exchanged who-gives-a-fuck looks.

"Anyway," Wraith said, "a fucked-up sleep schedule is something you pe—"

"The *reason*," Dire-horn said as Wraith rolled his eyes, "is that at roughly one thousand hours on ship, it is recommended that we debrief. This is an open forum to gain feedback and make adjustments."

I caught Javelin gesturing, and our raw scores populated a display in virtual. Shantu had his gambling face on, so he didn't know shit about this either

The air went out of the room when Javelin took in a breath. She held it for a moment.

"As of present, standard training milestones place this cohort at two standard deviations ahead of the mean, increasing the threat rating of *The Happy Marauder* by nearly one hundred points." She started in on a math heavy presentation about how we rank versus similar outfits.

These performance reviews were painful. Our progress from a standing start was huge, but we were still kilometers from catching up.

Thankfully, Sgt. Tok saved us. "Ma'am, I'm a grunt," he interrupted. "Two more months of training, and I'll take any four as my fire team. This stuff is over my head."

Wraith popped some berries into his mouth and chewed while

talking. "Javelin is trying to educate you on how we bid for jobs and how brokers and agencies see us." He gestured, and a comparative sheet appeared. "Some of these kids may make a life as a mercenary, hopefully here. These numbers make an' break crews."

She picked up, and the sheet morphed into a side-by-side comparison versus Handel Operations. The criteria listed mission success rates, contract violations, secondary objective completions, collateral damage rates, and so on. Alternating red and green to show profit and losses.

"We vote on the contracts we become bound to," she said. "This mission"—the example on the screen had them bidding low and winning the contract—"was uneventful. However, unprofitable."

She talked us through invoicing and profitability. By the end of the contract, Handel lost money. But I was not following. Maybe I was tired, or I was missing too many prerequisites to this class, but it all went over my head like a satellite.

While we were distracted by colors and numbers, the smell of sweet baked bread wafted around the room. I turned. Dire-horn pulled some fancy versions of pancakes out from the oven. They each were nearly a centimeter thick and jiggled almost playfully.

I didn't notice when the accounting lesson ended. Instead, I watched a two-hundred-kilo bipedal bull whose muscles had muscles stack flat cakes with the care of a surgeon. He hummed and drizzled some syrup down each plate as if he was caring for a child. He then topped each plate with whipped cream in a perfect cone spiral. It was beautiful. It was art.

Wraith served each plate. I watched mine jiggle for a moment. Soft moans of joy broke my reverie. I was the only one who hesitated. It was like cutting into a cloud. The fluffy pancake became creamy not soggy where it met the cream and syrup. Pure bliss.

When we came up for air, we all thanked Dire-horn and, by extension, Wraith.

"This should be a regular thing," Sgt. Tok suggested.

Dire-horn's ears swiveled and fixed on the sergeant. That was the equivalent of a raised eyebrow from the minotaur.

"Not to put pressure on you, Dire-horn. I can't cook for shit…"

"I only know how to cook scrambled eggs," Shannon added. She, our drone tech, was a shorter broad-shouldered woman who was well on her way to bulky. Her hair was curly red when we came aboard, but she now had several centimeters of blond showing.

"They're not that good either," Alexis added and received a slap to the back of their head.

The room fell silent.

"The culinary arts were a required course in finishing school," Saliut said in her oh-so-perfect high-born accent. "I would be delighted to lend my hand."

Saliut is a lithe, attractive woman with long black hair normally kept in a neat braid or bun. She was starting to bulk up with the rest of us.

Shantu and I remained silent because I don't think we had ever cooked anything, and that made this conversation uncomfortable for us. Well, for me at least.

"That sounds like a wonderful idea," Wraith said.

Dire-horn ear's perked.

Uvwewe broke the pause in the conversation. "How long have you been on the ship?"

I had recently learned that he was our resident anthropologist and seemed to bridge the gap between the grunt crew and the sophisticated pricks. A part of me wondered if he was here for his study abroad semester or whatever the fuck they call it.

Before anyone could answer, Gabe burst through the hatch, and Dire-horn spun to face him.

"NOT AGAIN!" Dire-horn dropped into a low guard, blocking Gabe's path to the food.

Gabe charged with wild abandon.

Dire-horn had no business having the poise and grace to sweep Gabe's front legs and follow the motion with a spinning backkick that launched Gabe across the galley. Gabe practically bounced off the bulkhead, and before he could take two more steps, Wraith tackled him from the side and locked his ankles around Gabe's massive rear leg. Gabe struggled against the restraints that bound his arms behind his back.

I didn't see how Wraith placed the bindings on Gabe or even where he had pulled them from. Dire-horn dropped his knees into the crook of that massive back leg. The shoni-vonti used his little inner arms to slap Wraith. Wraith wriggled around him, and Dire-horn expertly hog-tied Gabe, careful not to damage the small appendages.

The whole display was absurd. Wraith was then under Gabe, holding on to Gabe's shoulders. Dire-horn was between Gabe's front legs, who vainly tried to kick Dire-horn off, while his small appendages had started a tickle fight.

Javelin looked annoyed, but she always looked annoyed. She pulled what looked like a line of sausage links from the fridge, clicked her tongue, and dangled the rope of meat over Gabe's face. He stopped flailing, opened his mandibles, and followed the dangling food. The image of a baby trying to nurse entered my head. She fed the sausage thing into his maw. I could practically hear woodchipper noises as it disappeared.

Scout walked through the hatch, paused long enough to take in the scene, and stepped around the fray to serve himself coffee from the dispenser labeled —Scout's Coffee DO NOT TOUCH—. He leaned against the counter, holding the drink up to his face, just completely unfazed. Someone tried to greet him, but he just held up one finger while taking a long draw. That long draw continued into a slow, controlled chug.

"Good morning, everyone," he said as his eyes swept over us and then to the melee.

Javelin found a brick of ration concentrate and dropped it next to Gabe's head, making it clear she wasn't putting her hands near his face. The brick was like a hundred thousand calories and was meant to be run in a machine that would add water and flavors and turn it into like a week's worth of food. He looked like an ant trying to get a grip on a rock.

The sound of rocks grinding filled the room as Dire-horn helped roll Gabe off Wraith.

"Pre-flower shoni-vonti go through fracking, where their exoskeletons expand." Scout's eyes were almost closed as he refilled his mug. "It consumes most of their available biological resources, so they become very impulsive. Feed him, let him rest, and he'll be fine in a day or so."

His massive ears lifted like sails as he took another pull on his drink. I interpreted it as him savoring his morning ritual. I followed his eyes to see Gabe still working on the brick.

Dire-horn took out a water bulb and squirted some water on where Gabe was chewing. The brick swelled with the moisture. Gabe swallowed and fell asleep, and Wraith removed the restraints.

After that mini lecture, a giggle about the absurdity of everything turned into a riot of laughter. Even Scout's fuck-off-until-I've-had-my-coffee face became a meme.

After the laughter died down, Dire-horn began guiding the conversation.

"First and foremost, we are mercenaries with honors," he said. "In the modern age of surveillance, espionage has given way to direct conflict once again. The human idiom "ours is not to reason why" comes to mind. We don't ask." He let a pregnant pause fill the room.

"Not how that goes at all, Dire-horn," Wraith said with a thanks-for-trying look on his face.

"We investigate and follow the evidence. Since this work is

dangerous and expensive, we make it a point to diversify our specialties." Dire-horn continued walking around the room. "I specialize in contract law because we need to be sure our contracts will be honored. Scout is a psychologist, primarily for crew support, but he also builds profiles and provides Fourier analysis when appropriate. Wraith provides personnel intelligence. That taken in context with anthropological analysis gives us a good view of the local environment. These factors give us better situational control." His deep bass rumbled at the end to drive the point home.

"While everyone has their specialty," Wraith added, "we encourage you to diversify your skills. Even if you suck at something, go ahead and suck. A shitty passing familiarity is better than dangerous ignorance."

21

SOCIAL DIFFERENCES

"JAMES," SHANTU SAID.

Fuck! Who died?

My butthole puckered, my palms got all sweaty, and my heart pounded. Like the time he got shot, the time he had an impacted… You know what? Never mind.

I learned about this the other day. It was called classical conditioning. My name was paired with terrible experiences.

I stared at him like I was looking down the barrel of a gun.

"Cut that shit out. This isn't bad."

I forced myself to relax as much as I could, which wouldn't be a lot until it's sorted.

"Saliut has a thing for you."

If this ever becomes a movie, I want a record scratch right here. I will also accept a clip of a spit take.

"That uppity bitch likes me?" I asked.

"Yeah, and she doesn't know how to approach you. So, she's been talking to Piper, who's been talking to me, and now I'm talking to you."

"Wait a minute. You and Piper?" I asked, and his grin was shameless. "Dude, like a week ago, you were crying over the aesthetician."

"Nothing gets over the last one faster than the next one," he said as if he's trying to sound pleased with himself.

I knew he was lying. "No. Spare me that bullshit. Are you okay? I don't want you fucking everything in sight, making this place toxic, and getting us kicked off the ship."

"Bring it down, scramble nuts. It's not like that at all. We talk. They're interesting. Granted, I asked that question. It's a process for them to change their physical layout. The slower it goes, the fewer complications. It's more a psychological sense of identity sort of thing. The gendered language is our problem, not theirs. Their native language is imagery—the whole scene—with very little encoding. Makes me think about getting an implant."

I thought on that. I had never really considered how differently people thought. Not just unique perspectives but that whole different mechanisms were happening in their heads. Daydreaming and visualizations aren't how people communicate. Well, I guess memes count.

"Interesting," I said after way too much time had passed.

"Saliut?" Shantu prompted.

"Oh, um… Tell her to grow the fuck up. Stop being a bitch, and we can start from there."

"Bitch, and we can start from there." His mouth moved more than he spoke. He had been doing that more nowadays, talking through his typing and reading.

"You messaged her?"

"Uh-huh."

"Good man." I hated preschool back-and-forth bullshit.

The following day, we had close quarters battle (CQB) training, which was a fucking riot. Like fighting in a bathroom during a rock concert.

For the introduction, Wraith hid in the galley while all us new people, save Sgt. Tok, entered through one hatch to get him. Sgt. Tok acted as a proctor. We were given jelly blasters, which shot bouncy balls that stung on exposed flesh but wouldn't damage anything. A bot would recover the ammo. The padded body armor that simulated the weight of real armor albeit bulkier was enough warning that we were going to get our asses kicked.

We tried to stack up like something we had seen in police movies. And it went exactly as well as you would think for someone's first time.

Wraith, alone with a pistol and a grease pen, eliminated all of us.

"Welcome to CQB," he said. I had given up on trying to place his accents. "You have failed your first shoot-house as most planet siders call it. You will continue to fail. Not because you did anything wrong but because you're playing fair. Combat is not fair. Ideally, we save the fléchette and stab the target's neck while they're asleep." He smiled, but no one laughed.

Sgt. Tok took over and played a video from an action movie that had been edited with slides to explain the concepts. "Entryways like these are everywhere and are an obstacle that must be overcome. Lesson one: stacking."

After the presentation, we shot at target drones. Gabe, Sgt. Tok, Javelin, and even Dire-horn rotated around, shouting corrections. Then we took turns as attackers and defenders. Then it felt like they were just rolling dice to show us how many different scenarios they could make up.

Good times!

After the debriefing, I was almost in my room when Saliut accosted me. I like that word. *Accosted.*

She looks like a magazine cover, and she knows it. She swings her hips when she walks and tilts her head so her hair swings ever so gracefully. I want to kick her right in the head and tell her to get over herself.

I wondered if she was genetically edited to fit her parents' idea of perfect. Ugh.

"That's not how it's done," Saliut said out of fucking nowhere.

"Yes, it is," I said with no fucking idea of what she's talking about. My brain was still playing with the fatal funnel scenarios.

"Why do you have to be this way?"

I stopped myself from repeating it back to her because the interpersonal mindfulness briefing had explained why my success rate with that had been somewhere between zero and negative one. "What are we even talking about?"

"You know…"

"No. I don't know. What I do know is that this is important to me. Being here is important to me. I'm not…" I stopped myself before insulting her. "You can just take that bullshit somewhere else. I have shit to do."

Literally. That was why I was going to my room.

"You're going to leave a woman outside?" she asked.

I rolled my eyes so hard that my neck cracked. "Who the fuck taught you this shit? You prattle on about the schools and the competitions, and this is what you pull? We're on a spaceship. Your room is right over there." I pointed down the corridor ramp. I actually didn't know where her room was, but that wasn't the point. "I'm not leaving you in the wilderness to die."

"It is exceptionally rude for a woman to not be invited in."

She did that. Applied whatever victim filter to get her way.

"See, that's the problem right there," I said. "You expect me to give a shit. I don't give a shit." And if this drags on any longer, there will be a shit in play. "I'm going to my room, and you're not invited! Oh, and leave Piper and Shantu out of this!"

You know, what the fuck is wrong with me? Save Brittany, this is par for the course. Whatever that means. My last semi-serious partner would get drunk or high and then yell at me for making her cheat on me. Or get mad that I wasn't losing my temper.

But I didn't care then because I was either too exhausted from choosing food over sleep or because I knew she wasn't into monogamy. Yet I'm the asshole for not losing my shit on someone I knew wasn't going to keep it exclusive.

FUCK!

Sorry.

Less than twenty minutes later, I received a very formally composed email. The kind of shit I imagine gets sent to parents for an arranged marriage to consolidate family assets or some shit. I have a lot of emotions about this. This woman put a lot of effort into this correspondence. Either she has been planning it or this kind of writing comes naturally to her.

What the fuck am I talking about? This is *Saliut*. She probably had classes that covered formal and personal writing.

I respected the effort. The language was like chewing glass though. I had to look up half the words, only to realize they were embellished and completely unnecessary. It was nebulous beyond comprehension.

Maybe… No, never mind. I was going to upload it, but this thing doesn't receive file transfers, so just take my word on it.

If I removed certain sentences, it said she wanted to have a no strings attached physical relationship. The inverse was almost exactly true, save some words that would have to be left in as a pivot point.

Anyway, I looked up her home system.

Diadem was super heavy on social formalities, rituals on introduction, and the use of intermediaries. Apparently, it worked very well by local standards because there were very low domestic violence reports, and self-reports of partner satisfaction were high. I fell neatly into a checklist of a working relationship. We worked and lived near each other, and we were aligned in age and orientations.

Well, fuck. Now, I was half an asshole. One ass cheek anyway.

I sent her an email, apologizing for my cultural insensitivity. Then because my sensitivity doesn't last that long, I reminded her that she should have also taken in cultural differences when expecting courtship.

Such a foolish word for trying to explore a relationship: *courtship*. Courtship should mean the ship that carries the royal court. That makes more sense to me.

These emails went back and forth for two excruciating days. She would use plain language just long enough for me to think I knew what she wanted. It went about like this.

Saluit: James, I acknowledge that we come from very different backgrounds. I draw on the Nui Community Method and would be happy to pass my knowledge along to you to find a place in the new community growing here.

Me: My course load is full.

Saluit: This is hardly the time for you to neglect your interpersonal communication practices.

Me: –Calander-Link–   Interpersonal   Professional Communication (Course H00124). 520.152.0930

I had very little free time because we were just now earning our professional certifications for the ship. Many of which needed introductory courses that I was taking through the ship's library because I didn't have them.

I looked Nui Community Method up anyway. It's a whole lot of formal meeting practices for different personality types. It feels cult-y. I didn't go in depth but there were a lot of —all-your-problems-exist-because-you-didn't-buy-our-book-and-do-what-we-tell-you-to— vibes.

Maybe they're right. I don't know. I know I don't have the time to read self help books though.

You can imagine my surprise when she slid down my hatch. Her face was so angry; she had blown past pissed and ran into livid.

I was still preparing myself to deal with an angry woman who is used to a lot of cat and mouse. Whatever that means. Do they make noises at each other, and that's why it's synonymous with banter and flirting? I don't know.

She leaned in. I honestly thought she was going to headbutt me; she has a mean one, which I've regrettably learned from sparing. But instead, she went in for a kiss. When I retreated, she grabbed my hand and placed it on her breast.

Now, I am a strong-willed man. But I have no control.

Don't get me wrong. I enjoyed myself. There wasn't any back-and-forth. No communication. She came here for something, and she got it.

What really hurt my ego was the strength gap between us. She didn't look like it, but she could have held me down. It was clear as we, uh, progressed in the activities. She was letting me have input that was subjected to her discretion.

I assume that is what surfing is like. The wave is going to do what it is going to do, and the best you can do is get in position and hope it doesn't crush you.

I didn't look up if she came from a higher gravity planet or if she was augmented. I couldn't get access to her medical records. But the experience left me a little frightened. I didn't like the feeling of not having any control.

All that being said, I really liked it. Maybe it's the lack of companionship. Maybe it's the pile of drugs I'm on. It doesn't matter.

Something is a whole lot better than nothing.

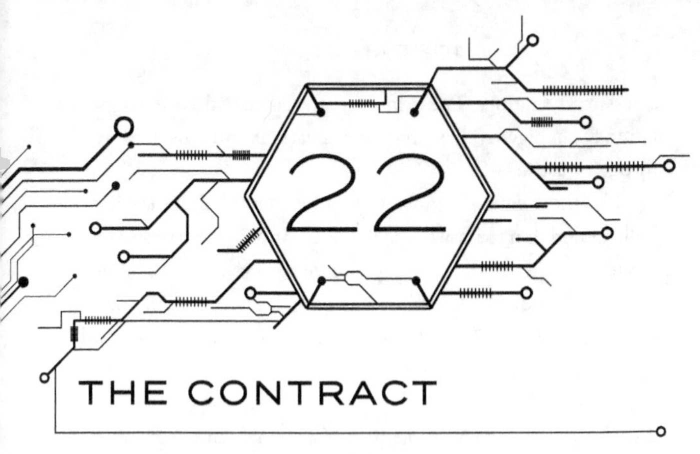

22

THE CONTRACT

520.301.0823 FTS *The Happy Marauder*, Interstellar Space

THERE WASN'T MUCH to keep up with there for a while. I'm getting good at the sub-vocalizations.

It's going good. Real good.

Let's see. Saliut and I have all but stopped talking. I became her booty call. It does bruise my ego to recognize that she is calling the shots, not me, but I'll be long dead before anyone reads this log, so I'll be as honest as I can.

Shantu and I aren't in the slow lane for physical training anymore. We're not caught up, but we're kilometers ahead of where we were. I can run a 10K with gear in under an hour. That was a big milestone for me.

Piper told me where we were. All I can remember is six months toward Commonwealth Space from Vanguard on the recommended trade route.

We had a new training specialist, this Quitilliziga Tu'chupa. The PhD who signed off on our training modules. That turned into weeks of scenarios for various skills assessments for some standardized ratings. The firm she represented had a brutal reputation for being merciless in their evaluations and thus preferred by big industries.

I like the briefing we got. It could be summed up as: don't bullshit and don't kiss ass. She'll do her job as we'll do ours.

Our ratings as tier three paramilitary private contractors, among a laundry list of other specialties, were finalized. Saliut had to do a bunch of testing for her accounting stuff. Shantu and I got ratings as load masters and air lock technicians.

FTS *The Happy Marauder*'s public profile was updated and disseminated. Then we had to do insurance and registration with a bunch of agencies that *The Happy Marauder* has contracts with.

Didn't take a week after the proctor-doctor-lady person… I'm not going to say her name again. Once was enough… Anyway, a week later, we were negotiating a contract. When I say *we*, I mean the senior crew. Most of us just exchanged looks as they went over the briefing packet and projections. We had some academic ideas but no practical knowledge of what a good mission was.

Something else that shows never talk about: insurance companies keep free trade ships in the sky. If a ship has a failure, insurance calls us to show up for repairs. Maybe the policy is only for certain cargo. If a ship or colony goes dark, insurance calls us before they pay out. Those are ideal. Ninety percent of the time, it's a drive-by, and we either sell them a fast packet drone or tell the insurance to pay out. We don't really have to get involved.

This is a good place to explain how comm beacons work. You put a computer server in space, and everyone going that way gets a small fee for carrying message traffic. They pop out of warp and slow just enough so that the doppler shift doesn't degrade the data and move on. Heavily trafficked areas turn into full-blown space stations or get raided before they get there.

It happens.

We're flying faster than light but basically doing the same thing as a cowboy going from town to town, reading the help wanted board outside the post office. If no good jobs come along, we trade some stuff and keep flying.

The good life.

The training briefings are over. We have one profit and risk management briefing a day. Then we take turns presenting available contracts and picking them apart. It is starting to sink in. I'll give my example.

I picked an overdue ship contract. Now, I'm converting to Vanguard planetside credits (V) because that's how my brain works. We get paid in commodities through brokers, and there's a whole thing where we give lists of acceptable payments and specifications, breach conditions, and penalties. That's Javelin's, Dire-horn's, and Saliut's full-time job, and I don't fucking want it.

Anyway, A to B would be six months. Flat fee of 100,000V to fly it. For easy numbers: this ship burns roughly 1,000V a day in operating costs. So, if we don't find anything, we're out roughly 80,000V. If the ship is dead in space, we don't have salvage rights. So, we're still out 80,000V. If it's reparable, it's 10,000,000V plus repair costs.

Flutter is good, but our repair ability is limited. That ship was a semi, and we are a pickup truck. You get the idea.

If we could get salvage rights, it would be worth it.

Their insurance had low rescue and rescue in place rates. Which implies the ships should have multiple redundant, air, food, and water sources at a minimum. Heat isn't a big deal like they make it out to be in the shows because vacuum is the best insulator anyway. So, we would lose money if we gave them survival supplies.

We broke down the numbers and decided it was unlikely

profitable. The risk was way too high, and it wasn't the way we were going, so it was not worth the detour.

The New Horizons Developmental insurance contracted us to investigate a colony as an affiliated third party. The colony's fast packet drone had been intercepted and tampered with. We were given a copy of their internal verification software. Basically, messages and records would now have to be verified by us.

It was the space version of drive over and trouble shoot some old ladies' computer and install new antivirus software because doing this over the feed wasn't working.

It was close, but the money wasn't good enough, so they sweetened the deal by diverting the ecology team that was already enroute. Our mission was to deliver the ecology team, check out some satellites and send a new fast packet drone.

I was hoping to get to meet the ecology team. New faces. Someone who I couldn't recognize by their farts at this point.

But alas, disappointment.

They were pod people stacked in with the rest of the cargo. We just strapped into gravity couches and hoped no one would shoot at us while the drone jocks transferred the cargo.

There's a special deck just forward of the bridge that's set up as a lifeboat. That's where our gravity couches live. I don't know why they call them couches. They're more like loungers or a nice office chair mounted onto a deck to overhead sturdy gimble, so if the ship accelerates hard, we won't pop a blood vessel. The chair portion looks like an egg and will snap closed if Piper hits the maneuvering alarm.

The senior crew went to the bridge, and we annoyed each other on the lifeboat.

Xi, our cyber security tech, does this thing where she pulls out the sweetest kitten voice and then asks you to rearrange a core personality trait.

I like it.

"Saliut, I love that smell. What is it?" Xi asked in her kitten voice.

"It's my rose hip and hibiscus lotion." Saliut then prattled on about her scent collection for a moment.

"It's lovely but a bit much for confined quarters by about seventy-five percent. Oh, I have a great idea. Do you think you could help me dial that in with my moisturizer?"

I'm pretty sure that would have worked. But…

"So, it doesn't smell like a mall kiosk in here!" Ryan yelled. He's our biologist and environmental tech.

"All right, Turtle Tank!" Saliut shot back.

"Hey! You want to maintain the algae farm? You know what? I think I'll tell Javelin that I need help, and you volunteered."

DEAD SILENCE!

That was a cardinal sin. Javelin had a "do it right then and do it until you can't do wrong" approach. Involving her would force Saliut into a dual specialty. However, an accountant–excuse me, *forensic* accountant–who could maintain an environmental system would be invaluable.

Shannon broke the standoff. "Hey, if you need help, we can all put in some time. Take turns and check off some boxes for cross training."

Dramatic pause.

"If you smell like a turtle tank, she smells like stripper glitter," Shannon said.

We lost it.

We decided on Turtle Tank and Stripper Glitter as their names. Saliut was in an angry huff. By the time the dust settled, and the cross-decking was over, Shannon was now Gym Sock.

Anyway, a day or two later, I walked into the far side of the galley. The humidity was higher, and the smell was different. Like something from the botanical gardens. I've only been there once on a institute field trip

I felt like a cartoon character searching for the new smell.

The fridge door was open, a brownish green mass was crawling on the shelving inside, like a slime mold had gained sentience.

"Um, what the fuck is that?" I asked anyone within earshot.

"Check your messages," Uvwewe replied from the couch in the lounge area while scrolling through videos. "New crew. Environmental engineer."

His chill helped me find my chill.

"Uh, hey there?" I asked, near the fridge now. "Need something?"

"Ee-cha, needa foodie," the moss thing said. "Ea-cha harda wooka. Ee-cha eat dim nap nap."

"All right. What do you want?"

I went back-and-forth with him for a while before I figured out fermented eggs with vinegar and salt. The food processors could make a synthetic, but he was on his own if he wanted to turn some of the frozen stuff into his mom's home cooking.

Ship's manifest has him listed as Lamal, and he's a trip. He's a chinook, which looks like a moss-covered rock. Think a soft shell turtle but with more useful limbs. The old ones have seaweed stuck to their shell. His oily fur smells like grass, lilac, and burnt wood. Altogether, it's rather pleasant.

"EEEEGAAAHH WHAT THE FUCK?!" Ryan launched himself, from the table.

"Unny oo-man. Why oo on loor?" Lamal had replaced Ryan's seat.

There's a lot of Lamal working his mouth as he tries to make the sounds. His profile says he's certified in six languages and familiar with four others. I'm not even that good with Common, so I'm not going to say shit about him taking a moment to process.

Turns out, Lamal likes being sat on, and it makes him feel safe. After a bit of reading, I found that that is normal for a chinook. Makes them feel like a part of the group. We took to sitting on him.

The shit that becomes normal…

TIME TO BE AWESOME

520.320.2332 FTS *The Happy Marauder,*

"ACTION STATIONS! ACTION STATIONS! CLEAR FOR MOVEMENT! ACTION STATIONS! ACTION STATIONS! CLEAR FOR MOVEMENT!" blared into my ears and across my closed eyes.

My heads-up display –HUD– framed my vision in red, populated with the ship-wide emergency alarm. I silenced the alarms in my head to hear the same broadcast from the emergency system. My rally point was set to my garage.

Training took over as I dove into my HEPS and got moving.

I accessed my feed at a full sprint and found the alert was in response to a distress signal from our target colony. I played the signal and slipped into my AV by feel and muscle memory.

A terrified woman's face filled my vision. She spoke clearly, despite looking on the edge of panic. "This is Colony Stator Outpost Station 232. I am reporting a class one mega-fauna threat." She took a quick deep breath. "Aggression level is fucking suicidal. Several outposts and monitoring stations are unresponsive. They're tearing open the buildings and eating people. I don't know what else to say. We hardly have any weapons, just a small police force and a few big…"

The video cut off abruptly. Contract information scrolled across my feed. The colony had insurance money available for emergencies. The need to do something, anything, pounded in my chest. I skipped the details and voted for immediate deployment. My inner hero ripped open his shirt and went TA-DA!

I mean, at this point, I had been bouncing off the bulkheads in and out of my AV for six months. Part of me would fight an entire colony of fuzzy kittens just to avoid another slide presentation of slide presentation.

I wish I was joking, but we're taking a class called Train the Trainer. I think it's a subversive way to force people into specialties— just feed them drier and drier shit until waste management seems like sweet relief.

Sorry.

The colony satellite network was set to emergency aid, granting us general access. The current feed time stamped the information at over twelve hours old. Giant land animals, a cross between an elephant and a sloth, were tearing through the colony's structures.

Giant Pangolin? No, those were made up…

Two powerful claws on the forelimbs tore through the adobe-style dwellings with monstrous efficiency. When they found something sturdy—like a stove or a refrigerator—they brought it up to their multi-tentacle maw, which delicately probed it for anything worth consuming and tossed the rest away. Chitinous plates covered the rest of the creature like heavy armor. Wiry fur filled the gaps between the plates.

I pulled up the animal's ecology report. Its normal diet was several species of subterranean fauna, the local equivalent of earthworms, grubs, and beetles. All of which were supersized and weaponized. Reports of predation showed that the animals were fast for their size. They preferred a rolling, slashing, bunny kick kind of maneuver to escape predators, which were pack-hunting slug things. This was the first time they had attacked humans.

I scanned the information, looking for anything useful. An irritating plant or bug that might be an effective chemical deterrent. I was looking for pepper spray because I didn't like the idea of slaughtering animals.

"Giant fucking moles!" Shantu said, interrupting my thoughts. "Not what I really thought we were going to be doing on this mission."

"You can do them. I plan on finding some hot colonist to bang," I replied. "Seriously though, I'm looking for something like pepper spray." I added Turtle Tank to the feed. "Ryan, do you have any suggestions? I don't like the idea of killing a sub sapient."

"Busy," he said and disconnected.

Shantu gave a brief dark chuckle and then spoke in a more serious tone. "I don't really think that's going to work…"

He shot me a video clip. It showed one of the animals mutilating itself on some industrial facility's heavy hangar doors. The enraged animal broke its thick claws. Viscous orange blood poured from its claws, and it searched the building for a moment before ripping into the roof near some small vent. It extracted a human, whose leg was impaled with broken shards of a claw, and shoved the poor soul into its maw. It then went from enraged to frenzied. The mangled roof frame stripped the flesh off the creature's arms, while it tried to get any other humans below.

I closed the video. "Yeah. Fuck."

Before we went down a rabbit hole on how we were drastically unqualified for this, a cargo list populated.

"Uh, fuck. We're taking a drop shot."

The drop shot is a tin can with just enough breaking thrusters to survive planetary insertion.

"I got this. I got this," I said to myself, trying to clear my brain of everything that wasn't my problem.

But my brain wouldn't shut up about the forces at play during orbital insertion. Developing an embolism or stroke or pressure necrosis. I was a squishy thing who had a very narrow survival range, and all this was testing those limits.

Shantu and I did what we do. Stacked preloaded crates of food, ammunition, medical supplies and everything else based on some action list someone had prepared. We had done this so many times and this time it happened quickly that I stopped dead in my tracks. Waiting for Sgt. Tok to give me some corrections for this drill.

"Stow those AVs," Sgt. Tok said. "We're doing a coffin drop unless you've decided to stay on the ship."

That was it…

I had a choice. Fight or stay?

A glaring voting board appeared, obscuring my vision. Most were voting to save the little colonists.

Shantu didn't hesitate. "Time to be awesome! I'm not going down there without you."

"Time to be awesome," I muttered without any confidence. "What was a Marauder to do?"

I parked my AV on the second level of the pod with the rest of the heavy equipment. Drones welded frangible bracing into place. A few other drones darted in and out updating the inventory.

I hopped out and got a look at the shot pod. It was an ugly armored hexagon, four stories tall like a shipping container turned on its end. The mostly hollow interior was filled to the brim with equipment. We were even bringing a fabricator. A multimedia printer with a limited ability to assemble and refine.

The lowest level had the reactor, propulsion and all the shit to move through space. Above that we all cargo ever of things we hope we don't need but would suck to be caught without. Above that, we crammed the deck with a serviceable armory. The third level was filled with life support equipment to keep us alive in the coffins at the top of the pod. The walls folded down, giving the pod a limited ability to right itself if the landing went poorly. Drones attached the disposable fuel pods.

I wanted to protest that we hadn't trained for this. I fucking hated the idea of my lungs being filled with fluid that was used to keep my chest from collapsing and my ribs from being crushed and all the other terrible things these coffins do to keep me alive for this kind of trip.

STOP THINKING ABOUT IT!

Just a nice little sleep and then on the ground. That's it.

The Vanguard pathfinders were the ones who developed the coffin drop. They were a different sort of people. Their documentary interviews made their whole persona surreal. "Wake up in hell, ready to fight the devil" was not a bad motto. The video played in my head as I felt connected to people I had never met.

"We don't think about it. There's not time," a calm dark-skinned man with a pleasant smile explained. "Get in the coffin, and you'll wake up in hell. Then you have to make up a story that ends with you coming home. If you can't come home, do something so that someone else can."

"What about the thirty percent that never make it to the ground?" the interviewer asked.

"They're statistics. That's it. They didn't even wake up to have a story. The rest of us did." His face seemed to realize that that wasn't okay for anyone who wasn't a pathfinder. "I don't mean any disrespect to them. That's how we handle things. We find out where we can add to the equation, and then we get after it."

I climbed the ladder and found Shantu staring at his coffin with fear written across his face. I took my fear by the throat and shoved it into the ground. Anger at being afraid rose in me.

I didn't say anything. I just took off my HEPS and stowed it in the cubby. I pulled out my ear bugs and contacts, put them in the case, and stowed it too. In the coffin, I sunk into the little gel pillows that filled the interior.

"Ooh. This is nice," I told Shantu, reaching for levity that I didn't feel. "It feels like a hundred tongues licking me. Think I have time to rub one out before the drugs knock me out?"

Smiling, he slunk into his coffin as I activated mine.

24

DEATH WOULD HAVE BEEN NICE

520.321.0018 Rapid Planetary Insertion Pod, █████████

I SURFACED TO consciousness with hard acceleration and a sucker punch to the back. The roaring noise vibrated my bones together, and an underwater afterburner threatened to rattle me into component atoms.

The acceleration didn't stop. I tried to clench my jaw as my chest got forced through my spine, but I couldn't because of the hard foam filling my mouth. I retched when a tube moved in my throat like a live snake trying to get comfortable. I gagged and spasmed again and again against the hard tube.

Agony stitched up both sides of me. My ribs failed as the weight of my own mass piled on my chest. I tried to scream as each one of my ribs threatened to snap like twigs. A whirring vibrated through my mouth, down my throat, and into my chest, which moved the pain from my ribs to my lungs. My precious air sacs inflated like angry tires, and my diaphragm spasmed.

Pale green lights flashed through the coffin, and little fingers massaged my body with a constant pulsing rhythm.

I tried to squeeze my fists and accomplished nothing more than squishing the slimy worms around my fingers. The coffin waited for my strength to fail and pushed my hand back into position.

My heart and diaphragm were still dialed up to eleven. My left elbow and my left ankle burned.

RELAX!

Systems check.

I started at my eyebrows. They wiggled against the padding. My ears wiggled. My eyelashes weren't touching anything. I couldn't move anything, but I flexed and wiggled. Everything seemed to respond.

The roaring was oppressive. Like I was strapped directly to the drive bell. My joints ached. My muscles spasmed, a tingly sensation bothered my elbow, and my muscles turned into jelly. Which must've been a muscle relaxer.

Okay. The pods *were* survivable. The only thing that would kill me was if I stroked out because I was freaking out. So, stop freaking out. Which is a stupid fucking thing to say. Why do people yell "calm down"? They should be like "Look at your fingers and toes. You're here. You're safe."

I had found a new definition of uncomfortable, but I was safe.

Is that what arthritis feels like? Because, fuck, my joints hurt.

Yet, I embraced the void.

The machines released the pressure from my chest before forcing it back up. Every bone hurt, threatening to shatter. Have you ever sparred with someone and felt the sharp barb of an arm bar? The one that makes you tap out instantly lest they break it? I felt like that *everywhere*.

I sought solace in the memories of the classes I had taken on this equipment. I wasn't even breathing air. It was some supersaturated fluid that allowed gas to transfer into my lungs at g's, pressures and vibrations aren't survivable any other way.

A good portion of my blood wasn't even in my body. It was running through a machine that diluted it with preservatives, so my blood cells didn't get rattled apart and clot. I was expecting a ten percent overhydration when I got out.

At least I could pee without consequence.

There's a special numb you must find to let a machine breathe for you. Human instinct, though I can only talk for myself, views any intrusion into our breathing as a fight on sight. Overriding that instinct is not easy.

That panicked part of my brain would kill me via stroke, embolism, aneurysm, or something else if I let it. And I did not want to die like that. I put the animal part of me in the cage, shut the lid, and sat on it.

Next problem.

Don't think about my breathing.

I will bet my left nut that you're aware of your breathing. Having a rubber sock filling your mouth and a hose in your chest cavity makes you very aware of your breathing.

I retreated into a visualization of an AV cockpit. That's what a person really is: a brain piloting a meat vehicle. I tried to monitor my body in the cockpit of my mind. My imaginary status board lit up with alarms. Every joint hurt like stubbing my toe. That's not going to kill me. The burning sensations alarms lit up, and I wrote what I thought the injection was with a marker.

Sometimes, the drugs would be obvious when my heart rate skyrocketed, and tension filled my body. I wanted to fight everything. I think I was on epinephrine or adrenaline or whatever.

I didn't look at the breathing controls. Just don't look at them. There was so much else going wrong.

The drive cut off, and the momentary free fall left me feeling tingly.

Sweet relief.

The silence of the drive felt like a hit from a good drug. The absence of pain was almost euphoric. Maybe it was. I didn't know where the subsystem was that governed that, much less wanted to mess with it.

But the gyroscope in my brain cockpit was broken. I tapped on it and nothing. I had no orientation data.

I just hung there.

The coffin deflated the fingers, so I relaxed in a void, floating in oblivion. I waited and drifted, half sleep and half awake. Consciousness became nebulous. I became a concept explained in a paragraph at a galactic library.

I don't know how long I drifted there with only the occasional pulse of a green light breaking me from the darkness. Felt like forever.

Without warning, the pod began what I guessed was its breaking thrust. It was just as noisy and violent as what had brought me this far. My alarm board lit up just like before, and I changed all the bulbs from red to white. This was normal now.

The truck lifted from my chest, and the pressure lowered in my lungs. The coffin ran fluids over me, and the fingers agitated rhythmically. The feeling of getting flushed down a toilet mixed with laundry being run through a machine.

Perhaps an ultrasonic cleaner?

The fluid in my lungs was removed next, and it was like someone was flossing my major organs.

Too much time passed.

I had an oh shit moment when I had to manually operate my lungs until they ran on their own again.

An ice-cold slap to the brain stem with a wet dick hit me. I was ready to fuck the entire universe with my rock-hard cock on a mountain of conquered armies. All of creation was my bitch, and it was about to find out.

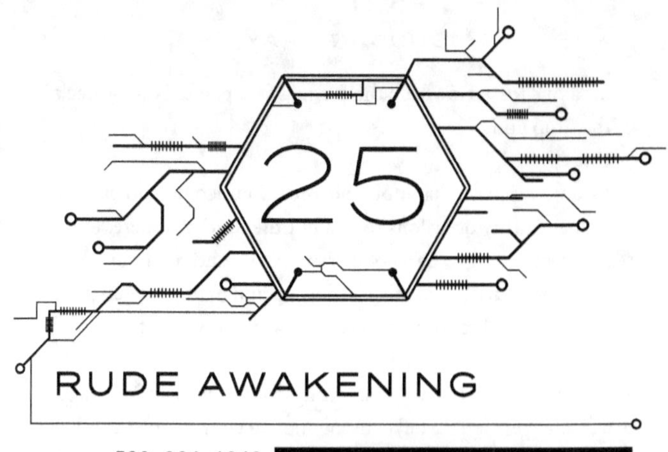

RUDE AWAKENING

520.324.1848

I FELT AROUND in the dark.

Bingo!

I jerked the coffin's handle. Euphoria was ripped from me as the machines wet-vac'd my lungs clear, and dry, sterile air refilled them. I hiccupped, coughed, and burped. The tubes tickling my major organs deflated and continued to suction as they retracted from every orifice. I retched. When I couldn't be anymore violated, the urethral and anal catheters ripped themselves out.

Naked, I was covered in goo on a plastic plate…

You know that last flake of cereal that sticks and dries to the bowl after you drink the milk? That was me.

Zero out of five stars. Do not recommend coffin travel.

Fuck that thing.

The coffin popped open, and the interior lights blinded me. I didn't even get a second to feel sorry for myself as a heavy thud shuddered through the pod and into my naked greasy body. The second one tossed me from the coffin. I face-planted on the deck of the drop pod.

I was pissed.

I wanted to have that moment where I curled up and cried. I don't have many occasions to cry, but the urge was there. I was ready. It was going to be a good cry to center and reset me.

But the metal deck of the pod flew up and hit my face instead.

Disoriented, I felt for my feed hardware. It was in the cubby where it was supposed to be.

Whoever is playing with the settings for my life decided to add in a challenge: air didn't like me anymore. I coughed up the salty, almost garlicky residue from the coffin. It had the consistency of oatmeal…from my lungs… I retched with the occasional hiccup into a burp.

I don't know how I didn't lose one of those tiny, delicate devices. I managed to get them in place while my lungs pissed off my stomach. Now my eyes burned because I didn't wash my hands for the contact lenses.

I glanced at the environmental screen mounted overhead. All green. I wondered if the zero humidity was helping or hurting me. I tried to access the pod's external cameras, but only a fuzzy, integrated image appeared where the cameras overlapped.

I asked my feed for the common name for these things.

"Colloquial nomenclatures denote diller," it answered as I stuffed my feet into my HEPS.

Collision alarms flashed, and the silhouettes of the dillers appeared as shadows through the bulkheads. A few dozen were stampeding toward the pod. The first one would impact in moments.

Where the fuck was everyone? Fuck!

I don't know how long it took, but finding the panel for the coffin control felt like forever. The big emergency revival icon took up a quarter of the panel. I hit it and the confirmation slider.

The first beast slammed into the pod. The whole pod shook. Part of me wondered if it killed itself, and another hoped it did.

I transitioned the hatches down the decks and to the lowest garage area with my AV. I slid down the ladder. My legs buckled, and I landed on my ass. I climbed into my AV and took it from standby to active.

"Open the door and close it once I'm clear."

My feed responded by highlighting a manual control lever that folded down the ramps.

FUCK!

I jumped out of my AV, aware of what was going to happen once that ramp broke its seal. My mind raced with all the ugly ways I was going to die here. I needed to somehow fight the dillers off or distract them until everyone else was awake.

Then a horrible idea hit. Maybe they would follow a blood trail like a predator. I ripped a first aid kit from the wall and found a shit ton of fancy devices that were not syringes. The trauma kit—that I was not supposed to touch unless I was the last one alive, and I was trying to resurrect someone—had vacuum rated draw kits that were compatible with my HEPS.

Someone was going to yell at me for this.

I pulled the sample. And because I didn't know what I was doing, I mangled the kit, trying to extract a raw sample. I then taped the sample to my fork as fast as I could, ignoring the silhouettes of red animals approaching.

The auto-stabilization mechanism flashed a warning in my feed before it collapsed the drive bell. The pod dropped three meters, bouncing me around like a bug in a can.

My HEPS kept me from smashing my skull into my AV, the deck, and at least two other things in the process. The fact I can remember the hollow THONK that my helmet made as it hit metal probably means my head would have cracked like a light bulb.

I shook off the double vision and cracked the ramp enough for my AV to climb through. Zoning in on how fast it was moving. I guessed how long it would take me to run from the switch, hop in my AV, and clear the ramp before it resealed.

The memory of playing this game calmed me. We had done this at Telex's. Hit the button and try to get out the garage door before it closes.

I was confident the few seconds would be plenty.

My exit from the pod was ugly. I think I clipped the edge of the ramp and fell into a rolling mess. I hope I didn't break anything.

Maybe I didn't have a feel for gravity here. Maybe the drugs and being stuck in a box for days was fucking everything up. Maybe one of the knocks to the head broke something loose.

I canceled my internal inventory when one of the dillers took my AV's leg in its mouth and dragged soil across my canopy.

That was the first time I had seen soil in person. It looked like the brown dehydrated mixes used for drinks. What did it taste like?

I fired my strut with enough power to do a flip. The industrial strut shredded its maw, tearing half its face off. The carnage shook me straight to the core.

"Stay in the fight!" Sgt. Tok yelled from a distant memory. "First, first aid is covering fire." His voice rose louder and meaner than his normal no-excuses-get-it-done tone. "When the plan goes to shit, get mean. Mean enough to keep everyone else alive."

Once I got upright, another diller reached for the still closing ramp. I set my weight, fired my stilts at full power, and speared the diller low behind the shoulder. Metal met flesh in a wet smack. Bones broke, and blood sprayed.

The size of these animals finally sunk in. Half again as tall and three times as long. They were wider than my AV was tall. Just massive beasts.

The diller's shell was fleshier and less armor than I had

expected. What were those gray things with the tusks and the long nose? No. The one with the pointy nose?

Fuck my head hurt.

I rolled off and skidded to a stop, spinning to survey my surroundings. The dillers were wandering off toward the town's scattered buildings. Take a big cow and get it shit-faced. That was how they moved. I didn't know anything about how they *should* move, so that might be a high speed for them.

"I need a head count and target priority," I told my feed.

It popped up useless fucking colony dates to remember, and I dismissed it.

"THINK! FUCKING THINK!"

I had my feed call the colony security directory until someone answered. I took to playing blocker as the inebriated herd passed the pod. I crushed one diller's skull with the shoulder of my AV, and the rest parted to pass by.

"You have reached the voicemail of..."

"Next!" I shouted at my feed.

The colony was on planes with spread-out buildings and homesteads. The way the roads were marked in virtual looked like they were planning to build a big city, but the clinic was two shipping containers glued together, and the shopping plaza was the field where they did a monthly swap meet. But the landing pad markers were spaced out, ready to grow into a functional spaceport.

The big processing facility a hundred kilometers away looked like a piece of a spaceship that had fallen from orbit and started growing there like a mechanical infection. To be fair, it was probably dropped from orbit. Just more delicately than I had said.

The rest of the buildings and homes looked like they were printed out of the local dirt with solar roofs.

Anyway, when the numbers thinned to the point where I figured they couldn't knock over the pod, I abandoned guard duty to sprint to the chemical facility from the video.

"You have reached the voicemail of…"

"Next!"

"You have reached the voicemail of…"

"Next!"

"H-hello," a small voice said. A child's voice. Maybe under ten?

I wasn't ready for a child to answer. I took a deep breath and calmed myself. "Hi, I'm James. I'm here to help. Is there an adult?"

"N-no." The little girl cried. "The dillers got them. They were nice before. Why did they get mean?"

Something slammed, and metal rent.

Fuck.

"Sweetheart, I'm new here," I said. "Can you tell me what your building looks like?"

When she didn't answer, something from a crisis class surfaced.

"HEY! I need you to listen to the sound of my voice. Tell me your name."

"Astrid," she blubbered out.

I tried to have my feed tell me the origin of the link and got an access not granted message. A myriad of network errors distorted the link.

"Good, Astrid," I said. "Tell me where you are."

"The hangar," she said so distorted that I could barely make it out.

I yelled for my feed to find me the hangar. It replied that the local map was unavailable.

It took a moment to get oriented; I was just off the clearing that passed for a landing pad. Astrid's hangar must be the only building with giant doors. It was the nearest structure, save a few outbuildings. I maxed every limiter I had and hardly touched the hard packed soil to close the distance.

I realized too late that I didn't plan this out at all. I spun so the back of my AV would hit the dillers attacking the hanger. Hitting backwards would keep my neck from snapping like a twig. Letting go of my controls, I crossed my arms to my chest, bracing for the impact.

There was a wonderful free fall moment before I slammed into the diller with sickening velocity. With that much momentum, their bodies behaved more like water balloons splattering across my AV and the building.

I was out cold for a second.

When I came to, my vision cleared but not all the way. It wasn't double vision either. Just not right. I laughed when I saw damage warnings for my meat-ware in my brain cockpit. I put the mental tool away and focused on running my AV.

The connection to the little girl had failed. But my feed had continued down the list until…

"Constable Chan, is this *The Happy Marauder*?" a hard female voice answered.

I circled the hangar and killed the rest of the dillers. "Yes. James, AV pilot." My voice sounded too calm and confident. "I need target priorities until everyone else wakes up."

My words were coming out professional, but the voice wasn't my own. The training in me moved without the need for my rattled brain. The rest of my mind wondered if this was real.

"What did you bring down with you?" She sounded like she had been crying.

I sent her the inventory list.

"Shit. Uh, I have five people trapped, uh, here." She sent me a waypoint, and I got going.

I finished the call with the constable and tried the little girl's number again. The call went straight to voicemail. I hesitated, but the memory of Sgt. Tok yelling at me during training pushed me forward.

I sprinted toward the waypoint.

Once I was away from the landing pad, the hard soil turned into grassland or a meadow. That's the best I got. Less than a meter tall grass that's sort of a sandy pink. I'm not sure if this sky and stars were any different from Vanguard through my helmet and canopy.

The colony was in shambles. Virtually every building had been damaged. The standing structures had dillers actively tearing into them. The waypoint was some kind of vehicle depot next to a destroyed jail or courthouse kind of building.

I slowed my pace to a reasonable disaster.

Four dillers were trying to dismantle the only vehicle depot building, but the heavy frame and integrated crane held. The siding was shredded, and the doors were mangled.

I drop-kicked the first diller and was rewarded with it flying into the next building. It slammed into a pathetic heap. I clamped the second one's ankles and tried to pull it away. It spun, raking my AV's canopy with its claws while kicking like a mule to free its legs. It turned into a whirling dervish of claws and anger.

Fuck this!

I launched myself into the air and landed on a third one, crushing it into the building's frame. The second diller blindsided me before I could recover from the leap. It chewed on my AV's upper arm. It found purchase and clawed and kicked in a way that would gore anything organic. But the hard composite of my cockpit resisted the blow with an oily smear.

I rolled and tried to free my AV, but it wasn't enough. Its grip pulled me off balance. Another one piled into me with a suicidal charge. We tumbled into a mess, and they found their feet first. They drug me around, jerking like hyenas trying to get a mouthful of meat.

Hydraulic alarms filled my cockpit. I found my opening when one let go to reposition. I managed to shove a clamp down its maw, and orange blood poured out. It hacked and heaved, scrambling backward.

No longer pinned, I righted myself, grabbed the first limb I found, and rolled my AV as violently as I could. Its limb twisted free with a sickening pop and tearing sound. Flashes of dismembered animals filled my vision. Blood and tissue covered my AV.

This was wrong. This was all wrong.

My stomach twisted at the carnage. Maybe, it was just twisting. I don't know.

A proximity incoming call link saved me from my mental spiral.

"Is it safe?" a man asked over the call.

I looked around. "Yeah."

A few minutes later, four people climbed out of the building through a tear in the side. They weren't wearing more than unarmored constable uniforms.

"Nope. Back in the hole. I can't take you anywhere."

A fifth emerged with a bundle of helmets and an armful of reflective safety harnesses. Through my cameras, I saw every diller in the area perk up the way a dog does when it catches a scent on the wind.

I turned to face the new incoming and spoke through my external speakers this time. "Nope. You're too squishy for this."

I extended my stilts, jogged, and promptly put my canopy in the dirt.

Fuck!

This planet was unstable.

No. *I* was unstable. The bright clear horizon wanted to tilt both ways at once, and it was too fucking bright.

Two more tries later, I moved up to speed in loping circles on the outside of the small colony. I slammed into the dillers with a roll. The report of a chemical projectile alerted my feed. The colonists were fighting back.

I got a good look at the few structures. Several dead dillers had carrion animals picking at their carcasses. I assumed they had been dead for days. But I knew way too little about life on this planet for any certainty.

There was a field of rubble that I assumed was residential houses. The solar roofing, occasional vehicle, and climate control unit were all that was visible.

"James, come in," the captain said while my feed reconfigured to a combat HUD.

"Go," I responded automatically, focused on keeping my AV's stride as smooth as possible.

"Sitrep."

"Uh, fuck, um…" I paused, trying to get my brain to remember combat communication protocol. "Status yellow. Megafauna group, uh…" I swiveled my torso and saw dozens in a mass behind me. "Maybe fifty behind me. Unresponsive to my blood. Fixated on the locals. Heavy damage to local infrastructure, um. End."

"Copy. We have you covered inbound."

My mini map populated with the other Marauders, the tagged drone coverage, and a bunch of shit I couldn't pay attention to. The pod erupted with weapons, and my HEPS polarized. Dillers dropped off the mini map, and I slowed my pace to a leisurely stroll and face-planted again.

The captain's line opened. "James, you just did a coffin drop awake. I need to know your status. No bullshit."

His use of *no bullshit* kept me from yelling that I knew because I was there.

I wasn't ready to rock the boat yet. "Um, not good. Uh, yellow and slipping to red." I wanted to puke, but yeah… Brain fog was getting worse. "I'm tired, rattled, pissed, and scared. I don't know what the fuck you want from me right now. I think I have a concussion."

"Copy."

The connection closed. I was given a waypoint back to the

pod. Weapons fired all around, cutting down the hoard with ease. Distantly, Sgt. Tok told me he had it from there.

I wandered back to the pod.

Someone had set up one of the medical beds, where I promptly passed out.

::EDIT:: I went back and watched the footage. I did all those things with the grace of a drunken ice-skater.

WHAT THEY CALL ME

520.325.0500

MY FEED CHIMED to wake me. It was one of those default alarm clocks that I had set.

Waking up was a mistake. My head was killing me, and all my muscles burned. I didn't know if I was hungry or wanted to barf. To top it off, mangling animals from the safety of my AV left me feeling fucked up.

I checked my feeds and found no pressing tasks. I took the time to stretch and take care of other essentials before checking in.

"Dude. You okay?" Shantu asked on an open channel. "Like, what the fuck are you made of?"

I opened the map. Everyone and Shantu were running patrol, with the constable, looking for survivors. Javelin was in one of their big chemical plant's towers. Dire-horn and a few others were trying to cut out the door for the hangar. Gabe was on the roof of the hangar while Scout and Turtle Tank were doing their best to act as medics inside the hangar.

"No shit, Shantu," Sgt. Tok said. "I had partial failure once and had to have high energy engram incoherence. I was not combat effective for several months. Most have ongoing traumatic stresses."

"Motherfucker bounced out of the coffin like Dracula," Gym Sock added. The drone operator was officially making me uncomfortable with all the attention.

"Dracula?" Alexis said. "That would make a good call sign."

"Can everyone shut the fuck up, please?" I knew it wasn't going to happen.

Sgt. Tok was lounging on crates near me, examining the map and placing icons. Normally, I couldn't see anyone else's feed but tac-link was active and it made everything all tactical. Mostly it made things feel like a videogame with the HUD.

I hooked into the pod's life support and ran a hygiene cycle. The warm fluids and pulsing air blasts made me shiver as they got into crevices that were reserved for formal bathing. I flipped the lever to let the helmet spin in its seal, careful not to disengage the seal. The padding at the back of the helmet inflated, and I used it to scrub my face.

"Perhaps we should call him box. As in stupid ass," Luanne said. I liked her because she's our no bullshit signals analyst. She gets a pass on being an asshole because it was usually constructive. "Dipshit didn't use his turrets. Instead, he wrestled with giant fucking armadillos."

I had forgotten that they had equipped my AV with point defense turrets. I think the safety plugs were still in place.

"We'll let you take the next coffin drop awake," Sgt. Tok said while the pad of my helmet mashed into my face. "Let's see if you'll think clearly."

I did my scrubby, scrubby dance, seeking the relief that I would get from a normal shower. Warm soapy water was nice, but it wasn't the same. I drained my HEPS and set the system to dehumidify. Warm dry air whirled around me, and my ears popped. The air steadily cooled until the cycle finished.

"I mean, my boy is stone cold," Shantu said. "How about Tombstone?"

"You can be Tombstone since you always have shit to say, and we know you didn't come up with it," I shot back.

"I have now reviewed the records," Dire-horn boomed into the channel. "I must admit, you have proven to be a monolith of professionalism."

Shantu guffawed into a choking fit of laughter. He drowned the channel for way longer than appropriate. "He called you fucking *professional*."

"I christen thee, Monolith and Tombstone, as my AV pilots," the captain said evenly. His location still had him on the ship, cheapening the moment a little. "Marauders, there we have it."

And that's how I ended up with the call sign Monolith.

TURNS OUT, I did have a concussion. The medical bot knocked me out for a day and gave me whatever the treatment is for a concussion. The Marauders waited for the med bot to clear me before we did the after-action report.

We held the report in the drop pod's armory. The room had barely enough space and was sealed so we could take our helmets off. I'll skip what you already got and move on.

Sgt. Tok started the failures section. "First and foremost, the biggest fuckup is mine, Javelin's, and Flutter's."

"Because Flutter is going to apologize," someone commented. I missed who.

He ignored the comment. "Monolith has a resistance to the sedatives in the pod. It showed up in his blood work twice. He was put through unnecessary stress during both his onboarding conditioning treatments and the coffin drop. Like the Marauder he is, he didn't say shit while we pumped his blood with blades."

I think that was a complement and an apology.

"Oh, fuck," someone murmured around the cramped room.

"Next, the auto-revive system failed," he continued. "We're still inspecting the unit to see if we can determine the cause."

"Hold up. Did we use the wrong equation and get the right answer?" Shantu asked, his voice shaken.

"If Monolith had not hit the auto revive within three hours, we would have suffocated when the battery packs ran down because the units were not connected to the reactor," Dire-horn answered.

"We jumped the gun, fucked up, and almost died through negligence on behalf of myself and Javelin." Sgt. Tok sounded cold and disconnected. "The pod was in cold storage, which included disconnecting the power from those systems."

"Wait," Saliut said. "Why did they come on at all if they were disconnected from power?"

He pulled up camera feeds from every point of view from inside the pod and zoomed in on the coffin control panel. He kept zooming in toward the top right corner of the pod's display. The little icon for the internal battery showed it was at ninety-nine percent.

"We placed those batteries from the *Marauder*'s inventory as part of launch prep," he explained. "I was mission lead. Javelin was responsible for this equipment, and Flutter was the engineer. It's still your lives that get spent in the crossing."

I was under the bus for not using the turrets mounted on my AV because my brain was fried from the drugs and the stress. It wasn't an ass chewing, more of a good-natured ribbing. I was reminded to always have a buddy and to stow the hero shit.

He then moved on to how this mission was a scramble and how we got lucky. He sent out updated procedures, so we didn't have to rely on luck for the next one.

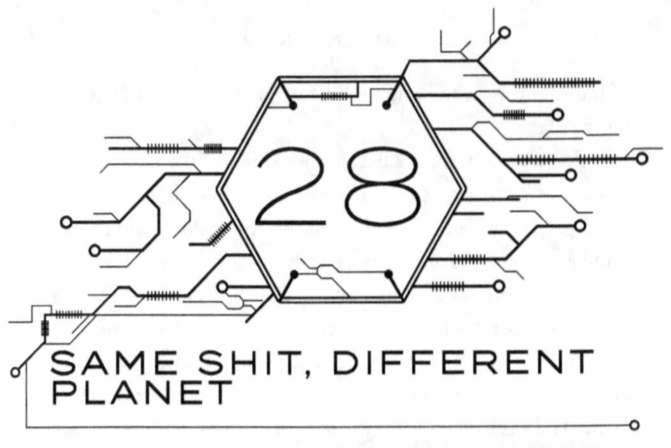

SAME SHIT, DIFFERENT PLANET

520.328.1901 ██████████████████████████

SO, HERE I am on a brand-new colony, building a fucking fence. Same fence I put up around countless construction sites.

Which is total bullshit! When do I get to make out with some hot colonist?

I'm on light duty due to, you know, a concussion and everything else. Sgt. Tok keeps reminding me to take my meds and scheduled naps.

It bothers me how long it's taking because I'm sleeping, and Shantu is basically working alone. Even with everyone pitching in, Shantu is spending more time chasing these highly educated assholes around than getting work done.

Here's the thing: Shantu and I are the only ones with real construction experience. This bag of degrees is suffering a massive case of paralysis-by-analysis as Sgt. Tok puts it. Therefore, Shantu is project leader by default.

Go fucking figure. Not that Shantu got the position. After months of being the dumb kid with all the questions in the back of the room we're the ones getting work done the moment we hit the planet.

It doesn't really matter because we were on the clock under the colony's insurance. Constable Chan wanted all the help she could get, and we were here. My construction people will understand a remote time and materials job.

While Shantu was tied up micromanaging a ship full of FNGs to construction I was the one actually working. I was dismantling the vehicle depot I totaled and feeding the raw materials into the fabricator so it could pump out shit for the fence. Then I would take the material for the fence to the working area where Shantu was watching people smash their thumbs with hammers.

At the end of the day, I am in my AV, building a fence.

Bitching aside, it is nice being back in my AV, doing what I know how to do. It feels good to be useful, being half of the heavy equipment team. I know that most of this is only possible because of the equipment we pilot. Sure, other team members may have power armor, but it still isn't rated for this kind of work.

Oh. Earlier, we did help Gabe and Gym Sock assemble a variety of equipment into locally powered sensor pods. It was mostly us acting as gofers because we didn't know what they were doing with electronics and networking at that level.

"What the fuck are you doing?" Sgt. Tok yelled at me over the open comms.

"I am staring at a flower, Sergeant!" I yelled back shamelessly.

I was in my AV in what could be best described as the downward dog. The flower was about twice the size of my hand, and the petals looked like fire, bright yellow fading into red on a thin green stem.

Absolutely gorgeous.

He maintained his sergeant voice. "Is it a nice flower?"

"Lovely, Sergeant."

"When you're done…" He gave me the next set of requests from the colonists.

Light duty did have its perks.

Shantu and I have been getting ribbed thoroughly for staring at the local flora. Everyone knew we were from a frozen city, and this was the first time we had seen wildflowers in person. It was all in good humor. By my standard, they were gentle with the jokes.

Once all that was done, someone—not me—declared it safe for the ecology team to come down. They took the leisurely approach to orbital mechanics because of how gentle you're supposed to treat spacecrafts, not to mention human bodies you expect to use more than once.

Anyway, not five seconds off the shuttle, the lead investigator of the ecology team, Douchebag Extraordinaire Karen McKevin, winded up into a full rant. "You savages couldn't have even attempted to save one. Do you monsters even…"

The line went dead.

The prompt for the communications went private and then secure.

"What the fuck is his problem?" Shantu asked over the common channel.

"He comes from a *civilized* world." Wraith almost spat the word. "Best schools with the worst education."

"Ah, one of those silver spoon idealist fucks," Shantu restated.

I knew he didn't know what the fuck he was talking about. He was just trying to coax more information out of Wraith.

Wraith grunted.

"Contact restricted with the following personnel," Dire-horn said. A list of the newly landed science people briefly cycled before folding its way into a menu. "They are considered high liability contacts. If contact is unavoidable, please consider the ramifications from a legal perspective."

A chorus of grumbles traveled across the local channel. All of us without orders found something else to do and somewhere else to be. Senior crew problem.

I closed out the channel and busied myself with the list of requests that the surviving colonists had made. The labor requests fell into two categories: billable and courtesy. I gave priority to efficiency, avoiding the greed versus bleeding heart argument. Back in my AV, doing mundane tasks, I feel safe.

The setting sun casts red across the clouds here. I've never seen clouds from below before.

THE FOLLOWING DAY, Captain Vatosh brought down the first of six modules for ecologist's lab. I wanted to see the shuttle and wondered— why the fuck hadn't I seen a space shuttle yet?

The lab had flat packed axles. Which sounds cool. Then you realize it's the big version of the toy you get from a vending machine. The kind that's just a plastic sheet, and you push the parts out to assemble a truck. That was what Shantu and I did for our morning. That and stack the ecology team's shit.

The joys of being an AV operator: stacking other people's shit from the beginning of time.

The captain then assembled everyone near the pod for a briefing now that the ecology team were out of their boxes and ready to be people again.

I don't know how bad it is to be in suspended animation, but I hear it's rough.

The briefing began in virtual, which I didn't care for because it made everything feel like a comic book. When someone spoke, their face expanded in floating bubbles above their location with an arrow pointing at their head. If they were out of my line of sight, a wire silhouette indicated their position. Everyone without cameras in their suits had an ID avatar that didn't move.

The briefing was like a bad cartoon.

I locked down the controls in my AV, unfastened my shock frame, and went boneless, lounging in my AV cockpit.

"Contract priority is now assisting the ecology team," the captain said. "Phase one is complete as far as site security and preliminary scouting. To the northeast of the mountain, all observation posts and drone stations seem to be functioning. We've reestablished contact with those field labs. To the southeast, the field lab is gone. Most of the observation posts are also destroyed. However, we've reestablished contact with a drone station."

A topographical map took over the meeting, a circle of red pins surrounded by green ones. It was animated to show the red pins attacking the colony and getting eliminated. A circle appeared over the origin of red pins, shading red to the center.

"The local fauna—colloquially known as diller—is our primary subject." The captain gave an acknowledging nod to Shantu and me, referring to us. "Armor. We're fabricating active restraints. The animals are normally docile, even to invasive sampling. However, given the circumstances, lethal force authorization will be granted or denied by Monolith and Tombstone. Beyond that, lethal force is authorized in the event of clear and present dangers. Armor, anything to add?"

Wow. No fucking pressure on me.

Shit.

"Now, if any of you trigger monkeys…"

The lead investigator was cut off.

Fucker stole my moment.

A very animated conversation ensued in pantomime between the captain and Douchebag Extraordinaire Karen McKevin. No one did a voice-over. That's much more disciplined than I expected. I'm kind of disappointed.

I perked when the outline of the lead investigator went from green, indicating team member, to gray, indicating bystander, to alternating red and gray outline of an unconfirmed enemy. The conversation must have gone poorly because the captain stepped away, and Dire-horn took over contact with the lead investigator.

The lead investigator took on an aura of yellow, and the hold fire order displayed in my feed. I popped up and locked my shock frame into place.

His silhouette went red, and bounty information flashed. He then went white, marking him as bounty awaiting collection, a second later.

I opened the bounty's information; five credits for a disturbing the peace charge.

Wraith had the lead investigator turned around with wrist restraints before anyone knew what had happened. Two of the local police were added as team members.

The captain picked up the meeting like nothing had happened. "Please welcome Deputy Parks and Deputy Wallace. They are going to be our local contacts. Please rely on their knowledge and expertise of the area."

I didn't know what conversations happened with Constable Chan, but that wasn't my problem, and the lead investigator was a dick anyway. Didn't seem right that he was arrested, but he was out of our way.

The message was clear: if the ecology team stepped out of line, the local government authority would come down on our side.

"Thank you all for everything you have done. Remarkable work!" a shoni-vonti said with a warm, friendly tone. The personnel identifiers indicated that he was the ecology team's new leader. Dagklakochakbak. There's some clicking and grinding noises in there that I don't know how to do.

Doctor, if you ever see this, I will happily take you to lunch, and you can teach me how to say your name appropriately.

"I do not share my, uh…" He mumbled something in his native language. "Predecessor. Yes, that's the right word. I don't share my predecessor's militancy toward martial occupations."

The captain interrupted the scientist with a polite throat clearing.

"Right. To work. We need scans and tissue samples from the healthy diller population to establish a diagnostic baseline, compared to the necropsies. Furthermore, I will advise against bringing the colonists because they are the primary loci."

The captain went on about mission parameters and assignments. Fairly standard stuff. The mini map updated as drones scouted ahead.

We got through the pre-mission briefing. Shantu and I had standing orders to deploy the Marauders, scoop up the cops and the ecology team, and then return to base.

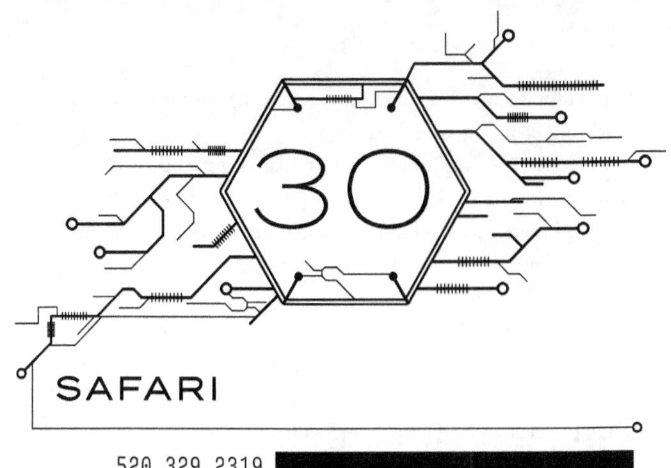

HERE I AM, in a new world, stuck in my HEPS. I want to go touch the dirt. I know how silly that sounds, but I have never touched soil before. Vanguard City is on a mountain-top. Everything there is frozen. If it's not frozen, it's covered in slime. Ambient temperature here is close to *thirty*. I want to walk around barefoot and climb a tree naked. But *no*, I'm stuck in my HEPS because of the unknown biological status of this planet.

Total bullshit.

Don't worry. I'm not going to be the guy who gets everyone sick. We are here, making money and doing some good. I have worked too hard to start going backward.

I wonder how much of my internal anger is built on years of bullshit. I worked in a system that never sought to improve me, just used what little bit I had, only to replace me with the next unfortunate soul.

Sorry. I have discovered I harbor a lot of resentment toward my previous occupations, and it may be inhibiting my ability to fully embrace my new situation because it's an invalid bench-mark… According to Scout anyway.

I was trying to appreciate the fact Shantu wasn't the only one watching my back. Sgt. Tok, Saliut, Alexis, and Gabe literally strapped themselves to mine. I had a pretty solid idea what they would do in a given scenario, none of which involved throwing anyone under the bus.

Shantu carried Dire-horn, Gym Sock, Uvwewe, and Luanne.

Eight of the ten ecologist team were between Shantu and me when we had cleared the fence. The hard-pack gave way to soil. Then the cleared land turned into a dense forest.

"I don't know the load capacity of the soil, so be careful with launches," I told Shantu casually on the open channel. "I already made a note to get a sensor package, so we can monitor the terrain."

"Careful with those GPR and IR systems." Wraith was refer-ring to the ground penetrating radar and infrared system. "They are beacons, even on shitty EM suites."

I have no idea where Wraith was. He wasn't broadcasting his location.

"Passive sonic systems might be your best bet for passive systems," Gym Sock added. "The impacts of your rigs are large enough they should give an analytical signature."

"I would recommend a sound dampening subsystem," Gabe said.

We used upgrades and modifications as tension eased into small talk. It was clear that everyone was on high alert, only paying partial attention to the conversation.

Dire-horn made the call to transition and put the ecologists on us because the humans were struggling to keep up. I'm guess-ing they're human, in a lighter version of our HEPS. The sho-ni-vonti was fine to keep walking.

The flora here fell within the Marburg-Santos spectrum. The Marburg-Santos spectrum went into detail about similar conditions that led to convergent evolution. But I didn't know one type of tree from another. These had clusters of eight heart-shaped leaves, green with a reddish-black bark for a trunk.

I didn't get to see much fauna anyway because I was twenty tons of walking metal that smelled like industrial cleanser. I'm sure the animals didn't want much to do with me.

An hour of tense walking ended with a diller digging under a tree, pulling a squid-looking worm thing from around a tree root and eating it. It didn't acknowledge Shantu or me taking up flanking positions. We were ready to pounce if the massive animal twitched wrong. The rest of the Marauders faced outward for unseen threats.

"Don't worry about me," the shoni-vonti team leader said. "I can leap clear if the need arises."

I believed him. Humans were no match for a shoni-vonti. Think of fighting a bear.

The diller ignored the ecologist as he touched it. It didn't even stop digging and slurping down the squid things when he jumped on its back. He pulled some spiny parasite from between the diller's armored plates and tossed it to his compatriot, who was behind him. The diller shook like a dog with a happy rumble.

"There's a big parrot thing with a long orange beak and an opossum thing that normally eat those. I don't think they'll be around with the mechs," Deputy Parks told us. "The only threat we've seen are the harpies. Pack-hunting bats that attack at noon. They're mostly in the plains. They can't swoop through this tree cover, so you guys can relax."

I didn't correct Parks when he called us mechs. True mechs copied the pilots movement from suits. We sat in seats and operated joysticks, and pedals. We were more push-button and less dynamic input. It wasn't the time or place for that conversation.

"I can't have my people developing bad habits now, can I?" Sgt. Tok responded.

"Why the shit didn't you tell us about man eating bats?!" Gym Sock barked.

"Well, y'all are scarier," Deputy Parks answered.

"They taste good," Deputy Wallace added, "and they eat these goat things, which tear up our crops. The goats are toxic."

"Are you saying you're hungry?" Saliut asked.

"No," he said defensively. "We're trying to fit two thousand humans into an ecological niche on a potentially hostile planet."

"Aren't you a cop?" Shantu asked with confusion in his tone. "Like no offense, but I thought your title means you, like, work under a sheriff."

He looked at me, and I pointed my pincers at Shantu.

Uvwewe threw Shantu under the bus. "Tombstone is pointing at you."

"Fuckstick," I said.

"Fucknuts," Shantu replied.

"That one," Uvwewe said to help the deputy out while letting us have our fun.

Deputy Wallace dropped all aggression out of his voice. "I'm a vested principal shareholder. I sold off everything to bring my family and a few friends here. I'm on the committee that hired them."

I have to assume Wallace was gesturing to the ecological team but i was looking at a vine with blue flowers.

So Pretty!

I missed who asked where he had come from, but long story short, he and most of the investors came from a planet that was at war with the local wildlife and corruption. He said the name, but I might have been looking at a tree.

Okay. I'm sure I was looking at a tree. I wanted to take my HEPS off, climb out of my AV, and touch it. I couldn't climb this one. It was too tall. I wanted to though.

Anyway, he and the other investors who organized all this were from the Commonwealth with plans to settle via the Zenith Planetary Model. I don't know shit about the Commonwealth besides that they were the ships that scattered after Vanguard took off with the bulk of the military. I need to look that up. The Zenith Planetary Model was based on Vanguard colonization practices. I complain about that planet, but they got some things right.

Right now, I have a tree to look at.

While we were playing Get-to-Know-the-Colonists, the diller kept working through the soft undergrowth for its meals. The ecologist handling the parasite unceremoniously disemboweled the creature with a wrist-mounted contraption.

Save the team leader, the ecology team was bipedal and the right size for humans. I could tell they were talking by their head bobs and gestures. A technician arguing about servos does the same bobbing as one talking about biochemistry, I suppose.

The shoni-vonti on the diller made himself comfortable; I assumed he was working in virtual. I did the opposite and turned up the gain on my sensor feed, getting familiar with the sounds of the marshy forest.

"Look alive," Sgt. Tok said. "They're going to take some samples."

Shantu and I turned to face the diller and looked like we were making fun of sumo wrestlers, ready to pounce. The animal only twitched as the team leader reached between its thick armor plates.

Images of the slaughter I had committed floated through my mind. This diller wasn't even defending itself from the increasingly invasive testing. It moved as the scientist sprayed something on the testing site, but it seemed more irritated from the spray, not the big ass needle.

"Look at how docile they are," I said. "That's a big fucking needle."

The indicator on my HUD turned the animal from green to gray, indicating that it was no longer a priority. The ecologist jumped down and began another round of bickering.

After a half hour or so, they opened a channel to us.

"We have found a significant variance in neurological active proteins," the team leader said. "Specifically in their hormone production and awareness centers—"

"The diller's abnormal behavior could be explained by a foreign prion," another ecologist picked up. "What we think is happening is a short segment of DNA equivalent is causing brain damage. It's speculation—not science—until the data is consistent. We want to take two dozen more samples from this area, if we can. Ideally, we would want to replicate the result but—"

Next off the chopping block for shit they don't show in movies: walking.

We broke into three groups so we wouldn't be working well into the dark. Then lots of walking. Our route was spread out over dozens of kilometers since apparently dillers like their space.

Wordlessly, our three groups took a least-time-to-completion path.

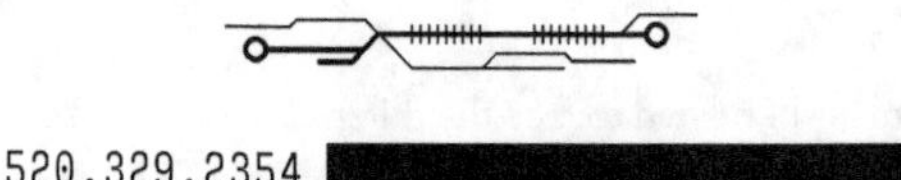

520.329.2354

::EDIT:: I got romantic about the local flora for about four hours there. Then completely stopped making sense.

During the walk, I learned the soil squids that the dillers ate, survived their trip through a diller's digestive system. They used the acidic environment as a breeding pool, according to Deputy Parks. They had a cryptocyst that would grow into a new adult after their body was digested. Eggs even hatched in the manure.

That information now lives in my brain rent free.

"Why don't y'all call them phoenix squids?" someone asked. I missed who said it.

It was the sky this time… I've been staring at the same bulkheads for months, and now there's an open sky that's so much nicer than hanging onto everyone's every word. The sky here is more brilliant blue. In Vanguard City it's mostly black unless its foggy.

"The name is taken," Parks answered. "We got a cease-and-desist from some video game company, and we didn't care that much."

After the third or fourth diller, even the scientists lost their enthusiasm. Each team collected samples from two dozen or so individuals before calling it a day.

The full combat warning then flashed, and our transceivers went manual in the off position. My HUD disappeared, and my ear bugs popped, powering off.

I felt exposed.

Just one giant target for a sniper. If anyone was going to get shot first, it was going to be me or Shantu. My butthole puckered, and I took a knee and put my reactor into standby.

None of the reasons we cut the feed were good. Let's go down the list: mines, missiles, and other munitions. It's the other munitions—like fucking auger drones that drill into armor—that scare me. The first two. BANG! Fuck, I'm dead. But that's it. Done. Getting my AV's knees drilled out and then having to bail only to have the drone come after me is some high-octane nightmare fuel.

I had a side arm, four mags, and one extra charge pack. I could get lucky while a drill of unknown design tried to kill me or to eat the bullet and spare myself from getting mauled. If I was not moving too much, it might leave me for dead.

I now have an anti-bucket list of shit I never want to experience.

My anti-bucket list:

Auger drones or equivalent

Goats

Getting stranded in the infinite night

Another reason we go silent, which is in the shrug category, is cyber security. Where the fuck was Xi when I needed her?

After an uncomfortable amount of time of us hunkering behind a tree, our feeds reactivated.

"Status?" The captain called on the common combat channel.

We checked in. The scientists quickly scurried to latch themselves onto me, and the rest of the team spread out in a defensive posture. Our priority would be to disengage as soon as possible and retreat.

Scout set his feed to public and ordered the science team to be allowed in. His feed showed decaying portions of an entry capsule.

The feed then presented a device mostly submerged in a stagnant, swampy area. Scout's feed populated tons of information, such as likely metal types based on albedo and known and possible components based on acoustic analysis. The device dropped gobs of goo into the water from a metal spout. Each time a gob hit the water, a cloud of small worms swarmed and devoured the mass.

The entire science team pinged for contact priority to Scout. Their icons cleared, and only the team leader's icon remained active. A task request list populated and hid behind Scout's icon.

Scout gave orders for the drone wranglers to execute the requests on passive sensors and positioning transmission only. He then retreated and retrieved a sterile sample kit from the ecology team. On all fours, he just glided over four or five kilometers in a few minutes.

He lived up to his name.

He returned to where he was and caught one of the goop drops before it hit the water.

A heat signature bloomed in the device, and it became slag. The EM restrictions were lifted, and the drones did active scans. Finally, Shantu was ordered to recover the device.

It turned out to be two meters of melted chemical processing equipment.

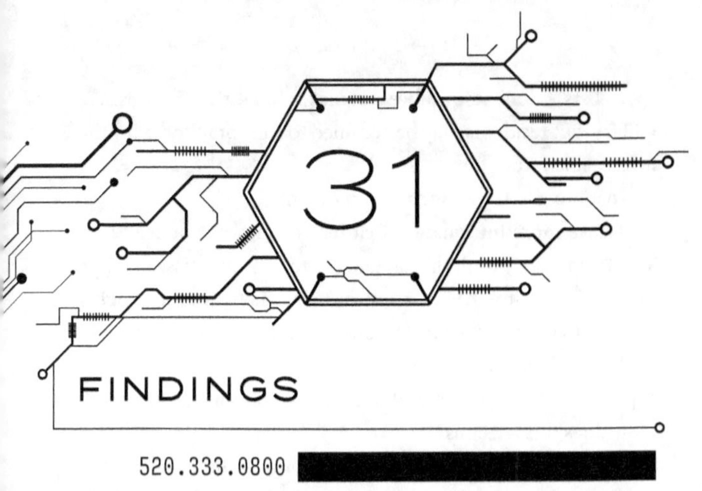

31

FINDINGS

520.333.0800

WE RETURNED TO base before dark and called it a night.

The following morning, the ecology team leader presented their findings. "The device produces compounds that appear to be mostly food for the local equivalent of mosquito larvae. The local mosquitoes mature on the availability of sporulates from the local fungi. The relative production rate by the device versus ambient levels in similar biomes is separated by orders of magnitude. Samples indicate that in roughly ninety hours, an unprecedented swarm will mature. We are still building our impact model."

"Thank you for your analysis," Constable Chan said. "As per our contract and colonization ecological provisions, I need a strictly thermal yield to minimize the contamination. I will entertain any alternative recommendations for the next seventy hours."

"As a word of warning to all the residents, we are not biowarfare specialists. I don't know if we can make a treatment for this. We will try, but residents may be confined to suits or indoors for the foreseeable future."

That hung in the air for a long moment.

"I have more information that may or may not be relevant." The team leader took the captain's silence as permission. "The mature mosquitos have several protein chains that are highly reactive to human-specific tetrameric receptor complexes."

"Doctor," the captain said. "In our line of work, we have an expression. B-L-U-F or bluff. It means bottom line up front. How does this affect us?"

The team leader seemed to think for a moment. "The evidence indicates that mosquitos would cause anaphylaxis in humans. While we are not lawyers, we know the loss of a colony or at least the personnel will have large repercussions in the economic arena. I bring to your attention that while the device and the delivery vehicle are cheap compared to a colonizable planet, the conventional materials and components give us reasonable parameters for a development time frame. Samples would be critical to its development. Even the most optimistic projections put a project such as this at the same age as the colony within a year or two, costing a quarter billion credits and two-and-half billion credits. Expertise and on-site monitoring are the main variables. Does that information affect our situation?"

"It does. Thank you. Please transmit your findings."

The feed booted both the colony and the ecology team. Communications icon went to combat protocol. The rest of the team dispersed.

"All right, boys and girls," Wraith said. "We're in the thick of it now. Do not trust anyone who wasn't in the drop pod with us. No unauthorized personnel in the pod. Stay sealed and only use the supplies we brought down with us. We're stepping over the line from our contract. We weren't hired to root out an insurgency, and the emergency provisions are running out."

Orders went out, and Shantu and I went back to rebuilding the colony. Internally, I was freaking out because I thought we were going to get into some spy game, cross examination, whodunit stuff.

Wraith spoiled by spy fantasies over the comms "A smart spy will go to ground until after we leave. *AAAnnnddd*"—he stretched the word out to match something he was doing— "a dumb one writes home. Aye, I got it. This local here has some interesting things in his room. Religious iconography matches The Dawning Flower. The religious group is secular, militant with a history of violence. This asshole was doing the data handling and burying it in the normal data stream." The icon for data recovery blipped. "Ships in system, minimal crew, strike team twenty to fifty in cold sleep. Ground launch capable. If someone's not jerking this guy's chain."

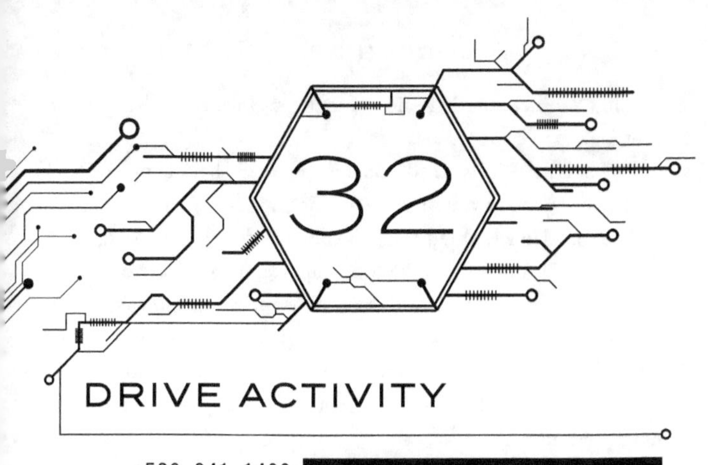

32

DRIVE ACTIVITY

520.341.1400

A LITTLE OVER a week later, Piper sent a message. "We have drive activity." They uploaded a two-hour old live feed.

The Happy Marauder was hiding in the moons of the local Jovian. This was one of those awkward situations where a bike was better than a car. In a parking lot, a bike could get moving and disappear before a car could get out of a parking spot.

I closed my eyes to see better and adjusted the feed to show a planetary orbit view. *The Happy Marauder* and its string of communication relays appeared as dots with circles indicating the range. An unknown spacecraft appeared as a thin white dot, and a line materialized, making its atmospheric insertion trajectory. Their projected landing site was less than a hundred kilometers from the colony.

Orders went out, and we assembled.

"We're APCs, man?" Shantu said as the teams mounted up.

"What?" I returned.

"You know, armored personnel carriers." He chuckled.

"Shh. You hear that?" I said in a quiet, tactical voice that got everyone to freeze.

"What is it?" Alexis asked from his spot in the back of my AV.

"It's the sound of you shutting the fuck up."

The squad link erupted in laughter before doing what I said.

Our HUDs updated, and a topographical map with two circles where Shantu and I were to deploy appeared. I looked at the mission timer and apologized to my passengers. We were to travel fifty kilometers in less than two hours. I know that doesn't sound bad, but we had to make it through dense mountainous jungle terrain.

Two drones shot overhead, feeding us detailed terrain data.

If I wasn't filled with prefight tension and focus, I would have been having a great time. There are few things I love more than to be cut loose in my AV and test the limits of my abilities and my machine.

Now, I was worried that a simple fall would kill someone.

We sprinted through the forest about a kilometer apart.

Someone from our team shouted, "YEE-HAW! RIDE EM, COWBOY!" But I was too busy watching my step and not killing anyone to see who was talking.

Shantu put on his creepy calm voice. "These things are twenty tons of moving metal with no computer assistance. We're moving over unfamiliar terrain at over one hundred kilometers per hour. So, if you wish to reach your destination as more than a smear on my frame, I suggest you refrain from screaming in my fucking ear. Mm-kay? Thank you."

We stopped a few kilometers from the projected landing zone. The sonic boom of orbital entry and contrail confirmed our location was good. I couldn't make out the craft because of the heavy foliage.

Our routes for approach updated with shadowing for a line of sight from the entry craft. Shantu's and my teams disembarked and moved to a wide firing line. We waited while Scout and Wraith did their recon portions.

I set the map to tactical mode. It took over my field of vision, shifting to high fidelity. Thin red lines showed the extrapolated data.

Scout sat in a tree less than a hundred meters from the landing craft. The craft was an ugly utilitarian thing with hard lines and spindly legs over a retracted drive bell. The single air lock faced away from us. It looked like a mass-produced crap can. Less of a troop carrier and more of a cargo pod for bodies.

"Ah, fuck. Cover and conceal!" Wraith barked. "It's Packard Interstellar Solutions. Xi, just found out the pod is full of kid soldiers, twelve to fourteen." He paused for a long while and then opened comms to the local net. "I need slave rights right now for any prisoners of war."

"Wraith," the constable started, "I don—"

"Constable, on that landing craft are three or four dozen children with full kit and kill switches in their helmets." His voice was ice. "They're going to die. If they don't die in combat, they will be executed because the fuel to transport them off planet is too expensive. Now, write it on a napkin. It doesn't matter. My crew needs legal grounds to operate."

He quickly walked her through the verbiage that was needed. Dire-horn slipped into lawyer mode to make sure we could fight a fine legal line. They were *staying ahead of the fact,* as it were.

A metal desk appeared on our HUDs, in grease pen was written: "FTS *The Happy Marauder* and crew have authority in all matters regarding security according to REDACTED. Acting under the authority of the acting Colony Administration Julie Chan." — Constable Julie Chan, Emergency Colony Administrator.

"Firing line, controlled suppressing fire only!" Wraith said. "Javelin, asset suppression! Armor, break tibia and fibula only!

If you break any other bones, you are likely to trigger the kill switches! Captain, can you go right with Gabe please? Dire-horn and I will go left. Sgt. Tok, the line is yours."

"Now that all the yelling's done, I get to be back in charge?" Sgt. Tok teased. He then spoke calmly. "Smoke and flares out."

A line of Marauders rained down the metal canisters, billowing multicolored smoke and flares across the landing zone. The forest erupted into fire. They depleted their charge packs into the trees, hitting nothing.

"One-half stun," Sgt. Tok said as soon as the panic fire slackened. "Armor out."

A laser raked across my canopy causing it to polarize. The hard thud reverberated through my cockpit, despite the noise dampening.

"Out runners, go!" Sgt. Tok ordered.

Shantu and I had maybe cleared half the distance before the next order came.

"Light suppressing fire. Second half, stun when they are fifty meters out. Armor, somersault in three…two…one…"

I did the forward roll, and the bulk of my AV blocked the thump of the stun grenades. We were roughly fifty yards away from the drop pod when it popped hatches with explosive bolts.

My shoulder turrets hummed. Weapons systems failed to deploy as they erupted with melted metal and that toxic orange smoke of doom. My shoulder turrets fired before they were on target, strafing lines that converged on the domed sensor module.

Three enemies too close to the vehicle lost their lives in a fraction of a second. One was decapitated by my point defense; another had a U-shape carved out of his chest. The last one lost his leg and most of his right hip.

Sgt. Tok had the line start intermittent suppressing fire. A pair of missiles harmlessly shot into the air, one after the other. Their operators were dead.

Dire-horn let out a morale-shattering roar—amplified to deafening levels by his armor. He wielded two long curved blades that hooked to his forearm. He locked them together, and a riot shield deployed.

Shantu and I stopped short, digging our feet into the soft ground. Soil and debris rained as we reached the enemies' line, and small arms rattled our AVs like drum rolls.

Dire-horn charged with the captain and Gabe on his heels, drawing fire. His point defense danced around the battlefield. The system destroyed weapons at a glance.

Shantu and I hesitated when the small arms fire stopped. We surveyed the tableaux. Those kids were outclassed by an order of magnitude. They found themselves in a shrapnel storm as battery packs exploded around them.

Their morale broke with their weapons.

The first few tried to run, but their helmets disappeared with their heads. Blood poured from their necks as their bodies flopped onto the ground. The rest of the kid soldiers locked up with indecision: fight us or die.

"Fuck!" Wraith yelled. "Get them out of their armor now. Charges are in their helmets and chest plates."

My canopy was still getting rattled with weapons fire. But an idea hit me like a lightning bolt. "Priority one action." That was tactical for "whoever can do this." The command also turned down the volume on everyone else's voice. "I need the kids to be target priority all shield and set the ambient area to fire for effect. Shantu, weapons free with me. NOW!"

The battlefield erupted with a grid of fast action laser and rail fire.

We were in a storm of superheated air, getting hit by supersonic fléchettes. The fléchettes exploded on the ground, showering everyone with dirt and debris. It was much more effective than any stun grenade.

Everything was silent for a moment. No one moved as the mushroom cloud climbed into the sky.

The captain's cold, controlled voice spoke over all channels in a general broadcast. "Keep your weapons in your left hand. With your right hand, remove your helmets and chest plates. You have twenty seconds to comply."

The sound of cracking glass held for a moment before they moved carefully.

Wraith followed with a countdown.

They really were kids: gaunt and bruised. They had a death stare that no child should have. They looked misshapen, like their growth had been stunted. I don't know.

The piercing sound of dozens of charges rang through the silence, and the kids didn't even flinch. Eight children fell: three still had their helmets on. Four were struggling with their chest plates. One was out of my line of sight.

I remember two of them. I couldn't tell their gender under their armor. But they looked at each other, and I knew their entire world with that stare.

Everything in their short lives had led to this moment of defeat. They were tired. Battle fatigued.

They had no home worth mentioning. A home implied comfort or care. Those words were strangers to these kids. They knew what would happen if they dropped their weapons, and that was okay.

It was the death of hope.

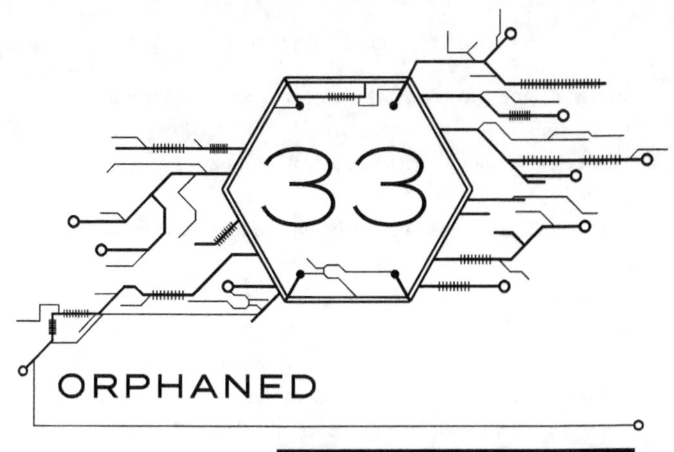

SORRY. I NEEDED a break. This shit is hard to get down.

I don't know who King Charles was, but I remember he got a painting done. I guess this was before cameras. The story goes that he wanted the best painter in the world to capture him, and I guess the painter was really good at making people look their best. But King Charles didn't want that. He wanted his face to have every blemish, warts and all. The way it was taught to me was that a thing was incomplete if you left out the blemishes.

That's what I'm trying to do here.

I locked onto the pair who decided they didn't want to be a part of this… A part of anything anymore.

I don't know if the spacer cocktail adjusted my neural activity, but things went into bullet time. I searched long and hard through every combination of every word I knew that could've stopped this from happening. I could stay in that moment forever. I wanted to be in that moment—because they were still alive then.

But closing a book doesn't change its ending.

Fuck.

They left this fucked-up life behind to move on to the next horror.

This little girl. She had piercing blue eyes behind a dirty face. She was smaller than the rest; her armor hung off her like she was trying to fit into her parents' clothes. She had her helmet off, but her tiny hand had struggled with the latch for her chest plate. Her left arm exploded in a gout of purple flames, leaving it in a burnt mangled mess. Blood poured freely from her chest. The back of her head then evaporated as the terror in her eyes was snuffed out. Her face relaxed, and her eyes went lifeless.

Someone had spared her from her misery. I didn't look around to find out who had the nerve to pull that trigger.

I didn't want to know.

"Wraith, you have command. Dire-horn, with me," the captain said as if he had a meeting to get to.

"Sgt. Tok," Wraith said, passing command onto him.

I don't know Wraith that well. He and the other senior crew keep to themselves like any other management who work on a different floor. I will say that I heard *murder* in his voice. Like he was going to get a hard drive, pull someone's address off it, slip into their bedroom, and quietly stick a knife in their neck for what had happened here. If it wasn't one person, he would take a skyscraper, put it in the basement during a morning meeting, and quietly sip coffee from across the street.

Maybe I've been watching too many movies lately. I don't know. That's how it felt.

Wraith stepped out from his armor, subtly pulled his sword from it, and attached the sword to his back. After a moment, it faded from view. Subtle transparent effects, like ripples on water, were only visible when I didn't look directly at it. He disappeared into their drop pod.

Twenty-three kids came with us.

They didn't speak when we herded them into a group. They just mechanically followed their commands.

They had been beaten long before we defeated them.

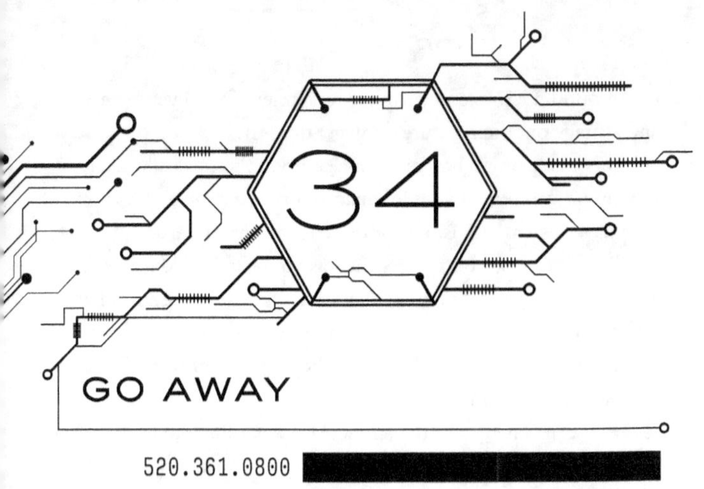

THE WHOLE SITUATION is a fucking shit show.

Let's start with: We were using a machine shop as a workspace. The table had been cleared of all its components. The abused surface and drainage trench running down the middle was an incongruous feature to the multibillion credit deal and interstellar incident being discussed. The single setting harsh light would be great for disassembling my AV, but here, it was just irritating.

Our stock plummeted from action hero to pariah.

"Baby killer!" random colonist number six yelled at us as we gathered for a meeting. Which pretty much summed up the current attitude over the last three weeks.

It was time to go. We officially had overstayed our welcome. But alas, no job was done until the paperwork was finished.

Contract Representative Jeff Brown was a nondescript male bureaucrat from indeterminate heritage. He was so pointlessly unremarkable that it was his defining characteristic. You could look directly at the guy, and he'd just kind of blend into the background. Picture every bank teller or clerk from everywhere and average out their features. You get this guy.

"This new colony has yet to enact any policies at all, much less define the complexities for unaccompanied minors," he said. "We have several provisions for our clients' personnel and their families, as well as contractors such as yourself. While we have a department set aside for captives exchanged in the event of a war, the combatants need to be a minimum of sixteen years of age if they're human. The blanket policy is to differ to the local government for orphan care."

Dire-horn fumed. On the surface, he was calm, stoic. But it was something I could feel. Like standing next to a live grenade. Maybe it was a change in his breathing.

"Let's come back to that topic later." The captain led the conversation from there with his patented diplomatic tone.

We Marauders all either sat on equipment or leaned against shelving while the captain negotiated the price of every round expended, every wear and tear on equipment. Anything that had a scratch was depreciated, and the drop pod was considered expended in service. Shantu's and my shoulder turrets were burned out and needed replacing; however, the price he negotiated was audaciously inflated.

The negotiations for "extenuating circumstances" took up the entire day, and I was not disappointed in how the spoils were divided up. Each share was close to four million credits if we converted them to V. On Vanguard, I would be living comfortably without having to work for several years.

Eventually, we circled back to the topic of the kids.

"Captain, there is no provision for me to handle the transport or guardianship of twenty-three minors," Jeff said.

The captain and Jeff stared at each other, a gulf of twenty-three orphaned children between them.

"If you would please, I would like to go off the record."

A physical time stamped non-disclosure agreement was passed around the table and attached to the contract and the code for the document that would be attached to our feeds.

Jeff's demeanor deflated. "Look, this whole thing is fucked up. We had taken to calling Packard Interstellar Solutions *piss* because they just piss on everything." His joke missed the mark. By a lot. He cleared his throat. "Anyway, we're looking at another corporate war because of their dealings with those Dawning Flower cultists. They were caught with their hand in the cookie jar and will scramble for damage control. The fast packet drones are already out. They might come after you"—he took a moment to look around the table—"or the kids, but we've already distributed information across our networks. They will either use whatever denial story fits the current political climate or sacrifice some lackey to the wolves. Time will tell."

Dire-horn grumbled like tectonic plates warning before a quake.

The captain spoke before Dire-horn could get a word out. "Think of the story here."

"I'm going to stop you right there," Jeff said. "I don't make those calls. Here's what I do know: the investors, most of whom are on this planet, don't want the battle babies here. Those children are a mess, and they don't want to deal with it. The colony wants to put all this behind them. I have access to two hundred tons of pure elemental titanium and a pellet fusion reactor. I'll pay out to you as an expediting fee."

I have no idea what those are worth.

But something changed in both men's demeanor that I didn't understand.

There was a lot of going back-and-forth about hubs where we could receive payment, acceptable commodities, and riders. If we don't get this, we want that. If we go to that place and not this one, we want an oil change and some air fresheners. I'm boiling all that down because I don't understand it enough to keep track.

"Five hundred tons, and you'll never hear from us again," the captain countered. "Or two-fifty and have us on your preferred contacts list."

"Seeing as you are a reasonable man, I would like to work with you again," Jeff said. "Two-fifty it is."

The captain and Jeff Brown went back on the record and ironed out the details.

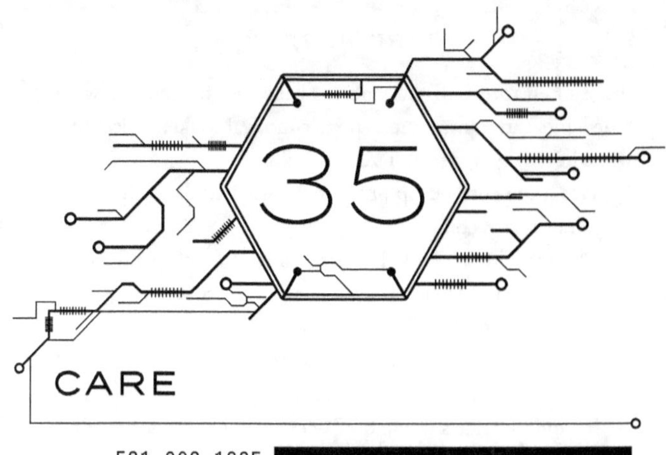

35

CARE

THIS MORNING, I woke up screaming in a panic so deep that it felt like I was drowning.

Thankfully, I was in my HEPS, or I would have cracked my head on my sleeping cubby. They're empty shock-absorbing computer racks. The foam is comfortable enough most nights, but tonight, it just saved me from another concussion and probably kept me from waking whoever else was sleeping in the pod.

I was yelling to stop the kids from killing themselves. It was me and Shantu trapped in coffins, getting chewed on by dillers. Tubes were stuffed down my throat. Unable to breathe, I hyperventilated, crying and holding my knees. Images of the three kids who died near that vehicle were now either me or Shantu.

This was the third night in a row.

I messaged Scout, and he told me he was available.

We took a walk around the drop pod, far out of earshot from anyone. He didn't wear armor per se. It was a matte skin suit that shifted to match the ambient pallet. Right now, we wore blue lights and transmitted in private mode. I walked awkwardly while he slowly sipped at his coffee bulb.

"Was it the coffin drop or the combat?" he asked. He took a long draw on his coffee.

"The casualties. The kids." I chuckled to comfort myself. "I know what all the veterans talk about in the media now."

"Is there any tension between you and Tombstone?"

The non sequitur confused me, so I answered honestly. "We're good. Is there something I don't know?"

"It would be news to me too," Scout said between sips of his coffee. "I understand that you two have been close for a very long time. I want to bring him in. I feel that it's for the best."

I shrugged.

A moment later, Shantu wandered up to us, fussing with his helmet to get his hair out of his face. "What's going on, Scout?"

"How have you been sleeping?" Scout asked.

He tried to rub his face through his helmet. "Like shit. Why?"

"Monolith is having nightmares from the conflict. As his medical contact of record, I'm letting you know. Furthermore, with your shared history, you're at a high risk of developing similar symptoms." Scout handed us HEPS compatible pill dispenser and auto-injector. "These will dispense sleeping meds, and you will have control of the doses within limits. Let me or Doc know if there are any problems, diet changes, constipation, and the like. You also need to wear the auto injectors at the port on your thigh; they have a stimulant for emergencies. I can trigger them remotely during an action station's alarm. I would appreciate if you logged your sleep, so we can fine tune your preferences."

"No psycho-babel?" Shantu asked, still half asleep.

"Only if you really want it… To clarify, I would be more worried if you weren't affected by these events." He ended things from there with a few pleasantries.

I woke up, feeling groggier than normal, but it passed quickly like the rest of the day.

We were here a lot longer than we had wanted, but we got to squeeze a few pennies out of the contract by repairing hangar doors and whatnot. That day was spent rearranging cargo containers into an ad hoc hydroponics, air, and water filtration. We were also taking on a colony of rabbits—partially for cheap protein and partially for the stupid amounts we can sell them for at any space port. On our way out of the system, we were also supposed to grab a comet or two for the water.

Anyway, never mind that day-to-day shit. Things fucking exploded…metaphorically… Is that the right word? It's not literal. There was no hull damage.

Fuck it. Moving on.

The captain and Dire-horn were arguing on the common ship channel for everyone to hear. This could have been happening in the galley. I was sitting comfortably in my AV not moving the pallets I was supposed to.

"We are vulnerable right now," the captain stated matter-of-factly. "Our max acceleration is 0.6 g, and it's going to take us almost a year to get to Fermi Station. Toshduan is where they get off."

"If we abandon these children, I will no longer have a place aboard *The Happy Marauder*!" Dire-horn roared in startling contrast to the captain's calm certainty.

"WHOA! Big guy," Wraith said. "We're not abandoning them. Bring it down a notch. Let's talk about this."

"I don't know much about human children," Piper added, "but we're really combat oriented. It doesn't seem like a place for any young ones. Dire-horn, do you really think this ship is the best place for them?"

"We have the resources, medical assistance, psychological help, food, water, and life support," Dire-horn retorted. "We can, and therefore, we should. The burden may be heavy, but we will be stronger for it."

"I thank you for the faith in my expertise, Dire-horn; however, humans with this level of trauma would likely need specialized care that I'm not sure I can provide," Scout said, sounding irritated.

But I do not trust my ability to read a different species' tone—especially one trained in psychology.

"Are you not willing to try?" Dire-horn grumbled, more like a seismic shift than audible words. He sounded betrayed.

"I didn't say that" Scout corrected. "I just feel that they would be better served by someone or a facility that specializes in this level of care."

"Are you unwilling to try?" he asked again, his voice almost a growl.

"My parents are human, so I think I know them pretty well," Gabe said. "These kids are pretty fucked up. They don't talk. They don't do anything. They just follow commands. We're waiting for the reports on their brains from Doc, but they need care, man."

"Mind if I chime in?" Sgt. Tok asked.

No one objected.

"I don't know what to fucking do here, but let's look at it from all angles. These kids aren't space rated. Shouldn't we put them back in the boxes before we take them up? Then where could we take them? Colonies don't have that kind of care. Developed worlds have strict immigration laws. Can we sponsor them or something? Gabe has a point that these kids are fucked up. Here, this lifestyle is maybe familiar enough to soften the transition until they're old enough to make their own decisions."

"I am willing to put forth *The Happy Marauders* resources to act as a patron," the captain said. "Maybe get them passage after Toshduan to a nice colony that is more developed. If that would satisfy you."

"It is not about my satisfaction!" Dire-horn thundered. He took a deep breath and calmed. "They have a tentative legal status at best. If we release them from our custody, Packard has legal grounds to regain custody in most developed systems. *The Happy Marauder* is the best place for them."

I wondered if this is what it was like when parents fought. Because I felt like this was.

The captain didn't falter. "They will die here, Dire-horn. Most humans don't do well in space. We're checking on the pods but inducing them is going to be a problem."

"Kalp!" Dire-horn barked so sharply that I feared I would pop an eardrum.

I replayed my log and found it. *Kalp* is an insult or an accusation. It translates into traitor by neglect, someone who can't be trusted. A fuckup. Usually, it's reserved for unruly animals and drug addicts. In polite minotaur society, using it would end in duels or alienation.

The captain snapped back with "Ogap!" He tried to match the minotaur's volume but not his tone.

Ogap translates to zealot or a fool who places unfair expectations on those who don't deserve it. It's usually reserved for priests who attack villages for lacking piety. In modern terms, it's usually a criticism for military commanders who mismanage a crisis with a civilian population.

They shot insults back and forth for a minute before things came to a head.

"The path we walk must be paved with our own two hooves." The minotaur expression meant do what is right even if it's not easy.

"*The Happy Marauder* is vulnerable," Wraith said. "They're not spacers. If we maneuver too hard, we'll kill them. Right now, it's point defense, missiles, and hope our shields hold. Even if we make it to Fermi, *The Happy Marauder* cannot be their home."

"Fermi Station would be a good place to take them," Piper suggested.

"I have made my decision. The loss in capability and profitability is not worth any morale stance," the captain pressed. "It is not worth the risk. We have always made it a point to not get sucked into a cause. Making one of your own is no better."

"Then I assume Toshduan is where I will get off," Dire-horn said, sounding deflated now. "I expect to be paid in full."

I looked up Toshduan. It was the nearest star with a budding colony. Relied on Vanguard for martial services. Light ship servicing facilities. Heavy meat exports. Kind of a backwater.

"Dire-horn, hold on!" Wraith exclaimed. "Captain, this is a step in the wrong direction. The math may not pan out at a glance, but trust me, it will." He said it with the kind of conviction that rallied armies. "Trust me. This is an *opportunity*. This is what Marauders do. We can find a way to make this work for us. First, let's stick Flutter on a redesign with updated manifest to make sure we can handle the new passengers. See if we can get them back into the boxes that got them here. Then see if we can find them a good home. Look, we'll try and find some political brownie points along the way. We'll make it happen. Won't we, Dire-horn?"

"How does taking in twenty-three strays help us?" the captain asked coldly.

"You took me in," Javelin said.

It felt like the air left the room even though I was watching the everything unfold in my feed from my AV. No one breathed in the silence, and there wasn't so much as a heartbeat for a long moment.

"Not forever, Captain," Wraith said, continuing without any acknowledgment of Javelin's comment. Like it was a dirty secret that would become too real if they looked at it. "Just long enough for us to find a good home, something Dire-horn will sign off on. Right, Dire-horn? *The Happy Marauder* is growing, Captain."

Something unsaid passed between the old crew.

Shantu and I had many of those moments, ones where we would glance at each other and reference that thing we did that one time. This was theirs.

"We should grow with it, Captain," Wraith said.

"We're due for an overhaul anyway," Piper added. "Fermi Station has been on our projected schedule for over a year, and at this rate, we'll still be on schedule. I'll kick a contract off the schedule. That's the closest major station with refit facilities. There's like a hundred billion humans; I'm sure we can find homes there."

The captain named another station I didn't catch which was closer and safer but didn't have a large human presence. The impression I got was that it was the same as dropping the kids off at a convenience store in a bad neighborhood.

Dire-horn did not like the idea.

"I will stake my back dues to the overhaul," Wraith said. "That being said, Captain, we can't lose Dire-horn like this. When we started this, how many years were we only keeping people on for one job at a time? He is an intangible asset. Scout, Piper, Flutter…"

There was a pause where he didn't say Javelin's name, but I heard it, nonetheless.

"The last fifteen people, we have recall retainers with. That WAS DIRE-HORN!" Wraith took a long, calming breath. "If Dire-horn leaves, I guess I'm going with him."

I shifted uncomfortably.

"I will wait for more information," the captain said, conceding. "If we can make this work, we can go to work. Fermi, it is."

I don't remember if there was a literal sigh of relief when the tension was over, but I felt like there should be one.

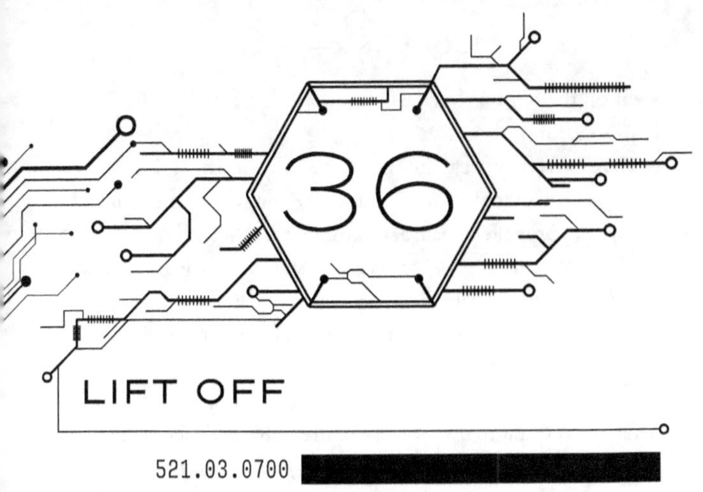

LIFT OFF

521.03.0700

HERE ARE SOME questions I should have asked a long time ago: what kind of shuttle do you use? How do we get up from a planet?

Down is a drop pod. Cool. I understand that.

Heavy lift shuttles *suck*. Bulbous ugly sons of bitches. Maybe there are cooler versions out there, but the two we used *sucked*.

Piper came down in one to pick up Javelin and deliver cargo. The shuttles had their autonomous guidance, but this was a good opportunity for Piper and Javelin to build up flight hours.

At first, it looks like a missile on a glide path. Then it flared its skinny wings like a dragonfly, lifted its nose up until it almost stalled, and then leveled out before hitting deceptively gently on fat ugly wheels.

It was the compromise, streamlined enough to take two shipping containers in the ass while having walking room around the side. So, where did we put all the stuff we needed, like landing gear and control surfaces? Just wherever. Gear went on the bottom obviously. Control surfaces could double as propulsion.

Here's why they suck: they have little baby electric turbines for the initial lift. Once they're in the air, the wings I had mentioned are used as propellers that rotate around the whole shuttle.

So, we're going to travel between the stars but use giant fans to get off the ground? Isn't there something better that can harness the planet's magnetic field to repulse a craft into orbit? Maybe, I don't know because I'm using a giant fucking fan.

What about an ion drive? They're no good anywhere near where you'd want to live because of the eighteen different kinds of radiation they put out. Once you're off a planet, the magnetosphere will protect the planet, but in the atmosphere, you're going to scorch everything. But at least they're not a giant fucking fan.

Or chemical rockets! Sure, there's a trade-off because you must account for the weight of fuel which quickly turns into a spiral of we-need-to-bring-fuel-for-the-fuel-we're-bringing.

Thus, the big ass fan we were strapped into.

The fans—excuse me, *propellers*—fold into wings during takeoff and landing, making the whole thing look like someone smashed a dragonfly onto a sub sandwich. We load up everything we're taking with us, including rabbits, feed, soil, seeds, and the kids. One trip just dipped into the atmosphere to gather free gasses.

I think these vehicles are stupid because it went like this:

I loaded my AV and secured it with the vertical and horizontal cross braces that come with these shuttles. Did some other loading and securing because that's why I'm here. Then I strapped myself into a hammock. The hammocks were the cheap solution to a self-orienting crash couch.

Jet noises whined as the turbines spun. It shuddered and wobbled, getting off the ground. More shuttering and wobbling as it got to speed. The whining jet noise was replaced by the propellers' BLAP-BLAP-BLAP. More wobbling and swaying.

It was chill for a while. Just hanging out in a hammock, swinging back and forth and trying to read stuff in my feed.

Then it was not so chill. Javelin gave zero warnings as she circled and pulled up hard, pushing three g's of acceleration. Do you know what happens before you break the sound barrier? The propellers break the sound barrier.

Stand on one of those industrial jackhammers. No, those are better because they stop to reposition. This fucking thing just kept getting louder until we made escape velocity. Loud and annoying doesn't begin to cover it. Both the hull and my ear bugs struggled to cancel the noise, but it was like fighting a wave.

I suffered for a few minutes, swinging around in my hammock, before the main drive kicked me in the ass.

How the fuck is this the best way to get to orbit?

If I had to braid grass to throw a lasso around a moon and climb it to get to space, I would do it so I wouldn't take another shuttle up.

BOARDING PARTY

521.005.2102

TODAY WAS PRETTY fucking awesome.

We spent the last three days ferrying crap up from the surface. Because one shuttle trip was enough for a lifetime, I had to do it six more times. Then got everything sorted and balanced until Piper was happy. Not the cool part.

Very uncool. Fuck shuttles.

We got the kids brought up and did some basic safety stuff. Then set them up so they could access the libraries. We updated security procedures and all that bullshit.

The senior crew then hurried us to the galley, which was covered in vibrant floral decorations. Most of the walls had prints that showed large fields of flowers with the occasional stream. The couches and monitor had been moved against the bulkhead to give room for folding tables and chairs. The furniture had cloth coverings that gave the appearance of rough-hewn wood.

Near the galley, Wraith wore an obnoxious apron that said "kiss the cook" with a set of stylized huge red human lips behind the text. He was running a cooking space that seemed to use burning plant matter for fuel.

"Congratulations," the captain said to us in the professional voice of a broadcast announcer that was simultaneously forced to be festive and professional.

Maybe it was his eyes, I don't know, but it wasn't genuine excitement. I assume it's the way a whore pretends to be attracted to you. My best guess was Javelin—or someone else—had coaxed him to put on a nice face.

His words were meant to rile children into excitement, but something just seemed off about it. "The senior crew and I will take care of everything for the next twenty-four hours. Take this time to enjoy yourselves."

"Step right up, boys and girls," Wraith announced in a mock rapid-fire salesman voice; I couldn't help but laugh as his dumb antics added to tableaux. "Not to forget the this and thats. Talking about you, Lamal."

That was the only cue Lamal got before a cooked piece of meat flew across the room and smacked his face. He quickly gobbled it up and licked the juices from the floor.

"Izza good, good," Lamal burbled.

"Because there's a Wraith at the grill, and he's firing up your fill," Wraith continued. "I have steaks, flanks, and ribs. Don't be shy. You better call dibs. Because it's all going on the fire, and it'll be everything you can desire."

He made an extravagant show of tossing cooking implements into the air and spinning to catch them behind his back. It turned into half juggling, half food prep act. "Find your seats and rest your feets. Dire-horn will be bringing around the corn."

Dire-horn set out light vegetarian appetizers and hors d'oeuvres.

I was taken aback by the hors d'oeuvres. A slice of cucumber served as a base, carrot slices were carved into flower pedals, and a savory cream sauce glued everything together. Cauliflower and broccoli made up the inside bits, and a dab of jam gave a contrasting splash of sweetness. By the stars, they were fucking delectable. When I popped one into my mouth, I took a bit of time to savor them and appreciate all the different flavors and textures.

The kids looked like kids. They had fresh sets of T-shirts and shorts all cut from the same pattern in a variety of bright primary colors. At a glance, they could be a school sports team. Someone had taken the time to get them cleaned up and cut their hair.

But they still had distant wide eyes that no one should have. They just sat where we put them like independent thoughts were burned from their brain. Or maybe we were using the wrong language.

Please don't think less of me or do. I think less of me. Anyway, the kids creep me out. Scout tells me it's the uncanny chasm. Kids are on the level of clowns for the creep factor.

I should have some sense of solidarity with my fellow orphans. But I didn't, and they made me uncomfortable. If they were angry, I could relate. If they were sad, I could try to comfort them. But I couldn't handle those wide eyes.

It was like they weren't really people.

That line of reasoning was derailed like a papier-mâché train in the rain when the smell of fresh cooking hit me. Hunger—the primal kind—awakened in me. I let go. I mean, really let go. My brain just turned off, and I guess I got to become the kid I never really was.

Wraith kept everyone's attention with his exhibition, tossing small cuts of meat across the room and using it to introduce the kids and crack their shells. The captain helped serve the meat dishes, and Dire-horn notably kept a distance from the animal products, or maybe the captain.

The kids ate ravenously before just staring off again. It took a lot of coaxing to get them to try the games. Gabe had printed ring toss, bowling, ski ball, and some others. Everyone seemed to be doing their best to coax to some enthusiasm but were forced to settle for participation.

The galley was more crowded than I had ever seen it. Shantu and I became flies on the wall. Whatever a fly is. Saliut was working with a boy who seemed to be the one with the most bruises out of all of them.

The captain passed through for a toast. "Monolith, that was a Marauder move. Saved twenty-three lives."

But I had killed three.

We raised our glasses and drank.

I saw Piper and Shantu kiss.

38

WORK TO LIVE, LIVE TO WORK

521.007.2230 FTS *The Happy Marauder*, Interstellar Space

WE SPENT THE day moving cargo and welding new air locks into place.

Everyone was pretty much scrambling. Flutter was busy with Turtle Tank and Lamal, trying to expand the algae farm and convert one of our training decks into a dorm. Scout and Doc were doing their best to get the kids' pods working. Piper was trying to find a comet that wasn't too dirty. They, Flutter, and the captain also worked on integrating everything into the existing environmental system. Dire-horn and Wraith were on babysitting duty.

Someone was running the plumbing. I don't know who. But trust me, it was a ton of work.

I was in my HEPS, going back and forth with the induction heater and the fusion scanner. Welding in space is a lot easier than in an atmosphere. Half the time, it'll cold weld with no oxide layer. Little heat and banging, and it'll fuse. No atmosphere to draw heat away or contaminate the weld. The problem was the amount we had to do. We were cutting apart shipping containers to use as raw materials. The workflow schedule had me doing thirty of these.

Gets old quickly.

"I thought this ship was able to crew hundreds," I bitched at Gabe.

"Originally," he said as chipper as ever. "*The Happy Marauder* is a lean mean fighting machine now. The time and the price were right, so we sold off most of those systems for this and that. If memory serves me, I believe we upgraded our point defense at the time. We moved from traditional lasers to multimodal-trans phasic directed energy."

"Do you see what we're driving?" Shantu said. He was prep-ositioning loads of metal near each hydroponics pod. "Back the technobabble down to ground-pounder level, will you?"

As cheery as ever, Gabe replied, "I have more infantry combat experience than both of you combined, so if anyone gets to play the dumb grunt card, it's me. But because I'm a gracious soul, I'll respect your wish anyway. The laser's medium can be changed by modulation in—"

"Dumber," Shantu stressed.

Gabe ground his mandible, the human equivalent of *uh.* They snapped together. "They can change their color to work better against shields and armor. Also, they can go wide beam to disperse chaff."

"Interesting," I said to keep Shantu from being more of an ass. "Seriously though, what do we do if we can't maneuver?"

"We can maneuver. We'll just kill all the rabbits and fuck up most of the new hydroponics. It's working hours that are the problem. These hoses, coupling and a bunch of other things, are going to get broken on the first maneuver. I'm trying to think of a human equivalent." He paused for a long while. "Snapping turtle or hippo. Large and dangerous but not swift. Before we were a lion or bear, apex predators. We were well balanced in firepower, maneuvering, shields, and point defense. Taking away our maneuvering leaves a lot to contend with."

He prattled on about calorie and phosphate conversions and a whole bunch of environmental concerns. All of it was like brain floss, removed my preconceived notions but wasn't sticking yet.

Eventually, I felt like an ass and said, "I haven't gotten to shield theory, and I'm pretty sure the media has never given an accurate representation on how they work."

Gabe didn't breathe; I'm really not sure if his respiratory system functions like humans do. "Our shields are dual layered non-Newtonian lattice ferrofluids. Play with some cornstarch and water from the galley. The magnetic netting deploys from pylons, and the shield fluid sticks to the nets. Space combat is all about energy. Kinetic energy gets absorbed by the shields and converted into electrical or thermal energy. The containers on the exterior of the ship can shrug off a puff of hot dust much easier than the same amount of energy in a metal slug. If things work the shields…"

And then he lost me.

I was paying attention, but if I try to quote him, someone smarter than me is going to follow up with shit about how what I said couldn't have been right because something about energy and velocity. So, here's my best try, and if I'm wrong, give me a break. I had one class on starship theory; it was a one-hour presentation, and I was really tired.

Let's see. Things hitting the shields… Missiles. Right. Most missiles detonate in a cone, and we get peppered with shrapnel. Most shrapnel get converted into energy as it burns up when it hits the shields. That degrades the liquid portion of the shields. Each impact changes the stable half liquid, half net thing into a mash of contaminates.

The movements of the ferrofluids generate an electrical charge that can be channeled into capacitors for use. Counter currents flowing into the nets can give it a more rigid or foamy structure on what the computer thinks is best for the incoming threat. A rigid smooth surface gives it a higher albedo—that means shininess—and is better against directed energy weapons but will be weaker against kinetic weapons. The foamy setting was for kinetics.

Point defense, active defense, and counter shot batteries are all interchangeable terms, just meaning guns that shoot at bullets. Those were meant to deal with missiles, shuttles, more than other ships.

There's a lot more to it, but what I took away is that I don't want to own a starship. I thought it was all sit in a cockpit and yank on controls and kill shit. No, it is *way* too fucking complicated.

Normally, anyone who talked this much would end up getting tortured by Shantu's and my antics, but Gabe seemed immune to it. We would talk shit, and he would move right the fuck along. Not ignore it. Just enough acknowledgment that we said something, call us assholes, and go right back to what he was talking about. His speed and laser focus were fascinating.

Here. I'll give an example.

"Each pylon's rigidity is modulated to the amount of energy needing to be dissipated and the current maneuvering strain," Gabe said.

"My rigidity definitely gets modulated to maneuvering strain," Shantu replied.

"Must be pretty lax because you have no maneuvers. But you see why large amounts of kinetic energy must be dispersed..." And just like that, he went onto why we need to be in shock couches.

Talking with Gabe was fun because he didn't get butthurt about anything. Plus, if you spend days assembling and installing air locks for an ad hoc environmental system, any stimulation is nice.

39

WORK INTERRUPTION

521.011.0111 FTS *The Happy
Marauder, Interstellar Space*

SHIT GOT KINETIC fast and with wild fucking abandon. There is nothing quite like getting bitch-slapped by a baffle to say, "Hey, sunshine. It's time to wake up."

I was deadass asleep when the maneuvering alarms went off, and a baffle deployed to keep me from going splat across my quarters, turning me into a mess for the next guy to clean up. Then nineteen—yeah, one nine—g's of hard deceleration tried to force my organs out of my mouth.

If I had shit myself, I would not have been ashamed.

Did you know there is at least a solid second before vision comes on after your awareness wakes up? I know this because I distinctly remember trying to fight the baffle while my asshole tried to merge with my mouth via the physics trying to kill me.

I wondered if my welds for the new hydroponics would hold.

The shit that goes through my head…

I made sense of the action station's glaring alarm. All hands alert ordered me to a sled. Which was nice in concept if I wasn't learning what a dick felt like in a condom.

The giant balloon of fancy plastic that squished me into my bed disappeared like my hopes for a good night's sleep. I dove for my locker, slithered into my HEPS, and went careening down the passage while still sealing the suit. I had bounced off the second bulkhead before I realized we were in free fall. Panic and conditioning mixed as I followed procedure. I landed in a seat and strapped myself in.

Shantu sat next to me, and we bumped knuckles. A calm washed over me. Everything was going to be all right.

A maneuvering warning blared as I fought to keep my senses oriented. Javelin was at the helm, and Gabe bounced in, taking the copilot's seat. He assigned the alpha team designations with her as team leader.

"Prepare for a barn toss," she said cooly as she went through her emergency launch checks.

Some things you need to know. A sled is basically an armored missile meant to carry people instead of a warhead. It does have a breaching charge in front that's meant to cut into the hull. No life support. No turndown service. And the seat I was occupying may not have been designed for anything with a spine.

Got it? Good.

A barn toss is a stupid-ass maneuver invented by psychopaths who want to watch people suffer and die. It involves rotating the ship on two axes and then depressurizing a bay to launch a ship. It is how rednecks and pirates get shuttles up to boarding velocities without a proper catapult.

So, there I was, in a suit that had the armor rating akin to cellophane, in a metal tube that wasn't meant to carry biological lifeforms, piloted by a woman who seemed as indifferent to a horrible death as the amount of space dust in one cubic meter to the next.

And what does my dumbass say? "What are we waiting for?"

In my defense, a strange amount of time had passed since Javelin finished her prefight. Prelaunch? Whatever… I'm not a pilot. I mean, I am a pilot, but I don't fly.

This was an emergency, right? Unless this was some kind of sick joke. Nineteen g's said it wasn't an exercise. If it was, it was an expensive-ass exercise.

"The mule," Gabe answered.

The mule was a drone, basic quadruped of exposed frame, batteries, and servos. It had been preloaded since I came onto the ship. There was an assortment of rifles and pistols, a few temporary air locks, and heavier launchers. The hypermobile limbs articulated in ways no biological creature would as it locked itself into a bracket on the deck.

A moment passed, and Alexis, obviously injured, rode another mule in and fell into the jump seat on the other side of Shantu. Her face was twisted in pain. The second mule was hers and bristled with antenna and sensors. Smaller drones fit into docking ports.

As soon as she and the mule were locked, the mission light popped green, and *The Happy Marauder* spun, nose over tail. She screamed and then fought the pain down to grunting growls.

I didn't know what was going on outside the sled, but I imagined walls of flack and wildly twisting flight paths. I focused on my breathing and maintaining my organs in their default positions. The sled spun into a spine-crushing brake. Then it jerked with a metal rending vibration and a final THUNK! A vacuum warning flashed around my HUD before framing the mini map in yellow.

That was the friendly reminder that if I get punctured, I'd die.

The weapons mule presented itself. That was my cue. It was a basic exo-frame with a smart holster, hardened gloves, a few tools, and an emergency thruster pack. It assembled my boarding kit outside my HEPS.

I'm cramming all this shit together because we trained a lot. However, kamikaze-ing our asses into a boarding action was not a part of it.

Sgt. Tok's CQB training led me forward as my brain took a back seat for this ride.

The mule repeated the process with Shantu and then armed us with default weapons load: a double tap, two pistols, one double tap, one cutting, eight zero g frag grenades, a hundred meters of cutting line, one brick of high explosive, and one thermal blade.

I went high, and Shantu went low.

My heart pounded in my ears. The movies always made it sound like a drum. The better ones used a recording from a stethoscope. I always heard a WHOOSH, WHOOSH, WHOOSH. That was the cue for me to calm *the fuck* down.

I took a deep breath. That did nothing.

I really hoped this thing wouldn't explode.

The breaching mechanism is basically a rope made of like ten kinds of explosives that can be tuned on the fly. On the fly... I mean as it's detonating. It's supposed to cut, weld, and push. This whole thing is a bomb that needs to behave in a very specific way, pushing layers of metal into place to form a tube that we can traverse. Any misbehaving, and this sled isn't even high-speed debris. It's just dust. The course on it is on the top of my independent learning list.

If I don't die.

"What the fuck are we doing here?" I asked, riding the adrenaline high.

"Follow-up," Javelin said it like it explained everything.

"Gabe?"

"We need life-support, stores, or systems. Everything we built to take the kids on just broke. We want anything that can offset the cost of the ordinance. We'll take the whole ship if possible."

I don't know who activated the breacher, but it exploded in a spiraling flash of plasma, and I didn't die.

The breaching mechanism burned into an air lock big enough for both our AVs. All I saw was a rapidly cooling tunnel of scorched and melted metal and unrecognizable equipment. Both hatches were destroyed, and the far bulkhead had been licked by plasma.

The weapons free order flashed, and we darted out of the sled, through the destroyed air lock, and paused before checking the corridor. Our HUD identified floating bodies as hostile.

Gabe ordered us down the corridor. If we had gravity, we would be climbing in the upper corners of the passageway to avoid the hatches. Our mini map tagged each one as an uncleared room to be explored later.

Gabe took point and led us deeper, toward the ship's interior. We manually overrode another air lock, destroying the electronics and forcing the mechanism. Workstations and observation rooms dotted the walls. A massive spherical reactor with all its accessories dominated space. Its metal bracing almost looked like an organ.

Squat, round vac-suited creatures scrambled hither and thither. We opened fire in double tap mode, picking off our targets.

It was quick and gruesome work. Gobs of frozen red-orange blood bounced around the deck as the creatures died. The breach in their suits made little jets, sending them bouncing around the compartment.

All I felt was the recoil.

Shantu and I went in opposite directions, slaughtering as we went. I think these were technical personnel. Maybe the people who ran the reactor. My silent feet told me the reactor was cold. I hope it was a graceful shutdown.

My HEPS helmet had a coating around the edge that went

opaque and was radio luminescent. It was the chemical version of a Geiger counter. My visor was clear, so I was good. If I didn't notice the flecking or glowing right away, I would have already been dead. It was there, so I could tell someone, so they didn't get dosed.

When we finished and came up for air so to speak, Alexis was directing the drones to cut into the equipment. She was focused on her work, so I let her be.

I asked my feed for a profile on the enemy.

The combat synapsis told me that they were galunkin, a hostile species with tribal mentalities that preferred to steal instead of produce. Their piracy and space tactics each had links to separate books.

"Skip," I ordered my feed before it read a book to me.

Galunkin were characterized as clever and dangerous, especially in numbers. They tended to be impulsive and short sighted. The nonmilitary cast tended to use improvised tension weapons as they saw them as more efficient than modern projectile or energy weapons. Their personnel fighting forces avoided individual combat, seeking strength in numbers.

My feed heavily warned about their use of explosive- and shrapnel-based improvised weapons that were used as area denial munitions. Small numbers of them will work themselves to a panicked death, prepping booby traps. They were almost ignorant of losses while rushing for an attack. Individually, they avoided direct contact and preferred to reunite with any of their own species.

I dismissed the helper tool and saw Gabe and Javelin wearing the most sophisticated armor I had ever seen. This was not what they wore for the colony mission.

Intricate moving plates covered Gabe. Dual shoulder turrets swiveled, looking for targets. I could barely see the small aperture sensors embedded all over his armor. From what I could tell, there must be hundreds. I could just make out the little thruster nozzles from between the plates.

His relatively low-profile backpack, more a bulge than a separate piece of equipment, had an embedded grenade slinger. The slinger was just a skinny arm next to the rail of grenades. I couldn't tell how long it was, but the idea was interesting as fuck to me.

Javelin appeared to be a pile of debris. Her silhouette highlighted in my identify friend or foe. Her suit relaxed, a loose flowing fabric. It was sophisticated stealth; right now, it moved with a disorienting glimmer versus the bay's harsh light. It was complete with a robust sensor on a stick and those mechanical tentacles that gripped onto things. She pulled her shroud into various little compartments on her body armor, but even then, she was hard to see with her smart camouflage active.

It briefly occurred to me that they were on the colony world with me, and I never saw them. Even on the shuttle, she was in the cockpit, and my ass was strapped in the back.

A stupid big rifle, attached by a heavy cable, appeared from behind her. It was almost two meters long. The cable detached from the rifle—or fucking cannon, I should say. It was hardly something practical for anything other than ship-to-ship actions.

Anyway, it dropped onto the deck like we weren't in zero g and landed on four stubby legs. Maybe it was the motion required for the thing to move, but I shit you not, it started *hopping* and turning this way and that. Like a puppy with a new trick that they had to show everyone.

There was a distinct possibility that I had brain damaged, but that fucking personnel portable planetary defense cannon was cute while it—I don't know—randomized its sensor sweeps or whatever the fuck it was doing.

Gabe and Javelin quickly rigged remote fire rifles with basic sensor modules on simple stands. Alexis carefully floated into the compartment, drones blossomed, and our mini maps colored with current information.

Javelin set me as her point, meaning I get shot first, with objective and took her place at a hatch. Javelin and I were tasked with recovery or destruction of the primary and secondary point defense control computers.

I didn't even look at the list of objectives she was asking. Instead, I moved to the overhead based on the tactics we had practiced. We moved quickly, not bothering to clear anything behind the hatches. We rounded a corner and found a gaping hole two decks high, fifty meters or so to our left. The entry hole was the size of my fist, and I realized we were at the wide side of the exit wound.

"What the fuck," I murmured, taking in the tableau of mangled hull and black sky.

"High energy capacitors." Javelin said it almost like an insult. She then highlighted some heavy cables that melted into a bulkhead and, without another word, updated the target priority.

She pinged my feed to accept information from her. I accepted, and much more detailed environmental information populated my HUD. She was getting component manufacturing information, materials quality, and ballistic information.

I found the menu to bring the information flow down to the grunt level.

Alexis' drones added their information to form a composite map. Large areas with known hostiles were marked red. The ship vibrated, and I tensed, afraid that I would be tossed into the void.

Next to the mini map, Javelin's feed discreetly gave the results of some sonic analysis in the form of an ambient information prompt. It showed a general class of point defense turrets. I let it fade as she commanded me to take point down another corridor.

She ordered a halt near a bay. I waited while drones circled the bay, getting a head count and an accurate map. It looked like a machine shop with a fabricator large enough to spit out entire vehicles. The fabricators and supporting equipment became marked priority salvage.

Another long moment passed while the drones did their drone stuff.

She gave me a prepare to breach order and disappeared up a level, cutting through the overhead with her thermal blade. It wasn't as dramatic as in the media. She had to stop and fling hot slag across the compartment.

Think of someone cutting through ten layers of cardboard with a pocket knife. Sure, they're getting through, but it takes a minute, and it's not glamorous.

I placed my cutting line on the bulkhead I was ordered to breach through.

And waited.

I checked my mini map. Gabe and Shantu had formed together and took off down another passageway.

And waited.

I practiced jumping back and forth from the deck to the overhead. I wasn't good at getting the heels of my boots to disconnect, so I was trying to fix that.

And waited.

I also was in complete darkness with my lights off. It was quiet. So quiet I could hear my own breathing and my blood pumping in my ears.

If I let the battle high wear off, I would be asleep in minutes. Fortunately, before I got too bored, the ready chimed, awaiting my reply. I got back into position and replied with my ready.

The staccato of high energy impacts reverberated through my boots.

Less than a second later, my –GO– order came.

I triggered the cutting line. Plasma flashed, and I tried to push my cut through the bulkhead.

And failed…

I didn't account for the dead space between bulkheads—where all the plumbing and electrical ran. A heavy electrical conduit was particularly stubborn. I tried to kick the chunk of bulkhead in and failed. The mass was considerable, so it drifted into the bay like a hungover coworker. It took two more unceremonious tries to get through.

I took the time to spot Gabe's, Shantu's, and Javelin's silhouettes, so I didn't strafe them by accident. I then opened fire, using the two meters of bulkhead as cover as I pushed it forward with my shoulder. A pile of shrapnel ricocheted off my cover and peppered the bulkhead to my left. The impact forced a hearty grunt from me.

Both of my brain cells worked together and let me know that much shrapnel would splatter me, not just puncture my HEPS. I pulled at the limits of my boots and gloves to keep my portable cover positioned and angled optimally.

Peeking around my cover, I found dozens—no, scores—of galunkin concentrating fire at various targets in the overhead. Our drones were falling off the mini map quickly while they redeployed. To my right were chemical processing equipment for the auto fab, and ahead were palletized and secured manufacturing materials.

I requested a scout drone to fly overwatch and map the maze of crap. By that, I mean I gave a panicked yell into the comms, and I'm not sure what words came out of my mouth.

My quick burst from the double tap only strafed the overhead and catwalk they were firing from. My HEPS helmet kept going opaque, leaving me ignorant for a second to save my delicate human retinas from laser backscatter.

I wonder what chemicals can do that. There were no electronics or sensors built into the HEPS.

I pulled a fistful of explosives from my kit, attached it to the floating piece of bulkhead, and added the detonator. I heaved it up and toward the gun emplacement.

This is where I fucked up because I'm stuck to the bulkhead and not deck.

I was going to dive and use the manufacturing materials as cover, but now I was floating up two stories from the deck on a lump of metal with some high explosive between my feet.

That would be a stupid way to die.

I rolled over into a crouch while looking at their silhouettes with my feed, checking galunkin's armor. They were high mass, low velocity torsion-based weapons. Some psychopaths improvised an amalgam of modern materials into dark age weapons. The flak flinger was a pile of salvage and a three-person team. The loader was on an exercise cycle that turned the crank to store the elastic energy.

I don't know why that pissed me off. Here, I was on a spaceship, and there was a little fucker riding a bike that turned a crank that pulled a basket that stretched some elastic material between two poles. Two other little assholes pivoted and turned the whole assembly to aim. It looked to be riveted directly to the catwalk they were on.

I don't know if I actually rolled my eyes, but I like to think that I did.

After finding the grenade assist, I practiced the toss until it turned green for the correct angle and velocity. I set the grenade for proximity and centered an area of effect on their slingshot thing.

I threw the grenade.

The zero g grenades had little gas thrusters to guide them but could only do so much versus a bad throw. My throw was spot on.

An awkward second passed, and I didn't get any return fire. I slung my rifle and scrambled like a roach over to the other side of my floating bulkhead. My training kicked in when I jerked to a stop halfway to avoid an uncontrolled spin.

So, there I was, floating on a plate of metal in the middle of a manufacturing bay like some kind of fish. The grenade had imparted a slow spin, and I would be coming into view soon. I readied myself in a low squat so I could launch myself somewhere if needed. I double-checked the release setting for the mag boots, fixed my previous fuckup, pulled the rifle, and set it to single rail.

And waited.

The grenade detonated.

Shrapnel shredded the fire team and several others around the bay. Chunks of the slingshot bounced around the bay like evil spirits looking for a life to end. A large piece bounced off my magic carpet, accelerating my spin with a painful clang that reverberated through me.

The galunkin on two different levels rotated into my firing arc, and I dispatched them with quick pops, stitching up their heads and torsos.

People talk about how it all happened so fast they don't remember things. But I remember everything.

Upside down and in perfect kneeling firing position, I was ready to leap with my rifle trained on the edge of the bulkhead segment when the first galunkin came into view. It was just poking its helmet around a console after the grenade had exploded maybe thirty meters away. Their domed helmets have opaque visors and no neck, more a blister over their barrel bodies.

I fired until I saw it burst with gas and liquids. I didn't know how many rounds would make it through the console, but the console was obliterated in a shower of brittle composite glass and metal. The creature beyond was nearly cut in half vertically.

A team of five or six were clearly intent on something in the center of them. They could have been assisting the injured or assembling a bomb. I didn't know. I peppered the group with individual shots, moving from one to another and punching clean holes in their vac suits.

On the catwalk above them, another one fired wildly at me with a pistol that didn't seem to fit its hand.

My shots severed that galunkin's left arm. Its friends were scattered around the bay, trying to riddle my segment with poorly aimed panicked shots. I got off two more shots when I flew off my segment. I didn't notice I was sliding back with the recoil. Until my vision tilted in an uncontrolled spin.

My back hit the bulkhead behind me evenly, and an ugly grunt was forced out of me. I sprayed the catwalk and ran toward the nearest sturdy-looking thing. It was the atmospheric processing or maybe fire suppression. Either way, it was big spools of the smart hoses and complicated machinery.

I exchanged fire with the galunkin for a few more seconds. They took quick chance shots and then pulled their limbs back to cover. I might have hit or grazed a few, but that wasn't what mattered. I just didn't want to get shot while I waited for my pièce de résistance. The bulkhead segment finally rotated, and I blew the gob of high explosive.

There was just a hard vibration, and then it was over.

One second, there was a catwalk with galunkin, and the next, there was twisted wreckage and red-orange mist filling the cargo bay. The wreckage of catwalk looked like an evil spiderweb trying to consume a segment of bulkhead, which was sort of bowl shaped now.

Most of the debris was only a few centimeters in diameter. The advanced composites were simply shattered, the hardened bits survived intact.

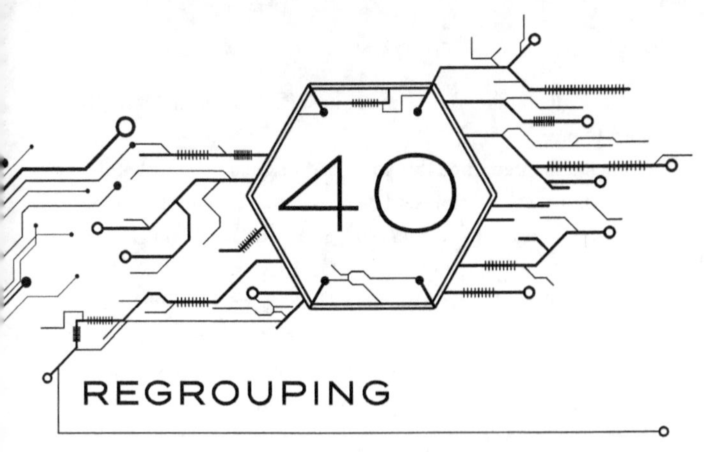

40

REGROUPING

AFTER THE FIGHT in the fabrication compartment, I didn't want to move. Sleep tugged at me as my adrenaline waned.

Marauders had been making slow progress to the point defense computers. But we had retreated twice to resupply. Alexis was working on getting replacement fléchettes. We had hurt the galunkin a lot, so they didn't seem to be in any hurry to come get us in the fabrication bay we held.

"So, what's the plan?" I asked, drinking from the straw in my helmet. I didn't even know what processed paste I was eating; I just wanted something in my stomach. At this point, I had been throwing myself from one end of the ship to the other.

Javelin didn't seem to be showing any signs of fatigue. "Uncertain. With resistance this heavy, I am thinking we reprioritize to disabling individual aft point defenses."

She shared a display of the ship. It was a massive star liner. The drive bell looked almost puny compared to *The Happy Marauder* as a reference.

"How much damage did the ship suffer?" I asked. "It looks intact to me."

She highlighted three thin lines that originated almost at the same point at the ship's nose. The lines divided evenly, punching out just forward of the engineering area. She then highlighted a sphere in the engineering decks. "The main reactor should be here somewhere. If it was damaged while operating at full capacity, it could destroy significant portions of the ship. Standard ship building practices have fail-safes that will initiate a safe shutdown in the event of catastrophic power failures.

"Anticipating your next question, Piper fired at the light. The practice of opening fire at an active sensor sweeps. The time delay in space combat gives the defending ship seconds, even minutes, before the returning light reaches the originating ship. That's why they fired at the primary sensor array; it was the only point of reference. We launched to board before damage could be repaired and secondary systems could be brought online. The point defenses we feel firing are targeting bird dog missiles that use drones to map point defense."

I studied the map for a moment. The reactor we boarded near was a subsidiary reactor for local power, according to the rollover feed. "How big are those holes? What made them?"

Her hard expression almost softened. The same way steel was softer when it was room temperature. "It is an ion cannon. Some call it a plasma cannon. Both are accurate. Ions are projected, and plasma is their energy state."

Because of my genius suggestion, I was on point again.

I was thankful that I didn't bitch through the knot and rope class we had taken. We made tow slings with ammo, grenades, and spare weapons. It was four hours of arts and crafts, pulling cable from everywhere we could find.

Fuck my life.

But we were blessed with a nice nap after that was completed.

Then back to work. Javelin sent me forward on point again. Climbing through the jagged hole, I slowly moved through bulkhead after bulkhead.

Scaling kilometers through the most decimated parts of the ship gave me a lot of time to think.

Thoughts like "Will this jagged piece of conduit puncture my suit?" and "I really need to learn more about ship-to-ship weapons" and "This is a long-ass hole for just one shot." More of my favorites include "I need to shower" and "That will definitely puncture my suit" and "Is that conduit hot?"

I learned a few things from my feed as we went through the hole, which ran mostly through the ship's primary superstructure. The ion cannon is not a laser because there is a stream of matter. Mostly super-freed hydrogen and magnetic metallic particles moving close to the speed of light.

Uh… Something about high energy chemical properties and matter superstates.

My brain made sense of it as a space water jet. It's not how hard it is; it's how fast it is going. Then water passes through a material. It gets polluted and changes how it behaves, which is why the hole we're crawling through is not the size of my fist but the better part of a meter.

Compartment after compartment, cut equipment after cut equipment, we drifted forward. The hole through the equipment must have had something to with liquid handling because of the thick fog that filled the area.

When my mind drifted again, I put on a racial profile learning helper. Outside their suits, the galunkin are naturally aquatic scavengers. Nearly deaf. Their large eyes can see unaided and with vivid light ranges in deep, murky water. They're prone to saturation blindness, dazzle, and long-term degradation.

I pinged Javelin for some flares to use as dazzle concealment. She sent me a lighting drone.

Galunkin are mostly biped, more like a tailless salamander. Their skin texture and colors range across the spectrum, following familial lines. The presence or absence of claws follow so many different genes that selective breeding practices have proven futile. The increased dexterity of those with claws either makes them exceptional or an outsider.

Socially, they are loosely organized in populations determined by proximity or specialization with fluid movement. Their language is highly contextual with little use of proper nouns. A group is often translated into Common as "those who specialize in" with clear signifying markings on their garments. Traditionally, every change in specialization will be placed over the previous with the amount of overlap illustrating either the time or importance.

The helper tool finished its monologue, and I went back to worrying about dying in a suit puncture.

"Are we going to exterminate them all?" The words just fell out of my mouth.

"Yes," Javelin said, emotionless. "Their survival traits do not leave room for coexistence. If we breached the hull, and humans were on the other side, we would have taken hostages instead of opening fire, negotiated an exchange for damages, and went on our way."

"Hostages? Really?"

"Depending on the crew's compliance, yes. That scenario has the most likely positive outcome. We would demonstrate that they would not survive in a fight against us. Limit every other option that doesn't involve compliance and execute dissidence."

I thought about talking about something more in-depth but decided against it. I wasn't in focus anymore. I needed to stay in the game, but it was rough while drifting in the dark, using only low fidelity cameras and ambient light. Zero g was a warm, comfy blanket when you're tired and sore from combat.

They never show that in the movies: someone dozing off while paddling like a dog because it's so easy.

"You're doing well," Javelin said without preamble. Her voice was a few degrees kelvin, but for her, it should have been the core of a star.

"Thanks," I said.

A pause hung in the air like a primed grenade.

Javelin made a noise like she started to say something. Then nothing.

Another long silence stretched into eternity. My thoughts swirled on the infinite possibilities. It was so out of character for her to give a compliment—much less to me. Was she cunning enough to use a huge psychology trick to keep me stay sharp and awake?

If she was, that was clever! It was working!

Hard hits of mind-fuck circulated in my brain. It wasn't fair how the fuck those three words could consume my brain and send me down a waterfall of thoughts and emotions. Complete bullshit. I didn't know what made it more infuriating or intriguing. She had plausible deniability if I called her on it. Worse, I would be an asshole for reading into such a mundane compliment.

What the fuck do you do if you're trapped in a laser hole with a woman who just gave you a compliment but also has you up front to take incoming fire because you're junior to her?

I had never felt so awkward in my life.

Fuck, I was tired.

I was almost excited for the scout drone running ahead of me. Javelin chimed a halt, and we took a moment to investigate the little golf ball's findings.

Two dozen galunkin went back and forth, rebuilding some kind of energy handling apparatus. They were salvaging any-thing with better conductivity than a potato. Arcs of welding flashed, drowning out the lights they had scattered around the compartment.

Javelin flashed a melee icon, and I released my makeshift bandolier and secured it between two pieces of bulkhead. There was a service corridor we would have to cross before reaching the compartment. A team of four maneuvering a crate that's auto guidance seemed to be fighting them.

She flashed a cover icon.

I moved to the right bulkhead and held position. A dim red flashed from her position, and the team stopped moving where they were.

She flashed an enter and cover order, and I jumped across the corridor. The hole here was smooth, melted metal. I gripped it to fling myself around and plant my feet on the bulkhead, and then I slipped into the shadows—unnoticed.

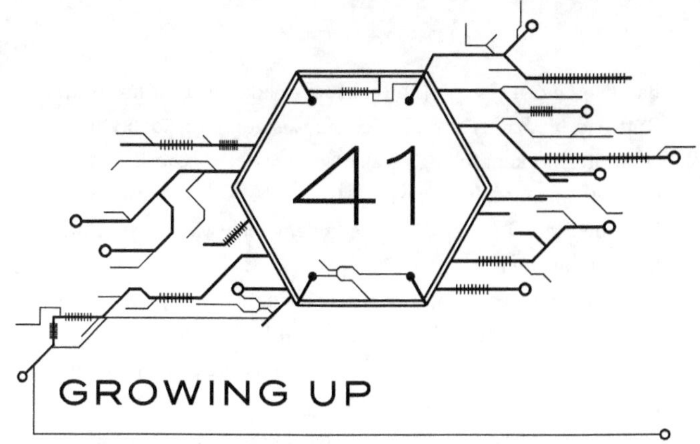

41

GROWING UP

I WAS MAYBE ten now. Shantu and I were inseparable at this point.

At the institute, several crews ran one thing or another, trying to claim something. One ran a gambling ring, another ran a drug trade, and another could get out of the institute to go on adventures. That last one, we had spent time with, trying to plan our escape, but it didn't look good.

One of the older kids who was about to age out told us that we had tags somewhere in our bodies, and CE could pick us up anywhere in the city if we were noticed missing. He had a doctor's appointment to get it removed.

With that thing in our bodies, there was no running. And we were tired of fighting.

Shantu and I waited. We had been trading and fighting and starving to get this knife. It was the best knife, the kind soldiers used.

We were waiting for a kid named Rott because he had killed

Barkly a few weeks ago. The staff said Barkly had hit his head. Rott had hit Barkly's head. No one was going to do anything about it. Rott kept telling us that we were next because we told everyone that he killed Barkly.

At bedtime, I reached for the knife, which was stuck in the plastic of my bed.

Our dorms were two rows of bunk beds along each wall with a bathroom in the back. Simple beds. Six beds on a side. Shantu and I were near the door. Staff should be at the door, watching us sleep.

"Stay in your fucking beds, you ugly bitches!" Rott warned us when he barged into our dorm hours after lights out. He liked to remind us that we weren't pretty anymore. We had gotten too old and too ugly for him.

He then went after the youngest or newest. I didn't know who he had chosen, but the kid put up a screaming fight. I pulled the knife out of the plastic and gripped it tight. Waited for the wrestling sounds to move to the bathroom.

Pillows covered heads like that would stop the horrible sounds.

I didn't know where the staff was. They never stopped this.

I slipped under my bed during the struggle, slid onto my belly, and moved under Shantu's bed. I tapped his bed twice in a way that he would know it was me. We crawled like army men to the end of the bunk and waited. The plan was to stab Rott in the back before he could hurt anyone like he had hurt us.

The memory of when I got to the institute flashed through my brain. I didn't want that.

The new boy was fighting, fighting hard. He had brand-new shoes.

Rott liked to take shoes, so he would always have the nicest things. Even if the shoes didn't fit, he would take them. He'd say they didn't deserve nice, comfortable shoes because they hadn't earned them.

Only Rott could say who deserved what.

I saw Rott's pale, scarred foot and slid the knife across his heel. It smoothly glided for a bit, popped through something, and ground to a halt in bone.

The scream was so loud.

I knew it was Rott. He landed on his knees, clutching at his bleeding heel. He turned, saw me holding the knife, and lunged. I swung with the knife, cutting his hands as he reached under the bed.

Rage burned in his eyes. It wasn't rage as much as a mask of humanity shattering to show the animal underneath. His face twisted in a feral frenzy. He launched the bed across the dorm room, and the other kids screamed, no longer able to hide under their covers.

Someone jumped onto my back, crushing the air out of me. Rott lunged forward, pinning my knife arm to the ground. Out the corner of my eye, Shantu emerged from under his bed. I used what freedom I had in my wrist to flick the knife toward him.

Rott punched my face. My head bounced off the floor, and the world did somersaults without me. I could have smiled when the second blow landed; there was so much less strength behind it.

He let go of me to scramble for the knife, but I hung on tight, keeping him from Shantu.

Someone turned on the light. Blood covered me.

All the boys screamed at once.

Rott was weaker now, but he was still bigger than me and Shantu combined.

He fell on Shantu, trying to get the knife. I jumped on his back, clawing at his eyes and screaming. Shantu wrenched his hand free, slick with blood, and plunged the knife into Rott's chest so hard that I thought he would stab me too.

Rott fell back on top of me.

A second passed. Shantu panted on top of Rott's still body, on top of me.

It wasn't enough.

Rott never stopped when he was on top of me.

I don't remember getting out from under them or getting the knife. But I remember running that knife into Rott so many times that I couldn't move when it was over.

42

MURDER

521.011.0957 FTS *The Happy Marauder*, Interstellar Space

THE MEMORIES OF the only time I had waited in the dark with murder in my heart flashed through my head. I fought then, and I was going to fight now. But I was going to do it on my terms, so my friends got to go on breathing.

Javelin and I spotted light moving and approached, heading aft through the hole Piper had shot into the ship. The light reflected several times down corridors. In the deep dark, you would be surprised how far light could bounce down corridors.

More than a dozen galunkin were scrambling to repair an electrical system. Nets were strung across the compartment with tools and parts tied to it with string. A deep blue work light on a meter-long stick hid my entry through the rent in the hull. It was easy to slide between the crossmember and the bulkhead. I could hide and point my double tap at the back of their heads.

But I couldn't pull the trigger because we were after the equipment they were working on.

I concentrated on keeping my breathing calm and steady as

they moved around. I was in vacuum, but in my head, I could hear my breathing, and therefore, they could hear it.

Javelin and I were set in a two-person scorpion maneuver. I was the claws, meant to engage, while she was the tail, meant to strike and withdraw from a position of mobility. Beyond the basic tactic, I was ordered to cause as little collateral damage as possible to the tools and equipment.

Brawls broke out every few minutes over reasons I had yet to figure out. I was waiting for a bigger brawl or two at the same time. I wanted more of them to be distracted.

Half an hour passed. The fights calmed down, and a working pattern emerged. I tagged each individual with a number just to keep track. The final count was twenty.

As one presented its back on the other side of the netting from the others, I moved before I could think. The primal survivor part of me snapped out with my thermal blade cutting a shallow vertical line up its backpack to avoid the square piece that might be a battery. A few electrical flashes. But I didn't breach the interior of its suit.

I snatched it from the deck and maxed my magnetics, pinning us both to the bulkhead. The galunkin flailed for the auxiliary controls on its helmet, which were centimeters from my faceplate. Its panicked sloshing reverberated through my helmet.

I watched its colleagues for a reaction. The galunkin I held went limp, and I grabbed the next galunkin. And the next. And the next.

It was almost no time at all and all of eternity.

An emotional circuit breaker blew in my head. Numb. I worked my way around the compartment, murdering them all before they even found out I was there. Javelin let me work and managed the bodies for me.

The cold analytical portion of my brain realized I didn't get into their physiology and didn't know why they stopped fighting so quickly. I checked one's faceplate. Its eyes and mouth were half open, unresponsive.

"I didn't breach their suits. Are they really dead?" I asked absentmindedly.

"I know and yes. Stand by." Javelin quickly connected components in the equipment that dominated the compartment.

The AR workspace displayed detailed instructions on how to make repairs. I pushed thingamabobs and doohickies at her. They did stuff with electricity; however, I was far out of my depth. I just followed the pictogram and tried to send her the right items.

The control panel came to life.

After a few more minutes, I got twitchy. Drones had made steady sweeps of the immediate area, but I still wasn't comfortable.

The equipment powered up, and Javelin came around to the front and tapped icons on the display. She tapped one icon repeatedly until the display cycled to Common.

She fucked with the menus for a few minutes. "Reinforcements are on the way."

"What did you do?" I asked. "What do we do now?"

"I set the system to do a fault integrity test. Then power down for maintenance."

WAKING UP

521.011.1234 FTS *The Happy Marauder*, Interstellar Space

WAKEY WAKEY, SPUNKY McBitchFace," Shantu said, pinging my helmet with loose fasteners from around the compartment.

"Five more minutes, then I'll get up I promise." I mumbled.

For a moment we were in our first apartment together, and he was waking me up for work. But the illusion quickly faded as I slapped my faceplate, trying to rub my eyes.

"Fuck," Gabe said over the common channel.

"That's right," Shantu said. "Told you. Now give it up."

"What the…" I grumbled, opening my eyes to find a sword in one hand and a pistol in the other. I'm sure that's why Shantu kept his distance.

Javelin and I had made it back to the fabrication bay, and I had fallen asleep at some point.

"I bet Gabe that you would be all cute and shit when you woke up," Shantu said, on a roll. "You did not disappoint. I want to kiss you right now! This is so exciting!"

"Fuckstick," I grumbled.

"Fucknuts!"

"You watch me when I sleep?"

"Dude, this sword is so awesome: monoatomic electro dynamic cutting surface, ultrasonic destabilizer in the spine, active molecular spectrometer in the guard, biometric scanner in the grip—"

"How long have you been watching me sleep?" I asked.

I was, of course, ignored when Javelin chimed in. "Just like all of ours."

Shantu didn't hesitate. "Yeah, but this one was Gabe's personal weapon, not part of the ship's inventory. Look right here."

He turned the sheath to show where Gabe had written on it in permanent marker. —Gabriel Martinez's Personal Weapon. Do Not Inventory.—

"*Martinez?* Why the shit do you have a human surname?"

Gabe shrugged. "I'm adopted."

"When did you start watching me sleep?" I wasn't letting this go.

"What about my first name?" Gabe asked.

"I thought it was that thing that a lot of species do," Shantu said. "You know, where it's either a cultural or phonetic approximation. That or a nickname to save everyone a lot of time and effort. Honestly, I haven't given it that much thought. This is a weird conversation to be having sober."

"So, being intoxicated makes etymology and nomenclature appropriate?"

"No. It makes discussing them interesting."

"Fucking shit!" I yelled. "Will you two give it a rest? What is going on, and why do you watch me sleep?"

"Uh, no. We will not rest," Shantu said. "Going down these topic lines brings out the most obscure fucking details that no one gives a shit about. We can listen to generators run next to each other. Sure, they're making noise, and they're together, but that doesn't mean they're communicating."

I turned my helmet around to scrub my face on the helmet pad. Why the fuck was my best friend arguing with a guy who didn't need to breathe? Not to mention, he had like five different graduate courses. The only secondary education we had was mostly taught by him.

Un-fucking-believable.

I turned the volume down on their banter and reviewed the ship's map. Alexis was in the main reactor, chilling with the two mules and most of the combat drones. We had a point-to-point comm to her via the hole Javelin and I had drifted through. No one had bothered her or the drone we left on patrol in the machine shop.

"Javelin, when are the reinforcements coming in?" I asked. "And what's the plan from there?"

She highlighted a shuttle bay near us. Then highlighted the machine shop and the primary reactor. "Presumably, we will secure the ship, starting with isolating and firing up the primary reactor. Then we will print networked drones and purge the galunkin from the ship."

"You mean kill all the galunkin."

I couldn't see her roll her eyes, but when she sent me a file with documentaries, analyses, and interviews, I felt one.

The galunkin memory tended to be fickle things. Ship-to-ship actions tended to be remembered as a natural disaster. Something along the lines of "it was awful, but we survived." However, individual combat was taken very personally.

A technician defending their own life while cornered has started more than one war against star liner companies. Individual offenses often grow into crusades through constant embellishments in the retelling of stories. The practice of cold extermination of galunkin has drastically reduced the number of such crusades.

"Point taken," I said. "Then what do we do with the ship? Scrap it? Repair it?"

"I don't know. We need a full survey," Javelin said coldly. "Determine what we can and can't do. I do not want to speculate ahead of information. Concentrate on the goals ahead. *The Happy Marauder* needs environmental systems and food. We should be sitting on a good supply of both. Everything beyond that is not necessary."

I thought on that until my feed pinged me to head to the nearby hangar. I then realized I was a space door man. "Shantu, we really are moving up. A million kilometers from home, and we're getting paid to open doors for people."

"Quit your bitching," he said. "This is hardly a door. It's a three-stage recovery bay."

"Uh-huh. And what are you doing? Getting the door open for the boss."

He grunted, messing with some portion of the side of his mechanism. "Yeah. By dismantling the power mechanism. In zero g. In a HEPS." He gave a hearty grunt as he pulled a connection. "It's a whole new life," he added with exaggerated cheeriness.

"Seriously though, how are you holding up?" I said, prying off the same power conduits. I found something that looked like a safe plug, just shaped insulation.

"I'm okay. Gabe is a lot of fun. He really takes the edge off. This isn't like the games. But in some ways, it is," Shantu said. "Like it is just point and shoot. The games add in noises where there shouldn't be. It's all so quiet in a vacuum, you know. You don't know you're being fired at unless you see one of their goddamned crossbow things. I know we've never killed on this scale. It's full-blown slaughter here. At one point, I cut through a window, stuck my rifle through it, and used the barrel scope to shoot. They couldn't hit back, you know. They tried, but the window was pressure rated."

When he stopped talking, I filled the space. "I killed like

twenty of them by disabling their suits and holding them down while they drowned in their own piss."

"What?" he asked between grunts.

"I looked up the configuration of their suits and what I was disabling was the mechanism that filters the fluid they live in. When it loses power, it releases everything into the suit. They have a manual backup on their helmet, but they must activate it. I held them, so they couldn't. I held them for the rest of their lives. After the first one, I thought one of them would notice, and a firefight would break out. It took me almost two hours, but I killed them all without ever alerting one."

"Is that how you got the point defense shut down?"

"Yeah. Javelin said something about a testing and maintenance cycle. We had a plan where once it got kinetic, she was going to dive in, but it never did. I'm sure she thought that would help my combat rating and just left me to it."

"Gabe never let me out of his sight. It was nice, you know. He takes things to the face that would kill a human by g forces alone. But after a little while, I thought he was getting reckless. I guess he got a good reading on their weapons and took off down a corridor, spinning and shooting. He was way above normal human reaction times. I watched the video slowed down. He took a lot of direct hits, but his armor adjusted the plates to ricochet. His shoulder turrets did the most damage with their independent targeting. Scary stuff, you know? But we need some armor like that."

"How much do you think that armor costs?"

Shantu thought for a moment. "Millions. But I don't think it's that simple. There's support equipment. I just assumed the senior crew kept their armor in their cabin."

"Makes sense. I never looked into armors because we're always in our AVs. Never thought I could afford one. I should watch one of those before-you-buy videos. I do like the idea of a layered system. Like a skin suit that has detachable plates to make it lightly armored and then a heavier one with all the toys like Gabe's. I have no intention of carrying around a sniper rifle set for orbital bombardment."

"Well, sign me up for a copy except I want the light plates part of the armor. Like the captain's when we met him."

We talked about preferences and mostly bullshit. It was good for us, just to talk while we work.

But that went to shit when Shantu was Shantu. "So, did you try to fuck the ice queen?"

"First off, you're an asshole. Second, she's *senior* crew. Third, we've been in a hard vacuum since we got here."

It kind of spiraled out of control from there, and I endured. Mostly, I was a sounding board while he honed his jokes and repartee. He often said he didn't give a shit what people think, but that was because I didn't. He cared a lot. Mostly, he wanted to entertain people.

Maybe in a different life, he could have been a comedian.

OPENING DOORS

GAABBEEE!" SHANTU YELLED into the common channel with the whiniest affectation he could muster. "You have power armor. Come help us crank. We're tired."

This was the third time.

Shantu and I dismantled the automatic drive mechanism and were using the manual release. This door was the size of a stadium field. It was designed to allow entrance and egress of passenger shuttles.

Hundreds of manual release handles lined the door's periphery in a complicated cam system. But only two of us were working them like ski poles. It had been three hours, and we had moved the several hundred-meter door six fucking centimeters. At this rate, it would take us like thirteen hours to clear the pressure interlock, and that doesn't include a break. This thing was designed for a crew of thousands.

"You're doing great. Keep up the good work," Gabe answered with the best affectation to an absent father figure from TV.

"Quit your bitching," Alexis said. "The first set of servos are on their way. Thank Javelin that she found them and the battery packs. You two idiots, listen up because I—"

"What?" Shantu and I asked in unison while looking at each other.

"Listen because—"

"Huh?" we said together.

"List… You fuckers. Here!" They sent a basic workspace sketch over the feed on how to rig the servos and a few notes about tolerances and performance. They had done the wiring with a few spare components and more than a few guesses. All we had to do was weld it in place and turn a dial.

A drone climbed into the bay, dragging an odd bouquet of parts behind it. Relief flooded me as I kicked off the deck to meet the thing. It was a simple frame with four magnetized legs, a lightly encapsulated body, a few sensors, and a little antenna in the center.

"Thanks, little buddy. Never mind that big bad person who controls you," I said to the drone to trigger Alexis.

"Super fucking weird when you do that," they responded.

I ignored them and petted the drone like it was a puppy. They tried to maneuver it out of the way.

"Oh sorry. I can't play right now, cutie. I have to go to work, but I'll see you later."

Shantu laughed.

I undid the clip that held all the parts together and freed the little device. "Bye!" I said with what I hoped was an uncomfortable amount of enthusiasm.

"Still not okay," Alexis said.

An hour later, Shantu and I had them rigged and on. I switched to thermal to see both the batteries and the electric motors alarmingly rising in temperature.

"Uh, Alexis, how confident are you in your wiring?" I asked.

"Not. I'm happy they came on and didn't go out in a blue smoke of doom," they replied. "Go live."

I did.

They mumbled while trying to do math. "Fuck it. Max them out. Either we'll deplete the batteries, or they'll explode. Either way, we're going to get as much energy into opening those doors as possible."

"If they go, will they take out the mechanism?" Shantu asked, oddly the voice of reason.

"Fuck, I don't know. I'm not even sure if they're really batteries. I doubt it. Doesn't matter. I need you here."

A red arrow appeared on the mini map, and I zoomed in. Javelin and Gabe were moving to flank.

"We're on the way. Tell us what you know," Shantu said, maxing out the last of the servos before following me.

"Gabe and Javelin have been killing a few here and there, trying to expand our parameter forward," they said. "They've been finding a lot of booby traps and secured doors."

I zoomed in on Gabe, who was actively using his grenade flinger to depopulate a compartment. The corridor he was retreating from was a mess of bodies and debris. Large chunks of metal just big enough to fit float down the corridor. The random mess made it impossible to fight. Dead bodies absorbed shrapnel from the grenades. The metal chunks deflected the rail and moved too much for a laser to burn through.

A mass of pissed off galunkin charged down a three-by-three service corridor. The occasional outrunner would charge forward, pushing and dispersing the mess further down the hall. One wielded a hand cart like a giant shield while its wheels spun wildly without gravity.

Gabe gave a quick burst, and the runner died, but the mob pressed forward. Javelin calmly welded heavy chunks of metal in place, completely indifferent to the carnage barreling toward her.

A black circle appeared in the mass. Not a circle. A tube. Maybe a plumbing pipe. What the fuck were they doing? Were they going to use it as…a battering ram? It coughed white vapor, and chunks of metal and ceramic crap flew down the corridor in a shotgun blast.

Gabe launched himself into a ball, seemingly to defend Javelin with his body. He grunted as the shrapnel slammed him into the bulkhead. He bounced off another bulkhead as his thruster system and magnetics tried to bleed off his kinetic energy.

Shantu and I picked up dangerous amounts of momentum, floating down the corridor and toward the center of the ship.

"Calm down, boys. My armor can take it," Gabe said in a soothing, slightly entertained voice. "That trick isn't for things with bra-ains in coconuts." He grunted with another bounce.

Shantu and I slowed our pace, and he uncoiled himself just in time to land belly down on the bulkhead, opening rail fire with his rifle right down the center of the pipe. He traced a slow circle around the outside of the pipe. Red fins deployed. Fluid circulating in tiny channels that almost looked like vascularity.

A grenade flew from over his shoulder and went down the barrel of their makeshift shotgun. He launched straight up and stuck to the opposite bulkhead, only as his previous position got mutilated by shrapnel from his own grenade.

Javelin stood to look at her work, almost seeming proud. She ducked into a compartment, and Gabe launched himself after her. They hurriedly worked the blast doors closed until the mechanism slammed to a stop. She calmly strolled to a valve in the pipework and gave it a yank. All the drone feeds on that side of the door ended, engulfed in blue-white flames.

After a ten count or so, she jerked the valve closed. She and Gabe worked the door open with significantly more effort than it took to close it. The door ground to a halt less than halfway open.

Alexis sent a drone through as Shantu and I reached the door on the opposite side. The corridor was scorched in a nightmarish hellscape. Everything was bowed and melted in a swirling twisting style that made the hard metal corners look organic. The service corridor looked like the inside of burnt intestines.

"What the fuck did you do?" Shantu asked.

"I rerouted an emergency chemical thruster down the corridor," Javelin said calmly, like she was reading from a technical manual. "Please be aware that you'll have to decontaminate before you enter a habitable area because the residue is quite caustic."

45

MANAGED EXPECTATIONS

521.012.1922 FTS *The Happy Marauder*, Interstellar Space

YOU HAD TO go and fucking say something! *Had* to just say *if there is no counterattack*," Shantu chided Gabe on the common channel. "You couldn't have just kept your big mouth shut."

The galunkin had been pressing us in a hundred different ways. There was a feed about iconography on the left side of my vision that would probably explain everything if I had time to read it.

"Will you shut the fuck up and kill something?!" I snapped at Shantu.

"Oh, I'm going to kill something," Shantu said. "I'm going to—"

"SHANTU!" I shouted, and I didn't give a fuck who heard.

The galunkin had been doing hit and run attacks, trying to draw us into an ambush or lure us away from the reactor. It had turned into a war of movement, and we were all tired and wearing out.

Shantu had been reminding Gabe that he jinxed it, but I was tired of the distraction.

I guessed the galunkin security forces were responding, not the technicians, because they were in powered armor that could shrug off a lot of damage and had thruster packs that helped them move. Real weapons too. Not that homemade speargun shit. Worse, they were smart and disciplined enough to not over-commit to an engagement.

We struggled to keep up with the constantly shifting points of contact. I would be engaging ten, and then it would just be one of them firing down the corridor. Javelin's armor and a couple of the drones identified the weapons by the laser signature. That was how we noticed what they were doing.

It was a horrible tango as they tried to find a hole in our defenses or make one. Move and countermove. They had the advantage of numbers and mobility. Their people could rest, and we couldn't.

The math said we were going to lose.

The homing grenades they used worked against them. So, I didn't count them as one of their advantages. Galunkin had short arms and couldn't throw the way humans could. They had to underhand toss, exposing them for way too long.

Our combat link had kept count and assigned individuals serial numbers. We had identified, with low confidence, at least three hundred of them with no group over ten. Unless they were changing armor or some crazy shit, they were cycling their forces out to manage their fatigue.

They rotated with a relieving squad at about the two-hour mark. I wanted to rotate out.

My aim was going to shit. Even in zero g, I was sluggish and struggled to manage my mag boots. Everything hurt because of how many times I slammed into things.

"Gabe, I need situational awareness," I said. "Where the fuck is our reinforcements? How are we getting resupply? Where did they get their armor, and why didn't we see it?"

I didn't have the authority to order Gabe to do shit, but no one said anything.

"They have individual access denial weapons patrolling the outside of the ship," Gabe said. "We're getting our resupply from drones. They're pulling almost forty g's to get here, and they're taking out like one in four." A series of bursts crossed his mic. "I am working off the assumption that we killed the one that focuses on engineering, and now we're fighting their warriors. They know they're outmatched for fire power, so they're using guerrilla tactics."

"Well, it's fucking working," I spat. "We're all still breathing because of sheer fucking luck. Can't we bring *The Happy Marauder* in close and use her point defense or something?"

"No. Her point defense would shred this ship while we're still on it."

"So, either you or Javelin need to go out there," I said as flatly as I could.

"Javelin is the only one who has the optics for something like this," Gabe answered.

"If I change roles now, the loss of my active combat power will undoubtedly cause a shift in tactics," Javelin objected.

Okay. I was fatigued. We were all fatigued. Except maybe Gabe. But grouchy didn't even begin to describe how we were. The mental strain alone was enough to break people.

This is why I am falling in love with *The Happy Marauder*. My bosses and I are on the same page, and we're arguing the *details*. Arguing as in giving reasons or citing evidence. Not insulting each other and playing the blame game with a bullshit veneer of professionalism. My superiors are making sense, even if I don't agree.

"What's the transit time for the shuttle?" I asked.

"I see where you're going," Gabe said. "Ideally, thirty-eight minutes if Piper is flying. Twice that for the captain. Only the final approach matters. The last fifteen seconds or so."

"Can anyone else fly a shuttle?" This shit was above my pay grade, but I wasn't going in a bag because I didn't ask a question.

"Just me."

"You are not qualified to fly under combat conditions," Javelin said. She said it like if Gabe was at the stick, she would stay here and live longer.

"I'm barely through the basic class. So…let's put that under no other options."

I needed to learn to be this chill under combat conditions.

"Javelin, can you do that?" Gabe asked. "Buy them a solid minute to get into that bay?"

"If I do this, one of you will die," Javelin said. "Right now, we're steady. They are falling at an appreciable rate. I say wait and see if there is a decline in their combat power before we change tactics."

I was not in a steady state. Getting shot at was not a steady state. She was calm enough to almost make it true though.

Sgt. Tok had taught us how to monitor our fatigue. Not I'm-tired-and-I-want-a-nap fatigue. But the did-I-just-throw-a-grenade-without-priming-it fatigue. I was there. The next level was I-primed-the-grenade-without-throwing-it fatigue. I wanted relief before that.

"How about two hours?" Gabe offered.

Javelin clicked in the affirmative.

After fifty-eight minutes zipped by, the galunkin pulled something new out of their asses: a half meter metal ball. More like a medieval flail, it had spikes and jets that sent it bouncing down the corridors like something from a terrible video game. I didn't know what kind of guidance system it had, but it never seemed to target anyone directly. Nor did it follow a predictable ricochet path. I could imagine its programming being limited to "fuck up things in that direction, and don't come back."

As they exhausted their limited fuel supply, the metal balls exploded.

When I saw the first one, I was locked onto the overhead, lying down. Just my head and rifle peeked around the corner. The metal ball bounced off two opposing bulkheads like a bouncy ball. I didn't think. I just fired even when the fléchettes ran out. I ran half a power cell down the corridor before I did enough damage to make it explode. The white flash made me flinch, and my exo-frame pulled me back.

"New fucking problem." I tagged the threat for everyone and then wrestled my voice into something calmer, trying to be Gabe. "Javelin, if you could be so kind as to get us some cover, so we can get some relief."

The intercom chimed and cut out before she could reply. Gabe's line was active, so I assumed she was getting convinced by someone more qualified than me. I checked the mini map, and she broke contact as she left the ad hoc battle net.

I went back to my first cultural exchange with the galunkin. Then a thought struck my mind. "Gabe, are we the pirates here?"

I should not be having those thoughts as I was shooting murderballs out of the…corridor. I wanted to say *air*, but we were in a vacuum.

"That's a complicated question," he answered, sounding excited to have a philosophical debate. "The galunkin would certainly think so. But if we kill them all, not only will there be no one to contest our claim on this ship, we would be respecting their cultural traditions and practices, save the mutilation and cremation. There's still time for that."

"This ship is also a Wandathu design, a luxury star liner. They don't sell their ships. They lease them, but the bulk of their crew will always be Wandathu. Typically, the Wandathu would tout us as heroes if we gave the ship back to them. Quietly, they would go through whatever government is available to bill us for the damage."

"What the fuck?" I returned. "We blasted three big ass holes through the ship. I assume Piper didn't do that for giggle shits."

"What I got before we left is that we got a high intensity sensor sweep, indicative of a weapons targeting. Piper bracketed the ping because there was no hail. Think of shooting at a flashlight in the dark. When we get to Fermi Station, we'll get a broker and see what we can get for it. *Hulls*"—Gabe said the word with emphasis, like there was a large portion of economics involved—"are worth more than the materials. The whole-is-greater-than-the-sum-of-the-parts kind of thing."

I was watching the turret feed for a moment, trying to look for a weakness in their tactics. We had transformed the two decks forward of the engineering levels into the space equivalent of trench warfare with area denial turrets and drones. The galunkin kept us at bay with the bouncing bombs. They also probed our defenses by cutting through the decks, where we would have to respond. They had the numbers if they attacked in mass from multiple fronts. Maybe their communication gear wasn't that complex for a coordinated attack like that. Or perhaps they were afraid.

I was vaguely aware that my body was moving.

I bounced from cover to cover. What was my hand doing? Right. Reloading. I smiled as I realized all those drills in zero g off-loaded that task to something deeper like breathing.

In the ship's vacuum, I used a thick structural bulkhead as cover. The compartments between us had turned into mangled piles of death as explosion after explosion destroyed the soft dividing walls.

It was like I was a holy avenger, trying to keep the creatures from climbing up the depths. Standing, I looked down. That was the easiest way for me to fire from cover: just lean forward a bit and either take potshots down the corridor or try to throw a grenade. If there was power in the area, there weren't any surviving lights. Just a long hole with murderous fucks trying to get me.

With the last burst of return fire, I spun in a circle. I counted on them seeing my backpack and thinking I was fleeing. After setting a ninety-second timer, I waited.

The timer went off. I turned on my helmet light and mag dumped.

There had to be at least two dozen or two squads… whatever… down there. They all turned their big bulbous heads away from the light. Which were shredded by me pumping fléchettes into their faceplates. The powered armor helmet with no neck held for a few cycles before the combination of thermal and kinetic shock was too much.

I vividly remember how much pressure it took to work my double tap for the base where their faceplates met their helmets. I was missing more than I was hitting, but I tried to hit every target at least once.

I cut my light, threw a grenade, and leaned back to reload. Switch to double tap. Not full auto. Sidestep as many times as I could until the grenade exploded. The shrapnel vibrated my cover.

Light on. Lean forward. "GABE!"

The galunkin were using their dead as cover to rush me. I was target fixated, trying to shoot through the dead bodies as they flew toward me.

I was then in that place when too many things changed at once, and my brain took a moment to catch up. My targets were gone.

"You're welcome," Gabe said.

"What was that?" I asked.

"Missile." His weapon's fire chattered over the word.

"Oh."

Of course he had missiles.

We went back to trading potshots from a couple hundred meters away. I was so tired; my sense of time was slipping. It felt like hours. They started with their bombs again.

So many unknowns. Could they tell it was just me walking in circles, shooting down this hole, and waiting for one of their bombs to get me? Did they think there were a few people taking turns? Why didn't they just booby-trap the place and move?

Could Gabe smoke them with another missile?

I didn't want to move up because that was too far away from what resupply I was getting, and if we lost a drone, we were fucked. I looked at the map, trying to figure out if there was a reason they were pushing in one place and not another. What asset were they trying to defend or use? Did some lift tube provide access for mobility? Were they manufacturing these bombs to counter us, or did they have a stockpile?

Either way, there was an origin point and a target.

"Gabe, is there any way you can get them to stop throwing bombs down the corridors? Like—I don't know—kill them at their source?" I asked, wincing at how condescending it came across.

"Geez, Mono. I wish I had thought of that. Only they're deployed evenly across our lines, and we can't spare anyone to go hunting."

"Are they making them to counter us, or is it a stockpile?" I was annoying myself if I'm honest.

"Great fucking question. We don't know. Javelin and I had this talk already. They're made from local materials. They could have been stockpiling them for trade, or they have a good manufacturing ability. They've been consistent in their deployment. If you figure something out, let me know." He killed the connection.

Shantu reopened it. "Gabe, can you throw up a live assessment map? I know I'm slipping."

A tab appeared near the mini map. It gave a general combat power numerical score for us and them, based on all known criteria. Our scores fluctuated pretty evenly with theirs. Individually, we were faster and more accurate, but their armor could take a lot of punishment.

And the projections sucked. If they managed to suppress Javelin and shoot down three resupply drones in a row, we were fucked. If any one of us fell, we were fucked.

They were surviving, so whatever advantage we had there really didn't matter.

"Fuck. Can we get some armor piercing rounds, missiles?" I asked out of frustration for the cold indifference staring at me in the form of data.

"This is a terrible place to use missiles, and the AP load got shot down," Gabe said. "A mixed load will be here in four minutes."

"Oof. Fuck," I grunted as a drone slammed into the back of me. It quickly discharged its supply of ammo and exchanged power cells into my exo-frame before disappearing back down the corridor. "What the fuck?!" I yelled at Alexis.

My heart stopped when I realized nothing came back.

I quickly checked our battle link. A drone showed that they had left their position in the reactor compartment. They were fucking with an area denial turret at the junction of a primary lift and two of the largest corridors for that deck. Two larger tracked drones intermittently fired up the shaft, covering them as they worked.

Alexis fixed whatever the fuck they went there to fix and started back down the shaft. The drones spewed death in the way only machines could, cold cycles from one target to the next. The galunkin fighters weren't feeding their bodies into the meat grinders; they were launching their damned bombs.

A red emergency alert flashed across my HUD. Red was very bad. Fix-it-before-someone-dies bad.

Alexis' icon flashed red. I took cover to see them and switched views, struggling to get their suit's banana out of the slot—the ones used to amputate a limb. They pulled the banana, and their left leg was severed in an angry red flash of sparks. Their leg was held in place by the exo-frame as the last of the blood vaporized out the hole in his ankle. Their icon went from flashing red to orange.

Orange means it's working but not for long.

Alexis' icon went black and dark. It was subdued and fell behind the torrent of other combat data.

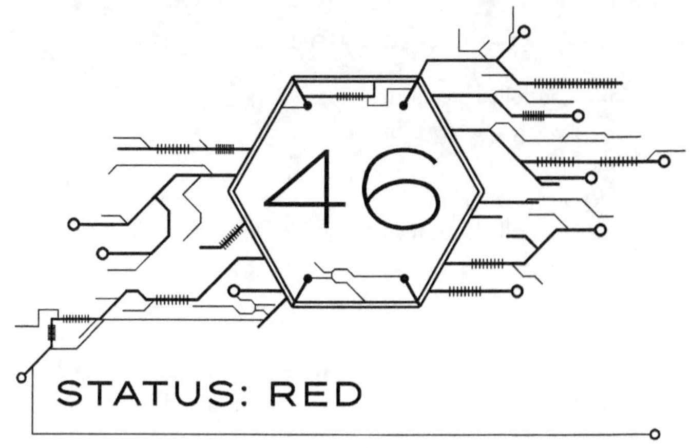

STATUS: RED

HEY, FUCKNUTS. I can't keep up. I'm too tired," Shantu called to me from a distant place in my mind. I think it was the common channel. "Fucker, fall back! We've done enough! Reinforcements are here!"

Shantu was yelling at me. Why was he yelling at me?

My body slapped me with its exceeded limits. Every muscle ached—no, *burned*. My face plate fogged from my breath, and sweat swam in my visor. I braced against a bulkhead with a pile of galunkin warriors. Nothing moved under me, so they all must be dead.

My sword was stuck, but I couldn't let go of it. What was my left hand doing? I couldn't turn my head to see it, but it was holding something. My body told me not to let go of that either. I took a deep breath and tried to will my heart to slow down. My lips were numb, and my vision was narrow. I tried to see the analog gauges on my HEPS, but my eyes wouldn't focus.

Deep slow breath in.

Long controlled breath out.

Just like Sgt. Tok taught us.

One.

Deep slow breath in.

Long controlled breath out.

Two.

When I reached five, I could see and think again. "Ah, fuuucckkk."

Violent, painful spasms racked my body. I tried to take a pull at the nipple inside my helmet, but both water and paste were empty.

"It's okay, buddy. I'm here. Let's see." Shantu patted my HEPS, applying pressure seals. "Patches are holding. Your oxygen medium is good. Barely touched your spare tank," he lied as he replaced a tank on my HEPS. He patted me down. "Your frame is beat to shit. Oh, here's the problem." He added that last line with a frightened tone.

"What?" I asked. "Is there another hole?"

"You're a crampy little bitch." He tried to pull me from the pile. "Let go of the sword."

"I can't."

I guessed he was going to peel my hand off when he looked at the blade. "No shit," he said with disbelief. "You fused the grip with your glove. How the fuck did you do that?"

Fatigue warred with pain for my attention, and my head swam as I tried to focus. "How the fuck should I know?" came out as "Hiuko."

"You take a nap," my best friend said. "I got you."

HONORABLE RETREAT

521.014.1200 FTS *The Happy Marauder, Interstellar Space*

I WAS SLAPPED awake in the way only pharmaceuticals could jumpstart your brain.

Dire-horn hovered over me. No, he was floating in front of me. Long lines of fibrous brown material floated away from him to a spool.

Was he crocheting?

I was on the bulkhead in the med bay. The beds were configured against the bulkheads because of the zero g. Shantu was in the bed next to me between me and the hatch. The overhead had the deployable medical beds stowed between the lights with other medical supplies filling every nook and cranny with high-capacity auto straps.

I wasn't in any pain.

Wait. I couldn't feel anything other than my face. I looked around. My left knee was encased in a clear box while little mechanical arms sunk long needles into it. My right hand was in an egg of gel.

"Good afternoon," Scout greeted me, holding a squeeze bulb up to my lips.

I coughed and then took a drink. He waited patiently.

"Status?" I asked after draining the bulb.

I don't know if it was a racial trait or his job to measure my reactions, but he seemed to be flatter than calm.

"We lost Alexis." He paused. "You, Ryan, Xi, Uvwewe, and Shantu are wounded and combat ineffective. All are expected to make a full recovery. *The Happy Marauder*'s life support system is overloaded. Preliminary salvage reports show supplemental equipment is available, pending securing the ship."

"Can I see my medical chart?" I asked.

Scout pulled a tablet from a slot on the wall, attached it to an articulated arm, and placed it in my view on my left side. "How is that?"

I nodded, and he hit the icon for it to use my eye movements as a cursor. I took a second to calibrate it before reading.

Right hand, 1.5 percent, complete palmar aspect to include digital surfaces, thermal contusion with chemical features. Blah, blah, blah. I burned the fuck out of my right hand and poisoned myself by melting the HEPS glove. I also tore up my left knee by bouncing around in zero g and got two holes punched into my left calf, turning it into hamburger. Give or take the cryo and hard vacuum damage done before I could patch the holes in my HEPS.

Doc had a nerve block in my spine, so he could operate on me while I was awake. The prognosis projections showed two days of surgical rebuilding and three months of rehab.

I checked Shantu's tab. He took two pieces of shrapnel to the abdomen and lost a chunk of his bowel. Scheduled for a follow-up surgery in a month. He would be fine.

"All right, Scout. I know why you're here," I said. "What questions do you want to ask?"

"How are you?" he asked in a way of eliminating bullshit.

"I'm fucked up." I glanced around the med bay. "We lost Alexis, and I thought our line was going to fall. We were going to die. I thought that if I dug a little deeper, each kill would buy me another minute to live, you know?"

He didn't respond.

"The next thing I know, I'm cramping up, and I can't use my right hand."

"Yes, your thermal blade battery failed," he supplied. A long silence passed as Dire-horn placed a hand on his shoulder. "I'll be available if you need me." He excused himself.

Dire-horn stepped up and took a long sniff up my neck and the side of my head on both sides. His whiskers tickled my face. I wondered if my butthole was puckering because I couldn't feel it.

What the fuck was he doing?

"I would know the scent of a true warrior," Dire-horn said.

I knew I was giving him the freaked-out side-eye, but he continued.

"For my people, when a weapon appears in your hand at a needed time and brings you home safely, it is known as Tet: a friend who will walk with you. Tombstone is your Tet. This is your Tet." He produced a piece of scrap metal that was vaguely shaped like a hatchet or an adventure climbing ax thing.

He turned the tablet and pulled up drone footage of my thermal blade frying.

My memory coalesced with the footage.

I was gassed and burned. Go ahead and stick a fork in me because I was done. I had crashed through hard limits and kept going. Intermittently blacking out because my HEPS couldn't cycle fast enough to strip the carbon off the oxygen. I rode that line just enough to see my next target and then swung with everything I had.

Alexis fell. The resupply drones started falling. I was next.

Someone called for a retreat. I didn't know who. Might have been me. We did our best to fall back to the hangar. The turrets were running dry, and our line was falling. It was only Gabe, Shantu, and me holding key points without those turrets. We would get flanked, and no one would even know my story.

I rounded the corner to a corridor where the galunkin were cutting through the overhead. Dust covered everything from the circular saw kind of thing they used.

I couldn't see shit, save the sparks overhead. I guessed at where to stab by the sparks and rammed my blade straight up through the overhead. I wanted to kill the operator. Maybe even the machine.

Two explosions. The first fried my thermal blade. I guess I hit the power pack or something because the overhead violently deformed, bouncing me off the deck. Saw stars from that hit. I'm sure my exo-frame was the only thing that kept my neck from snapping like a twig. I couldn't feel anything. My hand just went numb. But I could smell burning meat in my HEPS.

Bacon. I smelled like bacon getting cooked.

The second explosion forced the overhead to peel downward like a blooming flower. The overpressure cleared the dust, and there I was—in a perfect position to make a difference.

I don't remember grabbing the chunk of metal. But there it was in my left hand. My right hand was ruined, the thermal blade fused into the overhead.

I caught the the first galunkin off guard completely, hooking the pick-ax under its armpit. It didn't puncture its suit. I maneuvered it into range, wrapped my legs around it, and pulled with everything I had. The armor buckled just enough to break the seal. I used the dying galunkin as a shield, shoving that one into the group that was already drifting down the hole. Their canceled momentum made it a crawling furball.

A hand gripped the flowered deck metal. I seized it and yanked it toward the overhead so hard that my boots broke contact. I used my side arms to shoot visors at close range.

It was surreal.

Armored heads looked down from opposite sides of a hole. I planted my feet to swing around in a stripper pole drop kick.

I should have pulled the banana. I didn't think of it, I was so exhausted.

Breeched galunkin flailed and bounced off every surface in the narrow hole. The drone didn't show the panic I felt or the galunkin that nearly broke my ankle with their powered grip. It only showed me jerking my leg back, dragging the galunkin with it, and firing at the elbow and shoulder to free myself.

I stopped the video to see what Dire-horn was doing. He had wrapped the bottom third of the handle in a beautiful organic weave.

"It was there when your other weapons had failed you," he said. "I have wrapped your handle, to honor the occasion. In the weave, you will find the words *one step closer*. To your ears, it should mean *closer to home and closer to perfection*. It will show you as worthy to any minotaur." His rumbling bass ended with a kind of reverence. "These are my ways; I invite you to them."

"Thank you. This means a lot." My discomfort translated into my voice. "Uh… You've given me a lot to think about."

He used a general latch to secure it to the bulkhead near my bed.

I drifted off to sleep before I realized it. The good drugs sleep.

A buzzing noise woke me.

Scout shoved Doc and hit something on a console. "Preparations incomplete." His ears were up and flushed with pulsing blood in the thin membrane. Almost like in panic. "Data processing not secured. Defense and reactionary measures will activate."

"What the fuck?" I crossed my eyes and tried to move my head away from the drill that was a centimeter from my forehead.

He sighed in a very human way, shifting gears. His ears pulsed with blood and then waved before going down. "You have a few aneurysms. Doc…changed his schedule, and I'm glad I caught it in time. The praportorian buds don't understand terms like"—he paused—"*freak the fuck out* because he's drilling into your skull while you're sleeping."

I would have given him the side-eye for matching my words almost exactly, but my head was clamped into braces. "Can we pretend I'm giving you the side-eye?"

His mouth opened. I guessed that was his smile. The pulsing in his ears seemed to slow.

"Are they bad?" I asked. "The aneurysms?"

"They've reduced your g-rating to three g's. I wouldn't recommend combat."

"I haven't noticed any headaches or anything," I said flatly, turning my lips down in a facial shrug. I had never noticed how much I talked with my body until I couldn't move.

"You shouldn't. They're more weak spots than true balloons. I imagine you understand why we stay ahead of potential problems."

We had briefings over this, complete with videos and reports. A self-guiding little tool was going to enter the vessel and scrub them a little to get them irritated so that they would start healing. Then the tool would squirt some juice on the weak spots, which will reinforce them until they naturally heal. The goo should get broken down over the next couple weeks.

The filaments shouldn't ever touch my brain and stay in the blood vessels. I would be awake, so Scout could monitor for changes. Like if I suddenly forgot how to talk or started to have a stroke. A team of neurologists should be doing this, but Doc was qualified. Even if his bedside manner was shit.

"I think I'm ready. What do you want to talk about?" I asked. "Thank you, by the way. I would have freaked out."

"How are you enjoying your time on *The Happy Marauder*?" Scout asked.

I rolled my eyes at the default question. His large pupils came down from full dilation when my eyes came back around.

"I'm not going to give you hell about doing your job." I sighed; it was only half as deep as normal because some muscles weren't doing their jobs. "It's weird for me. I probably know you know more about me than I do with all the testing and background checks and all that. I'm sure you have a program that can predict my behavior accurately."

"Individual predictive models require implants to be effective." He relaxed a bit more, seeming happy to talk on a subject in which he was the expert. "I need to monitor brain activity, chemistry, and external exposure response to build an accurate model. Right now, in a game or two, I should be able to predict your chess moves. However, removed from monitoring, the model would be useless in a day or two. Cumulative effects are especially difficult to predict, even harder under combat conditions. It's easier to just ask you how you're feeling. Not to mention, ethical and cheaper."

Doc turned the machine on, and a needle poked to numb the area.

I tried to allow a polite amount of time before asking, "What do you do when someone starts to crack? I know there are signs or whatever."

Scout ballooned his chest with a deep breath, sending a wave of blood through his translucent ears, and relaxed. "It's all case by case. You understand. The policy is we remove them from active combat or vital duties. Which only determines our combat power for future contracts. As you can see, times like now, we need everyone we have. If the signs warrant it, we monitor, confine them to quarters, and then sedate if necessary. In most sapient species cases, they ask for sedated transport."

My eyes almost crossed as the drill vibrated my skull. It was kind of fun, the way driving over a bumpy road jiggled your body. Then my nose itched, and I tried to wiggle it, working my mouth back and forth.

Scout's big eyes dilated. "Monolith?"

"Yeah?" I shot him a weird look.

"Is something wrong?"

That scared me. "I don't know. Is something wrong?"

He started barraging me with questions. After a moment, I recognized the cognitive assessments and stopped him.

"Scout, is this from me doing this?" I worked my mouth back and forth again, trying to wiggle my nose.

"Yes. What is that?" His ears lifted up and down with what I guessed was anxiety.

"Yeah. My nose itches." I crossed my eyes to see the tip of my nose. "Would you mind?"

"Would I mind what?"

"Scratch my nose. The squishy part at the end jiggles, and now it itches."

Scout's ears went flat, and he gave me the side-eye. I would like to think being overly concerned with an itchy nose was a great way to ignore someone drilling into your brain.

"Isn't touching a human's face reserved for intimacy?" he asked, still mimicking the human side-eye.

I rolled my eyes again. "Yes, but this is a medical setting. I have a spinal block, and I can't move. Help me out here, will you? If you don't want to touch me, grab a cloth and just wipe from the bridge of my nose to the end with light to medium pressure."

He did as I asked with the awkward deliberateness of a medical student.

I thanked him. "What is your species anyway?"

Scout made a croaking noise. "Uniform, Romeo, Golf, Lima, Uniform, Romeo, Kilo." Then croaked again. He did his open mouth smile and waved his ears. "We have served on *The Happy Marauder* for months, and you never knew what my species?" He chittered or squealed excitedly; I was thinking that chittering noise was a laugh. "How delightful!"

"Uh…" I was taken aback by his uncharacteristic outburst. "I take it that's not normal across many planets?"

"Normal is without definition, across the galaxy. What was the name of your planet?"

His words were a slap in the face. That the place I had spent my whole life was just a brief stop in a ship's route.

"Vanguard," I supplied.

"Ah, yes. Delightful if I remember the system correctly." He seemed to be pulling something up in his memory. "Do not recognize non-organic sapience and have convoluted ways to bind them as property. Conversely, in the common sector, as you would know it, slavery of organic beings is widespread under many different guises, usually economic stratification and servitude."

I made eye contact with him and gave him a deliberate pause. "Vanguard was pleasant to you?"

"Ah, yes."

I stopped him before he could get into it. I didn't want to ruin his version of Vanguard with mine. "You know what? It doesn't matter. How are the kids doing?"

He seemed to take a moment to transition between topics. Another deep ear flapping breath. "They are not well. The combat cocktails they were given, along with various forms of abuse, have taken their toll on them. We—and by that, I mean the captain, Dire-horn, and I—had to make some tough decisions. There are certain medications that might be beneficial. However, we need a supply for combat injuries. I'm invoking some questionable liberties by sedating them while we get the pods ready. I'm already justified because two died when the main gun fired. I'm doing my best to use the ship's database to catch up on human developmental psychology, but my specialty is group and interspecies dynamics focused on community goal attainment."

Doc or the machine finished or whatever without so much as a courtesy beep. I only noticed when my head drifted to the side because the halo was retracting.

"Thanks, Doc," I muttered. "Great bedside manner."

Scout was almost scolding. "He doesn't understand the concept of sarcasm or any emotional nuances. I was originally hired in conjunction with him to act as an adjunct to his medical skills."

I wasn't going to stop him from sharing. "That was all for me, Scout. How did you get saddled with the responsibilities of ship shrink? Affectionately."

"I completed what you would know as my post graduate work, spent a standard year or so in a clinic. I hated it. It was everything I had wanted since I was a hatchling. Star blood, they call it. As in *you have the stars in your blood*. Planets aren't bright enough for me anymore." He seemed to drift off in his own thoughts.

Dire-horn entered before things got awkward and placed himself in front of Shantu's bed. It took me that long to realize I didn't have my contacts or ear bugs in.

"Can y'all see our medical schedule?" I asked Scout.

"Yes," he replied. "I have administrator access as lead clinician. Though Doc is the healthcare provider."

I felt like he was going to explain the obvious, so I stopped him. "Yeah. I don't think he cares about administrative responsibilities." I leaned my head in as far as I could. "So, I have a question."

"Feel free to ask me anything," he said, completely missing the point.

I rolled my eyes. "First, the lean in and change in voice is for confidence." I realized how many different meanings that could have. "I mean, trust and discretion. Moving on. Do praportorian—"

"My dame and sire would find you worthy," Dire-horn said to Shantu, derailing my question. His voice was dripping with profound reverence. "I would invite you before them when the time comes."

What the fuck?

Shantu completely ignored Dire-horn's tone, and his eyes narrowed. "Are you asking me to meet your parents?"

"Fuck," I said, my eyes widening as much as they could.

Scout's ears perked.

Shantu's eyes smiled at me.

"Shantu, don't!" I tried to yell, but there was no volume to it. Like I only had so much pressure for my voice.

"Aw. Big guy, you're so sweet. I think you should buy me dinner first."

Dire-horn remained completely serious. "I have made many meals for you. Is there something specific required?"

Shantu made a bashful face and fluttered his eyelashes. "I didn't know it was a date, out in public for everyone to see."

How the fuck could someone wake up from surgery and be an asshole?

I gave a deep defeated sigh. "Scout, if Wraith isn't busy, he should watch this. Sgt. Tok too."

Scout looked confused as well but gestured to his feed.

"This would be a matter for celebration; therefore, a public venue would be appropriate."

I wanted to cry for Dire-horn and his confusion.

"What are we celebrating?" Shantu asked, maneuvering for his next joke.

"You have shown your decency to your brother," Dire-horn said.

"I have done no such thing," he lied and feigned indignity.

"But if you're interested in my decency, I think I should be able to rally for a show."

This fucker.

"Scout, tell Dire-horn to lick Shantu's face from chin to hairline," I said as urgently as I could. "Please. This is an emergency." When Dire-horn's ear flicked and he hesitated, I spoke sotto voce. "It'll mean a great deal of honor to me and Shantu."

Dire-horn did it—in all his massive glory. A big ugly long lick from a tongue that was much longer and flatter than should fit in his head. Gobs of saliva dripped down Shantu's face.

I idly wondered if Dire-horn's tongue was prehensile.

Dire-horn looked at me with big cow eyes like *did I do good*? The lawyer infantry was adorable.

What the fuck do you do with that?

I smiled and nodded my approval to Dire-horn.

Shantu tried to kill me with eye daggers. I smiled the biggest shit-eating grin I could. Then I saw the wet hair with Dire-horn's sputum standing straight up and lost it. I laughed as hard as I could. Which was more of an awkward giggle given that half of my thoracic muscles were paralyzed.

Shantu looked at me, completely flat faced. "I have a cow lick, don't I?"

I laughed to the point of tears, and by the stars, they were nice to have. Scout and Dire-horn looked completely confused. If Doc didn't have more control over my body than I did, I'm sure I would have hyperventilated.

Shantu's face went from anger, to admiration, to defeat. For all his faults, Shantu, my biggest asshole, was a gracious loser.

"Dire-horn, I apologize," he said with as much respect and deliberate language as I had ever seen come out of him. "I was not taking the situation seriously, making jokes. Ja— Monolith. Monolith stopped me from disrespecting you further by having you do that. I would be honored to learn more."

I wanted to hug him.

If Scout was thinking out loud, I imagine it went something like: "Fucking human, erratic pain in the asses. That's racist. These two are such a pain in the ass. It's repulsive how effective they are. Like children with nukes."

What Scout really said was, "Let me know if I can be of service." Then left.

When Dire-horn left, I turned to Shantu. "What the fuck was that about?"

"When you passed out," he said, "I stayed with you and took a round to the gut for my trouble. Dire-horn thought it was the greatest act since The Fleet Resignation."

The Fleet Resignation was a historical event that led to the founding of Vanguard. The short story is that the civilian fleet government, after the evacuation of Earth, ordered the invasion of some habitable planet they came across. The planet turned out to be inhabited. The military said that they weren't going to fuck up some natives and then proceeded to tell the civilian government that they weren't really a government because they were exceeding their authority, and to go fuck themselves. There was a war. In the end, the military took off to eventually settle Vanguard.

"So, you're going to join his clan or whatever it really means?" I asked.

"I need to know if it's all spiritualism and combat focus. If I'm joining the minotaur military to get shipped somewhere stupid, fuck that," Shantu answered plainly. "What the fuck happened to your hand anyway?" He pointed with his chin.

"I think I stabbed one of those big saws that the galunkin were using to cut through the decks. It blew the power cell in my thermal blade. I'm going to be here for the next two weeks. What about you?"

"I'm out in a few days. Then I go right back into that shit hole. All soft tissue. No bone involvement, you lazy shit."

"What the fuck is wrong with you two?" Turtle-tank asked from my other side. "Don't you know how big of a deal it is to be honored by a minotaur?"

"What the fuck are you on about?" Shantu asked before I could.

"If Dire-horn invites you to meet his parents, that means his clan leadership."

Shantu and I made faces at him while he prattled on about honor and dignity and other shit that gets you killed when you're not paying attention to who's holding a knife at your back.

I didn't even try to stop Shantu.

"If you have that glory dick in your mouth…"

"I'm gay," Turtle-tank said, trying to divert the conversation.

"Pussy. No, cunt. Anyway, it needs to be gross, uncomfortable, and for someone else's pleasure. Armpit, tentacle—I don't give a fuck. You don't like it. My point is that all that honor and glory shit gets you killed while someone else makes a profit. Worse yet, it lets them charge you less for your life."

Memories of my rant to the Vanguard recruiter floated in my mind as Shantu beat Turtle-tank over the head with our experiences at the institute and in the slums of Vanguard City.

When he started to be too rough on Turtle-tank, I intervened. "Did you read up on the galunkin?"

"No," Turtle-tank said. "I've been in and out of surgery for the last few days. My pelvis was crushed."

"That sucks. Anyhow, they have the tendency to rally behind martyrs. Mind you, they almost never make their own ships. So, the martyrs are usually some assholes who got killed in a boarding action. However, when you kill them all, there's no story, no retellings with embellishment. Therefore, it doesn't go viral. It's just one less group to harass space goers. So, we don't get hunted down or get a bounty on our heads. We're going to kill them all because that's what the smart money says. Now, the minotaur are likely going to have something against what we are going to do. It's ugly and necessary. Tombstone here might not want to get his hopes too high."

Shantu's face went wide-eyed. "I didn't think that far ahead. I just wanted to give Turtle-tank shit. I know he admires Dire-horn, and I wanted to dig at him for being a twat. I didn't expect you to go on a fucking tangent about social relativism."

"Oh." I turned to Turtle-tank, "You're a twat!"

A good-natured laugh went around the bay, and I noticed Xi was awake beside Uvwewe.

"Xi, what happened to you?" I asked to invite her into the conversation.

"I had my console in my hands when the baffles came down, and it snapped both of my forearms," she said. "I'm out in a few hours. Looks like I'm headed over in the next rotation. How bad is it?"

Shantu and I exchanged looks.

"Right. One dead, and you two wounded in action." She took a deep breath, looking nervous.

"Just take it one corner at a time," Shantu offered. "Do it slow and right. Just like we trained. This is not the place to experiment."

"That's not what you five were doing," Xi countered.

"Yeah. We dealt with the shit show, so you wouldn't have to," I said. "Honestly, I think they'll try to get their fabricator going to start pumping out drones."

She only looked slightly relieved.

"It's the zero g, isn't it?" Shantu asked.

She nodded.

"Let them know and do your best. We did all right, and we had less training than you. Weren't you in the Vanguard fleet?"

Xi looked away. "As a network engineer…"

She was a citizen with a second tour in the Vanguard fleet.

In theory, she should have at least two engagements during her initial conscription and then whatever they did with the fleet. Shantu and I avoided Xi to avoid conflict. I think maybe we were wrong. She never did anything against us, and now despite being a few years older, she was looking to us for advice.

We weren't in the habit of sugarcoating things.

"I don't know what your orders will be. If you can, take some time to get used to bouncing around with a loaded exo-frame," Shantu said. "Don't work yourself up. Remember our training. Slow is smooth, and smooth is fast."

"Yeah," I said. "I almost blew myself up when I mag locked myself to a piece of bulkhead instead of the deck."

Her eyes went wide, and I regretted telling her that.

"Deep breath," Shantu said. "Take your time. Get more confident with your maneuvers. Let them know how you're feeling, so they can decide where to put you."

True. Javelin and Gabe didn't let us out of their sight. We got shot, and they stayed in the fight.

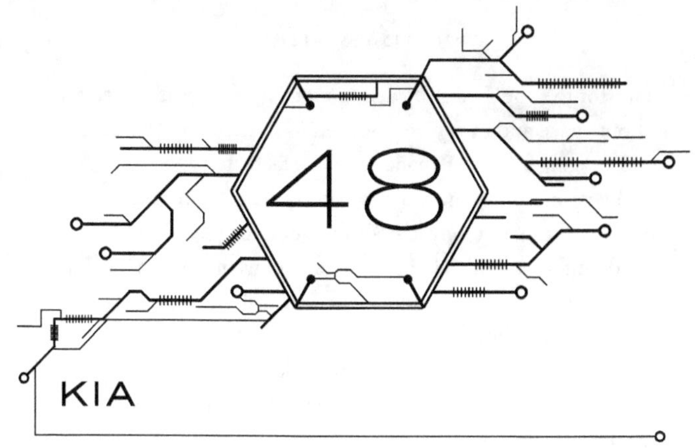

521.024.0800 FTS *The Happy Marauder*, Interstellar Space

I SPENT TEN days or so in the med bay, having my right hand rebuilt. It had the base neural tissue rebuilt, but the signal conductivity was way down or some shit. It would go from tingling to burning at times. The real problem was that my hand shook and twitched.

My feed alerted me of a change in status: Lingenfelter, Shannon S. KIA.

Gym Sock. That was her name. She took the name in good humor. She was always smiling while looking at herself in the mirror. Not in a conceited way. Like a painter trying to figure out where to put the next brush stroke. That was her thing. She liked working out for the art of it.

We had all spent time in the gym with her. I was trying to catch up fitness-wise, and she helped a lot. Always close at hand to go through a *movement*. That was what they were: *movements*, not exercises. That was what she had taught us. Movements.

She was always in the gym, doing her own thing. One eye on

a mirror to spot if we struggled too long, but she was respectful of our space and own goals. She led us in fitness with a gentle, encouraging hand. She made everyone feel safe.

"Everyone in a gym is there to get better," Gym Sock would tell us. "If it's good for the body, it's good for the mind, and it's good for the soul. It's a journey to find out what you can't do but want to. These couple meters we occupy is all the space we really control. Take control of it."

She had wanted perfection in her body, not for anyone else's sake but for her own. It was her happy place, and everyone was welcome.

I wish I had gotten to know her better.

The gym felt like a room now.

Gym Sock was the one who wanted the gym displays and did the work to build profiles that helped us track our progress. Not everyone used them, but it was thoughtful. I used mine, and it really did help. It didn't matter that I was still one of the slowest and weakest onboard; I had improved a lot. I was stronger, faster, and more coordinated because of her.

Now, there was a spot in my memory where Gym Sock lives because she wasn't keeping an eye on me in a mirror anymore.

Scout did his best to coach me through the exercises. He wasn't Shannon, and I didn't have a right to compare. She was just the one who I wasn't ever going to see again.

I should have told her how grateful I was.

He watched me, holding a probe to test sensation in the pink new skin in my hand. "Do you want to continue?"

"Yeah," I said to the empty place where Gym Sock used to be.

49

BACK TO IT

521.016.2000 FTS *The Happy Marauder*, Interstellar Space

I THREW MYSELF into requalifying. I generated a new subsection of profanity with every bump, bounce, and missed target. My right hand shook and felt like I was gripping a live wire. But I didn't have time to work through it.

Left would be my primary.

I was already offhand qualified now. I just had to hit minimums for primary. It took two days for me to requalify, and Gabe might take a giant shit on me for not maintaining the range. But I'd deal with that later.

I hated the idea that each death was one less person on the environmental systems. It made the pain comforting, an electric shock to my brain that I wasn't a waste of oxygen and protein. And that made me hate myself more.

I wanted to get this over with. I didn't want to be hanging out in the infirmary when someone died.

I don't remember the shuttle; this one wasn't rated for atmosphere.

When I rotated back to the star liner, Gabe had managed to

fabricate some half-assed armor that would fit over our HEPS. It was heavier than our standard kit with enough strength augmentation to mostly offset the weight.

"Ugh." The armor resisted my jump for too long and fired off all at once, sending me crashing into a bulkhead. I clenched my jaw against a fresh wave of agony. "Fuck, Gabe. Is this better than just the kit?"

The armor was glitchy as hell.

"I don't have time to troubleshoot it to your exact specifications," he said. "Figure it out because I don't want you getting shot again. I'm enabling your IFF lockout, so you don't fucking shoot someone we care about."

IFF is identification friend or foe that uses our tac link to keep our weapons from targeting each other.

That was my training for field fabricated equipment.

Fuck me!

Sgt. Tok's words echoed in my head. "Worry about things you can control. Right here, right now. Then work your way to other objectives."

I don't even think he was talking to me. I was just present.

I surveyed the fabrication bay while trying to troubleshoot my armor. That was an exercise in futility because none of the servos were labeled. The code managing everything was raw. Think of all the symbols on a keyboard you never use and try to read that. I needed a few hundred hours of training to even find out what was a sensor and what was servo. Then I could start managing their relationship.

Fuck that!

I tried to do something useful and found that the whole supply chain management process was a fucking mess. Some was my fault. Several servers and consoles that would have integrated the whole compartment into a magical machine of production were damaged in my initial breach.

We had stand-alone multimedia printers, large enough to print out server components, but we were quickly running out of the media that came in specific cartridges. We had a recycler that could break anything down into base elements, but they were designed to use the ship's water supply for cooling. Which wasn't working. The robotic arms that could assemble components from the printers were folded into their cradles because I had shot or blown up their control system.

It wasn't all my fault. Javelin, Gabe, Alexis, and Shantu were all in this firefight.

My HUD flashed as I synced into the battle net.

"Monolith, Tombstone, Saliut, under Dire-horn," the captain spat. "Secure materials for transport to *The Happy Marauder*."

A list of crap populated our HUD before disappearing into the mission bar. My icon was yellow with a green center, showing walking wounded.

I synced into Dire-horn's team chat. He set himself as ready location and set the formation as single file, active moving cover. I was third in line, right guard since I had to fire with my left hand. Saliut was second with Shantu acting as rear guard.

I used the time it took me to get to Dire-horn to get up to speed with the tactical situation.

The shuttle bay was covered by the heavy antipersonnel drone that floated more than a kilometer away, covering the ship's exterior on that side. It had a perfect butter zone where it could hit without being hit.

A portable generator powered the machine shop, which was spitting out pieces of surveillance drones that would also serve as routers for the ad hoc comm system. Xi was doing her best trying to do Alexis' and Shannon's job while working on getting a network set up.

Right now, we were reliant on the senior crew, meaning the captain's, Gabe's, Javelin's, Wraith's, and Dire-horn's armor to provide a network. Their expensive specialized armor was built for battle space integration, and their range was little more than line of sight through the ship's massive superstructure.

The good drones that we brought with us that had survived this long only provided coverage between the shuttle bay, the fabrication bay, and the primary reactor. This meant we had surveillance at most of the ship's three big compartments in the aft of the ship. A ship that was almost two kilometers long and over a kilometer in diameter.

Incidentally, I found out the ship respected the golden mean in compartment organization. I don't know what to do with that information, but it lives in my head now.

It was also over six million cubic meters of space with an unknown number of enemies onboard. Of which, we had coverage for a few hundred meters.

Wraith had scouted the ship's exterior, and the large portions of the forward section had power, heat, and pressure. The forward half of the ship and the entire opposite side had its defenses still active.

I had the feeling of an ant trying to eat a whale.

The ship's current map was almost all dark, meaning we didn't know what was happening there. Red lines showed the forward edge of our territory, where galunkin had attacked and retreated. Black lines displayed where we had scouted and returned. Simple icons marked things like water tanks, stand-alone power sources, server compartments, and other resources.

"Xi, I'm asking a dumb question," I said.

"I can't reach the ship's intranet from here," she said. "We don't have any power in the sections we control. Even then, it's going to take some doing. Right now, we need to secure the sections we control, and there's at least one reactor powered up. We know they were transmitting in the clear for days before Wraith killed the dish. Let me work on getting our own network up and drone coverage." She closed the line.

Okay? That was a lot more information than i asked for and now I forgot what i was going to ask…

I drifted up the bay and saw Dire-horn on the overhead, standing in all his glittering glory.

His seamless armor was reflective in that gold majesty that said *fuck your laser*. Dust on the overhead had created a ring of electrostatic fear that wouldn't dare to soil his armor. A mirror spun so quickly on his left shoulder that it looked like a solid trans dimensional orb. It was the targeting aperture. The laser on his back would be a team serviced weapon on a human. The cannon on his right shoulder followed his head movements.

If he was here on the initial shuttle, maybe Alexis and Shannon would still be alive.

Or maybe we would have gotten shot down on approach.

I found my position wordlessly, and he cycled out through a maintenance hatch meant for bots. He had to hug his knees to his chest and fight his way into the lock. I wondered why one of the smaller members of the senior crew didn't come for this.

We passed into the hollow between the decks, where conduits and pipes and shit runs. When ships were operational, the mini pressure vessels were mainly to hide subsidiary and emergency systems.

We were told to go dark and relied on Dire-horn's armor to give us an artificial image, which wasn't tuned to our HUDs. I guessed his armor was sophisticated enough to transmit with a low probability of detection.

The good false image didn't calculate my position, I slammed my knuckles into handholds or missed completely. I turned the fidelity down to a grainy mess to get my brain to distrust the image. Then I turned it all the way down to a faint shadow, enough that my suit's glowing analog display seemed bright.

This compartment had pressure. I should have noticed when I transitioned the air lock but didn't.

We moved through the hollow until we found pipes and conduits converging around a beam. The beam had a rail with latching points for bots to get transported around the ship.

Dire-horn forced the pressure door open, using some kind of specialty key mounted to a hand drill. Like the kind you see frontiersmen using in the preindustrial videos.

The false image was provided by his armor's telemetry.

"What is that?" I signed, using tactical hand signals. Technically I signed *identify* and *left hand*.

"A key to a combination lock." He signed *code*, but I assumed he meant combination.

He followed his answer with a brief video clip that rendered the complicated tumbler system that was the vacuum seal's locking mechanism. These weren't air locks. Just the emergency seals that shut when the system lost power. After a minute, he got the seal to release and manually opened it.

My HEPS squeezed me with new pressure. "What's this air around us?" I signed.

He gave us a feed for atmospheric composition. This compartment was filled with pure helium. I didn't know how or why.

We spent six hours drifting in the dark with only a soft glow from the indicators in my helmet. Nightmarish silhouettes danced in the dark as my eyeballs tried to make sense of stray cosmic rays.

We were doing a sort of spiral through the bowels of the superstructure, checking every nook and cranny when we hit pay dirt. The canisters we needed were standardized for the printers and food processors. Iron, carbon, gold, nickel, and printer chemicals. We found them filling the walls around a hangar. There had to be hundreds of them.

I guessed they would become secondary blast resistance if

something went wrong in the hangar. I don't know who designs this shit.

Dire-horn turned on his lights and active sensors, and I winced at the sudden brightness.

Full combat link was established, and the mini map synced. This was a dead space deck. The place where you run your plumbing and electrical but with enough space that if something exploded in one compartment, the next has a fair chance to survive. The pervasive grime coated everything except where the bots traversed in their mechanical paths; otherwise, it was that eerie perfect coating. I found some signs of habitation when my feed translated galunkin profanity etched into the grease.

The map showed we were near another print shop and adjacent hangar. Gabe and some others were searching the areas for another bot hatch.

Another four hours later, we found a route through the maze of compression chambers, auxiliary atmospheric holding tanks, and other shit that lives between the bulkheads of kilometers-long ships.

Dire-horn instructed us to fan out to look for electrical and physical junction boxes. If the star liner was working properly, the canisters of materials would be shuffled around the ship, almost taken for granted like turning on the tap. Now, we were trying to hijack the system to send them to our print shop, where we could work in peace.

It was better than getting shot at, I guessed. Though doing boring, tedious tasks let my mind think about how boring and tedious the task was.

When you're getting shot at, it's all like AAGGGHHH! Then it's over.

Then you go "Holy fuck. Did that just happen?" Then you get to think about how things went.

Sorry. I think the drugs are still fucking with my head.

Moving on. The fabricators were ramping up to a useful production rate, starting with the assembly drones. In a day or two, they would be pumping out sensor pods to fill in the gaps.

Motherfucker, the games and media lied to me again.

The shows always showed a like ten-minute fight. Then boom, they have control of the bridge and everything. We didn't even know where the bridge *was*.

Bridges are stupid. Let's take everyone controlling everything and put them in one room. First off, that's not possible. Reactors and drives are big ass pieces of equipment that will need a fuck ton of support. Most of it, you can disable with a hammer. So, fuck that heavily guarded room with ten levels of security and an army of minions. I'm going to smash the cooling equipment that has the structural integrity of old spaghetti and make the ship stop anyway.

That whole fucking concept needs to go.

Things got interesting a day or two later when a priority update went out. Wraith had population estimates at close to ten thousand.

Our estimates had their fighting strength at a few hundred, who were now focused on securing key assets in a defensive posture. Defensive posture means we know they have booby traps, and we don't have the drones or equipment to find the traps and disable them.

The term *defensive depth* entered my vocabulary. The galunkin had lots of it. Their sappers were quick at deploying mines and trip wires just out of our lines of fire. We knew they were working because every once in a while, one blew themselves up.

So, we bounced around in the dead space, trying to find options.

The fruits of our labor were Dire-horn finding a way straight to a hangar that was warmer than the ambient hull. He chanced drilling a pinhole that he could stick a camera through and used some goo to seal it before a leak was detected.

He then shared his feed.

It looked like the galunkin had every vac suit in the hangar getting makeshift armor, and they were all getting trained in combat.

Dire-horn had us pull canisters of print media and return to base. In the print bay we were using as an operations center, we consolidated reports.

Wraith found two other reactors and the functioning service deck that kept the bulk of the population alive. The term *force multiplier* came to mind when I read his mission report. He had been among them somehow, waging a guerrilla campaign to give us the time we needed to work. He sabotaged everything he came across in ways that could be easy to explain as stress fatigue, battle damage, and improper maintenance. He did this while picking off every trapper team he could find.

On top of that, he was returning to his sabotaged areas and throwing the trapper teams in the compartment to make it look like much bigger battles had taken place.

"My fuck," I said as my feed finished reading the report to me. Then it occurred to me that I sleep on the same ship as this guy. He killed while keeping his documentation up to date.

Was that my future?

Is that a bad thing?

Should I fear or admire the effectiveness?

I scrolled the video back. There were hours of Wraith wandering and touching the bulkheads with a stick that had a tennis ball on the end. Just casually walking around enemy-controlled territory, taking measurements.

Skip all that shit.

Javelin spent twelve hours preparing a round with her pet murder cannon. If the cannon was a dog, in its belly was munition fabrication hardware. She made five rounds in total because the first four didn't pass quality control.

If you ask me about her quality control criteria, I'll send you the link to her expense report. The report is so dense with materials science and physics it's about to start fusing.

Just no.

She fired her magic round aft. It shattered two sensor pods, changing its trajectory each time and popping secondary charges to maintain momentum. The round now flew toward the bow in line to enter the hull through one of the exit wounds Piper had shot. It skimmed a mangled cross member that adjusted its course just so it entered a pipe like the lethal injection it was.

The round exited the pipe and penetrated the terminating equipment. The exterior layer flashed into plasma, melting the layer below that mixed with the layer below. The lower layer reached saturation and released its energy. The energy was split between adding to the round's momentum and deforming a half-melted metal plug to stop atmospheric loss.

The magic bullet penetrated three more bulkheads. It entered the back of the galunkin's main leader, general, shaman guy's head, and its helmet exploded with the overpressure as the round deformed its body tissues. The round landed in the middle of a display table, now resembling a sunflower spinning with the last of its energy. Surrounded by stunned galunkin military leaders.

Javelin was facing aft and hit a target eight decks below her to her right and behind her.

Insane.

Wraith had bugged the room and attached a video to confirm the kill. Everything else about the flight of that round was math, science, and more math. I didn't do any of that; I watched a simulation. Javelin's projection ended as the last of its kinetic energy expended into the target's head.

Shantu nudged me, getting me out of that report. There was still a meeting going on.

"—with their leader eliminated," Uvwewe said. "From what Wraith has gathered, I don't think infighting will happen. Mind you, the margin of error is large here without a trained interpreter. This guy"—he put up a seemingly random picture; I didn't know one galunkin from another—"is in position to take charge."

"Let's call him Prince Asshole," Shantu interrupted.

"Okay. Prince Asshole is using the chaos to eliminate rivals and blaming us or to execute them publicly as spies. I'm projecting consolidation of power to take less than a week, minus a day for every push we do. Prince Asshole thinks there are two or three hundred of us."

"Their numbers are fair." Javelin explained in-depth combat ratings and equipment.

We got off track for a little while, while they talked about language profiles and numbering systems. I wish I could give more details, but it was turning into like six different conversations, and I didn't know what was happening.

"Suffice to say, the galunkin have a reasonable estimate of our static combat power," the Captain said. "We need to make up the difference in the dynamic. We're Marauders; we don't fight fair."

::EDIT:: That was getting ugly and technical. This is how I'm going to do it.

Imagine your mayor gets assassinated. Now every restaurant owner and rich asshole wants CE with them at all times. That's because they're *so* important that they might be next on the hit list. Now your city has no CE. Everything is going to shit because everyone is panicking.

That's the galunkin.

Now we just had to kill them all.

Purging a ship of civilians was not on my agenda when I got on this ship last year. They were sapient, intelligent, and more concerned with their day-to-day shit than an existential threat. I was that threat, and we were casually looking at ways to murder everyone on this ship.

Can I get some extra fuckup with my situation? No, not on the side. Just dunk that shit.

The background app in my brain that looked for conspiracies popped it head up and said that we had some issues here. We were going to casually exterminate a civilian population. Were the senior crew fabricating or cherry-picking data to feed us?

::ERROR::

That didn't feel right with everything that had happened aboard. Dire-horn would lose his shit. I would put money that he would relieve the captain and take command. Shit, he was down here running the ops.

How the fuck does he do it? Dire-horn was arguing with the captain over the orphans what felt like yesterday. Now he's running missions in full slaughter armor. Someone please start consolidating this shit for me!

Javelin made sense. She was just looking at the numbers. Maximize profits. Minimized expenditures. Path of least resistance. All that shit made sense. I wasn't exactly comfortable with executing people as a negotiation strategy, but that was a thousand meters from slaughtering non-combatants.

The ship's library, mostly from Vanguard and The Commonwealth, had extensive literature on how to manage or deal with the galunkin, and the answer was the same: just kill them. There were a few cases of humans surviving capture and managing to co-opt the ship over the course of twenty-odd years or about two galunkin generations. But that was not the option we were taking.

Shantu nudged me again.

"What?" I said over a private channel.

"Focus."

"How can you tell?"

"You kind of go rigid and start spinning. I've been keeping you facing the right way."

"You're a good friend."

"Uh-huh."

Wraith was talking about pumping a chemical they were using to secure the decks into the hangar. After turning their own defense against them, it turns out that pumping things in zero g is a pain in the ass. To move a compartment's worth of fluid—gas or liquid—to another, you need an intake and exhaust fans to start the cycling process. They would need to be something like atmospheric flight turbines, which would be destroyed by a caustic fluid. Long story short: it would be a lot of work with equipment that wasn't practically available, especially when you're trying to stay on the offensive.

Instead, we would use neutralizing torpedoes…according to Wraith. He used a stock image and labeled what he wanted. *Torpedoes* are a stretch to the term. We would be using cheap box fans rigged with a battery for propulsion. The payload was containers of soft drink concentrate bladders wrapped with rubber bands. Yes, *rubber bands* would squeeze the syrup out pin holes for a dispersed delivery. The fans were the biggest hiccup because we had to pad them so that they wouldn't make so much noise as they bounced around. They then had to be laminated with a resistant material.

Our tactical advantage came from fast food concentrate and office supplies.

This was absurd.

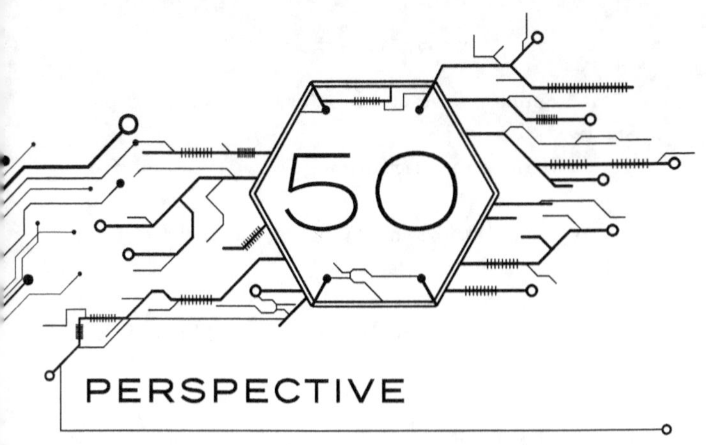

50

PERSPECTIVE

THIS WOULD MAKE a great show," Shantu said in the open channel, shoving a meal packet into its receptacle. "I mean, we get everything."

"What the fuck are you on?" I asked, slightly irritated by him interrupting my reading. Especially because I was about to doze off.

He didn't acknowledge me. "Let's see. We've had mutant wildlife, tragic space orphans, and now a long campaign against evil space goblins. Gabe, you've done a great job as the comic relief who brings out the best in me."

"Thank you," Gabe said.

"You're very welcome, Gabriel Martinez. I hope we get to do a season where we explore your backstory. The foreshadowing shows that Dire-horn's up next season."

"Are you framing recent events in terms of a serial show?" Javelin asked.

"N-not if you don't like it," Shantu said, his voice full of fear.

"Please continue," she said evenly. "I'm curious to hear your perspective."

"I-I was getting to the fact that we have a vat of acid on a spaceship."

"It's not acidic," Wraith said. "It's coolant, and it's alkali."

"It's caustic," Shantu countered.

"We're in free fall," someone added.

"They're using it for area denial, and it's working," he said. "It's a vat of acid."

"That…makes sense," Wraith said, sounding surprised. "Okay then. Who am I in all this?"

"You're that mysterious badass with a heart of gold!"

It broke orbit from there with Shantu, Gabe, and Wraith dominating the conversation. Others would float in and out, sometimes to make a joke or to point something out. I had to give it to him: morale soared regardless of the shit we were doing.

51

PREPARED GROUND

SGT. TOK IN his infinite wisdom had us practicing breaching, mop up, and emergency first aid. Sarcasm aside, he did find some pretty big liabilities.

The strobing and EM interference of the FLICKER grenades caused an error in our networked targeting. If we were firing off one of the senior crew's suit data, our feeds didn't have the processing power to update the silhouettes to give us real-time targeting information. Good to know before an engagement.

Sgt. Tok made us practice drawing fire and coordinated maneuvers by using large heavy pallets of materials as simulated cover. The training did help us get used to maneuvering in poorly balanced glitchy-ass armor.

Someone explain to me how this guy's barking made CQB feel like Tuesday.

After the dry runs were over, we were in the walls of a hangar.

Things were getting weird. Days ran together, sleep was a shadow only seen out the corner of my eye, and the clock jumped. I was getting comfortable sleeping in a prone firing position. It didn't seem like a skill anyone should have.

We had been in the dead space between compartments for like sixteen hours. Drones kept up a façade of compartment-to-compartment fighting. Sgt. Tok and Scout put this plan together, and we were taking advantage of the galunkin *Social Environmental Threat Response*. If it sounds like a military handbook, it's because it is. Prince Asshole was attempting to restructure their people into something militaristic.

We were going to throw a wrench in that.

Wraith was somewhere in our hangar, doing whatever a Wraith does. The false image let us see into the compartment based on his suit's sensor data. The head count and target priorities were less important than his fire disposition analysis. The primary asset denial we were after was removing their space worthy suits.

Asset denial. Fuck me. The training was sinking in. I would kill for gravity and six hours of solid sleep.

This is bullshit.

We waited, watching two hundred of the galunkin do their calisthenics with rubber bands and formation practice. I was effectively a fly in the wall, watching the army practice to kill me. This mess was what anthropologists were talking about. I had seen ice junkies fuck with more organization. I didn't know how long it would take the galunkin to get into something formidable, but it wouldn't be soon. Fights would break out; then others would get drawn into it when they tried to break it up. The military personnel would peel through the dog pile until one or two of the troublemakers were removed. I wanted to toss a grenade into the fat juicy target. Five military or dozen civilians would be a great opening salvo.

I held my position, and the animated conversation from their soldiers showed their morale was low. I didn't know what they were saying, but if their body language translated to human, they didn't want to deal with their trainees while we still posed a threat. I guess the civilians weren't transitioning to a militia well.

Wraith set the standby order and updated our threat analysis, and we redeployed accordingly. The captain sent the prepare order. We placed cutting lines to burn big sections out of the hangar's bulkhead. Next, we placed explosives to send the pieces flying. We then moved to our firing positions, so we didn't get killed by shrapnel.

Wraith had control of the devices. Let's talk about trust. We had backpacks of primary explosives. Wraith, Dire-horn, Javelin, Gabe, and the captain could kill any of us with a gesture.

The *are-you-sure* prompts seemed a whole lot less stupid right now.

What am I worried about? I'm worried about being the one whose line doesn't cut right. That there was some flaw in the manufacturing process years ago and everyone is going to think I fucked up. You know, because I botched cutting with explosives once already. Javelin had corrected my technique but we couldn't spare explosives for trial runs.

Anyway, we got on with our preparations. We had managed to cobble several turrets and got them mounted in useful locations all around the hangar. The plan had the turrets on sweeping patterns for low power lasers and then slaved to senior crew for directed rail because of the limited ammo. The element of surprise should give the impression of scores of troops breaching for just a few moments.

Something changed in the…air? The galunkin were starting to organize? I think they were trying to line up in rank and file, in their own shitty way. It involved more shoving and animated gestures but no brawls.

A tag for Prince Asshole appeared at the hatch opposite us. He entered with an entourage of maybe twenty-five additional military.

"Uh, is that a threat?" I asked on the open channel.

"I'm not really sure," Sgt. Tok said with venom. "He's always making some big fuss, I don't speak the language, but my impression is he's some bureaucratic blowhard. As a personal request for my time in service in the Commonwealth Fleet, can I kill that guy?" He asked.

We were stunned into silence. Sgt. Tok never talked about his time in fleet service.

"Sure. Why?" Wraith thankfully asked because none of us were.

Sgt. Tok's voice was gruffer than normal, almost a growl. "I spent years of my life staring at the back of someone's head, letting some silver spoon commanders feel important."

That was the only personal thing I knew about him.

Things I knew about Sgt. Tok:

Hard-ass trainer

Hates excuses

Hates military formations

I didn't think he had the capacity to drop his professional persona. Maybe it was in his contract.

It was open knowledge that he was onboard to keep friendly relations with the Commonwealth. That was a standard operating procedure for free trade ships. Hire locals to act as guides to avoid, so a ten-credit administration fee didn't blow a billion-credit contract.

"He's all yours," the captain said. "At your discretion, Sergeant."

The —Weapons Free— icon illuminated. My assigned target list populated and cycled based on conditions I only had a cursory understanding.

Sgt. Tok didn't hesitate longer than it took to let his rifle's redundant telemetry confirm his target. The laser burned through the bulkhead. The rail shots were textbook. Clean holes in the chest.

The galunkin were stunned and confused for way too long after blowhard died. The gasses escaping from his heavily decorated vac suit made him flop and bounce like one of those inflatable flailing advertising aids.

The bulkheads we rigged exploded, cutting bigger swathes through their number than they should have. If they had practiced their emergency operations at all, it was likely that half wouldn't have been cut down in the initial breach. They ran into each other, trying to escape the high-speed debris. The turrets we rigged didn't draw hardly any fire because the galunkin were fighting over weapons instead of distributing them.

The rest of the engagement went as planned. Javelin picked off the tagged military and then any heavy weapons. The junior crew, me included, provided fire support and a distraction as Dire-horn charged through with his psychotic energy weapon. The captain and Gabe were on his heels.

The bay's atmosphere turned toxic and charged. Lightning danced around the bay as equipment fried. Most of their infantry, conscripts, trainees, whatever…died, choking on toxic gasses. Too slow to seal their gas exchanger things.

I didn't see most of the targets I was shooting at. Too much debris and smoke.

Xi was the cost of the victory. In the confusion, something exploded, and a chunk of a container hit her section of the bulkhead. She was fine for a few minutes but developed blood clots that ultimately killed her a couple hours later.

The way she died bothered me.

Xi was doing her part, scared and rattled like the rest of us. Then her feed flatlined, flashed her icon red for medical emergency, and faded to gray. We were helpless in a toxic atmosphere, and some bruise sent a blood clot somewhere her body couldn't handle.

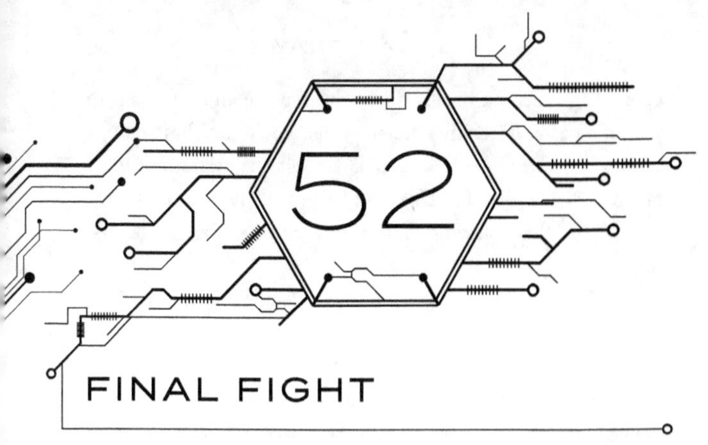

FINAL FIGHT

THE SHIP WAS secure. Can we leave it at that?

Please?

Thank you…

Flutter had upgraded *The Happy Marauder's* life support systems with the other ship's much more robust equipment. It took a bite out of a cargo bay and made the existing system an emergency backup, but *The Happy Marauder* could now support over a hundred oxygen breathers. It was super overkill, but there wasn't a middle ground with the equipment we had on hand. In a week, Dire-horn would be serving fresh fruits and vegetables from hydroponics, and we could stop eating ration paste.

People don't talk about how much it sucks to eat ration paste day in and day out while shitting liquid into a tube to drink it again.

Well, I'm talking about it.

In the HEPS, your shit and piss get dehydrated. Then you get to drink the water. The byproducts get concentrated into this capsule. A machine breaks down the capsule and refeeds it to you in a paste. It's really efficient when you're on short rations but fucking awful. And that actual flavor is chalky, buttery, mustardy…fish? Maybe. I don't know. It's gross. The texture is thick and oily. It's like packing your mouth with bearing grease. Just unpleasant.

Just think of that shit next time you decide you want to be a space adventurer.

Now that that's out of my system… Sort of.

Flutter was on his way to start assessing the other ship's damage and decide if we should strip it of valuables or try to bring it with us. It was his show now.

He arrived in a pod that reminded me of a bad video game villain. Four overly long, articulated arms stuck out in all directions. They looked frail and spindly. The whole thing was more a snow globe than a space suit. I guess osheran didn't lend themselves to space easily. Perhaps this pod had the equipment he needed.

The rest of the transport shuttle was filled with maintenance drones and a controller unit. The good expensive ones you would hide in a firefight.

The osheran were almost impossible to have a conversation with, but in a virtual workspace, they were fantastic. The workflow models made sense. No micromanagement. Clear, easy to understand tasks. I don't know if it's Flutter, the osheran as a whole, or a feature of the translator, but my workflow chart was in color-coded animations.

Right now, our primary goal was to get the ship underway. Which meant firing up the nuclear disaster that was the primary reactor. Which meant we needed the cooling system operational before we could turn on the controller or the diagnostic subsystem.

I'm not getting into how one of the local reactors was radioactive slag. That reactor was supposed to power the startup systems for the primary reactor. There were a lot of other people dealing with that mess.

Glad it wasn't me.

Thus, my day started with me vacuuming the coolant up into this big centrifuge thing to be filtered and refined before being returned to the cooling system. In my head, I was the dancing office janitor in those shows, just happy not to be the one welding shielding into place for a melted reactor because fuck that.

I swear, if you give Flutter two coffee cans, a bowl of rice, and a screwdriver, he could build you a starship. He whipped up the coolant purifier dingus out of the scrap from around the ship. He and a few others were chasing the coolant lines for leaks and isolating the system to just the primary reactor, the reservoirs, and the radiators.

Two days of wrestling with cables as thick as me. Okay. The heavy maintenance bots did most of it, but I helped. Now, the primary reactor was ready to start pre-fire testing.

I learned that the small ancillary reactors ran on gaseous hydrogen in a fusion reaction that *vent*. *Vent* is what they put on the brochure to make it sound safe. Like the paired reactor that was *consumed* in a twenty-kiloton explosion that canceled the force of the venting. If the venting wasn't balanced, the ship would disintegrate in a high energy spin. The containment walls get enriched with all the energy they absorb as they fail.

Long story short: don't shoot reactors with particle beams. It makes a radioactive mess.

The big reactors use helium three and metallic hydrogen. Though I think the hydrogen has something to do with super-conducting. It's a bunch of complicated shit that uses math and physics I don't understand, so I'll spare you my butchering explanation. The big reactors don't melt with discharge energy; they explode with enough force to turn most ships into shrapnel.

Important safety lesson kids. Also the reason why Piper did their best to not shoot that.

When we successfully isolated the cooling and the power grid, we ran the pre-fire pressure tests. Something was wrong because Flutter shut it down and directed the bots to tear into the supporting equipment. He seemed flustered. Then directed the repair efforts to life support and resealing the reactor compartment. So, that was what we did.

I didn't understand how much ships flex and warp with major collisions until we gave up on repairs to do a more thorough survey. Now, we were running back and forth, repairing severed conduits. The next thing I learned was that the Wandathu ships tended to be very flexible and used pressure inside the compartments to control how the ship flexes and to limit passenger discomfort during maneuvers and docking.

The aft engineering decks were designed to depressurize to protect the reactors and drive system from pressure waves from impacts. The shock absorbers built into the frame for the primary reactor and drive were keeping everything in safe shutdown.

I don't understand why, but also, I don't design starships.

"When do we abandon this piece of shit?" Shantu asked no one in particular.

"You tell me," Gabe answered. "Do you want to leave several trillion credits of a vessel because you want to go play with your reproductive organ?" He had been hanging out with Shantu too much.

"Trillion," I said. "Like with a *T*. Tri-illion."

"You're forgetting the space tax."

But that didn't curb my enthusiasm. There's always someone willing to buy. We just need to sell it before the Wandathu find out because they'll be pissed.

"Fuck em," Wraith chimed in. "They want this ship? They can come get it, and we'll just take the primary drive and duct tape it to *The Happy Marauder.* Cheap sons of bitches. It was recovery of a shuttle, same day kind of mission. They used the local port authority to charge me for towing back to their hangar after I found it for them. Didn't make any fucking money. They wouldn't release the controls so I could fly it. They wouldn't send someone to get it. I even offered to pick their pilot up to be a good sport about the whole thing. No. They wanted a *tow* and fucked me on the contract."

I wanted to say, "who asked?" but thought better of it.

"Is spite that much of a motivator?" Gabe inquired.

I almost heard the shrug from Wraith. "Yes. I would very much enjoy it when the table is turned."

The order came down. We would start patching the hull. Three holes, two kilometers long each… Who knows how much secondary damage?

Fuck my life with a barbed dick.

In the same notification came that *The Happy Marauder* was taking off to get a comet or two for the gasses.

"All right. What the fuck do you know when there's months of hard work ahead?" I asked the common channel but meant it to Gabe or Wraith.

"Days to weeks," Gabe corrected. "We're not fixing this whole ship by hand. We're going to have a production ramp up, survey, and more production ramp up. Then either we fix it, spear it, or scrap it. We have what we need and more; we won't hang around on dwindling potential. This ship is a treasure trove because of its scale, but if Piper and Flutter say it's a no-go, we'll tag it and take off."

"We can sell or auction the trajectory based on our survey data," Wraith added. "We would be lucky to get a ten percent value. There is a lot of research and negotiation that goes into it. Fuck that. It's the captain's, Dire-horn's, and Javelin's problem."

"Good because I feel like I've lost twenty kilos," Shantu

commented. "I can't wait for one of Dire-horn's meals."

"Yeah. Me too," I said. "Wait. What do you mean by spear it?"

"*The Happy Marauder* basically will ram its nose up the ass of this ship and push." Wraith sighed. "Not my area of expertise. That's about all I know."

Flutter, who was clearly on the line, released projections with velocities and acceleration rate parameters. Then added two other sets of data, one using the known values for *The Happy Marauder* and another using the upper and lower limits of the other ship's Alcubierre drive. But the pretty color-coded chart didn't mean shit to me.

Thankfully, Gabe translated. "Yeah. It'll take us eighteen years, using *The Happy Marauder*. If we get this ship running, it'll take three to six months optimally."

"Why wouldn't we keep it and start a fleet?" Shantu asked a fraction of a second before me.

"This ship is going to be radioactive when we reach Fermi Station." Wraith was being polite but in a harsh way. "We're *mercenaries*. This ship is a heavy fucking prize. A prize that we can't use and can't defend. There are enough big fish at Fermi Station to take the ship from us. Once we start telling people there is a ship up for grabs, it'll be blood in the water. Oh, and believe me, we're going to chum the water. The idea is to hook the biggest fish we can without getting eaten by a shark. To drive this metaphor home, the ship is the bait, and the payout is the fish."

EVERYTHING'S GOING TO BE FINE

521.094.2000 FTS *The Happy Marauder*, Interstellar Space

YOU KNOW WHAT your reward is for doing a good job? More work. We had months of work ahead of us. Today, we're surveying. There's a lot of that to get done. When that's done, we're going to install a sensor shroud. Not stealth anything. We just need to change the lines of the ship's silhouette.

That's fine.

Everything's fine.

I don't know how to explain this to anyone who's not a merc. Maybe military people get it. It's not the things we do; it's who we do them for. It makes sense until you say it out loud. Then it doesn't, and that's fine too.

I am a mercenary, not because I want fame and riches but because this life appeals to me. If I tell you it's because I wanted to escape the economic shackles on Vanguard, it would be a convenient truth to tell someone who isn't ready for the whole truth.

I'm not sure how my training and experience stack up versus the toughest in the galaxy. I could look it up, but honestly, I don't care. I don't need to be the toughest, the strongest, and the fastest. I survived, and that's enough. What's more important is that I didn't let my friends down. That's everything.

Shannon, Alexis, and Xi died, and I'll process that on my own time in my own way.

If I'm struggling with it, that's fine because I have people who will help me.

I'm where I belong.

ABOUT THE AUTHOR

Jordan Gray is a base-line human aside from decorative pigmentation. Pre-first-contact Old Earth is a dumpster fire social stratification and resource hoarding. Old Earth is a far cry from the Mother Terra described in certain religious texts.

Jordan found comfort with a close group of friends who enjoyed tabletop RPGs. It was during these gaming sessions that the first embers of The Infinite Night began getting stoked. His notions of good and evil were challenged by perspective. How does a person determine how much of a necessary evil is tolerable? The books started to take shape as mental exercise to deal with the mind numbing tedium of various occupations.

Then the day came as one venture failed and priorities changed and breathing life into *The Infinite Night* became not just possible but a necessity. He hopes you enjoy exploring the universe as much as he enjoyed creating it.